A. R. O'Brien is the up-and-coming author of the romantic thriller, *The Homecoming*, and is excited for the next phase of her writing journey. She has lived in Idaho, Utah, Montana, Wyoming and North Carolina and is the busy mom of three boys. When she's not writing she can be found at her kids' never-ending school events, the occasional football or basketball game, hiking the trails of North Carolina, or out with her best friend at local bars. She loves reading thrillers and might even be found swooning from time to time at a decent romance novel. She loves coming up with a good storyline and putting it into words and hopes to one day be a bestselling author.

Truth Hurts

A. R. O'Brien

Truth Hurts

VANGUARD PAPERBACK

A CIP catalogue record for this title is available from the British Library.

ISBN 978 1 80016 692 9

Vanguard Press is an imprint of Pegasus Elliot Mackenzie Publishers Ltd.
www.pegasuspublishers.com

First Published in 2024

Vanguard Press
Sheraton House Castle Park
Cambridge England

Printed & Bound in Great Britain

To Steven, my love. You have both inspired, as well as supported me on the persistent journey of writing this book. I'm not sure I could have done it without you. To my family and friends who have offered support and encouragement as I trudged through the process of this book, thank you. To my boys, I'm so grateful that I have each of you. You inspire me every day! Finally, thank you everyone at Pegasus for believing in my work and giving it a chance to shine. I will do my best to do you all justice.

Chapter 1

Sylvie Dunlap took a deep cleansing breath of the cool mountain air and turned to survey the breathtaking scene below. She tightened the jacket that was tied around her waist in case it got cold on the long hike and grinned happily down at her old friend.

"God, it is beautiful up here, Duncan. I had forgotten just how much you know." There was awe in her voice as her brown eyes took in the rolling green and blue of the hills and mountains below. Off in the distance far beneath them she could see the small blue circle that she knew was the lake, as they had hiked by it a mere two hours ago.

Duncan Jamison grinned up and squinted slightly against the sunlight that shone over the cliffs and rocks above. "I told you it would be worth it," he said, sounding smug.

Sylvie stared hard at him for a long moment before forcing her gaze away. He was still every bit as good looking and sexy as he had been when they were teenagers in high school, and she found herself feeling drawn to him the same way. He looked even better now, she had to admit, if only to herself. His dark hair had grown just long enough to curl slightly at the nape of his neck under the tan cowboy hat he wore on his head. His blue eyes were dark and enigmatic, at once both drawing her in and warning her off at the same time. His lean body was hard and unyielding and though she remembered he had always been that way, he seemed even more angled and stronger than she remembered. She supposed long years of hard ranch work would do that to a man out here in the rugged mountains of Idaho.

Sylvie reached for the water bottle she had tucked in the side pocket of her backpack. She pulled the top up and tipped her head back as she took several swallows to distract herself from watching him. She felt his eyes watching her now and lowered the bottle to meet his gaze.

There was something there in his blue eyes and she wondered what it was. Before she could figure it out though, one side of his chiseled mouth turned up slightly and he tipped his head as he reached for his own water

bottle. He drained the half empty plastic bottle and then slid the backpack off his shoulders to pull out another and slid it into the side of his bag to replace the empty one.

"I'm glad you got out, you know," he said in a low tone.

Sylvie turned back in surprise to meet his gaze. When they were in high school, they had constantly talked about leaving the tiny one-horse ranch town they had grown up in to see the world. She found herself wondering once again why he hadn't left as well but shrugged. "I needed it you know? With everything that happened graduating year it was too much for me to handle. When my mom suggested I go away for college I didn't think twice about it, just jumped at the chance."

Duncan nodded. "I remember." His tone was low and mild. "You never even said goodbye."

Sylvie felt a surge of fresh pain wash through her. She met his engaging blue eyes with her own brown ones. "I'm sorry." She knew it sounded lame but couldn't help it. "I honestly didn't think you cared all that much."

Surprise widened his eyes slightly before he covered it with a calm devil may care smile. "No reason to apologize for doing what you needed to do." He waved a hand as though none of it mattered any more. "Ancient history, as you know."

He wiggled his eyebrows suggestively and grinned. "Now, are we going to finish climbing this mountain or what?"

Sylvie felt tension in her belly but let it go. "I suppose we are going to run out of daylight if we don't get going, huh?" She replaced the water bottle and turned her back to him as she made her way up the steep rocky slope. Deep in thought now, she watched the rocky cliffs above them as they hiked ever closer. She found herself dragging her feet as the daunting rockslides and sheer smooth cliffs came into focus. Squaring her shoulders, she took a deep breath. They had come up here so many times growing up that even now she knew the area like the back of her hand. But as she approached the solid rock, her heart thundered wildly as though it might jump out of her chest.

It had been her idea to come up here, though she had secretly hoped Duncan would talk her out of it. Instead, he had assured her over and over that she wouldn't regret it. It had been eight long years since her sister, Elaine, had died tragically in these mountains. Sylvie wanted to hike to the top the way they had when they were kids and place a small memorial at the top for Elaine.

Elaine was two years older than her. She and Duncan had dated on and off all through high school, though they had been off when Elaine died. Duncan was two years older than Elaine and he also had a younger sister, Jackie, who had been best friends with Elaine.

Sylvie had always been the youngest one of their little group and had never heard the end of it. Though she traipsed happily along everywhere they went, they constantly teased her about playing with kids her own age. She had idolized Elaine though and had a pretty severe crush on Duncan anytime her sister wasn't dating him. She would never have admitted that to anyone, but it was true.

Tears filled her eyes, and she blinked them away. Now, her sister was gone. Had died eight years ago up in these mountains. There was a long search for her sister when their parents first realized she was missing. Then when search and rescue had found her body at the bottom of a cliff, a long investigation had followed. After the six-month investigation it was finally ruled as an accidental death and Sylvie's parents had encouraged her to go to the east coast for college.

There was nothing she could do at home and the constant nightmares and night sweats of their youngest daughter had them both worried. She needed some time away from this place and all that had happened here. Gratefully, Sylvie had agreed and when her parents dropped her off at the airport she had promised to be back for Christmas.

A tear slid down one cheek as she remembered her promise. She hadn't come back for Christmas or New Year's Eve. When she still hadn't visited for her birthday the following year her parents had packed their bags and come to her in North Carolina, where she was studying pre-law.

At first, they had visited her every few months but after two years of her not coming home, they finally packed up the old farmhouse and moved to the east coast to be near her. Sylvie hadn't really given them much of a fight when they came. Instead, she had focused on school and her new friends. Her mother got a teaching job right away and her father, who was a police officer, simply transferred to the local police precinct.

She had reached the base of the cliffs now and she hesitated as she stared up at the daunting slick rock face. She felt, more than she heard, Duncan come up behind her and she willed herself to keep moving. She had climbed the steep rocky face countless times in her youth and knew exactly where the safest pathway up and through the cliffs was. She stepped forward and placed one rubber sole of her hiking boots on the slick surface.

Her vision blurred and she felt like her world tilted to the left before righting once again. Sylvie blinked and then squeezed her eyes shut for a long moment. She jumped when she heard Duncan's deep voice behind her. "Are you okay, Sylvie?" He sounded concerned and she tensed as he reached out to take her arm in a gentle grip.

She nodded and swallowed the lump in her throat. "I'm fine. It's stupid, you know I have climbed these rocks a thousand times before and never hesitated and yet for some reason I feel like I can't breathe."

He looked down at her with worry on his face. "Why don't we take a break?"

She shook her head. "I'm fine." But even as she said it, she couldn't seem to get her feet to move forward. She let out a loud sigh of frustration and forced a little smile. "Okay, fine but only five minutes." When he raised an eyebrow at her she said quietly, "I really want to place Elaine's stone up there while it's still light."

Duncan nodded but took off the pack and unzipped a pocket.

"Okay five minutes. Here, why don't you eat something."

Sylvie started to shake her head but stopped as she met his steady blue gaze. He had that stubborn set of his jaw that she remembered meant he wouldn't budge. She reached out a hand to take the granola bar from him. His fingers brushed against her palm as she grasped the bar and she shivered and then stepped back quickly. He stared down at her for a long moment and then smiled. "Are you cold Sylvie?"

She shook her head quickly and ripped open the bar and shoved it into her mouth for a quick bite. She didn't look up at him though she knew he was still watching her. She stared below instead at the peaceful view with pine and birch trees tangling across the mountains. The rolling hills looked lush and green in the early summer air. Rockslides and random clusters of cliffs were the only thing that interrupted the lush green view and even those looked majestic and beautiful. The lake they could see earlier was now out of sight over a rocky edge. She turned back to face Duncan. "I really have missed this place," she admitted.

He looked out at the view and then back at her. "Me too, actually." Sylvie looked surprised. "You don't come up here all the time?"

He shrugged. "I make it up about once a year is all." When she didn't look convinced, he shrugged again. "I'm busy. The ranch has me spinning my wheels and then there is Jackie and her kids. I help out when I can, but it leaves me with very little spare time."

Sylvie smiled. "Wow, Jamison, you are all grown up. Look at you go." A look of sadness crossed her face and she turned serious. "I wish Jackie could have come with us. Elaine would have liked that."

Duncan chuckled. "You and her both. Ren and I pretty much had to tie her down when she heard what we were doing. She tried to come anyway, eight-month-along belly and all. It's too dangerous for a pregnant woman out here, even without climbing these cliffs and rockslides and Ren wouldn't hear of it." He looked down at Sylvie and gave her his famous heart-throbbing grin. "I reckon she'll be out first thing next spring when the snow melts off."

Sylvie nodded. "Maybe I will come back again for it. We could all go up there together then. I honestly don't know why it has to be now." She looked off into the distance deep in thought. "At the back of my mind I have been wanting to do something like this for years, but it just didn't feel quite right. Then spring came this year, and I haven't been able to stop thinking of her and suddenly I felt like, it was time." She turned her head to look at him. "Does that sound crazy?"

Duncan smiled gently. "Not at all. I get it actually."

With that comment Sylvie choked on the bite of granola in her mouth. Coughing ensued and she was soon bent over gasping for air, with her eyes watering. She gratefully accepted the bottle of water Duncan held out to her and took a couple quick sips. Finally calmed, she turned to him and nodded. "Thanks."

Then she remembered why she was choking in the first place. "I'm so sorry Duncan. Here I have been talking all about how Elaine died that year, and I haven't even mentioned your mom."

He looked away and out at the wide mountainous view. "She died that same year, you know."

Sylvie nodded in agreement. Shivers took her shoulders for no particular reason. She watched Duncan as she wondered how she could have forgotten something so important and vital. She knew Mary Jamison had died here in the mountains that year. It had been part of what had broken her and yet she had somehow wiped that part from her memory. Something teased nervously at the edge of her consciousness, but she couldn't seem to focus on it.

Mary Jamison and her husband, Arthur, had been out for a hike in the spring of that year and she had slid off the edge of one of the cliffs. Though they had brought in a helicopter and flown her to the nearest trauma center it hadn't been enough, and Mary had succumbed to head trauma shortly after reaching the hospital.

Guilt surged through Sylvie at the memories. "I really am sorry, Duncan, all this time I have been so focused on my own pain and overcoming it that I have been a really crappy friend. Your mom died that same year and then Elaine." Her voice broke. "I know you cared about her too and yet you stayed all this time." She looked at him and tears shone in her bewitching brown eyes. "I should have been there for you and Jackie."

Duncan shrugged. "I had to stay and help Dad with the ranch. With Mom gone we were a bit short-handed. She did all the accounting for the ranch and Dad didn't know a formula from a shape. I had to step up and do it. Then there was Jackie and she needed both of us after losing her mom and best friend."

"I wish I could go back again and do it all over," she said wistfully.

He shook his head, "When I saw you yesterday and I could see how happy and healthy you were, I was grateful you'd left. I worried about you that year, even before Elaine died, you know?" His eyes searched her face as he continued. "It was like something changed with you and you didn't really laugh or talk any more. Then after Elaine died, you left, and I was afraid for you."

Sylvie's eyes scrunched together. "Really? I don't remember that, I guess." She shrugged her shoulders and shook her head. "I don't remember much of anything that year besides Elaine missing and then cops coming and going all the time from the house. When I got accepted into Duke my mom urged me to go and I didn't push back." A look of regret passed over her delicate face. "I should have made sure you guys were okay first though."

Duncan reached for her hand and squeezed it. "It's all in the past now, Sylvie, and I never blamed you for leaving. Truthfully, I kinda wished I could leave too."

They both smiled at his comment. They had after all had countless conversations about them all doing just that. She wrapped a slim arm around to give him a spontaneous hug. "Well, I'm back now and realizing just how much I missed you." She shaded her eyes with a hand as she looked up at him and promised. "I'll make sure I spend some time with Jackie too before I go."

Duncan nodded, "She would like that. Friends are sparse here as you know."

With a happy smile, Sylvie turned back to the rocky cliffs above.

"We better get moving before it gets any later."

She heard Duncan sling his pack over his broad shoulders even as she placed first one boot and then the other on the slick black rock and started upwards.

They hiked up the cliff edge, making good time and still it was an hour later when they finally stepped off the solid rock and onto the last stretch of the trail before they got to the summit. Clouds were gathering at the peak and above them the sky began turning a dark ominous grey. Duncan stared up at the sky with concern. When Sylvie stopped for a drink of water and to catch her breath, he looked up at the sky and frowned. The weather could change dangerously fast up here, and they didn't want to be trying to make their way down the slick rocks and cliffs in a lightning or rainstorm. He saw that Sylvie was looking at the sky as well and asked, "What do you think?"

She hesitated and then said quickly, "I don't know when I can make it back out here. I only took a week off work and who knows when I will be able to come again. Do you think we can make it if we hurry?"

Duncan watched the rapidly changing sky and shook his head. "I know this means a lot to you, but I don't want to spend the night out here in a lightning storm, and we won't be able to make it past the cliffs if it starts raining. It's too dangerous. I think we'd better get back down before we are stuck up here until the storm passes."

Sylvie looked longingly up the mountain. "We are so close, but I think you're right."

He nodded and turned back down. "How many times have we raced a storm down this mountain?" he asked as he turned to grin at her.

Sylvie looked nervous and his smile wavered. She didn't meet his eyes as she tried to smile. "We ran down a few times, barely beating the rain."

He took the lead and walked easily down the first rockslide. They heard thunder off in the distance and he lifted his head to look at the sky that was now so dark that it hid the sun. He picked up the pace, glancing back every couple of minutes to make sure Sylvie was still with him.

Once, when he looked back her face was stretched tight, and she looked terrified. With a low gentle voice, he assured her, "Don't worry so much, I will get you down off the mountain safely. I promise."

When Sylvie just gave him a blank look he pointed to her face. "You look terrified."

She shook her head. "It's not that. I know we will make it down. I just feel like my head is about to explode."

"I think I have some aspirin in my pack if you want some," he offered.

She shook her head. "Thanks, but no, it just feels like there is a lot of pressure in there, you know."

He didn't but didn't bother telling her that. Instead, he smiled a little and offered the only explanation he could think of. "Maybe it's the lack of oxygen up here."

She shrugged and pushed past him, making her way carefully down the rock and stepping onto the cliff's edge. She went slowly, taking her time to find good footholds before letting go with her hands. She was practically on her butt sliding down the steep surface one foothold at a time when the sky turned black. The thunder was constant now and she knew if she looked back, she would be able to see the scattered lightning bolts as they struck down toward the ground.

She didn't look back and only slid down at a quicker pace. She could hear Duncan behind her, so she didn't waste any time. Thunder literally shook the mountainside and she turned quickly to look up behind her to make sure he was okay. He grinned at her and that somehow made her feel better, even though the pressure in her head felt almost unbearable now. With a little smile she turned just as lightning flashed a mere mile away.

Thunder shook the side of the mountain again and she got up off her butt so she could move more quickly downward. Behind her, she heard Duncan laugh and yell, "We'd better hurry or the storm is going to catch us."

She gritted her teeth against the pain between her eyes and worked downward as fast as she dared go. She could see the bottom of the cliffs ahead and closed her eyes for a moment as dizziness made her queasy. She lost her foothold and slid a couple of terrifying feet before Duncan's hand closed firmly on her arm to stop her.

Heart in her throat, she turned to look up at him. "Thanks. I felt dizzy again."

He nodded and didn't let go of her, but loosened his grip so they could

work their way down, side by side. He wasn't about to let go until they were off the cliffs and slick rock. Lightning flashed again and thunder followed a mere second behind. They reached the edge of the rocks just as another lightning struck and then boomed nearly simultaneously.

Sylvie turned to look up at him as he stepped off the slick cliff-edge and onto the rocky path below. Suddenly she screamed and lunged toward him. "Watch out Duncan!" As she slammed into him, they both toppled to the ground, and she landed on top.

He came up fast, rolling over on top of her. "What the hell, Sylvie?"

She struggled to free herself and sucked air back into her lungs. "Didn't you see him? There was a man there behind you. He had a rock and was about to slam it into your head," she stammered, even as she looked frantically around trying to see him there.

Duncan looked around as well but didn't see anyone. "I didn't see him. Are you sure it wasn't just a shadow?"

Sylvie looked confused and lifted a hand to her aching head. "Maybe, and maybe I'm just seeing things because of this horrible headache."

He brushed himself off and stood, holding out a hand to pull Sylvie up. She grasped it and stood staring behind him. She could still see a shadow there, but it didn't make any sense because it didn't have a face, and though it looked like a man there was nothing she could see that identified it as such. Confused, she blinked as the shadow stood still for a long moment and then dissipated into a small grey cloud that floated away. She blinked again and then when she realized Duncan was pulling on her arm, turned to go.

Together they jogged at a quick clip down the mountain trail. The rain caught up with them about a mile before the campsite where they had parked the truck for the hike, and the last mile was slow going as they avoided slick spots on the trail to go around the long, less muddy route.

Shirt wet and sticking to his very sexy chest, Duncan opened her door and half lifted her into the front of his truck before running around to climb in himself. They sat there breathing hard for a long minute before he reached out to start the engine. He chuckled lightly and ran long fingers through his wet hair, shaking his head like a dog and spraying water all around. "Well, we almost made it," he said cheerfully, as he backed the truck up to turn around. "Now we just gotta make it down the muddy road outta here."

When Sylvie didn't say anything, he turned to look closely at her. Her face was pale still and she had dark circles under her eyes. He frowned and stopped the truck. "Are you okay?" he asked sounding worried.

Sylvie didn't know what she was, but okay was most definitely not the word she would have used to describe how she felt. Her headache had ebbed some, but she couldn't get that shadow out of her mind and she felt like she was losing it.

She opened her eyes and turned to force a smile at Duncan. "I'm fine," she lied. Then since she was going to hell anyway for lying, she added, "Just really glad to be off that damn mountain."

He chuckled and put the truck in gear. "Me too sweetheart, me too."

Chapter 2

They nearly got stuck on the mountainside in the truck. If it wasn't for Duncan's skilled driving down the steep road, she would have stopped and waited it out. It was well after dark as it was, when they pulled onto the highway a few miles from his family's ranch. He turned off the highway and drove under the hanging Jamison Ranch sign before she realized what he was doing. As soon as she realized where he was headed, she turned to him. "Why are we going to the ranch? I had planned to stay at my parents' place."

He shook his head. "No can do. Dad told me in no uncertain tones to bring you home to stay with us. He says your parents' place is a little run-down from these past years." He didn't tell her that he had been out there to periodically check on the old place himself.

Worry knit Sylvie's brow. "I don't want to put you guys out."

Duncan laughed. "I hope you're joking my friend, because as you well know, out this far in the sticks, any company is a party."

Sylvie laughed with him. She remembered how lonely it could be out here, sometimes going months at a time without seeing anyone new. She caved, but only because she was still wondering how she had forgotten that he had lost his mom that same year. "Fine, but I'll stay on the couch."

He only shook his head again. "Jackie's room is empty, so you'll stay in there."

Sylvie thought about arguing but she now felt like someone had taken a pickaxe to the side of her head, so instead she merely nodded. "Thank you."

He nodded and didn't say more until they pulled up outside the large log cabin style home that had been in his family for generations. Sylvie eyed the place through the eyes of someone who had now seen much more of the world. "It looks older than I remember," she said

bluntly and then regretted it as she saw his eyes narrow. "I'm sorry, I didn't mean to sound rude, it just always seemed so huge and fancy when we were younger."

Duncan relaxed. "It is pretty old at this point. My great-great grandfather built it. I try to keep up with the place but with everything else going on it gets a little neglected, I'm afraid." He stared out as the heavy rain slowed to a drizzle. "Maybe we should make a run for it in case it starts up again?" he suggested mildly.

Sylvie nodded and slid right up next to the door of the truck before opening it and jumping out to run toward the wide front porch that was lined with wide pine pillars that held the roof up. The old stone and concrete stairs were showing their wear with several of the stones loose or missing and chunks of concrete gone, leaving holes in the walkway.

Duncan ran up behind her with her bags in tow. She blushed feeling foolish. She had forgotten her bags were there in the back seat of the truck. "I'm sorry, I forgot about my luggage."

He grinned and shook out his wet hair again and she looked away. He was all too familiarly sexy this way and she didn't like that she noticed it. She reached for her bags, but he held them out of reach. "Hands off, okay?" He made his way toward the solid wood front door. "You're going to make me feel like less of a man. Is that what you want?" he teased, as he hefted the heavy luggage onto the stoop next to the door.

Sylvie tried to step around him to get to the door at least but he stepped backward just then and bumped into her. She lost her balance and toppled precariously toward the concrete stairs below. She gave a little squeal once and then again as his hands closed over her shoulders to right her just in time. "I was trying to get the door for you, but instead I just got in your way."

He shrugged. "At least you're in one piece. I wouldn't want to come scrape you off the concrete in the rain."

She laughed and hurried forward to beat him to one of the bags. He dove ahead, but she laughed and shoved it to her side and out of reach. "At least let me get one of them. I hauled them around on the trip here, so I know how heavy they are. Besides, don't you know that women are taking a stand for these things now?" she joked.

He didn't fight her then but turned to open the door in front of them. When Sylvie stepped inside she felt like she had taken a step back in time. Her head spun again for a long moment and she paused, looking around at the open rooms inside. They stepped directly into one corner of the front room and she could see that the furniture was all still the same as when she and her sister had visited countless times before.

The only difference was that now it looked worn and dusty. Off to the right side was a long dining room and a sturdy looking wooden table and chairs. Straight back and kiddy corner to the front room stood the wide-open kitchen. The only thing that separated the space was the long bar which was now covered in used coffee filters, dirty dishes and what she could only imagine must have been eight years' worth of old newspapers.

Duncan saw where she was looking and groaned. "Damn. I forgot I was going to clean all that up."

Sylvie smiled widely at his embarrassment. "Believe it or not I've seen worse."

He gave her a disbelieving frown. "Your mom was always so tidy. I can't imagine it ever getting this bad."

She didn't look at him as she walked toward the open fireplace that was blazing warmly. She stuck her hands out toward the flames to warm up her icy fingers. "I don't know if you heard, but Mom passed away."

Duncan was silent for a long while before coming up behind her and wrapping her in a tight hug. "I hadn't heard. When did that happen?"

Sylvie shrugged against his chest. "It was a couple of years ago now. She had cancer and we didn't catch it until it was already too late to do anything more than make her comfortable."

He was rubbing his hands up and down her arms comfortingly. "Jesus, I'm sorry. I can't believe no one told me."

She knew she should step away from the warmth his hard body offered but instead she leaned back and against his chest. "It's probably my fault. I haven't been the best at keeping up with old friends and you know how Dad is. He can barely remember where he leaves his gun."

Duncan did know how Reagan was. He had practically grown up with two fathers back then. Everyone had teased her old man about his lack of memory and awareness, but he was quick with his gun when it counted. "How is he doing with losing your mom?"

Sylvie held back tears. "He's been a mess, but okay, I guess. He doesn't know what to do with himself, so he takes as many extra shifts as he can and spends all his spare time down at a local bar. I finally taught him how to use Uber since I was getting so many calls to go down and pick him up." She turned to look up at him.

Duncan looked thoughtfully into the flames. "Dads take it the roughest, I think. My dad fell apart when Mom passed, and he hasn't been the same since. Sometimes he does things that don't make any sense at all."

Sylvie wondered what things he was talking about but didn't ask. From her vantage point looking up at him she could see his wet dark lashes fanned out from his eyes and he looked more handsome than she ever remembered him being. She flushed a little and tried to wiggle out of his arms. He turned his blue gaze down to hers and she watched as a knowing grin spread across one side of his face. He held onto her so she couldn't go.

Heart pounding suddenly, she stared helplessly up at the man she had long ago thought she would like to marry someday. She shook her head a little. That had been such a long time ago and now they both had lives that didn't include each other. For all she knew he had a girlfriend or even a wife.

He chuckled. "No, I don't."

She stared up at him. "No, you don't what?"

He grinned and took in her beautifully tanned face. "I don't have a girlfriend."

"Okay," she said breathlessly. "But I don't know why you're telling me that."

He chuckled and his breath brushed against her cheek. "You just asked if I had a girlfriend."

Her eyes widened and she shook her head. For all that she was now a fully grown and sophisticated woman and had traveled the world, she fell back into childish speak before she could stop herself. "Did not!" She said in denial.

There was a glint of something in his cobalt eyes then as he leaned down toward her and said mere inches from her lips, "Did so."

They both laughed and she pulled back as he let her go easily. Even with the warmth of the fire, she was starting to shiver in her damp clothes, so she turned to him again. "I don't mean to be a bother, but I'd really love a shower if it's not too much to ask."

He looked at her wet clothes and grimaced. "God, I'm sorry. I guess I'm really not very good at this hospitality stuff. Come on, I'll show you up."

She followed him up the familiar wide staircase that turned halfway up making a balcony above the lower-level front room. He led her to Jackie's room, which looked as though it had been recently cleaned and put her bags inside the door. "You remember where the bathroom is, don't you?" he asked as he crossed the hall and opened a door to look inside. He frowned and then closed the door again. "Better yet, you can come use my bathroom, it's just inside my bedroom." He said as though she might not remember.

She looked at the door across the hall. "This one is fine, I'm not picky."

He shook his head adamantly. "I don't know what has happened in there, but I definitely wouldn't recommend going in."

She laughed and made a mental note to look inside later. Quickly, she gathered some dry underwear and a pair of grey sweatpants and a purple tank top. Items bundled in her arms she followed him into his tidy room. The log post bed was the same as it had been back then, only now she saw that it was merely a queen-size frame when it had always seemed so huge. There was a shirt thrown over the side of a leather armchair and she wondered if it smelled like him or if it was clean. The two tables on either side of the bed held brown and gold lamps and looked dust free. Compared to the kitchen, this place looked spotless. She wondered at that phenomenon as she made her way past him and into the bathroom that was connected to one side of the room. She smiled uncertainly at him and set her bundle on the clean countertop that ran the length of the sink cabinet and then another one on either side. "Thanks so much for all this," she said lamely.

He nodded and started to close the door. "There are fresh towels in the bottom right drawer."

She thanked him again and quickly locked the door behind him. She had forgotten shampoo in her haste to come in here, but noted with relief that he had a big bottle of it on a shelf next to the tiled tub/shower combo. She turned the water on hot and hurriedly peeled off her wet clothes and stepped under the hot spray and sighed.

She spent longer than she should have but used the excuse that she also had to shampoo her hair out. She rinsed it well and was reaching for the nozzle to turn off the tap when she thought she saw something move from the corner of her eye. She turned to stare at the window with blurry glass as a frown crinkled her brow. She could barely make out the outline of a face there. She shivered and lifted her hands to cover her breasts as she rinsed soap from her eyes and then looked again. There was nothing there now and she forced a relieved smile. She had obviously imagined whatever it was. She watched for a long while as the water slowly turned lukewarm, but she saw nothing. She shook it off and feeling a little guilty for using all the hot water, stepped out onto the plush blue rug that cushioned the beige tiled floor. She reached for the drawer and a clean towel and then she saw the blue one hanging there on the rack. She wondered if it had *his* scent on it and moved closer to smell it. It smelt clean and fresh with a little woodsy scent that she would have recognized anywhere. She grabbed it with a guilty smile and dried off.

It took her another ten minutes to brush through her hair and then she opened the door cautiously to head out. She didn't see Duncan in his room so she hurried out and took her wet things into Jackie's old room to hang them across the arm of a chair so they could dry out. She felt a little chilled, so she slipped into a soft sweater and then stepped back out looking around curiously. She walked toward Duncan's room and called softly, "Jamison? You in there?"

She heard nothing so she walked back down the hall and toward the stairs. Her nose perked up. Someone was obviously cooking, and she sniffed the air in pleasure as she made her way quickly down the stairs. She didn't see him at first as the kitchen was hidden from view but as she walked around the corner, she saw him standing on the other side of the bar. She walked silently toward him and whatever deliciousness he was cooking. "Something smells good," she said, and watched as Duncan jumped and knocked his head on the stove hood.

He cussed and rubbed a hand through his wet dark hair. "You startled me," he complained but turned to her with a smile. "Hungry?" he asked.

Sylvie smiled. "Starved but I didn't mean to startle you." She stepped closer. "What on earth is that heavenly smell?"

He held up a long cast iron griddle and grinned. "I don't know how to cook a lot of things, but I have gotten pretty good at some steak."

She stared in appreciation at the two huge T-bone steaks that were already seared and were now slowly cooking. "Those are the kind of steaks

I'd pay fifty bucks for back home."

His eyes widened before he cocked a grin. "I think I'm on the wrong end of this food chain then, because I raised this beef myself and I ain't never seen close to that price for it."

She laughed. Most of the people who lived this far out of the city owned ranches. "Maybe you aren't selling to the right company then."

He laughed and turned to her. "I do all right."

She wondered what he meant by that but didn't ask. Suddenly she realized he was in dry clothes and had obviously taken a shower already.

"When did you shower?" she asked in surprise.

One side of his mouth turned up in a lopsided grin. "As soon as you went in, I raced for the one down here myself. I had a feeling I might not have hot water if I didn't hurry."

She raised her eyebrows. "Why would you think that?

It's not like I take marathon showers."

He didn't miss a beat. "So, I'm guessing there is lots of hot water still then?" He turned to the sink to turn it on to prove a point and she laughed.

"Okay, you got me but it's probably only because you showered too." He chuckled. "Nice try, sweetheart, but I have a sister. I know the gig." Sylvie smiled and walked around the bar to stand near him. To her surprise, this side of the kitchen was quite tidy. The counter tops were clean and shiny, up until it got to the bar. She stared at the mess for a minute before forcing her gaze back to her friend.

He was staring at her with a funny look in his eyes. "It's a little strange, right?"

Sylvie shrugged; she didn't want to assume she knew what he was talking about.

He looked at the bar and then back at her again. "Dad doesn't like me to clean that part of it. He gets all worked up anytime me or Jackie try to clean it up. We can clean everywhere else in here but that has to go untouched."

She thought of her own father struggling, to make it through each day and said gently, "It really is so hard on them, isn't it."

Duncan only nodded his agreement and turned back to flip the steaks. He opened the oven and pulled out a pan filled with fresh cut potatoes, carrots, broccoli and green beans to check if they were ready.

She raised an eyebrow. "Steaks are the only thing you know how to cook, huh?"

He didn't look at her as he slid them back inside when the fork he held refused to pierce the red skinned potato. "I did have to learn a few tricks to survive you know. Steaks are great, but they'll only get you by for so long."

She laughed and walked straight to the right cupboard to pull out clean plates and glasses. “I bet you tell all the girls that.”

He shot a look at her under his brows. “You bet I do. If they think I can cook, then they start thinking that I should do all the cooking and I simply couldn’t have that.”

They both laughed as he flipped the sizzling steaks onto the plates and turned off the gas burners. Then he pulled out the steamed vegetables that were done perfectly and loaded some onto the plates. He reached into the fridge and pulled a beer out for himself. Then he remembered his manners and asked if she wanted one too. “Are you one of those prissy wine drinkers now or would you like a beer?”

She smiled and said, “I’d take a beer if that’s all you have.”

They both knew she hadn’t answered his question as they made their way past all those dusty stacks of newspapers and to the dining room table.

Chapter 3

The rain had stopped the following morning when Sylvie opened the curtains to look outside. The sky was warm yellow with orange and red light coming up from the east, and she took just a moment to take it in. She had grown up here, spent her first eighteen years here in these mountains, and still she had forgotten just how lovely the mornings were. She could see cattle off in the distance grazing the hills at the base of the mountain and smiled. *Were those Duncan's*? she wondered.

Her parents had been some of the few around who weren't ranchers and she had always felt like an outcast because of that fact. They didn't go on cattle drives or have branding days like so many of the other kids in school. Still, Duncan and his family hadn't let that get in the way of their friendship like so many others had. She heard a horse whinny and turned to look at the barn and the open field beyond where the horses grazed on fresh grass. She saw the barn door open and watched as Duncan hauled a bale of hay to drop over the fence for the horses. She watched his shoulders and arms bulge with muscle and groaned. Several of the horses came galloping over and he took a minute to talk to them and pet them before turning back to the barn again.

She felt like she hadn't been near a man in years though in truth she went out quite often. She turned back to dress as guilt flooded in that she was here being lazy, when he had obviously been up for quite a while now. She quickly gathered some clothes and made her way to the bathroom across the hall. The door was locked now, and she stared at it for a long moment before turning and going into his room again. She tried to hurry but wasn't sure how long it took to brush her long hair out smoothly and apply light make-up. She thought she made pretty quick time and was proud of that fact as she hurried down the staircase. She smelled coffee and grinned as she made her way quickly to the kitchen. There was a fresh pot there and a note that said:

Help yourself to the coffee, I imagine you still drink that. There is toast on the table. Had a few things I had to do first thing, but I'll be back in a jiffy.

She smiled and reached for a mug, pouring steaming coffee into it before making her way back to the table. There was a plate with two pieces of buttered toast and a jar of Mrs Ginny's fresh jelly next to it. She reached for it with delight.

Mrs Ginny was the wife of a local rancher, who had a real knack for gathering berries from the wild and turning them into a delectable jelly that was known three counties over. Sylvie loaded a spoonful on a piece of fresh bread and took a bite, closing her eyes as she enjoyed the bursting sweet flavor. "My God, that is even better than I remember." She proceeded to spoon some onto the other slice of toast and took a swig of her hot coffee.

She was already on her second piece of toast when she finally saw the old man staring at her. She jumped and then set the toast down quickly. She stood and hurried forward. "Mr Jamison, it's so good to see you again." She looked around the house a little as she held out a hand. "Thank you for letting me stay."

He harrumphed loudly but took her hand and shook it, squinting down at her. "Elaine? Is that you sweetheart?"

Sylvie stepped back with an uncertain smile. "It's me, Sylvie, Mr Jamison. I came to visit for a couple of days."

He smiled then and nodded. "Sylvie, of course. Yes, Duncan told me you were coming. I had forgotten about that." He looked from her to the table. "I see you found the kitchen."

She nodded quickly and stammered, "Yes, thank you."

He turned without a word and walked silently up the stairs. Sylvie watched as he disappeared around the corner before turning slowly back to her breakfast. She found the last few bites of the toast and jelly to be a bit bland and hurried to finish so she could go out to find Duncan.

Sylvie donned new brown leather boots she had bought just for this visit and grabbed a light jacket to go over her white lacy top and blue jeans before making her way outside. She walked through the grass trying to avoid the mud as she made her way around the house toward the barn. She couldn't find Duncan anywhere inside, so she walked out and around the large red painted barn, to the back. She jumped when the horse whinnied nervously as she rounded the corner. With a start, the horse shimmied sideways, and she watched with concern as Duncan pulled hard on the reigns. "Whoa boy. It's just an old friend."

The horse settled and Sylvie shielded her eyes to look up at the man seated in the saddle. He wore a black and grey cotton button down with the sleeves rolled up to his elbows. He grinned and her heart beat a little faster. His jean clad thighs tensed and relaxed sexily as he held the horse between them. He whistled low from under his grey cowboy hat. "Well, now don't you look all fresh today."

Sylvie blushed a little and looked down at her brand-new jeans and boots. "It's nothing fancy," she murmured self-consciously.

He chuckled. "Around these parts that kind of clothing is about as fancy as it gets." He lifted one leg and slid down to the ground off his horse.

"Sorry to leave you alone this morning, but I had some things that need doing today."

She shrugged and then grinned up at him. "Thanks for the breakfast, I haven't had her jelly since I left. It was delicious as always."

He stepped close and she could smell the fresh mountain air on his skin. "I thought you might like that. Old Mrs Ginny's jelly has been a staple in our house since before I can remember."

Sylvie stepped close to the horse as he held the reigns. She reached out a hand to let the tall black stallion smell her before moving closer. He jerked his head back and sidestepped until Duncan pulled tight on the reigns again. "Whoa boy, she isn't going to hurt you. Just calm down."

She stepped back. "He sure is jumpy."

Duncan turned to smile easily. "I don't usually ride the stallions, but I picked him up from an old fella a couple of counties over and it's obvious he's been abused, so I have been trying to work with him to get him over the fear."

Sylvie nodded and made another attempt at the horse. She moved very slowly toward him. "So, you are a little afraid, are you?" she asked gently, as she stepped cautiously forward. "It's okay, I think you are big and beautiful, and I only want to rub you a little for now." She touched the star on his forehead lightly with her fingertips.

The horse breathed heavily and watched her but didn't jerk back again. Rubbing little circles, she stepped closer to let him get used to her presence. The horse stuck his head out and sniffed her jacket and then seemed to relax a little as she walked down the side running her hands along his neck and back. "See, I'm okay, aren't I?" she asked lightly, and smiled when the horse gave a nervous little shiver. "I'd like to ride you if you're all right with it." Duncan was shaking his head, but Sylvie had already stepped one booted foot into the saddle and then pulled herself up and over. To his surprise, the stallion stayed steady.

He lifted his head to look up at her angrily. "Are you insane? He could have stomped you or bucked you off and hurt you."

Sylvie only grinned down as she leaned into the stallion's long neck and hugged him lightly. "You weren't going to buck me off were you, buddy? You like me, don't you?" Her lips were puckered as she said the last and ran fingers through his long black main. She turned toward a worried looking Duncan. "I could tell he wouldn't throw me," she said confidently.

Duncan didn't agree. "He hasn't let anyone but me near him since I brought him here, so I don't know why he is so calm."

Sylvie laughed lightly as she continued rubbing the horse's neck gently. "It's because I smell like you."

Duncan raised an eyebrow in curiosity. "Come again?"

Sylvie chuckled again. "I used your shampoo last night so I'm guessing

I smell familiar to him."

Duncan grinned. He wasn't sure why, but the thought of her using his shampoo made him happy. He quickly changed the direction his mind was heading with long years of practice. How many times had he looked at Sylvie back then and wanted to kiss her? He hadn't though.

He had always kept his hands to himself like the good kid that he was. She was so much younger than him that it simply hadn't been okay. He grinned as he realized he hadn't changed his line of thought after all. He looked up at her curvy figure on his stallion with her tight jeans and boots and wondered if kissing her would be okay now.

He shook his head as he found himself wishing that he was the horse as her fingertips ran up and down soothingly. He felt himself harden and looked away. She would be out of here again in the next day or two and he would be left here missing her once again. He wasn't ready to feel anything for her now.

Sylvie held out a hand toward him. "So, are you going to give me the reigns or what, Jamison?"

He looked up in surprise. Her sitting on the stallion while he held the reigns were one thing, but he'd be damned if he was going to let her ride the thing.

"Are you out of your ever-loving mind, Sylvie?" he asked rudely.

She didn't take it personally. "Come on. You know he wants me to ride him. Don't you, baby?" she said gently as she ran a hand down his neck again."

Duncan's eyes darkened a little under his hat and he asked incredulously,

"Have you even been on a horse since you left?"

She laughed softly and shook her head. "No, but there is no time like the present and besides, it's like riding a bike don't you think?"

He snorted which made the stallion sidestep again. He held the reigns firmly and said, "No, I don't think at all."

Sylvie puckered up her bottom lip. "Please Daddy, come on. I really want to ride him, and he seems fine with me. This was my favorite part of growing up around all the ranches and farms here."

Duncan wanted to bite her bottom lip but instead said, "Fine, I'll saddle up one of the mares and you can ride out with me to check on the herd."

She looked thrilled. "Okay, here give me the reigns and I'll hold him here until you get back."

Duncan groaned. "You will be riding the mare, sweetheart."

Sylvie nodded mutely as though beaten. "Fine then." She swung her leg over and jumped down as Duncan looped the reigns around the post and tied the horse off before turning to walk back into the barn. He waited for her to follow. When she didn't immediately follow, he turned back.

“Are you coming?” he asked impatiently.

Sylvie shook her head. “I’ll just stay here and pet this big guy for a bit.” He swore under his breath at her stubborn streak and went inside to saddle one of their mildest mares. After eight years without riding, it was better to be safe than sorry. He took his time saddling the mare.

Minutes later, as he followed behind her and the stallion at a quick gallop while trying to catch up, he wondered how he had fallen for it. She raced happily ahead of him as the stallion stretched out his long neck and hooves flying across the grasslands. Duncan cursed and prodded the mare. Why had he picked such a slow horse? Now, he didn’t know if he could catch up.

By the time he’d walked out with the saddled mare Sylvie had already been long gone on the stallion. She left the gate unlatched for him as he jumped on the mare and tried to catch her before she got herself killed. After a long gallop she slowed the horse down and smiled back at him as she let him catch up. “He is beautiful,” she exclaimed joyfully and reached down to pet the horse again. “You’re such a good boy, aren’t you?”

Still angry, Duncan glared. “A dangerous beauty is what he is. I can’t believe you played me like that.”

Sylvie turned to look at him and met his flashing blue eyes, “I’m sorry, I shouldn’t have, but look at him. I really couldn’t resist.”

With her smiling and obviously so happy and apparently safe as well, he couldn’t hold a grudge. “You always could ride,” he said with an appreciative smile.

Sylvie laughed at his grudging tone. “Don’t sound so thrilled there, Duncan, or I might think you actually hoped this big guy would buck me off.”

A helpless grin took over his face. “And so damn stubborn.”

She laughed happily and let the reigns loose as she urged the stallion back into a run. He followed closely behind on the chestnut mare. When the horse began to feel tired, she eased him back into a walk and turned to watch Duncan as he rode up to the side of them. She felt more carefree and relaxed than she had in years. The sun was just over the mountain top now and the light hit his shoulders and chest and the dark hair that curled at the nape of his neck beneath his hat. She gave a little sigh.

“Did you know that I used to have a major crush on you back in the day?” She didn’t know why she said it, but she had and now wanted to see his reaction.

His eyes darkened slightly as he looked surprised at her candor before he hid his expression. “Really,” was all he said.

Sylvie wasn’t sure whether to be offended by that or not. She watched him for a long moment waiting for him to say more. He didn’t and she smiled. Somehow, that made his reaction more to her liking and she bobbed her head. "Yeah, I used to dream of what it would be like to kiss you."

He looked uncomfortable at her words which she liked a lot, so she continued. "I used to think I was going to marry you someday."

He wouldn't look at her now and that made her feel bold. "I knew you and Elaine would eventually realize that you weren't right for each other, and I would imagine you coming over and telling me that I was the one you liked all along."

He grumbled something low and unintelligible. She grinned as his eyes finally came up to meet her own. There was something hungry there and her heart missed a beat. "Then your mom and Elaine died and nothing else seemed to matter anymore." She took a long breath. "Did you ever think of kissing me too?"

He groaned and in a split second before she knew what was happening, swerved his horse close and wrapped an arm around her waist and pulled her onto his lap. His head came down hard over her surprised upturned lips demanding hers to part.

She had been so curious about him for so long that she wasn't about to stop him now. She had always wondered what he tasted like. He answered that question for her as his tongue swept inside and she got her first drug inducing lick of his spicy flavor. He tasted of coffee and fresh air and sweet, sweet spice, and she couldn't stop the shiver that ran the length of her body. He grinned a little against her mouth and then pulled back to stare down at her. "Does that answer your question well enough?"

Sylvie gasped for air and smiled. "Loud and clear, Jamison." And then because she was already floating on the precipice of disaster, figured she may as well jump off. "So why did it take you so long to do that then?"

He groaned and his mouth took hers again in a hungry kiss. Now that he had tasted her intoxicating sweetness, he didn't want to stop. She moved a little and before he realized what she was doing had turned around to straddle his waist. Then, she leaned into the kiss again, biting his tongue. He gripped her hips and then ran his hands up and down her back and sides unable to get enough of her.

When she began unbuttoning his shirt, he held her hands. "Not here sweetheart and not like this." He moved her hands away determinedly and held them in his.

Sylvie blinked. "I'm sorry, I got a little carried away."

He looked pleased at her apology. Her brown eyes were warm, and her dark lashes fluttered there against her half-closed lids. Her wide lips were pink and swollen from his kiss. The cleft in her chin prominent as she breathed in heavily. "You are goddamned beautiful, you know?" he said in a low voice.

She blinked at him again.

He grinned. He liked it much better when he was the one saying things that threw her off guard. He bent his head and touched his forehead to hers before giving her a quick peck. "Now, why don't we give this poor mare a break," he said as he lifted her off his hard erection and swung her around.

Before she knew what he was doing he settled her in the saddle and slid off and onto the stallion's back. He threw a grin over his shoulder and urged the stallion into a trot.

Behind him, Sylvie grumbled in surprise. "Hey, that's not fair." Then she prodded the tired mare into a quick trot to try and catch him. The mare was slow, and it took her a good while before she finally pulled up to his side. "What did you do, pick the slowest horse in the barn?" she asked accusingly.

He only grinned at her over his shoulder. "The herd is right over this hill. After I check on them, we can do whatever you want for the rest of the day."

With his taste still on her lips she smiled. She knew exactly what she would like to do for the day, but she wasn't sure he would go for it. She held her silence as the horse plodded slowly up the hill and then a little faster down the other side. She gasped as she saw the herd. There were what looked to be thousands of black Angus beef cows, steers, and calves that grazed lazily in the morning sun. She stared across at him. "Are all of these cattle yours, Duncan?"

He nodded and then held out a hand to wag it back and forth.

"Well, sort of."

She didn't know what to make of his cryptic response. "What I mean is, are these all Jamison beef?"

He turned and looked out over the herd. "In a matter of speaking. They all have our brand on them. But we do what we call an investment option for city folk or other ranchers that want beef cattle but don't have the acreage for them."

Sylvie stared at the herd in amazement, beginning to see what he was talking about. Then she stared at him for a long moment. "This was your idea, wasn't it?"

He grinned again and nodded. "When Mom died, and Dad started losing focus on the ranch I had to step up and take over things." He paused and then turned back to her. "It soon became evident that we were well on our way to bankruptcy. We had tons of acreage for grazing and plenty of room for cattle, but the herd was dwindling and there wasn't money to buy more cattle."

A smile dawned on Sylvie's face. "So you found investors?"

He nodded. "Of sorts. I didn't want to put any more acreage at risk for collateral so I couldn't go to the banks, but I heard a few of the farmers talking about how they'd like to grow a few beefs but didn't have the acreage to do it. It gave me an idea. What if I could get other people to buy the cattle for me and then I could run them on the ranch here until they were ready for market, and then we could split the profits? At first the old timers didn't trust it but over time we have built up quite a clientele. Now, several people from the city have also invested. We tag them for each buyer, but they are all branded with the Jamison beef brand. When they are filled out, the owners can choose to sell them on the market or even as many of them do, have one or two slaughtered for their own personal use."

Sylvie looked at the herd again. "So, most of these are actually owned by people who don't ever see them?"

He chuckled. "Only about half. It turns out there are a lot of wannabe ranchers in these parts who love telling their friends about their cattle in the country over cocktails and golf."

She laughed. "It is a genius plan. Do you guys come out on it okay?"

Duncan grinned and pulled off his hat to run fingers through his dark hair. "It works great for me. I don't ever have to pay money out for beef, but I rake in the profits at auction anyway. I've been able to pay off all the debts the last two generations racked up and have expanded our personal herd to three times the size it has ever been. It's also a plus for the local farmers as I have contracts with them to buy nearly all of their crops for feed. They give me a great price and in return have a guaranteed buyer where some years they couldn't sell before." He gave her a mocking grin. "Then we ship all the beef to the city where rich people pay top dollar for it. Their way of giving back, I suppose."

Sylvie wondered if it was a dig at her own law profession. "Isn't all this land and cattle worth a fortune?" she asked pointedly.

Duncan shrugged. "I suppose it's worth a bit, though I wouldn't say a fortune."

She laughed at his purposely vague tone. "Right," was all she said as they turned to ride back to the ranch house.

Chapter 4

Because the rain had most likely made the trail up the mountain impassable, Sylvie planned to spend her afternoon at Jackie's house. She and Duncan drove over after a light lunch at the Jamison ranch house. Sylvie was feeling quite impressed with Duncan's success in the cattle business, though he played off every compliment she gave him, as though it was a group effort with his dad. She didn't know what Mr Jamison was up to or how he had been involved, but it was obvious to her that something was wrong with him. She couldn't quite put her finger on what, only felt something off when he came again at lunch but only watched in silence as her and Duncan ate.

As they loaded a few things into his truck that Duncan wanted to take to Jackie's, she turned and once again saw him standing in the house and watching her from the window. She shivered a little nervously and turned away. Her headache was starting to come back, and she lifted her fingers to lightly massage her temples.

Duncan raised an eyebrow in obvious concern. "Is your head hurting again?" he asked as he shut the tailgate and came around to stand by her.

Sylvie grimaced and nodded. "A little."

Duncan opened her door and helped her inside before closing it and walking around to the driver's side door. She couldn't help noticing his broad shoulders flexing as he put the truck in gear. With a little smile she turned and buckled her seat belt. Duncan chuckled. "Sylvie Dunlap are you actually wearing a seat belt?" he asked jokingly.

She grinned. "Hey, when you see as many pile ups on the freeways as I have, you learn a thing or two."

He grinned as he buckled his own seat belt. Sylvie had never liked wearing the things when they were younger. No matter how much he and Elaine had begged her to put it on, she always wanted to feel free and unrestricted. "I get it," was all he said.

The air sizzled now with the electricity between them since their kiss this morning and had left them both a little on edge. He wished she hadn't told him about the youthful crush, wished he could put this genie back in the bottle. After all Duncan liked feeling in control at all times, but since she had called only a week before to say she was coming he felt like his world was off kilter. He was glad she'd come, no doubt about that. It was always good to see old friends and Sylvie was one he had often found himself wondering about.

He'd heard the rumors that circulated of course. Everyone in these parts was proud of the prodigy lawyer that she had become. He had also been proud though it had been bittersweet as she had left without a word and never looked back. When she had called him to say she was coming home and wanted to hike up and set a memorial for Elaine, he had been surprised. Then he'd realized that she hadn't talked to anyone else back home either. That at least had made him feel a little better.

But now here she sat in his truck as though eight years hadn't passed, only they had. And she was now a sophisticated version of the girl that had left. Her long hair was sleek, and sun bleached making her normally light brown hair shine blondish now. He caught himself wondering if she had professional highlights to get that look and forced his gaze back to the road. He had been doing just fine until she had gone and practically asked him to kiss her this morning. Now, he couldn't stop thinking about her legs around his waist as she leaned passionately into the kiss.

She cleared her throat. "So are we going to talk about what happened this morning or are you one of those no kiss and talk men." She smiled lightly as she rubbed at her head.

He couldn't help the easy grin as he turned and met her warm brown gaze for a moment. "I suppose I'm the kind of guy that can take whatever comes in stride."

His open honesty was refreshing, and Sylvie nodded. "I do believe that."

"Would you believe me if I told you I almost didn't call you?" He raised an eyebrow in question.

She sighed. "After leaving the way I did. Each year it became harder and harder to think of coming back. I actually wondered if you and Jackie would be either mad at me or have completely forgotten about me. I thought about renting a hotel in the city and driving out here alone to do the hike."

He pulled off the highway and onto a dirt road. "What made you change your mind?"

She shrugged. "I realized that Elaine meant something to you at one time as well and I also realized I was being a chicken."

He laughed. "If I remember correctly being a chicken is one thing you weren't. I don't think you ever turned down a challenge by any of us."

She turned and smiled at him. The light banter was beginning to alleviate her headache and she took a deep breath and put her hands in her lap. "No, I never could stand the thought of not being brave."

He pulled the truck off the road then and she looked around in surprise. There was nothing but open range on either side of the road. She turned to look at him, but he was already sliding out of the truck. She watched as he walked around the truck and opened her door. She didn't move then, only watched as he deftly reached around her and undid her buckle. Wondering now if he was going to kick her out of his truck, she stared up at him with concern. His eyes darkened as her gaze held his. She put her hands on his shoulders as he lifted her and easily slid her down his hard body.

Heat surged everywhere they touched, and Sylvie gulped and stared up at him. "What are we doing?"

He grinned. "It's less what we are doing and more about what *you* are going to do."

She raised her eyebrows in surprise.

He laughed, his voice low and throaty. "I dare you to kiss me."

She stared at him wide eyed. She didn't like being put on the spot. Was in fact, much better with putting people on the spot herself. She gave a little shake of her head. "I don't think that is a good idea right now."

His blue eyes darkened again as she backed away an inch. She backed into the truck and lost her balance. He caught her and easily righted her before taking his hands off her again. "Chicken," he rasped a few inches from her neck.

She shivered. "It's not that, Duncan. I just don't think it's a good idea to start anything right before we go to Jackie's. Besides aren't we going to be late?"

He merely grinned, "Jackie will be thrilled whenever we get there." He watched her, his blue eyes piercing as she squirmed. "It's not hard Sylvie, all you have to do is lean forward and kiss me."

She swallowed again. She tried to move toward him. Tried to give him a quick peck on the lips but couldn't will herself forward. She stared, transfixed as he lifted a hand to place on her shoulder and slid it erotically up her neck and back down again. "Does this help?" he asked.

Her mouth went dry. She couldn't focus with the shivers working their way out from her neck. His thumb lowered to run across her collar bone and then back. He held her gaze there in his own, unwavering one. His other hand lifted to thread into her hair at the back of her neck rubbing his fingertips there. Her neck arched back, and her lips parted a few inches from his own.

God, she wanted him to kiss her. He didn't move toward her however, only trailed those magnetic fingertips down her neck and her shoulders and then down her arms. Only to trail right back up again. She couldn't resist the urge to align her body with his even as her stubborn mind wouldn't let her lean forward and take what she wanted. She knew he wanted that from her, wanted her uncomfortable and off kilter.

Instead, she lifted her own hands to his shoulders and ran her fingers there. Heat enveloped her as she felt each muscle tense under her fingertips and power surged through her. Without thought, she lifted onto her toes and nipped at his lips.

He growled and his arms came down around her waist like steel bands, pulling her tight against his hard erection. She moaned as his tongue darted out to force her lips apart.

In the melding of heat and passion he knew her addictive taste and was afraid he would never get enough.

She melted against him and moaned, giving back as much as she got from the kiss. He pulled back suddenly, looking at once pleased and cocky. He lifted her back into the truck and buckled her seatbelt as she tried to kiss him again. He gave her a gentle kiss on her forehead. "It's not quite the same when you aren't in control, is it?" He drawled lazily and closed the door as he walked back around the truck and slid inside.

Sylvie breathed heavily, feeling hot and used. Her temper flared as he threw her a cocky grin. Golden sparks flew from her brown eyes as she met his gaze. "What in the hell was that?"

He grinned and started the truck. "I figured you could take as good as you gave this morning."

She couldn't even begin to understand what he meant by that. She turned to stare out the window as anger burned hotly through her. Had he been trying to prove a point? Hurt followed closely in the wake of the anger. She had been wanting to kiss him since she was fifteen and now she wished she had never been honest about that. She should have left well enough alone.

He reached out and took her hand then and slid his fingers between her own before she could pull back. In a calm serious tone he said, "I'm sorry if I offended you. I didn't want that, but Sylvie?" He waited for her pained gaze to meet his own. "I don't like to be played with."

She looked away and at the floor. "I wasn't playing with you," she sounded hurt.

He held her hand snugly in his. "No? Are you planning on hanging around these parts then?"

She looked up at him then. "Of course not! My whole life is in North Carolina now."

He nodded. "I'm occasionally okay with the casual relationship here and there."

Sylvie nodded. "Exactly, we could just have a casual fling while I'm here."

He shook his head. "Never with you."

She wasn't sure whether or not she wanted to know why so she didn't ask. Instead, she gave him a miserable nod and turned to look out her window. "Can we please go now?"

He didn't say anything, only let go of her hand and put the truck in gear. They drove the last three miles in silence. He didn't like that the spark was gone now from her face and eyes, but it was better than getting involved with her only to have her turn around and leave again for the next eight years. When he'd lost his mom, then Elaine and then Sylvie all those years ago it had almost broken him. Jackie was the only thing that had given him the strength to keep going. He wouldn't play around with Sylvie now, only to lose her again.

She slid out of the truck and hurried to the back before he'd even put it in park. He cursed under his breath as he quickly shut off the engine and caught up to her before she could load both boxes he had in the back into her arms. He clucked his tongue and hefted them away from her. "I've got these if you can get the door," he said.

She didn't look at him, only turned to walk ahead of him up the concrete pathway to the concrete steps ahead. She had never seen Jackie's house and looked around with a smile. "It's nice."

Duncan grunted as she quickly stepped up the stairs to the front door of the brick house. She reached out a hand to knock but the door swung open to reveal an older and much bigger, smiling Jackie. Sylvie hesitated but Jackie flew out the door and wrapped her in a warm hug. "My god, Sylvie. It's so good to see you again."

Sylvie hugged her old friend back as well as she could around the well-rounded tummy. "Thanks for letting me come over. I'm sure you don't feel much like company this far along."

Jackie let out a cackle of laughter. "Are you kidding me? At this point in my pregnancy, I look for every distraction I can get." She stepped back to look Sylvie up and down with a low moan. "How can you look so good after eight years while I look like an overstuffed cow," she complained as she wrapped an arm around her friend's shoulders and turned to usher her inside.

Sylvie laughed. "You look charming and lovely, and you know it." She wasn't lying. Jackie's dark hair and blue eyes, much like Duncan's, shone and her face had that glow that pregnancy always seemed to lend. Her face, though older, now looked smooth and radiant with fulfilled joy.

Jackie smiled. "While that is very kind of you, I feel huge."

Her body looked slim and elegant with the bump of her unborn baby sloping graciously out and downward before tapering at her hips. Sylvie gave her a perusing look. "Well, if that is huge at eight months may God grant me the same leniency if I ever get pregnant. How do you feel?" She looked concerned as Jackie reached a hand and settled it on the curve of her back.

Jackie shrugged. "As good as it gets after eight months, I'm afraid."

That had them both smiling and Duncan grunting grumpily to catch their attention. "Where do you want this stuff, Sis? Or should I just hold it all day."

Jackie turned as though seeing him there for the first time since they'd arrived. "Oh, hi Dunc. You can just set them on the table over there." She pointed to a large square room that looked like it doubled as a living room and playroom for her two older kids. "I'll go through it later."

Duncan walked over to carefully set the boxes down before turning back to give his sister a hug. "How is my nephew feeling today?" he asked as he leaned down towards her protruding belly.

Jackie glared, "Better than me as he won't stop kicking up a storm today." She turned suddenly. "Hey. How did the hike go? I really wish I could have been there for the memorial."

Sylvie met Duncan's gaze for only a minute before shaking her head and saying, "We didn't make it to the top before the storm swooped in and chased us down the mountain."

Jackie's eyes twinkled. "I have so many great memories of running down to beat the storm."

Both Sylvie and Duncan smiled as they too had those memories. Suddenly Jackie looked sad. "It's so strange, isn't it? All of us being here together without her?" She got twin nods of agreement and continued. "Elaine was like the nucleus of our little group." She smiled at Sylvie and then said happily, "Now you are some kind of big shot lawyer, aren't you?" She walked over and put an arm around her friend's shoulder and turned her toward the kitchen. "Come in and tell me all about it and we'll say hello to Ren."

Sylvie allowed herself to be pulled along into the bright red painted kitchen with bright white cabinets and silver countertops. It was warm and cozy while also looking spectacular. She looked around and smiled. "It looks great in here Jackie."

Jackie beamed at her and pointed toward the dining room where a tall blond-haired man stood next to two toddler girls, obviously trying to feed them. "This is all Ren's doing," she gushed happily. "He spoils me and the girls and has put so much work into this old house. It's practically new again."

Ren turned as he heard their voices and set down the spoons he held in each hand. He walked toward them with a warm smile. "Hello," he said, holding out a hand to Sylvie.

Sylvie liked him instantly. "Hi."

Jackie moved toward him, and he wrapped an arm around her shoulder.

She smiled at Sylvie. "This is Ren, Ren this is Sylvie."

He had cobalt blue eyes and a broad handsome face. "It's so nice to finally meet you, Ren," she said warmly.

He nodded. "And likewise. Jackie has told me so much about you over the years. I'm just happy to finally put a face to the name."

There was an ear-shattering screech from the dining table across the room, which had Ren and Jackie turning in unison. One of the girls had a spoon in one hand which had somehow got tangled in the other girl's hair leaving apple sauce in its wake as she tugged on it trying to pull it out.

Jackie moaned and rushed forward. "Oh no, Olivia! You guys already had a bath tonight." She extricated the spoon carefully, trying to remove as much of the sauce as possible. Ren had already gotten a clean washcloth wet and was walking over to help his girls.

Olivia who had dark straight hair like her mother, immediately puckered up. In a slur only a three-year-old can make, she complained. "But I was twying to give Owiana a bite." Jackie rolled her eyes and smiled at Sylvie in sorrow.

"I know sweetie, Mommy's not mad. We will just have to clean Ariana's hair again."

Ariana, Olivia's twin sister, sat still as Ren tried unsuccessfully to wipe little splotches of apple sauce from her blonde hair. Her eyes teared up and finally she turned and threw herself at Ren. "Owivia got my hair awl dirty Daddy," she exclaimed as sobs shook her shoulders.

"I'm sorry, Owiana, I didn't mean to." Now Olivia was in tears and threw herself at Ren as well. Sylvie watched in fascination as he lifted one on each arm and stood.

"There, there girls, it's all going to be okay. Why don't we just finish our food and then you can go back in the tub with baby shark and your toys for a bit?" Both girls bobbed their heads, and he settled them once again on their chairs. "Do you girls want to hug and make up first?"

Both heads shook in unison and Sylvie grinned. She felt Duncan behind her and turned to see him watching her with those unnerving blue eyes. "They are really something else, aren't they?" she asked, remembering when her and Elaine had fought in much the same way.

Duncan grinned. "Little she devils is what they are. When they get a mind to work together, they manage to get everyone wrapped around their fingers."

She laughed softly. She remembered that too. A fresh surge of pain came with a memory of her and Elaine ganging up to beg their dad for a new doll when he took them to the store. Their mother had already told them no, but their dad couldn't resist when they both puckered up together. Tears filled her eyes for a moment, and she looked away.

Duncan noticed but didn't say anything. Instead, he hurried over to give both of the girls puckering kisses on the cheeks and a pat on each head.

Both girls squealed in delight. "Unca Dunca," they said in unison as they realized he was there. Both climbed up to stand on their chairs and

reached their arms out to him much to the frustration of Ren who was trying to get them to take bites of food. Finally, he stood up from his slouch and said with a grin.

"Why don't you girls let Uncle Duncan feed you then."

Two nods of happy agreement had Duncan sitting down and plopping one on each knee as he reached for their dishes. "All righty then, which of you can eat the fastest?" Both girls lifted their arms in the air emphatically. "Me, Unca Dunca, me." With a playful laugh and a little tickle for each of them he settled in to feed them bites in quick succession.

Ren came over to stand by her then. "He has been a godsend with the girls."

Sylvie turned and met his gaze. "I bet." Then because she couldn't help herself, she muttered. "He always was good with the ladies."

Ren raised an eyebrow at the last. "Am I sensing a little bitterness there?" he asked gently.

Sylvie shook her head and looked away. "Not at all, as you know he and my sister Elaine used to date."

He nodded and smiled. "I hear a similar story from nearly every girl around these parts."

She chuckled. "He did make the rounds."

Chapter 5

When Jackie started pulling things from the large stainless-steel refrigerator, Sylvie rushed over to help. They made lasagna with meat and veggies, loaded in cheesy layers with red sauce and noodles. Then Ren pulled out French bread and sliced it so they could toast it with a garlicky butter spread. Jackie and Sylvie cut vegetables for a fresh salad together while visiting about the old days. Silence settled over the room for a long moment after Ren took the girls from Duncan to the bathroom for a fresh clean up.

After a quiet moment Duncan asked, "Are you going to try hiking up the mountain again tomorrow?"

Sylvie nodded. "That will be my last chance since I have a flight out the following morning."

He frowned. "I don't want you going up alone. If you wait until I can get a few things done in the morning, I'll come with."

Sylvie stared hard at him. What was the point? "I don't mind going alone."

Jackie watched them with a frown. "I don't think it's a good idea to go up there alone, Sylvie. Look what happened to Mom and Elaine. I couldn't take it if I lost another friend because they chose to go up into the mountains alone." She looked tired and stressed, so Sylvie nodded.

"Fine." Then when she saw the small smile on Duncan's lips she added. "I'm going up first thing though so if you really want to come, you'd better be ready."

He stilled, and his eyes held her angry ones for a long time before he finally gave her a curt nod. "I'll be ready."

Jackie looked between them again. "Is there something going on here that I don't know about?" she asked conversationally.

Both Duncan and Sylvie shook their heads, but Duncan was the one who answered first. "Nothing out of the ordinary. Sylvie just thinks she still has that stubborn streak from back in the day. I'll keep her safe though, don't worry about that."

Sylvie rinsed the knife she was washing and turned away. She made a show of digging through her purse and checking her phone before she remembered there was poor reception here in the mountains. She didn't know why she was letting Duncan get to her so badly but admitted that he did, if only to herself. She was usually a direct person and in North Carolina people seemed to be okay with that, even admire it. Here, she felt like Duncan was punishing her for her directness and she didn't like it.

Jackie came over to stand by her. "Are you okay?" she asked gently. Sylvie looked up to meet her blue eyes and smiled. "Of course."

Her friend studied her expression. "I know it's been a really long time, but I do remember that you would always clam up and get quiet whenever something was bothering you."

Sylvie wasn't ready to admit to anything, so she changed the subject.

"Do you like living all the way out here?"

Jackie smiled widely and with obvious joy. "I never was like you and Duncan. I always wanted to stay here. The mountains are in my blood and when Ren moved out here after he left the service it felt like fate had brought him to me. Speaking of which." She turned in the direction he had disappeared and said, "I really should go help him with the girls."

Sylvie nodded and Jackie hurried out. She looked down at her hands avoiding Duncan and whatever he was doing. He came to stand closer than she wanted him to, and she backed up a step. He advanced and lifted a hand to her chin to force her gaze up to him. "Are you mad at me, Sylvie?" he asked seriously.

She looked away and shook her head. "Of course not. Why would I be mad?" she asked, sounding as though she couldn't fathom the idea. She was after all a lawyer now, and half of being a good lawyer was the innate ability to convince a judge and jury of her convictions. She swung her gaze up to meet his steadily.

He let her go and stepped back. She was lying through her teeth. He really didn't like this version of her. "I'm sorry if I offended you. I was only trying to prove a point. I know you aren't planning to be here long, and I don't want a casual fling with you."

Sylvie gave a firm bob of her head. "Message received, Jamison."

He groaned. "No, it isn't, dammit." He advanced on her again. "I spent so much time thinking about you and wondering how you were after you

left. But things were hectic here and I couldn't leave and go check on you. Now, here you are again and you're sleek, and beautiful with a sophisticated air and all I want to do is take you to bed." His eyes darkened with intent. "The problem, is that I'm not sure I can handle watching you walk away again."

Sylvie's brown eyes clashed with his. "What the hell do you want from me, Duncan."

His eyes narrowed and his gaze moved to her lips before coming back to rest on her eyes again. "I want more than a one-night fling," he said simply and closed the distance between them. As his head came down over hers, he said in a pleading tone, "The problem is, that I can't keep my hands off you."

Her lips parted as though to respond and he took advantage, sliding his hot tongue inside to rub against her own, building heat and friction there. It took her a minute to relax, but when she did, her arms slid up around his neck and she leaned into him and the kiss. Her brain turned to mush as he threaded his long strong fingers into her hair and deepened the kiss.

He backed her up against the counter trapping her there in the mindless pleasure, the surge of passion shimmering there between them. She moaned and his hands ran down her back, cupping her jean clad butt and pulling her tightly against him. She whimpered against his tongue and a low growl erupted from his throat as he lifted her hips to sit her on the counter and she wrapped her legs around him. He wanted her here and now.

"Well, I guess you two left a few details out, didn't you?" Jackie asked with a little laugh. They jerked apart so fast that Sylvie nearly fell to the floor. Duncan righted her shoulders and then stepped back again as they both turned to see Jackie and Ren each with one twin in hand, watching avidly from the hallway.

Ren grinned and met Jackie's gaze for a moment before turning back to the two adults with guilty expressions. It was, however, Olivia who broke the silence. "Unca Dunca kissed that girl, Owiana."

Ariana nodded her head with wide eyes, whispering. "I saw it too." Both girls pushed against their parents until they let them down and rushed toward Duncan.

A little suspiciously they skirted a wide trail around Sylvie and then threw their arms around Duncan's legs. "Unca Dunca?" Ariana asked and he reached down and patted her back.

"Yes Ariana?"

She looked very serious. "Why did you kiss that stranger?" Her lips puckered into a pout. "You posed to kiss me and Owivia."

All the adults burst into laughter as he lifted them and kissed them each on the cheek. "Sylvie here isn't a stranger, girls, and sometimes we have to share." He gave Sylvie a quick wink.

Ren rushed forward with a horrified look. "I'm not sure sharing a kissing buddy is exactly the kind of information these girls need, Duncan."

He only grinned and let the girls go to their father. He held Sylvie's gaze for a hot moment before turning to his sister. "On that note, I wonder if the lasagna is done." He walked over to open the oven and look inside.

Jackie smiled. "Oh no you don't, Duncan. You aren't getting out of this that easily."

Sylvie blushed and then she laughed. "I agree with Duncan. That lasagna is looking delicious."

The girls played with dolls on the floor while the adults ate and visited. It was a wonderful afternoon all in all for Sylvie who very rarely had such dinners, unless it was with clients and then she felt like she was always putting on a show. She was very grateful for the warmth and laughter.

She said goodbye to Jackie, Ren and the twins just after eight o'clock and asked Duncan to drive her home. As he started the truck and drove down his sister's driveway, Sylvie turned to look at him. "I think it's probably best if I go stay at my folks' place tonight." He had kissed her again, and she was beginning to feel like she was in over her head. He had been pretty clear about not wanting a fling. She had no intention of staying here in Idaho past her scheduled vacation, so all in all she figured it would be best to put some space between them. He hadn't said anything, so she shrugged and looked out the window. "I can't stay here so I don't see the point."

He drove for a while in silence before finally saying, "I'd feel better if you stayed with us."

She turned back to him. "My parents' place is perfectly adequate, and I don't want you to feel like you have to put me up."

He pulled into the ranch lot and parked near the log house. She beat him out again and he groaned and ran his fingers through his hair as he followed her inside. His dad was nowhere to be seen but that wasn't unusual these days. He watched her hurry up the stairs and followed. "Sylvie, wait up. Can we just talk about this?"

She shook her head and practically ran into Jackie's old room and began throwing her stuff into her bags. "I am leaving on a flight in two days Duncan, I don't think there is much else I can say."

He swore low and walked toward her. "Sylvie, I'm not asking for a commitment here."

She saw him coming and rounded the bed keeping it between them.

"Good, because I can't commit to anything."

He shook his head as his blue eyes narrowed in frustration. "Fine," he said in a clipped tone. "I'll drive you over."

She met his gaze then and nodded. "I really wasn't trying to make things complicated. You have to believe me on that." Her tone turned pleading. "It was just a momentary lapse of judgment because you're good looking and I haven't dated in a while."

He looked insulted. "Is that right?" His tone was hard and unyielding.

She nodded emphatically. "Right. I'm ready to go now," she said as she pulled her packed luggage down to the floor. She marched right past him with her nose in the air.

He groaned and followed, hurrying to catch her and relieve her of her bags. As they came down the stairs, he thought he heard the kitchen water running. When he turned and looked, however, his father wasn't there. He sighed again and followed her quick stride out to his truck. He hefted the bags easily into the back and walked around to open her door. She gave him a wide berth by hopping onto the seat and moving nearly to the center away from him. He grinned and closed the door walking with a fast stride to slide inside himself. She was now on the far side near the door, with her seat unbuckled. He grimaced. "I'm not going to attack you, ya know."

She didn't answer but turned and gave him a ghost of a smile.

He drove the ten miles in silence. Sylvie didn't seem inclined to talk and he didn't know what else he could say. The old white framed house with wood siding was dark as they pulled in and they both leaned forward to look up at the place. She raised an eyebrow. "Looks okay to me. I'm not sure what you were talking about. My dad told me he has a local guy taking care of the place."

Duncan didn't say anything, only nodded. He climbed out and went straight to the back to get her luggage. He was tired of trying to beat her to the door. She sat in the cab for a long minute, and he laughed harshly under his breath. Of course, now she was taking her sweet time. He set the luggage down and reached for the door handle.

She was digging through her purse, and he waited patiently. Finally, with brows furrowed she said, "I could have sworn I had the keys in here." She shrugged then. "Oh well, there is always the spare one under the planter." She slid out without so much as a thank you and walked ahead as he hauled her bags.

She fished out the key and unlocked the front door. *So far so good,* she thought as she replaced the key and held the door wide for Duncan.

He nodded and moved past with her bags. "Where do you want them?" he asked quietly.

She was staring around the house as though in a trance. "It's so strange.

I remember being here, but it doesn't feel like home the way it used to."

He smiled. "I imagine not, it's been a long time since you were here."

Sylvie wasn't sure if it was her imagination, or if there was a slightly angry undertone beneath that smile. She sighed, "Well, why don't I take the bags upstairs while you head home."

He shook his head stubbornly. "I'll haul them up. You want them in your old room?"

She nodded absent-mindedly as she walked over to stare into the kitchen and attached dining room on the left side of the large front room that started inside the front door. She listened to him make his way up the stairs and stared in estranged curiosity at the space that had once been the centerfold of her family's laughter and life. Most of the photos had long since been removed so the old, papered walls were bare except for the occasional item. Most likely her parents had taken them all to their place in North Carolina.

Tears filled her eyes at the memory of her mother baking while she and Elaine joked and laughed nearby. She wiped her hand impatiently across them. Somehow everything had changed and fallen apart since those warm heartfelt days. Now, both of them were gone, leaving her alone to try and keep her father reeled in from the edge that he seemed ever drawn to.

She didn't hear Duncan come in but didn't flinch as he slid his arms around her waist from behind and pulled her back into him. "Are you okay?" he asked gently as he used his thumb to wipe the tears from her cheeks. "It's hard coming back here, isn't it?" he asked as he gently ran his hands up and down her arms.

She nodded mutely. "I don't know why I thought it would be easy after all this time."

He didn't say anything for a while. He held her there in his gentle embrace and allowed her the space to cry it out.

Sylvie was a little embarrassed when the tears flooded over and ran down her face and chin. He turned her into his arms with exquisite tenderness and laid her head against his shoulder. She didn't know why but that made her cry harder and before she could stop them, her shoulders began shaking uncontrollably as great sobs shook her from the inside.

She didn't remember crying much when they'd found Elaine's body. She hadn't cried much even as she had said goodbye to her mother and then watched as life seemed to ebb out of her. Her father had been wracked with grief and she wanted to stay strong for him. With Elaine it had been her mother she was worried about.

Looking back now, she couldn't ever remember crying much at all. Yet here she was in these mountains once again, alone. As Duncan held her it seemed that all of the pain she had been holding inside for the last eight years came pouring out.

"Just let it all out, sweetheart," he crooned softly.

She would rather not, but it seemed that her heart and body wouldn't listen to her as she cried, anguished, there in the protection of his arms. After several long minutes she calmed again and stepped back awkwardly. "I'm sorry, I don't know what's wrong with me. I don't usually cry like that."

Duncan smiled and she couldn't help noticing the tiny shimmer in his own blue gaze. "I remember. I never saw you cry when Mom or Elaine died. I always wondered how you could hold it all inside that way."

She looked down at her hands as she clasped them in front of her and shrugged. "My parents needed me to be strong."

He didn't say anything for a long moment and finally she looked up and met his gaze. "Here with me it's safe to let it all out," he said softly, and lifted a hand to tuck a blonde strand of hair behind her ear.

Sylvie looked away and out the window into the darkness. She didn't know why but the fact that she had been able to cry there in his arms, bothered her. She would be leaving soon, and Duncan had a life here. This couldn't really go anywhere. Maybe that was the reason she had been able to finally release all that pain.

She saw an odd flash of light in the darkness and leaned forward to look closer just as she heard the sound of splintering glass and then something punched her left shoulder and threw her back. She screamed at the flash of pain and felt herself falling backwards toward the floor. Duncan caught her before she landed on her flailing arms.

She was confused. She had seen something out the window before the glass splintered but couldn't imagine what. "Fireworks?" she asked in a high-pitched voice.

Duncan was turning her to face him even as he shook his head in denial. "It sounded like a gunshot," he said. Sylvie went limp in his arms, and he watched in horror as a small red splotch on her shoulder began blossoming out into a wide puddle as blood seeped out. Instinct took over, and he laid her on the floor even as another shot sounded and hit the wall behind where they had been standing. He crouched over her and put his hands over the seeping wound, staring in disbelief. "My god, someone shot you, Sylvie."

She laughed a little and shook her head. "Why on earth would someone shoot me?"

He was wondering the same thing as he watched her eyes roll back in her head and she went limp. "God damn it, Sylvie, you need to wake up." He held the wound hard with one hand and shook her with the other. "Damn it all," he swore under his breath as he reached for his phone. He stayed below the window line as he dialed nine-one-one. As soon as he heard the operator begin to speak, he interrupted. "She's been shot. I need an ambulance now."

The operator didn't hesitate. "Sir, can you tell me where you are now?" Duncan quickly told her the address as he adjusted his hand on her shoulder. Blood ran through his fingers and the world tilted for a moment before he forced it right again. "I don't know what happened, but I heard a gunshot and then she jerked. My god, it hit her in the shoulder and there is way too much blood."

"Sir, an ambulance is on the way but as I'm sure you know, it will take them at least thirty minutes to get to you. I need you to check for a pulse. Can you check for me please."

Duncan reached one hand up to her neck and felt there. He took a deep breath as he felt the gentle thudding. "She has a pulse, but she blacked out."

"Sir, can you check the wound and see how much it is bleeding. Is there a large area covered in blood or is the bleeding slow?"

Duncan looked down at his hand covered in blood and noticed the puddle that was there under her shoulder. "It's too goddamn much blood," he swore under his breath.

"Sir, can you find something and hold pressure against the wound?"

Duncan laughed coldly. "I'm already doing that but it's not helping enough. She will be dead in thirty minutes at this rate. Can't you send a helicopter out here and life flight her to the hospital?"

There was a long silent moment at the other end of the line. "Life flights are very expensive, sir, and we don't like to send them unless it is absolutely necessary because then it could mean them not being available for another emergency."

Duncan ground his teeth together in frustration. "I don't give a fuck how much it costs, and I am telling you she is not going to make it if you don't get a medivac helicopter here now. Do it."

There was a series of beeping sounds on the line. "Sir, I will send one now. Is there an open place nearby for the chopper to land?"

"Nothing but fields for miles," he said, and put his other hand over the wound on her shoulder trying to keep the blood from seeping out around it. "Just get them here."

"The chopper is on its way, sir. I need you to stay on the line until they arrive, okay?"

Duncan didn't respond. He stared down at Sylvie's pale face and bit a curse back. He leaned his face close to hers. "Come on Sylvie, sweetheart, I need you to wake up," he said as he willed her eyes to open. She lay there still, unmoving, and he swore a long line of curses. "You can't go, I won't let you." He put more pressure on the wound. "Come on sweetheart, wake up," he said in a cajoling tone.

"Sir, before the medics get there, we need to make sure it's safe. Has there been any more gunshots?"

He hesitated. There had been that one shot after, but that had been a few minutes ago, and he didn't dare tell her about it. He couldn't do anything to stop them from coming for Sylvie or she would die. "Just the one shot. I'm guessing it's just a hunter that wasn't being cautious enough or something like that." He had thought that it was most likely one of the hunters from the city that seemed to flock out here for hunting season and often lost their way in the hills and mountains.

"The police are on their way as well, but I just need to make sure I'm not sending medical personnel into a warzone."

"I'm sure the hunter is either long gone by now or has realized it was a bad shot." He prayed that what he was saying was true. He didn't want to be responsible for anyone else getting hurt but he also wasn't willing to take the risk of losing Sylvie. Not the beautiful, strong-willed girl that had grown into an intelligent, gorgeous woman. He had lost too much already. Though he hadn't seen her in years the fact that he had known she was alive and well had given him at least some measure of comfort.

"Sir, the chopper should be getting there within the minute. Can you hear it yet?"

Duncan perked his ears and listened but heard nothing but the slightest whistle of wind through the round hole in the window that spider webbed out from the center.

Sylvie moaned and tried to lift her head as her brown eyes opened to stare up at him. "What happened?" she asked and tried to reach for her shoulder and the throbbing pain there.

Duncan met her gaze, looking worried. "Someone shot you. The helicopter is on its way."

She shook her head. "That isn't necessary. I'll be fine."

Duncan's jaw set and he looked down where his hands held her tight against the checked vinyl floor. "I don't think so, sweetheart. Try to keep looking at me and stay awake though. You scared the hell outta me when you blacked out."

"Sir, the pilot says they are almost there now."

Duncan didn't move even as they heard the loud swoosh, swoosh of helicopter blades as it neared the house. He saw light sweep across the window from outside and then the swooshing got a little louder. "I can't let off the pressure so tell them to come right in the front door," Duncan instructed the operator.

"Will do."

He heard a door slam against the wall and still held the pressure.

"In here," he hollered in a raw voice.

Two medics rushed to them and unzipped a bag. "Sir, can you step back please, I need to assess the damage."

Duncan shook his head. "No can do, I think it hit an artery because its bleeding way too much."

One medic, a middle-aged looking, balding man came around to kneel by Duncan. He held a thick pad of gauze on a bandage and said firmly, "On my go step back and away and I will take over."

Duncan didn't want to let go but he wasn't a medic, and he didn't know what to do for Sylvie. He nodded tersely.

"Ready, set, step back, sir."

Duncan felt the blood ooze out against his palm as he released her shoulder and moved back. The medic quickly placed the compression bandage over the wound and held down on it. The other medic started an IV and Duncan rushed around to kneel by her head. He saw her eyes roll back in her head again and his heart thundered in his ears. "Can't you do something to keep her awake?" he asked.

Both medics ignored him as they lifted her a little to check her back before lifting her onto a stretcher. He watched as they grabbed their bags and wheeled her out. He stared down at his bloody hands and then rushed out behind them. "I'm coming with you," he yelled but they shook their heads.

"I'm sorry, sir, but that just isn't possible."

"Where are you taking her?" he asked in a voice thick with fear.

"To St Luke's Hospital," was all he heard as he watched them quickly slide the stretcher inside and climb in to slam the doors. He stared, paralyzed in the darkness as the chopper lifted into the air and flew off. He watched as it went up over the mountain and disappeared on the other side.

Chapter 6

Duncan stared at his bloody hands as he waited for the cops to show up. Anger settled inside. "Where the fuck are they?" he muttered under his breath anxious to get driving to the hospital. It was a three-hour drive from here to the city and he wanted to get going right away.

He heard a siren in the distance and sat on the front step to wait. Two police cars screeched to a halt in the driveway, and he watched as four uniformed officers climbed out, opening their holster tops as they walked quickly toward him. He stood and held out a hand. "Duncan Jamison, officers. Thanks for coming."

One officer reached for his hand and then stopped and stepped back. In surprise, Duncan remembered his bloody hands. "I'm sorry about that, I forgot," he said hoarsely. "Why don't you all come inside, and I will show you what happened."

They nodded and followed him in. "We had just gotten here. I took her luggage upstairs, and then I came back down here. She was in the kitchen, so I came in behind her." He hesitated, unsure whether or not he should tell them she had been crying. "She was looking out the window there and I heard a pop and the glass shattered. She jerked backward towards me, and I caught her but then I realized she was bleeding, so I laid her on the floor. It was a good thing I did too since the second shot landed right where I'd been standing with her." He pointed to the wall behind them.

"Sir, I'm Officer Charles and I am in charge here. Did you happen to see who was shooting?"

Duncan gave a pointed look at the black night beyond the window. "No," he answered in a clipped tone. "It was probably some drunk asshole that thought he was hunting. That's about all we get out in these parts."

Two of the officers turned and were looking closely at the wall and the bullet buried there. The other two skirted the puddle of blood on the floor and walked close to the window to examine the broken glass.

Duncan watched them numbly for a moment before turning. "I'll leave you all to it. I'm going to the hospital." He turned, intending to walk out.

"Hold on, sir. We need more information." The cop raised an eyebrow at his fellow officer. "We also need to take some pictures of your hands and clothing in case it becomes pertinent to the investigation here."

Duncan sighed and turned back. "Could you hurry it up then, because

I want to get over there and make sure Sylvie is okay."

The officer pulled out a notepad. "What is the victim's full name?"

"Sylvianna Dunlap." His tone was clipped and impersonal. "Her family used to live here and still owns this place."

The officer wrote for a bit and then met Duncan's eyes. "And what is your relationship with the victim sir?"

Duncan shrugged. "Friends, I guess. We all grew up together. Why?" His gaze narrowed.

The officer smiled. "This is all standard in this kind of situation. What is your full name, sir?"

Duncan's gaze turned slightly chilly. "Duncan Rayne Jamison. I own a ranch not far from here."

The officer nodded and wrote some more. "So, you were here with her the entire time then?"

Duncan lifted a hand to rub tiredly at his face, saw the blood there and dropped it back to his side. "Look, no disrespect officer. but I need to get going so if you don't mind, we can go over all of this after I know my friend is still alive."

Officer Charles nodded and turned to his partner. "After Officer Kershaw here takes some photos, you are free to get cleaned up and go but you need to keep in touch, and we will want to do a full interview later."

Duncan did as he was asked, holding out his hands and arms as photo after photo was snapped of his hands, arms, and even a few full body ones. When he was done, they asked him to remove his shirt and pants and he watched as they bagged them carefully. This was all beginning to look a little suspicious and he quit answering their questions quite so easily. He held the officers' gaze and asked quietly, "Do I need to get my lawyer down here?"

The officer watched him for a long moment. "I don't see a reason to, but it is your right." He held Duncan's hard blue gaze. "Is there something you might need a lawyer for, sir?"

Duncan didn't blink. "Not at all, I have nothing to hide. This is all just starting to sound a little like an interrogation."

The officer smiled charmingly. "I know these things can be a little difficult. I just want to make sure we are looking at every angle here. I'd hate to see anyone else get hurt."

Duncan gave him one short nod. "If it's okay I'd like to run upstairs and see if I can find a change of clothes." His grey boxer briefs and tank were a little light in the chill of the open door and the cold night air.

"That should be okay. I'd like to ask a few more questions before you go though."

Duncan nodded and turned on his heel to leave. He looked first in Elaine's old room hoping he had possibly left an old sweatshirt or something there. The room had been cleaned and mostly emptied so he turned toward her parents' suite. To his surprise there were quite a few clothes left in Mr Dunlap's closet and he reached for a grey sweater and tan slacks that looked like they might fit. He washed up in the master bath and then quickly slid into the clothes before making his way back down.

It took another hour and several more cops showed up before the officers finally let him go. He turned his truck around and fishtailed out the gravel driveway. Once he got on the highway he sped up and hit his sister's number on the truck's phone system.

She picked up after one ring and he quickly explained where he was going and asked her to check in on their father and the ranch if he didn't make it back until tomorrow night. Jackie promised that she and Ren would take care of it and then asked if she shouldn't jump in and come with him.

"Let me get out there and see how it goes first. If things get worse, I'll give you a call and you can come down, but you ought to get some rest while you can."

She harrumphed but left it at that, and he said goodbye. He glanced at the clock on his dash. It was ten o'clock and he quickly did the math in his head. With a little luck he could make it just after midnight. He rolled the window down a crack to let in the cool night air and took a deep breath. Sylvie would be okay. She had to. He was simply unwilling to think of any other possibility.

He rolled into the hospital parking lot at twelve fifteen and parked near the emergency room. He wasn't sure where she had ended up but the emergency doors were unlocked all night so he knew he could at the very least gain access to the hospital this late. A receptionist behind a wide desk inside, informed him that Sylvie had been rushed into surgery and she hadn't heard anything since. She told him to wait a bit while she found out more and motioned him to a chair. He didn't sit, however, but stalked the room, unable to sit still.

He heard her on the phone and turned as she held up a hand and motioned him back over. She covered the mouthpiece on the phone and said, "I guess they are about to take her to the ICU now if you want to head up there, sir."

He nodded and swallowed hard. ICU meant she was still alive, didn't it? He walked quickly down the hallway in the direction she pointed. He soon saw a sign and an elevator and took it up and then followed the signs down several hallways until it finally ended at locked double doors. He pushed the service button, and a nurse came on, asking him who he had come to see. Duncan quickly gave them Sylvie's name and when they asked if he was family, he said yes.

The doors opened and he hurried through to the desk ahead on the left side. A nurse there gave him a bright smile. "You said Sylvie Dunlap, right?"

Duncan nodded. "Yes, she was flown in a few hours ago."

The nurse typed for a minute and then finally looked up. "It looks like she made it through surgery and is on her way up. It could take a bit before you can see her. If you want, there is a small waiting room just down there." She pointed down the wide hall. "I'll come and get you when she is settled."

He nodded tersely and walked to the waiting room. He sat and held his head in his hands for a long moment. He was starting to feel the fatigue, having gotten up the previous morning at four so he could get some work done before Sylvie woke up. He closed his eyes and leaned his head back.

He heard the glass shattering again and again and saw Sylvie's body jerking back. His eyes opened suddenly, as he wondered who in the fuck had shot her? And why?

He replayed it over and over in his mind, eyes narrowed. At first, he had thought hunters, but now here in the quiet, that possibility seemed to be losing its edge. The bullet had nearly gone through her heart. If she hadn't been moving just then she would probably be dead. A long chain of curses flew from his lips in a low tone. Someone had intentionally shot at her. That pissed him off and he started thinking about who might be able to shoot from that range. Then he gave a low unamused laugh. Nearly everyone here in these parts knew how to shoot both rifles as well as handguns. They all hunted. They also all lived in the mountain climate where being able to shoot wolves and bears on the loose, could mean the difference of life or death. His jaw tightened as another possibility crept in. Someone could also have followed her here from North Carolina.

He sat up straight, racking his brain. He had heard about some of the court cases she had been a part of at her job with the district attorney's office and wondered idly if she'd made enemies there.

A nurse came into the room and looked around before walking toward him. "Mr Dunlap?" she asked. Duncan smiled; he hadn't told them he was her husband, but if they had made that assumption, it was fine by him, as it allowed him access to her.

"Hello," he said and stood.

"We got your wife all settled, sir, and you can come see her if you want," she offered in a quiet voice.

He nodded and motioned her in front of him. "I'll just follow you then, ma'am."

She gave him a ghost of a smile and led him out into the wide corridor. There were glass fronted units with sliding doors along three walls of the square area they entered and a large rectangular nurse station right in the middle. Each room had a number and then a little sticky note of who was inside. She stopped in front of one and he glanced over to see 'Dunlap' written just below the number.

"She is here, sir." The nurse slid the glass door open and then motioned him inside before silently closing it behind him. Memories of walking into just such a room with his mom before she'd died had his heart rate speeding up. He saw Sylvie's fresh gorgeous face and stepped determinedly around the half-drawn curtain.

The constant bleep, bleep, bleeping of the monitors felt soothing somehow and he squared his shoulders and stepped to where he could see her. He felt like a truck ran into his gut as he saw her there. She looked frail. Her skin was a pasty white color and her hair looked stringy. She had a tube running under her nose and several others ran under the white and blue hospital gown she wore. Even with the gown he could see the wide bandage on her shoulder. He groaned and hurried over to take her hand.

He bent over her and gently kissed her forehead. "God, sweetheart, you look like shit," he said in a pained tone. She didn't move and he bent to kiss her hand. He held her hand between his as memories of her, full of life, reeled through his mind like a fishing pole on steroids.

There was Sylvie running happily down the mountain ahead of him, Elaine, and Jackie, turning back to stick out her tongue and grin. "Catch me if you can." He remembered her saying as the sun shone brightly on her hair and skin, as she turned and booked off down the mountain.

Then he remembered a particularly gory horror movie they had all watched together. They'd all sat in silence processing the terrible film that had just ended. Suddenly, Sylvie stood and laughed. "Come on, guys, you look like everyone you love just died. Buck up, I thought this was supposed to be a party." She had turned on some lively music then and had gotten all of them up and dancing with her, as she twirled playfully around the room.

It seemed that through those years they had all teased her about hanging out with kids her own age, but she had persevered and in the end was usually the life of their little party.

Guilt teased at him. She had been that lively fun girl again on their horse ride even as she had practically taunted him to kiss her. He had given in to that urge and then had been angry, because he'd felt pushed to do something he wasn't yet comfortable with. So, he had made her pay the price when he kissed her again. He'd tried to make her feel as out of control as he himself did. It hadn't been fair of him. He could see that now.

He bent his head to her limp hand again. "I'm so sorry I couldn't keep this from happening to you. I should have seen something," he said through his teeth. He straightened up as a doctor in a white coat walked around the curtain.

"Mr Dunlap." He nodded at Duncan and then walked over to look at the machines behind Sylvie. "She came through surgery, though it was a little touch and go for a while there," he stated in a no-nonsense tone of voice. "The bullet went all the way through but because it was large, it left a lot of damage in its wake. We had to repair the brachial artery as well as some of the surrounding nerves and muscle before we closed her up, so it took a while."

Duncan nodded.

"She pulled through courageously. Fought to live, I thought you might like to know that. She coded in surgery, but we were able to get her right back. We ended up using four units of blood by the time we got the bleeding under control, so she is lucky to be alive. If you hadn't insisted on the life

Flight, I'm confident she would have died en route." He nodded approvingly at Duncan.

"Is she going to live, Doc?" he asked in a low voice.

The doctor met his gaze, held it for a long moment. "She has a good chance, sir. We are still monitoring her for complications but so far it looks good. We should know in the next day or so. In the meantime, you should go get some rest."

Duncan shook his head. "I'm fine, but thanks."

The doctor grinned. "I'll have a nurse drop off a pillow and blanket. If you can rest in the chair at least, do it. She has a long road ahead of her and she is going to need you strong."

Duncan nodded and pulled the chair next to the bed where he could hold her hand and sit. With a little sigh he pulled out his phone and updated Jackie. Jackie immediately sent him a thumbs up emoji with a heart and a hug. He smiled at his sister's peculiar habit of only using emojis to text and leaned back in the seat.

He stared hard at Sylvie's face, willing her to wake up even as he knew that she wouldn't. She was, after all, still sedated and would be for a while. Still, he stared, hoping that she would open those bright brown eyes and smile at him with that happy light way that she had. He fell asleep wondering how long he could stare at her frail body before he went insane.

He was awakened by a gentle hand on his shoulder. His eyes burned as he looked up through blurry orbs at the man standing there by his side. "Dad? Is that you?" he asked and rubbed a hand across his eyes before looking up again.

"I just got here, son. Jackie called and told me what had happened. I wish you had called me so I could come with you. This must be so hard for you after everything that happened with your mother."

Duncan shrugged. "A little, I guess," he admitted, grateful that his dad was obviously having a good day. Those were so few and far between these days that it was nice to get a glimpse of the real man. He smiled, "Thanks for coming, it can't be easy for you either."

Arthur Jamison smiled gently. "No, it isn't," he agreed and walked around to take Sylvie's other hand. "She looks so frail now, doesn't she?" he asked softly.

Duncan nodded. "It is so bizarre to see her like this as she has always been so vibrant and full of life."

His father nodded and gently patted Sylvie's hand. "Such a beautiful young girl. So sad about her sister too. She has really had a hard time through it all." He looked down at her for a long moment and then up to meet his son's tired gaze. "You both have. Do you talk about it to each other?"

Duncan blinked. His father hadn't seemed to be aware of much going on around him for the past several years. The fact that he was so aware at this moment took him by surprise. He grinned but shook his head. "Unfortunately, not. I haven't seen or talked to her until a few days ago when she called to tell me she was coming."

Arthur smiled gently. "Maybe you should. Sometimes it can be a comfort you know, to talk to others who have gone through the same ordeal."

Surprised once again by his father's obviously clear mind he laughed.

"Like you have, Dad?"

That startled a cackle of laughter from his father's dry throat. "Believe it or not, son, I have spent a lot of time talking to other men who have gone through the same things as me. It makes me feel much better."

This was news to Duncan, and he raised one eyebrow suspiciously.

"Are you talking about an online grief counseling group?"

Arthur grinned and walked back around the bed to sit in the second chair behind Duncan. "Even I need to talk to someone, son."

Chapter 7

He cursed into the darkness as he watched that bastard Duncan Jamison lay her on the floor, effectively removing her from his scope. He had tried a second shot, but it was too late already. The first had hit a little too high, because she had lifted her head and shoulders as he pulled the trigger. He watched for a long while with his finger on the trigger, ready in case he got another shot. He saw nothing.

After another five minutes he packed the gun into its case and tossed it into the back of the truck he was driving. He looked back at the house consideringly. He could go over there and make sure the job was done. He shook his head. He had to play the long game. By now, the bastard had likely called in the cavalry, and it wouldn't do any good for the mission if he got caught and thrown in jail.

Reluctantly, he slid into his pickup and started the engine, being careful not to turn on his headlights before his front end was turned away from the house. He drove quickly away. He hadn't worried about the shells, and he wasn't worried about the bullets being tracked back to him. They were, after all, one of a kind that he tediously made himself. They were virtually untraceable unless someone found his equipment.

He smiled into the darkness as he remembered her body jerking as the bullet ripped through her. He preferred more up-close personal work, but this time he'd had to settle for the bullet. It was the job after all. Besides that fact, Sylvianna Dunlap was far less personal than the others had been. He cranked an old rock hit on the radio and drove down the road and away. He drove the direction that he knew the police units would come from, just for the thrill of passing right under their noses.

He wasn't disappointed as two screaming units with flashing lights flew past, going well over the speed limit. He grinned and took a right

turn onto an old winding dirt road that eventually led to the cabin he was staying in while he completed his mission.

He whistled a happy little tune as he unloaded the rifle and hauled it inside to tuck into a closet where it wouldn't be noticed by anyone who might happen upon the cabin. He thought of his mark and wondered which hospital they would take her to and thought about going there. Soon, he thought to himself, he would go there, and his mission would be finished.

He whistled a good old country song as he walked to the fridge and opened it to look inside. He was thirsty and hungry after his long night of watching Sylvie with her friends and then casually following at a distance while she went back to the ranch. He was planning to shoot her then but hadn't had the chance as she had soon emerged with her bags. He'd followed them again and finally ended up at the old house that he was aware was her parents' place. He'd taken his time setting up his rifle and getting everything perfect.

He would go in the morning, he decided, and reached for a beer and popped the top off. He walked over to the table and sat, thinking of Sylvie Dunlap. She was a beautiful swan in the lake of his mission. He licked his lips in anticipation. Soon, she too would be his forever.

Hours later, unable to stay away, he paced the halls of the hospital. He was wearing a baseball cap but not because he needed it to hide his face, but instead for the simple reason that he liked baseball caps. Liked the way they covered the top of his slightly balding head, giving him a much younger look. It helped him get the ladies; he knew. He swore inwardly as he paced.

He'd changed his mind about the hospital after drinking a couple of beers. Impatience had set in, and he wanted to get this situation handled so he could go back to his life. He had gotten here pretty quickly but not quick enough as he had soon discovered that Duncan Jamison was here by her side. He had waited patiently as visitors came and went but the damn fool hadn't left her side. It had now been five hours and Duncan had yet to emerge from Sylvie's room.

He found himself wishing he could keep Sylvie alive for himself. All that shiny sun-kissed hair with her milky brown eyes and that gorgeous leggy body, would have been a happy addition to any man's bed and he was no different. She was a loose end now, though. She knew far too much and though he had no clue if she would tell anyone what she knew, he couldn't take the risk.

No, she had to die. Though now that he was thinking about it, he could take her away for a while and enjoy some time with her before he carefully strangled her. His loins began to ache, and he smiled. Yes, wouldn't that be nice. He gritted his teeth impatiently. If only Duncan would leave her side long enough for him to get to her.

Once the thought of taking her alive settled, he turned back down the long corridor. If he was going to successfully take her, he had to have a better plan. Unlike slipping into her room and carefully inserting the syringe in his pocket into her IV, taking her alive was much more complicated. He would have to wait, and watch, and plan carefully to do it right.

He took a deep breath and smiled pleasantly at a nurse who walked past. He could play the long game here. After all, hadn't he waited this long already?

Chapter 8

Duncan woke with a start and sat up in the chair looking around curiously. He stood and walked over to the sliding glass door, looking out and around. Nothing was out of order, so he shrugged and walked back to Sylvie's side.

After waiting for a long while with him, his dad had finally left to get a hotel for what remained of the night. Duncan hadn't seen anyone else come, though he had finally remembered to call Sylvie's dad.

"What in the hell is going on?" Reagan Dunlap had asked in a somewhat drowsy tone. He'd been awakened from a deep sleep after three scotches, so he was fighting the fog. "I keep telling her that if she remains involved in these high-profile cases that she is going to end up pissing someone off."

Duncan went silent and then asked quietly, "What high-profile cases?"

Reagan had cleared his throat and sighed. "Every case she takes. Dammit, she is like a dog with a bone. Once she sniffs something out, she doesn't think smells quite right, she doesn't quit digging until she unburies the truth. Which can be a real problem when you're dealing with drug dealers and digging to find their bosses." He sounded like he was moving around. "Are you sure she is okay?"

Duncan smiled. "As good as can be expected after getting a huge hole blown in her shoulder."

"I'm going to catch the next flight out there. Keep me updated in the meantime okay, son?" Reagan said and hung up to call a cab and the airport.

Duncan sighed and hung up and walked back to Sylvie's side. He couldn't believe he'd forgotten to call her dad until now. He groaned as

he ran his fingers through his dark hair and rubbed the tension in his neck. He hadn't been looking for anything to change in his life. The ranch was finally taking off and really starting to do well, and he had his hands full with that and his sister and her twins, not to mention the new baby she would be having soon. Sylvie had come and it appeared that she had brought a whole load of shit with her.

He almost wished she hadn't come. Almost. That tiny little curious place in his brain that had wanted to know what she was like now, still lingered. So far, she had seemed much the same as the adventurous fun girl that had left. He thought of drug dealers and shook his head. She couldn't be the same girl if she was pressuring drug dealers to give their bosses up. He laughed low and shook his head, trying without success to picture the young girl he'd grown up with, even talking to criminals.

He had apparently been very wrong when he'd thought she was much the same. Duncan stared at her face and willed her eyes to open once again. The doctor had informed him that he'd cut back her meds and she could be waking up anytime now, though he hadn't seen any sign of that yet. "Come on Sylvie, wake up sweetheart. We need to know what you were into, so we can figure out what you dragged back to the mountains with you."

She didn't respond though he felt a tiny bit of pressure on his hand as she squeezed weakly. He smiled. "Are you waking up, miss big shot lawyer?"

She didn't open her eyes or squeeze his fingers again and he began wondering if he'd imagined it. He frowned and pulled a chair back to the side of the bed and sat heavily. "Come on baby, I need you to wake up and tell me you're okay."

He leaned back against the chair and closed his eyes tiredly. He was exhausted, but more than anything he just wanted to hear that smart tone of hers when she curtly informed him, she was fine.

"Oww," she said as she opened her eyes, fighting the fog that threatened behind her lids.

Duncan stood up so fast he nearly tipped the chair backwards.

"Hey beautiful. You *are* awake."

She closed first one eye and then the other as though trying to clear her vision. "What happened?"

He looked at the door nervously. "Maybe I should get the doctor," he began.

Sylvie shook her head and then closed her eyes, wishing she hadn't. "Please Jamison, don't," she pleaded. She opened her eyes again to meet his bright blue gaze. "What happened, Duncan?"

He shrugged. "I'm not altogether sure yet. Do you remember anything?"

She eyed him and frowned. "The last thing I remember was shortly after we got to my parents' place. I remember looking around and being sad. Then nothing."

He hesitated to tell her more. He wasn't a doctor and wasn't sure if it was better to tell her what had happened or if he should let her remember on her own. To his relief a nurse came in with a smile. "Good, you woke up. Welcome back Mrs Dunlap."

Sylvie tried to sit up and then collapsed again. "Miss," she corrected automatically.

The nurse turned to stare at her and then at Duncan. "I'm sorry, miss, I thought you two were…" she hesitated. "Anyway, I will just check things quickly and then go get the doctor." She threw an accusing look at Duncan who only grinned. She shook her head and began writing notes on her pad.

Sylvie saw the exchange and raised one eyebrow at Duncan though she didn't ask. She groaned loudly as the nurse prodded at the bandage on her shoulder making it burn like it was on fire. "What happened to my shoulder?" she asked as she lifted the opposite arm up to touch the bandage. The nurse turned in surprise. "You don't remember what happened,

Miss Dunlap?"

She shook her head. "I don't remember coming to the hospital either."

The nurse smiled. "I'll let the doctor know. He should be coming in a bit to talk to you."

Sylvie turned to look back at Duncan with a pleading look. "What is going on?" She sounded panicked and she immediately calmed her voice.

The only reason she wasn't throwing a huge fit by now was because Duncan was there, and it had calmed her down. "Please tell me Duncan."

He looked at the nurse who shrugged and hurried out. "You got shot, Sylvie."

She laughed a little but when he was still there holding her gaze with a serious expression she stopped. "I'm sorry, I thought you said I got shot."

He nodded. "You did." He ran his hands through his hair in agitation. "I thought you weren't going to make it for a while there." He said it without emotion, and she studied his face.

"Who would shoot me Duncan? That makes no sense."

He shrugged. "Your dad thinks it might be someone you helped put away recently or something related to one of your cases."

Her voice went up an octave. "You talked to my dad?" She tried sitting up, but the pain was too much, and she collapsed back down. "Dammit Jamison, you shouldn't have done that. He has enough to deal with without worrying about me."

Duncan didn't smile though her high pitch was now beginning to grate on his very tired nerves. "Sure, yeah, I get it. You're here in the hospital from what could have easily been a deadly gunshot wound but let's not tell your dad."

She went cross-eyed. "You have no idea what these past couple of years have been like for him. This could send him over the edge." She glared hotly at him.

He did smile then. A warm ghostly smile. He met her eyes and asked, "How long has he been drinking himself to sleep?"

She looked away. Shame? Or something else he couldn't quite place, he wondered, as he moved closer to take her cold hand in his own warm one. She finally met his gaze again. "I don't know. I noticed it getting a lot worse about a year after we buried Mom."

He nodded. "My dad has been through it too. I watched him change right in front of me from a strong hard worker into this shell of what he used to be. It was like the things that mattered before Mom died just didn't matter anymore." He didn't mention his or Jackie's names, but she knew when she looked at him, that they were what hadn't mattered any more to him.

He brightened. "Good news though on that front, he actually came to see you earlier. He spent some time here with us and then went to a hotel. He said he would check back in later on."

Sylvie smiled. It looked good to see a little joy in his tired eyes. "I'm glad he came. I'll have to thank him when I get a chance." She thought guiltily of how she had forgotten his mother had died a few months before Elaine and stared down at her hands. "I'm sorry I didn't keep in touch. It must have been so tough for you and Jackie going through all of that with him, on top of losing Elaine."

He bent and lifted her chin with a hand to hold her gaze in his own. "Don't be sorry, Sylvie. Every time I felt weighed down by the work and the ranch, I thought of you and how you had gotten out. In a way it was what inspired me to keep going."

Tears shimmered there in her brown eyes and his gut clenched. Before he realized what he was doing he lowered his head and took her lips in a deep kiss. He pulled back a few minutes later when she was clinging to him with her good arm, and he was good and hot for her. He told himself he had done it to distract her, but he wanted to do it again, and she didn't need to be distracted now so that excuse went out the window. He grinned smugly down at her.

She attempted a breathy smile. "What was that for?"

He didn't know the answer, so he leaned down and distracted her again. This time he pulled back when the doctor cleared his throat. Duncan backed up three steps and turned to smile at the man.

The doctor stepped over to Sylvie. "Hello Mrs Dunlap, I'm Doctor Gerard. Do you know where you are?"

Sylvie nodded. "First, it's Miss Dunlap, and I'm at the hospital in Boise, right?"

The doctor nodded and glanced at Duncan. He didn't make any expression and the doctor turned back. "You were flown in late last night with a gunshot wound to the shoulder. Do you remember that?"

Sylvie shook her head. "The last thing I remember was being in my parents' home before the shooting, as I told Duncan." She was staring hard at Duncan. "Why does everyone keep calling me Mrs Dunlap?" Duncan only shrugged so she turned to the doctor who had busied himself with the machines. She waited until he looked in her direction before she asked again, loudly. "Why does everyone keep calling me Mrs Dunlap, Doctor Gerard."

He gave her a small smile and looked at Duncan again. "Because, until a moment ago I was under the impression that Mr Dunlap here was your husband ma'am."

Duncan grinned and held up his hands. "I never said anything of the sort."

Sylvie rolled her eyes. "But I bet you didn't correct that notion, did you." Then for the sheer pleasure of watching him squirm she asked sweetly, "Are you looking for a sugar mama to share her last name with you, Duncan?"

He chuckled low in his throat which only stoked the lingering warmth in her belly from his kisses. "I'm not, but if you'd like, I'd be happy to be your sugar daddy." He wriggled his brows suggestively as the doctor once again, cleared his throat.

"I'd like to examine you now miss. Duncan here is welcome to stay if you want, but it's your choice." He walked around her bed and pushed a couple of buttons.

She met Duncan's warm blue gaze with her own dark one. "I'd like him to, but only if you want to." She aimed the statement at him.

He smiled and nodded. "I'm fine here, Doc."

A nurse hurried in, apologizing for taking so long and the two of them began messing with monitors and checking her vitals. They had her wiggle her fingers and then squeeze their hands. They looked into her eyes and asked a million questions. Most of which Sylvie didn't know the answers to, as she couldn't remember. She wasn't used to being asked so many questions she couldn't answer, and it was beginning to get under her skin. She opened her mouth to tell them off, but Duncan beat her to it.

"That is the third time you have asked that exact question, Doc. Aren't the police going to come and ask all the same things?" he asked coldly. "She already told you she doesn't remember and asking over and over isn't going to bring her memories back."

Sylvie lifted her head and gave him a wide happy smile. "What he said, Doc," she said with a pointed smile. Then she looked the doctor deadpan in the eye and asked, "And can't a girl get real painkillers in this hospital? My shoulder is throbbing unbearably and here I thought doctors were rumored to over prescribe, not under." She snapped her fingers.

The nurse hid a grin and turned away as the doctor adjusted her morphine drip. "That should help a little Miss Dunlap, but I should warn you that too much pain medication can be addictive."

She gave a short little laugh. "I'm an assistant district attorney in North Carolina so I'm well aware of the downfalls of opioids, but thanks for being vigilant."

The doctor grimaced. "I can already tell you are going to be a fun patient, Miss," he turned on his heel and strode out.

Nurse Mepham turned and grinned at Sylvie. "I like you. Dr Gerard can be a little pompous from time to time, so thanks. You did all of us nurses a favor today." She smiled and gave a little wave and promised to be back to check on her in a bit.

Duncan was grinning and Sylvie couldn't resist smiling back. He pulled the chair close to her bed again and said reluctantly. "I forgot what a firecracker you can be."

Laughter tinkled out before she could squelch the urge. Her shoulder shook and the laughter turned to a curse. She looked at him with a brilliant smile. "It still hurts. Can you just scoot right over there and click that morphine button up a couple of notches?"

He laughed and held his hands in the air. "I'm sorry but that, I won't do. Call the doc in if you want more."

A look of distaste crossed her face before she stopped it. "Fine then, but if I suffer, you will be suffering right along with me," she promised in a lethal tone that had the hair on the back of his neck standing up.

He scooted back a foot. "Don't shoot, miss. I'm unarmed."

She laughed again and then swore before turning to glare hotly.

"Hey, you did that on purpose. Now that's just mean, Jamison."

They were both smiling when Reagan Dunlap came rushing in. He stopped short, looking at both of their smiling faces. "And here I was worried sick about you sweetie." He rushed over to her side and bent over her for a hug. He looked clean and freshly showered when he turned to Duncan. "Last update you sent said she was still out," he accused lightly.

Sylvie jumped to Duncan's rescue. "I just woke up, Daddy. Now calm down. I'm fine and you shouldn't have come all this way and missed work." He 'tsked' her with his tongue as Duncan rose and politely hauled a chair around the bed for him to sit. "Nonsense, Sylvie. As you well know I haven't taken vacation days in two years, so I have a boatload of paid time off." He sat in the chair Duncan set behind him and patted his daughter's hand. "So now, Sylvianna Dunlap, just what kind of a mess have you got yourself all mixed up in this time?"

Sylvie faked a wounded expression. "Now, Daddy, you know I would never," she began.

He threw his hands in the air and stood up to his full six-foot two height. "Young lady you are always getting your hands in pies best left alone and now you have gone and pissed someone off. Don't give me that innocent little ruse. Who have you been trying to put away now?"

She smiled at her dad and then threw a helpless smile toward Duncan. "I can't think of anyone who would go to this length to get at me, Daddy." He 'tsked' at her again and turned to Duncan as though really seeing

him for the first time. "Hello again son." He stood and held out a hand across Sylvie's lap. "You sure are all grown up now, aren't you." He seemed to think about that for a bit. "How are your family and your father?"

Duncan smiled warmly, "Jackie is good, she is eight months along with number three. And Dad is doing all right. Actually, a little better of late."

He met Sylvie's eyes when he said the last.

Reagan smiled and turned back to Sylvie. "See, honey, I've been telling you haven't I, that it's time to settle down somewhere cozy and start a brood of your own. If little Jackie Jamison can do it, so can you."

Sylvie laughed and lifted her knowing gaze to her very intelligent father's brown eyes, which were not unlike her own. "Little Jackie is two years older than me, Daddy, and you know it. I'll get to that when I'm ready." She held up a hand to stop him when he would have argued. "I'm not just talking about my career either, okay? I still haven't found someone to settle down with." She avoided looking at Duncan as she said the last.

As skittish as he had been when he thought they might have a meaningless fling, she was worried about how he might take that news.

Chapter 9

Sylvie was a terrible patient and had the whole hospital staff avoiding her room by the following day. She complained about needing real food, getting stronger meds, and wanting to get out of the hospital asap. Though Dr Gerard wouldn't sign the paperwork to clear her for the long flight back to North Carolina, he did finally offer to send her home to heal for the next few weeks. Sylvie had agreed readily and gave both Duncan and her dad glaring dares to tell him that it was a three-hour drive home.

She was done being in the hospital room and let them all know it. She put her foot down when all three men began arguing which one of them would drive her back. Duncan had his truck and apparently his dad had driven his as well. Then Sylvie's dad had also rented a car that he wanted to drive her in. She took one look at all three of their earnest faces and laughed. "I'm sorry guys but if I have to pick two of you to let down it's not going to be my dad."

Her dad beamed happily at her. "That's my girl. Of course, you will ride with me." He threw a warning look at Duncan and Arthur. "She is after all *my* daughter."

Duncan held his hands in the air and hid a grin. "Fine with me, Mr Dunlap. She really is a complaining grump you know. That way when she wines about the pain and yells at you whenever she needs anything on the three-hour drive you will be dealing with it instead of me."

Reagan, who'd had a triumphant look on his face, paused. Duncan had a point there. She had been awfully bossy the last day. He looked uncertainly between Duncan and Sylvie. Then he asked gently, "You'll be a good girl now won't you, Sylvianna?"

She nodded without missing a beat. "An absolute angel, Daddy, just like always."

That had him scratching his head and turning to Duncan. "Didn't you mention how much more room your truck might have than my rental car, son?"

Duncan grinned. "I did make that rather obvious deduction, yes." Sylvie was shaking her head even as his eyes twinkled in triumph.

"Daddy, I don't think that is a good idea." She widened her eyes and threw him a pleading look. "I really think it would be so nice to go with you." She snapped her fingers suddenly as she had a great idea. "I know, let's make it like one of those fun road trips, you know like we used to have back in the day? It'll be fun," she declared as she eyed Duncan suspiciously.

He had been by her side nearly every moment since she had awakened in the hospital, and it seemed he was getting far too comfortable around her.

Reagan was backing slowly toward the door as memories of those road trips plagued him. The girls all picked the music then blared it loudly while they sang along until a fight started. Then they would pause said music just long enough to finish fighting before telling him once again that one of them needed the restroom. He imagined helping Sylvie into the ladies' bathroom with her bandaged shoulder several times and shook his head in denial. He bumped into a chair near the door and said hesitantly, "Sylvie honey, don't you think you might be more comfortable in Duncan's roomy truck?"

Arthur stepped forward with a quiet smile. "You are still welcome to ride with me, too."

Duncan looked at his father thoughtfully. It was really good to see him feeling so much better now. He smiled at Sylvie who was staring directly at him. "It's all settled, Dad. She will ride with me, and you all can go ahead and make sure things are ready for her."

Sylvie looked at her dad. "I think I should just ride with you, Daddy." She pulled out her phone. "Here, I'll even make one of those special road trip playlists before we go, like we used to do, you know?"

Reagan was shaking his head. "That is a great idea sweetie, then you and Duncan can listen to it on your way."

Sylvie was confused. Not five minutes ago she'd had her pick of three rides and yet now it seemed like her dad wanted her to ride with Duncan.

She groaned and reached for her shoulder. It really did hurt so she only felt a little guilty as she said, "My shoulder has been so painful and I wish I could just ride home with you, Daddy."

For some unknown reason her discomfort only seemed to make her father shrink further away. Duncan was giving her that devilish grin of his and she scowled.

He chuckled and moved over next to the bed. "In case you haven't noticed, you can be quite a pain in the butt. I'm not sure your pain is going to get you the sympathy from your dad, but I promise I will make it up to you." He winked and bent to kiss the top of her head.

He was feeling far too confident and though it was sexy as hell, it made her uncomfortable. She met his eyes and gave a little smile. "I'd just really rather go home with family. You know how it is."

He nodded wisely. "I do. Haven't you heard the staff call me Mr Dunlap? I'd say that makes us family."

She laughed nervously. "I'm not going to win this one, am I?"

He shook his head and bent to her ear so only she could hear what he murmured. "I'd like to know more about this guy you are looking to settle down with."

Sylvie shook her head and blushed a little. "I'm not. I only said that to keep my dad off my back. I'm actually dating someone back home."

He watched her silently for a long moment and then finally asked, "How serious is it?"

She looked at her hands in her lap. "I think it could get quite serious, if you know what I mean?"

He stared at her again trying to decipher how much to believe her. She had openly kissed him and that didn't seem like something she'd have done if she was hot and heavy with someone back east. He remembered in high school she was always dating two or three guys but never serious about any one of them. He grinned suddenly. "Which one of them are you serious about?"

She gave him a blank look. "Which one of which?"

He chuckled and lifted her chin, forcing her gaze to his own. "Which one of the guys you are dating is it getting serious with?"

She shrugged and held his gaze steadily as her chin inched out a notch. "I don't know what you are talking about."

He let her go and stepped back. "I'm guessing there are two or maybe three guys you are stringing along out there, right?"

She had the decency to look a little ashamed. "There are only two I'm dating right now but don't tell my dad. He doesn't know about them."

He grinned, "You ought to tell him soon if you are getting serious with them."

She punched his arm with her good one. "Don't be an ass, Jamison."

He turned to see both of their dads standing near the door in a serious conversation. He gave her one last wink and strode over to them. "I'm going to pull my truck around so it's there when the doctor releases her."

They nodded and smiled gratefully at him before turning back to whatever they had been engaged in. Duncan made his way outside and squinted up into the sun that he hadn't seen for two days. He looked around the building and made his way quickly around to the parking lot.

Once he was inside the truck, he took a moment to call Jackie and update her. When he asked how things were going at the ranch, she laughed and told him for the millionth time that he really should hire some of the cowboys that were always looking for work.

He smiled, "Okay then. Set up some interviews for me and I'll hire a couple of them." He hung up before she had the chance to make a big deal out of his concession. She had, after all, been trying to talk him into it for the last several years.

He didn't stop to consider why, after all this time, he suddenly felt willing to let strangers onto the ranch. Back in its former glory it had been a well-staffed ranch and they had a large building just for the ranch hands. He had let all the help go when he'd seen the financials after his mother died. It was in fact the first thing he'd done to cut costs. It had meant long hard days in the sun to do all the work himself, but he hadn't minded so much since it meant saving his family's legacy.

The ranch really was a lot of work for one man and his dad had long since been too tired to help out. He'd always intended to hire some cowboys again someday when he wanted to settle down with one of the local girls. Now he found himself wondering why he'd thought he should wait until he was ready to settle down. He may as well enjoy more time to himself now. He could get up on the mountain more often.

He parked his truck near the exit that he knew they would be bringing Sylvie out and then reached for his phone again, dialing his sister.

She sounded irritated. "You hung up on me."

He chuckled. "I wasn't sure I wanted to hear what you were saying."

She harrumphed. "So rude. Anyway, what I was wondering is what made you change your mind after all this time?"

He shrugged, though he knew she couldn't see him. "I guess it just seems like a good time for it."

She laughed, "Right. And I don't suppose any of this has anything to do with Sylvie coming back home?"

"Of course, it does," he agreed easily. "She was shot and will need someone there to help her out but beyond that then I'm worried she is in real danger, and I intend to make sure we don't lose another friend too young."

"I hear you; you really are a great man, Duncan. What did you call me back for?"

He grinned into the phone. "About those cowboys, do you think you could just hire some right away?"

He heard the sharp in drawn breath on the other end of the line. "Yes, I could. Ren actually knows a few guys that are dependable and looking. What about salaries?"

"We can afford it. Figure out what is fair and offer them that with a ten per cent raise after the first year if it goes well." He noticed one of his nails were broken and reached for the clippers he kept in the glove box.

"Are you sure you want me to do this Duncan? You haven't hardly let me be involved in the ranch before now." She sounded a little offended when she mentioned it.

He turned back to the phone. "Correction Jackie, I didn't want you worrying about the ranch when you have more important things to do."

He sighed heavily. "Is this too much for you right now? You are pretty far along."

She harrumphed again. "You know damned well I'd love to do this. I have wanted to be more involved since I moved back after school. You send me all those damned checks every month of my portion and I feel like

I haven't earned it."

"It's your ranch as much as mine," he stated matter-of-factly. "Besides, I risked a lot and if we'd lost it, it would have been your loss as well. I'm just glad it's all worked out so far."

"That's because of your hard work and genius ideas, Duncan, and you know it. Don't play coy with me. We both know I wouldn't have been able to go to school if you hadn't stayed here to take care of things. If one of us deserves any credit here, it's you. You are the one who sacrificed everything."

He laughed softly. "No regrets here. I've done okay with it all."

She laughed. "What you've done with what you were dealt is nothing short of miraculous and you know it. I love you."

He sighed. "I love you too, sis. I would appreciate it if you could handle this for me. I don't want to leave her alone until they have identified the shooter."

There was a long pause and then Jackie sighed. "Keep her safe, but most of all, stay safe yourself, okay?"

He smiled as he clicked off the clock. "Will do."

He slid out of the truck. He didn't know how long it would take for Sylvie to check out and he didn't want to wait out here all day. Feeling relaxed now that he knew the ranch would be taken care of, he walked easily to the cafeteria and got three large coffees. They all had a long drive ahead of them.

He walked into her room just as the doctor handed her a clipboard. "If you just fill the paperwork out you are good to go."

Sylvie smiled at him and then reached for the pad. Duncan beat her to it. He snatched it from the doctor. "I'll help her with these," he stated and scooted a chair to her bed and sat. Together they filled out the forms. He couldn't help noticing her hesitation to answer some of the questions and raised an eyebrow at her. She only shrugged and answered them vaguely.

Soon they were making their way down in the elevator. She was in a wheelchair and of course, complaining nonstop. He rushed ahead when the elevator opened. "I'll pull the truck over," he said and jogged the last hallway ahead of them.

By the time her nurse and their parents made it to the exit, he was waiting outside with the passenger door swung wide open. She stood slowly and made her way out of the chair. He hurried to loop a tall shoulder under hers and helped her to the truck. She squealed when he bent slightly and lifted her legs to settle her inside. He only gave her that damnable grin and strung the seat belt over her lap to click it in place. He gave a quick nod to their parents. "See you there," he said and made his way around the truck to hop inside.

Sylvie raised an eyebrow as he reached automatically for the cowboy hat on his dash. He only winked as he put the truck in gear and pulled away. He watched as both Reagan and Arthur walked off in different directions and pulled out onto the street. He pulled off the side and put it into park again for a minute as he reached into the glove compartment. "I forgot."

He dumped a few ibuprofen tablets into his palm and then handed them to her with a water bottle.

She frowned. "I have a prescription for much better stuff than those."

He smiled, "Not any more, I'm afraid. I tore it up. I'm afraid you are stuck with over the counter from here on out."

She cursed. "That ain't cool, Jamison. I need those." She patted her shoulder as though it should be obvious. "Do you want me to be in pain?" she puckered her bottom lip.

He chuckled. "No, I don't, but I need you focused and on alert. Most of them make you drowsy or high and I need you paying attention."

Her bottom lip popped back in, and she studied him for a long moment as he pulled back onto the road. "You've been putting a lot of thought into this haven't you?"

He didn't smile but he did glance sideways at her. "I don't know if this was a fluke hunter or a targeted hit, but I'm not taking any chances, which means you are going to have to man up and deal with the pain."

Sylvie wiped a tear from one cheek. It meant a lot to her that after she had more or less abandoned her friends, they were here now caring about her safety. She didn't want it to go to his head though, so she didn't mention that to him. Instead, she settled into the bucket seat and looked out the window. "Okay I get it, but for the record, I'm objecting."

He chuckled low and she turned to glance at him. "Objection noted. So now that we are finally alone again, I need you to tell me who might possibly be after you."

He'd switched the subject so fast she had whiplash, and she faltered slightly before pasting on a warm smile. "I don't know. I think it must have been a hunter because I honestly can't imagine who else it might be."

He nodded as though satisfied with her answer. "All right then, I guess when your dad and I go over your files we might find something that you don't remember."

She swung her gaze to his relaxed pose and blinked. "What files?"

He shrugged. "Your dad pulled some strings and had all your past and current cases shipped so that we can go through them and figure out who the bastard is that shot you."

Her cheeks flushed pink, and she swallowed. "Who do you think you are? You don't just get to insert yourself and do whatever you want. Those are my cases and have privileged information."

He didn't disagree, only turned his blue gaze to stare her down for a long moment. "I'd say when you nearly get shot on my watch, that makes me privileged, wouldn't you?"

She glared hotly. "Not even close and that isn't what I meant."

He shrugged. "Like it or not, I'm in this now Sylvie, and I don't have any intention of backing off until the bastard that did that…" He looked pointedly at her shoulder. "Is either dead or in an eight by ten cell."

Her chin jutted out stubbornly. "None of this has anything to do with you, Duncan. I'm going back as soon as they will let me on an airplane, so you should put it out of your mind."

His jaw hardened and she saw his eyes narrow slightly but then he grinned. "If you didn't want me in your life then you shouldn't have come back. I won't walk away now." His tone was harsh and low.

Her eyes filled with tears. "Of course I want you in my life. I just don't want you getting involved in all this nonsense."

He saw a gas station ahead and pulled off the road to park at the end of a white rectangular convenience store. He turned to face her and then reached for her chin and turned her gaze across to his. "I won't be leaving you to deal with this alone. I care about you. You may as well be honest about who you think is behind it."

She blinked and shook her head. "That's the thing though, I honestly don't know who it could be. I wasn't lying about that. I'm smart enough to know it probably wasn't a hunter, but I haven't been able to come up with anyone I've dealt with that would go to these lengths to get at me. There are some who were angry at being put away, but I didn't feel like they blamed me for it. They were criminals after all, so they had to know it was coming, right?"

He shrugged. "Sometimes people are unreasonable." He pointed to the store. "Do you want anything while I'm in there?"

She gave him a tiny smile. "The bathroom?"

He laughed and walked around to lift her carefully from the truck. "Fine, but I think you should just invest in one of those funnel things that they make for girls. Then you can just go behind the truck."

They walked slowly inside to the sound of her tinkling laughter.

Chapter 10

He watched and waited. They finally left the hospital and that young bastard Jamison, insisted on driving her home. He swore under his breath. His patience was wearing thin. He wanted to slit her throat here and now but hadn't yet been able to get to her. All the men who seemed to cling around her never left her alone except when she went into the small bathroom off her room, and even then, he couldn't get to her. He briefly considered killing the men too but didn't want an FBI manhunt after him. After all, he had managed to work under the radar all these years and it would be a damn shame to end up being hunted now.

It wasn't that he was afraid of the hunt. He just thought it would be much harder to complete his missions if he had people on his trail looking for him. The idea of outplaying them all appealed, but he let that go. He couldn't think like that. He had to stay focused on the primary objective.

He watched her climb into Duncan Jamison's truck and swore under his breath. He would follow, of course, but wanted to be closer to her even now. He would rather her have an 'accident' so no one was looking for her killer, but he simply couldn't afford to wait for that. There was no way to know if she had already told someone what she knew. Even if she hadn't yet, she might now that she had survived the shooting.

He slipped away to his own truck as the men all went their separate ways. He walked quickly so that he could follow at a safe distance. He couldn't afford to get caught now. There was too much on the line. He thought of all the ways he might kill her, and his loins tightened.

It seemed the thrill of the hunt was the only thing that got his junk up these days. He laughed harshly and lowered his hand to rub there. He may as well take advantage of the rare opportunity.

At just the perfect moment the red truck ahead pulled off into a service station. He followed, but quickly pulled around the back looking for a little privacy as he stroked himself, face taut with need. He needed Sylvie Dunlap like he needed air, and since he couldn't have her yet, this would have to suffice.

He missed them as they pulled back out onto the highway, but it was no matter. He knew where they were headed anyway, and so he took his time catching back up to them. He saw an outdoor fishing and game store an hour later and pulled off to grab a few things he might need. He could catch them again long before they got back to the ranch.

He underestimated the time and when he pulled up and parked on the road just outside the fence with the long drive to the ranch house, Duncan's truck wasn't anywhere in sight, and he swore viciously. He had hoped the bastard was going to bring her back here in an effort to protect her. Cover to hide and watch was better at the ranch than her parents' home which was much closer to the small town and more visible from the highway and people passing by.

He would find a way. He had no choice. He squared his shoulders. First, he'd drive over to the grocery store one town over and get some water and supplies to hunker down if he needed to. He whistled along to an old country song as he made his way back to the highway and then made a left toward town.

Chapter 11

Duncan spent the last hour of their trip trying to persuade Sylvie to stay at the cabin on the ranch with him. He wanted to keep a close eye on her, but she insisted that she would prefer to go home with her dad. He drove over to the old house with his shoulders tensed.

The police had called him to say that they still hadn't located the shooter or the spot where he had shot at Sylvie but that they were still searching. Having nothing else on him they were pretty much at a standstill in their investigation.

Duncan had made arrangements with a local handyman friend of his to have the window replaced the day before but was worried about the potential danger of the shooter coming back for another attempt. When Sylvie refused to go to the cabin with him, he made up his mind. He wasn't leaving her side until they had the guy in custody. When he had informed Sylvie of that fact, she had looked across at him and asked through her teeth. "How do you know it isn't a woman?"

He shrugged; he wasn't going to let the feminist question get to him. He had no problem with women, but his gut told him that this was a guy. Instead, he turned and met her brown eyes. "Just a feeling. Why? Is there something you know that you aren't telling me?"

Her lips spread into a wide smile, but she shook her head. "No, of course not."

He turned back to the road as they pulled off the main highway and started down the gravel road. A quarter mile later he turned onto her folks' driveway, and they drove slowly up it. He scanned the mountains and hills around as he pulled up to the old painted house. Nothing seemed out of place now, but then again, nothing had seemed out of place then either.

"What are you looking for? I'm sure the hunter is long gone by now," Sylvie said ironically.

He put the truck in park, and turned to stare at her for a long moment. "Are you sure there isn't something you aren't telling us?"

She shrugged and looked at her hands for a moment before finally meeting his gaze again. "I honestly can't think of anything. I don't know who took a shot at me." There was sincerity there in her warm brown eyes, but he hesitated to believe her. Wasn't it her job to put on a believable show for people after all?

Finally, he asked quietly, "Would you tell me if you did remember?"

She grinned and then looked out the window. "I think so… I mean unless it was a confidentiality breach of client privilege."

That pretty much summed up that. One corner of his mouth turned up as he opened his door and climbed out. "I hear you."

He hurried around to open her door and then help her out. Her dad's car was nowhere in sight, and he sighed. "I guess we beat everyone here."

She didn't say anything as he lifted her gently down and then offered support as they moved toward the front of the house. He reached for the knob, but it was locked. He swore.

Sylvie looked at the door and then at him. "I forgot; I don't have a key." They had left in such a hurry neither of them had thought to get her purse and now the police had locked up the house and taken the spare key.

Duncan gave her a little smile and muttered, "Look away for a sec." She complied with a laugh as he pulled his wallet from his pocket. She heard the clink of the knob as he wiggled it and turned to gasp as he slid a card into the slot and wiggled until the door slid open. He frowned, "We had better do something about the security right away. Anyone could easily get in."

A car pulled up the drive and they both turned to watch as Jackie parked and then slid her huge belly from behind the wheel and hurried toward them. "Oh my god, Sylvie, I'm so glad you're okay." She wrapped her old friend in a hug and then pulled back as she caught sight of the bandaged shoulder. "You are okay, aren't you?" she asked a little uncertainly.

Sylvie smiled and nodded. "I'm all patched up and I gotta say it doesn't hurt any worse than a broken leg."

All three smiled at that comment and memories of the four of them running down the mountain until Sylvie tripped and tumbled, crushing her leg against a large boulder. Duncan had hauled her the last half mile down the mountain that day. It was when she first realized she had a crush on him. He was strong and handsome, and from her viewpoint up close, his blue eyes were striking, such that she had wanted to lean in and give him a kiss. She was only fifteen then, and of course, hadn't but the memory had her looking up to meet those same blue eyes.

Something deep in the depths of his eyes made her uncomfortable as he smiled back at her. She looked away and met Jackie's smile. Together they all walked into her old front room and Duncan quickly closed the door. After helping both women get settled onto the couch, he walked stealthily through the house closing all the curtains and pulling down shades. He wasn't going to make the mistake of letting someone have another open shot at her.

He walked back downstairs just in time to hear his sister say, "I totally forgot, I brought some dinner over." Jackie wiggled around trying to get up off the couch.

Duncan hurried around the couch as he urged, "Stay here and rest, sis, I'll go out and get it."

Jackie smiled gratefully. "Really?"

When he nodded, she relaxed back onto the couch with a groan. "It's in the back of the van in a tote." She lifted the keys and tossed them to him. "Here you go."

He caught the keys out of the air and strode to the door. At the minivan he lifted the tote from the back and then pressed the button to close it before walking back to the house. He was walking up the front stairs when he heard Reagan's car pull into the driveway. He turned and gave him a quick wave and then walked back inside.

The women were chatting happily, and he only nodded as he walked past and into the kitchen. He set the tote on the table and turned back to the front room. He heard Sylvie as she said hello to her father. Jackie squealed in delight and wiggled happily out of the couch. "Mr D, it's so good to see you!" She rushed him for a big hug.

Reagan Dunlap smiled widely and stepped back to study his older daughter's best friend who was all grown up now. "Jackie, so the rumors are true," he said as he took in her wide belly. "It's good to see you." He cast a look over at Sylvie and then grinned at Jackie. "Maybe you can convince my Sylvie that it is the most wonderful thing in the world to settle down and be a mom."

Jackie laughed and gave him a little wink. "Sure thing, sir." She turned back to Sylvie. "It really is the most wonderful feeling in the world." Then because she also loved her friend she added, "It is also the most exhausting, terrifying experience you can ever have."

Sylvie smiled pleasantly. "Daddy has been trying to get me to settle down but I'm not quite ready yet." She turned to her father, "I'll get to it when I'm ready, daddy." She reached out a hand and patted his own.

Duncan stood watching the exchange from the doorway. He hadn't had a decent shower in days. He had been using the resident's bathroom for quick showers before rushing back to sit by Sylvie. Now that she had people around for a bit, he wanted to go get cleaned up and make sure things were going well at the ranch.

He cleared his throat, and everyone turned to look at him. He hesitated; he really didn't want to leave her here where he couldn't be sure she was safe. Finally, when Sylvie raised an indolent eyebrow at him, he said, "I think I'll go get a shower and a change of clothes unless you all need something else right now."

Sylvie met his worried frown with a smile. "I am fine here Duncan. Go, take care of yourself."

Jackie wiggled to stand again. "I should go too. I left Ren home to deal with the twins alone. The food just needs throwing in the oven and your dad should be able to do that." She looked at Reagan hesitantly. "Unless you want me to hurry and do it all before I go?"

Sylvie looked at Reagan with a frown and then turned to Jackie. "You should have just brought the girls and Ren with you. It would have been nice to see them again before I go back home."

Jackie smiled. "I didn't want to overwhelm you."

"Not at all, you are all more than welcome. Why don't you call him and have them all come here for dinner?"

"Yes, that sounds lovely," Reagan added with a wide smile.

Duncan, who was halfway out the door, turned back. "I can stop over and give them a ride back if you want, Jackie?"

She smiled and nodded. "Please do. I'll call and see if he wants to and then text you. Go," She commanded Duncan, who was finding it hard to walk away.

He nodded abruptly and closed the door behind him. He wasn't going to examine just why it was so hard to leave now because he already knew it was his concern for her safety. He drove home and took a hot shower before loading up a bag and tossing it in the back of his truck. He slicked his hair back with his hands and walked out to the barn to check on things.

There was a young man who looked to be about twenty-five mucking out the horses' stalls and he nodded and made his way over. He held out a hand. "Duncan Jamison. Thanks for coming to help out. Things have been a little crazy and I appreciate the help."

The blond-haired cowboy tipped his hat back and looked up at Duncan as he took his hand. "Randy Kilgore, sir. No problem, I need the work and Ren says you're a good guy."

Duncan grinned. "Well, we'll see about the last, but welcome aboard." He dug in his shirt pocket for a minute and then pulled out a card. "Here is my cell number. If anything comes up don't hesitate to give me a call. You guys all settling in okay at the bunkhouse?"

Randy nodded. "All good. Jackie stocked the fridge and the guys all seem to be getting along."

"Good then, I gotta roll out but give the guys my number and don't hesitate to call if you need anything." He turned to leave but then turned back. He pulled a pen from his pocket. "I'm going to give you the number of the house I'm going to be staying at. Cell service is spotty sometimes." He reached for the card Randy held out and scribbled the old number he still apparently had memorized on the back of the card before giving it back to the ranch hand.

"You got it boss," Randy said with a grin and Duncan gave him a small smile before turning to walk out. For eight years he had been doing most of the ranch work alone. Only getting help for the few things he couldn't do himself, like branding and bringing in the herd. It had meant the world to him to be able to say that he was doing it all on his own, and yet now that he had caved and hired hands, it seemed easy, and natural to walk out and let them do it. He frowned, wondering why it felt so different now?

He shrugged it off and walked to his truck. He saw two other guys on horseback riding in from the back pasture and tipped his hat. They both tipped theirs in turn and he slid into his truck and drove away. Funny how years of needing to be in control of the ranch had turned so quickly, and now he was happy to drive away and let them shoulder the back breaking labor. He grinned and cranked the radio as he drove to get Ren and the girls. Ren had a truck as well, but Duncan figured it would be easier if the couple could ride back together so they could both help with the twins.

Ren was ready when he pulled up. There were two booster seats and a large diaper bag loaded with only God knew what, next to the driveway.

Duncan grabbed the boosters and set them in the back seat of the truck as Ren hauled the girls out in each arm. "Duncan." He nodded.

Duncan smiled and met him at the front, taking Ariana after he had kissed both girls' cheeks. "Hello my favorite nieces. Ren." He nodded at Ren and grinned at the girls.

Olivia pouted. "I want Unca Dunca too, Daddy".

Ren sighed in exasperation. "I will let Uncle Duncan get you out when we get there, deal?"

She nodded but kept pouting as the men buckled them both into their seat belts.

With both girls strapped in, Ren grabbed the bag and tossed it on the floor under Olivia's feet, before carefully closing the door and sliding inside the front. Duncan put the truck in gear as he closed his door and put his own buckle on. "So, how is Sylvie Dunlap doing?" Ren asked as he turned to look at Duncan.

He shrugged. "She is alive and healing. I can't wait to get my hands on the bastard who shot her though."

Ren grinned and nodded in understanding. "I hear you. It sounds like she was lucky you were with her."

Duncan's blue eyes darkened, and he scowled. "She would have bled out pretty quick."

Ren nodded seriously. "I wasn't sure I was going to be able to keep Jackie from driving to the hospital until you asked her to handle things at the ranch. Thanks for that. The doc says she shouldn't be going on long trips at this point."

Duncan grinned and nodded. "I knew she would be going crazy. I appreciate the help you guys got out at the ranch."

Ren only nodded once. "They are happy to have work. It's getting harder and harder for the local guys to get jobs, with all the big commercial ranchers coming in and taking over. Those big ranchers always bring in most of their help from other places and it leaves the locals without work, so they have to move away to find a decent job." He paused and looked at Duncan who was nodding in understanding. "Frank is the eldest and he has a family a few miles over. He should be a good foreman for you. The other two, Randy and Jordan, have worked off and on with my crew, but their hearts are in ranching so it's really a favor to them."

Duncan grinned. "As long as they know how to do ranch work and aren't lazy. It is not an easy lifestyle." Ren chuckled. "No, it isn't."

They drove in companionable silence until Olivia suddenly burst out crying. Within seconds, Ariana had joined her and both men looked helplessly back at the crying girls. Duncan asked if they wanted to listen to a song. Ariana cried as she shook her head and Olivia nodded. Duncan eyed them both warily, unsure what to do. Under his breath he said, "Remind me not to ever have daughters. They are complicated and hard to handle."

Ren only grinned as he reached an arm back in an attempt to soothe his darling girls.

Chapter 12

Dinner was a rather loud affair as everyone sat up at the long table that sat at one side of the kitchen. Since there weren't enough chairs for everyone, the twins sat on their parents' laps. Jackie had made fresh rolls and whipped cinnamon, honey, and butter together and prepared a green garden salad for an appetizer. Then there were chunks of chicken, potatoes, broccoli and carrots all baked together, sprinkled with butter, garlic and fresh herbs for flavor. The food was delicious, and everyone told her so as they cleaned their plates.

Just when they finished eating, the timer on the oven dinged, and Jackie jumped up. "Oh, that will be the peach cobbler now." She rushed over and pulled out a steaming glass baking pan. Then she went to the freezer and pulled out a quart of vanilla ice cream. "I thought some dessert might be nice." She carefully set the hot pan on a pad in the center of the table and went back for the ice cream and a scoop.

Duncan licked his lips. "Dinner was great, Sis. Thanks." He eyed the bubbling cobbler with great appreciation. "You guys don't know this yet, but Jackie makes the absolute best cobblers."

Sylvie watched him with a small smile. The hungry way he was staring at the pan made her own mouth water, though not necessarily for the dessert. She had been sitting next to him all night and was hyper aware of his every move. Their arms brushed occasionally which left shimmers of electricity running up her arm each time. She had originally sat across from him but then when his dad, Arthur, showed up, they had added another chair on her side and Duncan had quickly hurried around to make room for his dad.

It was a welcome throwback to the old days when the two families had barbecues and birthday parties together. The only sad point was the feeling of those missing from the family. Ren and the twins helped fill that void, but it still felt a little surreal to be eating here in this house with Jackie and Duncan once again. She asked about how Jackie and Ren had met and sat back to listen as together they spliced the story into one funny but beautiful picture.

Jackie had first met him at school where they hadn't liked each other at all. Then, years later, they had been set up on a blind date by friends. They had both laughed together as they realized their friends really didn't know them well at all as they were a terrible match. Together they decided to make the best of it and at least enjoy dinner at the very nice restaurant they had both dressed up for and driven a long way to.

Throughout the meal they talked about the weather and the mountains. When they both realized they loved the mountains they talked about that for a long while. When sports came up in the conversation, they found out they liked the same football and basketball teams, and upon further investigation, knew they liked those teams for the same reasons.

At that point they had both gone quiet for a while until Ren finally looked up and met her blue gaze. "So, I'm man enough to admit that I may have been a bit hasty in deciding I didn't like you."

Jackie had laughed with amusement and then with a little shame as she nodded. "Yeah, me too." Then because she was Jackie and she was spontaneous she said under her breath, "So why didn't you like me then, handsome guy?"

He stared hard at her, and she saw something deep in his blue eyes as he shrugged one shoulder. "I do like you. The reason I didn't back then, was because I had been in a few bad relationships with beautiful women who I thought acted like you. The girl I'd just broken up with actually even looked a little like you, only less beautiful, and she was a grade A bitch. Then there you were, even prettier, looking like a million bucks and I thought, if Eve was self-centered, imagine just how self- centered this chick probably is." He eyed her for a long moment. "I gotta say you really don't seem all that spoiled."

Jackie had thrown her head back and laughed at his comment. When he only gave her a charming grin she smiled and admitted, "Same for me. All through high school I dated this guy that was every high school girl's dream. He was handsome, funny, and knew how to make all the girls drool over him. When I graduated though, he suddenly asked me to marry him, and he didn't like the idea of me going off to school.

"He actually said that a woman's place was in the home having children and taking care of the house for her husband." She'd met his gaze head on then with a bit of a challenge. "I'm not one of those kinds of women, you know?" She watched him carefully, gauging his reaction to that comment. He only grinned and nodded so she continued. "So, then I walk into my stats class that fall, and there you are all handsome and all the girls are giddy and wanting you to ask them out."

His brows went up at her comment and he asked, "Really? I didn't know."

She laughed again and told him, "By the end of the year some of the girls were starting to suggest that you might be gay, and it was such a loss." His head went back at that admission and a low rumble of laughter rolled out. She laughed with him in good nature and then they both reached for their water. She eyed him over the top of her glass and then, because she couldn't resist, asked, as she watched through her dark lashes. "So, does all this mean you aren't gay then?"

Another roar of laughter slid from his lips, and he wiped a hand across his eyes as people around them began watching their table with interest. Finally, he leaned over toward her and in a loud whisper said, "You tell me. I happen to find *you* very attractive, and I'd like to do a lot more than look, if you know what I mean." He wriggled his brows in suggestion and then grinned.

Breathless, she shook her head as a warm blush warmed her neck and cheeks. "You have no shame, do you?"

He only smiled as he reached for her hand and slid his fingers against her own until shivers ran up her spine. When she blushed, he smiled and leaned in for a kiss. She didn't pull back and they left the restaurant before their food had even been served.

Jackie beamed happily as her and Ren exchanged a long hot look. Duncan cleared his throat. "I think it's time to change the subject. There are underage girls present."

Everyone laughed and the moment between them eased, but Sylvie didn't miss how Ren reached out to hold Jackie's hand tenderly with his own as the conversation turned to sports.

She and Duncan groaned at the same time. A little surprised, she turned, and their gazes collided. Her dad had once been a long-time fan of the same team as the Jamison's. But now she knew he was all in with their local team in North Carolina and a debate would soon follow. Duncan moved his thigh and brushed it against her leg leaving a trail of heat and longing there. She swallowed and reached for a dessert plate that Jackie handed over.

She had been perfectly content to have a fun fling with her old high school crush while she was here, but he obviously hadn't wanted that. Now, here he was, luring her ever toward some undefinable ledge that only he understood, and she didn't like it one little bit.

If he didn't want to have casual sex with her, then why did he keep getting in her space and all up close and personal? The whole thing made her nervous, and she vowed to steer clear of whatever he had in mind. If he wanted to date her long term it was going to be a problem. She simply didn't have time or room in her life for a boyfriend.

She scooted to the far side of her chair away from him. He turned and grinned at her, and she scowled back. He chuckled under his breath and asked quietly, "Is something wrong, Sylvie?"

She nodded quickly and swiped the ice cream scoop from his hand as she reached for the carton. "Just excited to try this so-called amazing dessert."

He laughed again softly and then leaned close. Under his breath he whispered, "Whatever you say, chicken."

She didn't even respond to his taunt. Only dished some gooey hot cobbler on her plate and then plopped a scoop of ice cream on top. Feeling rather piqued at him she quickly scooted the carton and scoop to Arthur who sat on her other side, out of reach of Duncan. He could go without dessert.

His hand snaked out to clasp her wrist, but it was too late. Arthur had already taken it from her fingers. She turned to smile sweetly up at him. "Did you need something, Jamison?"

A wide feral smile turned up one side of his mouth. He looked down at her and his eyes held promise as he said softly, "Nothing I can't get later." She shivered and heat blossomed somewhere inside her core. She forced a confident smile. "I'm sure the dessert won't be gone before it comes back around."

He didn't blink, only stared as a wide smile split his mouth.

"I wasn't talking about the dessert."

Luckily for Sylvie the conversation had indeed turned into a debate and her father was very invested in describing in detail what made Carolina's team so much better. Arthur was loading dessert onto his plate unbothered by the exchange but both Jackie and Ren had disbelieving frowns on their faces. She couldn't look at Duncan and wasn't about to get into the sports debate. Instead, she picked up her spoon and licked her lips as she made a show of taking a juicy bite and then enjoying it for Duncan's sake since his plate still sat empty.

The dessert made it all the way back around, and Jackie started getting seconds before glancing around and then saying quickly, "Oh, I'm sorry Duncan. I didn't realize you didn't get any yet. Here." She handed it across to him.

Sylvie hid her amused smile behind another delicious bite and then dared a quick look at him. "Yes, Duncan why didn't you get any yet? After all of your talk about how good it is, I would have thought you would delve right in." She reached for the scoop and carton. "Saving it for those of us who don't get the opportunity often? You're such a gentleman." Her voice oozed sweetly.

He swiped them before she could and gave her a calculating grin before heaping a healthy serving onto his plate. "Like I said before, I'm a patient man."

Chapter 13

Duncan waited until the last of his family had said goodbye and left before he brought up the only thing he'd wanted to talk about all night. He grabbed a beer from the fridge and walked in to sit across from Reagan who had a glass of scotch in his hand. He waited patiently for the older man to look up at him before he casually asked, "So, where are these files you had sent."

Reagan blinked as though it took him a moment to process the question, and Duncan wondered how many scotches he'd already had. Finally, Reagan took a swallow of scotch and then lifted a thumb. "I had them all put in the den."

Duncan nodded and stood. "If you don't mind, I'd like to start going through them now." He didn't wait for permission but strode across to the other side of the front room where the closed double doors led into the den, if he remembered correctly.

He heard Reagan stand up behind him. "Hold on just a minute son, I'll come with you."

He ambled slowly across the room and Duncan turned and forced a smile. "You haven't had much sleep the past few nights sir, maybe you should just head on up to bed and I can fill you in tomorrow after you're rested."

Reagan hesitated for a second and then turned and looked wistfully at the stairs. "Are you sure it wouldn't bother you?"

Duncan shook his head and gave him a reassuring smile. "Not at all. In fact, maybe you should have another scotch first."

That got Reagan's attention and he nodded and smiled. "Maybe I will. I'll wait here to make sure Sylvie is okay first and then we can both go up together."

"Sounds good to me." Duncan nodded again and then slipped into the den closing the door behind him. Sylvie had needed to go to the restroom, but it served his purposes well for Reagan to usher her up to bed. With a satisfied smile, he reached for the white cardboard box on top and opened it. One by one, he pulled out files and scanned through them. For only three years of work there were a lot of cases that Sylvie had been involved in, in one capacity or another. He soon began making stacks on the emptied desk, separating the files by what he gauged could have been plausible suspects in her shooting.

He heard Sylvie speaking to her father and stopped to listen for a moment. She never even asked about him and he wondered if he should have been offended. He wasn't. Instead, he grinned and went back to work. The sooner he made a list of people who might possibly want Sylvie dead, the better. He could then turn that list over to the police and also start looking into them himself.

For a long while he could hear their quiet voices as they talked. He was grateful for the solid wood doors that hid the light in the den when he heard Reagan tell her they should head upstairs. She agreed, and he heard them walking about and then finally the creak of the stairs as they went up to bed. He didn't think Reagan had told Sylvie he was still here, and he grinned. She hadn't asked either, so it was as much on her as anyone.

He spent another hour sifting through files before finally turning out the light and slipping silently out. He made his way to the windows making sure they were all still covered and then looked out the front door into the dark for a while. He saw nothing to raise the alarm, and after a while, checked that everything was locked up tight, and slipped silently up the stairs.

He checked the rooms upstairs as well, with the exception of Sylvie's and the master suite. When he was confident everything was good, he stepped to her door quietly and knocked. He listened as the light brush of movement inside paused at his soft knock. Finally, she said, "Come in, Daddy. I'm decent."

He opened the door and stepped quickly inside, closing it behind himself with a quiet click. She was dressed in a pair of blue silky pajamas with a low-cut top and shorts that showed off her long legs. He smiled as she turned toward him. She swallowed hard and let out a curse. "Duncan, what in the hell are *you* doing here?" she asked, sounding angry.

He met her dark eyes and shrugged. "I'm keeping you safe."

She shook her head. "I'm fine and Daddy is here now."

He gave her a small grin. "And how many more scotches did he have before crashing into bed?"

She didn't smile at his question, only stared as though afraid of him. He stepped toward her, and she lifted her good hand as though to hold him off. He smiled gently and clasped her hand in his own. She tried to pull away, but he held on with a strong but gentle grip. She glared hotly at him. "Let go of me before I scream for Daddy."

He laughed then. "Scream away, sweetheart. I doubt an earthquake would wake him now. Besides, as you well know, I don't mean you any harm. I just want to keep you safe." He released her hand and stepped back. "I will be staying here with you until the bastard that shot you is in custody or dead."

Her eyebrows went up at his confident statement. "I don't need you here, Duncan. Daddy is here and packing. He is the police officer here and is perfectly capable of keeping me safe."

He glanced around her room. Someone had obviously gone through and removed most of the high school paraphernalia that had once hung on these walls. They were clear now except for a few scattered photos. One of Elaine and Sylvie standing in running uniforms for cross country. One of Sylvie with her parents. There was one of the four of them all with arms slung around shoulders standing next to a mountain trail. He grinned and reached out a hand to trace Sylvie's young face as though in a caress.

He heard the air hiss out of her lungs as she watched his finger run down her slender body in the photo. He turned back to her, eyes dark now with unspoken hunger. He met the milk chocolate orbs head on and felt the tension sizzle between them. His groin tightened painfully as he looked her up and down from head to toe. Sounding a little surprised at his own words he asked, "How is it possible that you got even more beautiful in the past eight years?"

She looked away and down at her arms. Her good hand was rubbing lightly across her arm that was in the sling. Finally, she forced her gaze back up and he could see anger there. "Why are you suddenly trying to seduce me now, Duncan?"

For years, back then she had wanted, even hoped, that he would notice her, and he hadn't seemed to see her as anything but a sister. When she first came back, she'd liked the idea of having a quick pleasure-filled fling with him before she went back home. He had made it clear that he hadn't wanted that. Now she was perplexed as to why he seemed to be trying to seduce her at every turn.

His blue eyes watched her carefully as though studying her every move. She swallowed the lump in her throat as one side of his mouth turned up in

a slight grin. "Let's just say I think I'm exactly what you need right now, sweetheart."

Anger flared her slender nostrils out at his arrogance. "Does that mean you have changed your mind and are now open to a sexual fling?"

His grin widened and he shrugged. "Something like that. What do you think, Sylvie? Do you want me to make long, hot love to you?"

His direct question had her looking down at her hands again. Heat soared from her core out but the fear there at the base of her neck tingled down her spine making her feel hot and cold at the same time. Finally, she shook her head. "I don't think I do."

He laughed softly and stepped toward her. "I think I'll be the judge of that."

She stepped backward and he stalked her until her legs were against the bed. She stared up at him, eyes wide as he reached out a hand to gently cup the side of her neck. His head lowered to hers in a hungry, demanding kiss that lit them both on fire. She moaned and leaned into him even as he wrapped one arm around her waist and pulled her gently against him. Her good hand went up into his dark hair and held his head as he kissed his way across to her ear and then nibbled his way down her neck to her gently curved collar bone.

He stopped suddenly and stepped back leaving her feeling bereft. His breathing was heavy, and his voice sounded a little hoarse. "I think we would both like it very much, but I won't take it unless you want it too." He raised an eyebrow in question.

Sylvie stared at his hard chiseled face with a shimmer of dark whiskered shadow across his strong jaw and chin. Her dark eyes met his blue knowing gaze and something inside reared its ugly head making her gasp for air suddenly. Panic seeped up and she began shaking her head even as she backed up a step. "No, Duncan, I don't want this." Her eyes were pleading now as she sat heavily on the bed. "I know we have this attraction between us, I won't deny that, but I think we will both be better off if we stick to being friends."

She saw the disappointment in his blue eyes a fraction of a second before he covered it with a smile. He nodded once and then turned away to walk toward the door. "I'll be right back."

She blinked. She hadn't expected him to go. It sunk in then what he had said, and she jumped up to rush after him. Her shoulder throbbed and she

gritted her teeth and reached a hand up to hold there as she slowed. "Wait, Duncan, why are you coming back?"

He didn't respond from the hallway as he disappeared from sight. She was about to close the door and lock it when he gently shouldered his way back inside. He had a large bag slung over one shoulder and he shrugged it off on the floor next to a grey armchair. She was staring hard at him as he walked back and carefully closed the door. He began pulling things out of the bag and her brows came together in frustration. "What in the hell do you think you're doing?"

He turned and threw a grin over his shoulder. "I won't force you into sex Sylvie, but I will damned sure protect you."

She didn't know where to even start with that idiotic statement. She moved toward him hesitantly. "Can't you do that from some other room in the house?" She hadn't meant to sound like she was pleading, and her mouth closed. Forcing a friendly smile, she firmed her voice. "What I meant is that there are other rooms you can stay in if you want to stay here in the house with us."

He shook his head. "Sorry but no. I was literally in the same room with you when you got shot and if I had been even seconds away, you might not have made it." His voice sounded raw as he said the last. "I would never forgive myself if something happened and I couldn't get to you in time."

She hesitated only for a moment. "There is always Elaine's room. It's just across the hall so you would be nearly as close."

He unrolled a forest green sleeping bag onto the floor and shook his head. "I would rather sleep in your bed with you, but since you don't want that, then I will sleep down here." He turned to look up at where she was standing. "Unless you've changed your mind?" She shook her head quickly and he grinned. "Then I guess I'll be settling in on the floor."

She watched, intrigued as he pulled out a small pillow and tossed it to one end of the sleeping bag. Next, he reached inside, and to her surprise, pulled out a black and grey Sig Sauer and laid it on the floor near the pillow. Her eyes widened and she sucked in a breath. "Duncan why do you have a gun?"

He looked up at her. "I told you, I'm here to keep you safe. I came prepared this time, Sylvie." His face was devoid of emotion as he lifted his arms and pulled off his shirt.

She stared at his broad muscled chest and arms for a long moment before she forced her gaze away. "Why are you undressing if you're sleeping on the floor?"

He chuckled. "I get hot at night. I usually sleep naked, but I'll leave some shorts on just for you." He turned and met her eyes as he stood and unbuttoned and unzipped his jeans and began sliding them off his hips.

She turned away as a wide muscled thigh came into view. In self-preservation, she hurried over to the bed and slipped under the covers there. There were several pillows, so she tossed them onto the floor. She took a deep breath and laid back just as Duncan asked, "If you aren't going to use those, can I have one? This pillow is nice cause it folds in the bag, but it really is crappy to sleep on."

She nodded and then realized he couldn't see her head, so she murmured, "Suit yourself."

He didn't come over to her and she wondered if he was waiting for her to bring him one. "Unbelievable," she muttered under her breath and started to slide out of the covers.

He grinned. "What was that?"

She jumped as she turned and realized he was standing next to the bed in all his nearly naked glory. He wore only a snug pair of boxer briefs that left little to the imagination. She swallowed and forced her gaze up past the V-line of his pelvis and then up his chest lightly sprinkled with dark hair over toned muscle and up to his eyes. She saw the amusement there and glared. "Nothing. I thought you wanted me to bring you a pillow is all."

He shook his head and reached a hand out to her. She stared at the offensive limb dumbly. Finally, he said gently, "You might want these. It might help you sleep through the pain."

She held out her hand in apology. "Thanks, it really does throb."

He nodded, "I bet." He held out a bottle of water and she wondered if it had also come from his bag.

She took it and drank as she swallowed the pills. He stood still for a long moment there in front of her. Sylvie refused to look at him but when he didn't go away, she finally turned and met his eyes. "Did you need something else?"

His jaw was taut, and his eyes were dark as his gaze raked over her shape even under the covers. He shook his head. "I just want you to know that if you change your mind, I'll be right over there." He threw a thumb toward the floor and the sleeping bag. He winked and turned to walk away, but over his shoulder he murmured, "I would be happy to scratch that itch, sweetheart."

Sylvie swallowed again and reached for the lamp. "I'm turning out the light now, Duncan. So if you need anything, now is your last chance."

He laughed low in his throat, and she shivered as heat filled her core again. "I only need you, and that I could have even in the dark."

She didn't respond, only quickly turned out the light and rolled over in bed. Her shoulder ached now that she didn't have anything else to think about and she moaned. Then she rolled to a different position to try to ease the pain. She thought of Duncan's hard body a mere few feet away and wondered if his skin was hot to the touch. She groaned aloud.

Damn him. He had made that comment about sleeping naked and hot and now that's all she could think about. At least it distracted her from the throbbing pain of her shoulder, she thought as she lay awake in bed. She wondered if he slept but didn't give him the satisfaction of asking. Instead, she forced her mind to stay calm and willed sleep to come. It was he who finally broke the silence. "Are you sure you don't want me to come over there with you? I'd be gentle and it might ease the shoulder pain a little."

Sylvie closed her eyes and pretended to sleep.

Duncan chuckled softly again. "So much for the mighty district attorney act, you really are quite the chicken, aren't you."

It was more of a statement than a question and though Sylvie wanted to rebut his comment she pressed her lips together in a thin line. He couldn't possibly know that she was still awake for sure.

As though he read her mind he said softly, "I can tell by your breathing that you are still awake, and a bit upset."

She sat up. "For god's sake, go to sleep, Duncan. I'm not going to change my mind."

He rolled onto his back and lifted his arms above his head to lay on them. "Your loss, love."

She rolled her eyes and tried not to fill in the shadows to accommodate for the darkness that his shape made. She lay back against the pillow and closed her eyes. No reason to make this all hard on herself. With a little sigh she asked, "Doesn't this all seem so bizarre?"

He shrugged.

She didn't wait for a response. "A few days ago I was in North Carolina at work and this life seemed so far out of reach. Just a few days later I'm

here with you, in this room and there is all this." She waved a hand in the dark to encompass the space between them. "I actually got shot and now this reality is beginning to feel more real than the other and yet I know I have to go back to that life."

"Hmm," was all he said.

She bit back a frustrated groan, "are you trying to sleep or something?"

He sighed. "I'd rather be not sleeping over there with you, but no I'm not sleeping. Just trying really hard not to think of what could be happening over there in your bed. It makes me all hard and uncomfortable and I don't know how long I can be a gentleman at this rate."

That shut her up and she swallowed and rolled over. Now, she was wondering just how much of what he said was true. A little sadly she said, "That really isn't playing fair."

She could hear the smile in his voice as he replied. "Playing fair must be out of the range of my gentlemanly attributes."

Even Sylvie smiled as he said it. She turned onto her good shoulder side. "Good night, Duncan. I haven't said this yet, but thanks for saving my life."

He smiled through the darkness. "I will find who did it, Sylvie." It was a promise in the dark and they both knew it.

Chapter 14

The next two days went much the same with Duncan and Reagan pampering Sylvie as though she was an invalid. Each day Jackie brought the twins over to see them and Sylvie began to get attached. They were lively and beautiful, full of life and excitement about even small things, and she found herself wondering what Duncan's little girl might look like. She squashed that thought immediately. She would not be staying here much longer, and she had to start distancing herself from her friends and their family or leaving was going to hurt a whole lot more.

That, however, was proving to be difficult, with Duncan solidly insisting on staying in her room each night.

Each night she found it more difficult to resist his persuasive kisses and the urge to invite him into her bed. He was extremely sexy with his broad muscled shoulders and chest with dark hair sprinkled across and sloped down to the V that disappeared beneath his waistline. Each night he would strip down to his boxer briefs that left little to her imagination and stretch out on the thin sleeping bag. She tried not to stare at the muscle that rippled with each movement but couldn't resist admiring his muscular abs and body. She wanted to touch and lick at each of those defined ridges and slide her body against his warm strength but was afraid to. She felt uncertain since he had made a sudden change from not wanting a fling with her at all, to suddenly trying at every opportunity to get into her bed. She wasn't willing to lie to him, and she still had no intention of a long- term relationship, so the point was moot.

Duncan and her dad spent most of their days going through files, and sorting out possible suspects that may have wanted her dead. So far, they hadn't found anyone who benefited from her being gone, and Duncan left the den in frustration. Each night, her father drank himself into bed and then Duncan would come up to her room to make sure she was safe.

That was the entire problem, she realized on the third day, after the police had come out to take their statements for the third time. If she could help him solve the problem in front of them, then maybe he would go back to his own house and leave her in unlusting peace. She had recently started sweating at night due to the heat she felt as she watched Duncan lie on the floor at the foot of her bed. She wasn't about to admit that to him, however. It would only make him cocky and then he might realize that she wasn't nearly as unaffected by his touch as she'd been pretending.

In truth, each brush of his hand against her own as he handed her food, water, or painkillers, left a warm tingling sensation running up her arm. Every time she turned and saw those steady blue eyes watching her from across the room, she fought a shiver of awareness. She was much closer to the verge of giving him exactly what he wanted than he could possibly realize. Today, she had woken to him propped against the wall watching her sleep and she fought the shiver of heat that washed through her core.

He had stood and walked over to her then, still clad in only his boxers. He sat next to her on the bed and grinned down at her guarded expression. "Your dad is already up and about this morning," he'd said quietly. Since they had beat Reagan downstairs each morning since Duncan had been staying in her room, they hadn't had to explain his presence at all.

Her eyebrows went up. "How do you plan to tell him what you are doing here."

He shrugged and gave her a lopsided smile. "I plan to simply tell him the truth."

She shook her head. "Duncan, Daddy really won't like that you have been in here each night. We should tell him something else, or he'll think there is something going on between us."

His blue eyes darkened as he stared hard at her. "There is."

She shook her head in denial and slid off the opposite side of the bed to the one he sat on, walking around to dig through her drawer for a pair of jeans. "No there isn't. As you well know, nothing is going to happen here." She turned back to look at him pleadingly. "I'm leaving as soon as the doctor gives me the okay, Duncan. You were clear that you don't want a fling and I don't want anything else."

He didn't blink, only stood and stretched his arms up over his shoulders before stepping close to say quietly down at her. "I've changed my mind. I'll take whatever I can get at this point."

Her cheeks warmed with discomfort, and she squirmed around him to walk quickly to her closet. "Well, I changed my mind too, you know? Idon't want to complicate anything with a fling at this point. It isn't worth it."

He laughed softly under his breath. "I disagree."

She ignored him as she closed the closet door and took her time getting into the jeans and a white off-shoulder top that showed her sexy shoulders. It also gave him access to the bandage there, for when he insisted on replacing it with a clean one as he did every day. She heard him moving about in her bedroom and sat down on the stool next to her shoes, waiting hopefully for any indication that he had left. She heard him walk to the closet door and she held her breath.

"I'm going downstairs, do you need anything before I go?" He sounded slightly amused and she resisted the urge to say something tart to him.

Instead, she shook her head and said loudly, "No, but thanks. See you down there." She waited for his footsteps to recede but heard nothing.

After a long pause of silence, he sighed. "This conversation isn't over, Sylvie."

She swallowed and closed her eyes hoping that he would just go away and leave her in peace. She also wished he would open the door and take her into his arms, but she fought against the need that surged to bury herself against his warm body. She stayed absolutely still and silent until she heard his receding footsteps and then finally the closing of the bedroom door. She was a coward, and she knew it. She wanted to let him make love to her. Wanted more than that, but she couldn't afford the 'more'.

She took her time brushing her long hair and teeth. By the time she made her way down the long staircase, Duncan and her father already had breakfast sitting on the table which was set with blue porcelain plates and white coffee mugs with shining silverware on napkins. She gave her father a kiss on his cheek. "Morning, Daddy."

He smiled and looked between her and Duncan thoughtfully. Then his smile widened as a happy thought flitted across his mind. Maybe Duncan was the perfect man to finally get his Sylvie to settle down and have a family. He watched Duncan as he stared at his daughter, willing her to acknowledge him. Sylvie seemed perfectly content to pretend that her and her father were the only ones in the room. With a little grin, Reagan sat and said, "I'm fairly certain you know that Duncan spent the night here, dear, but it's still polite to say good morning."

Sylvie's brown eyes, much like his own, swung up to meet his knowing smile. She blinked and then turned to give Duncan a little nod. "Good morning, Duncan."

He nodded and held her chair for her to sit down. "That's not necessary, Mr Dunlap. Sylvie and I already saw each other upstairs."

Sylvie's mouth gaped open in surprise. Had he intended to make it sound like they had spent the night together? Her eyes narrowed as Duncan turned his gaze on hers with a grin. She cleared her throat and started to explain. "What Duncan means, Daddy, is that I saw him upstairs before he came down here."

Reagan fought a grin at his daughter's obvious discomfort. Not many things managed to shake her nerves any more, and he was somewhat intrigued by the fact that Duncan Jamison could apparently get under her thick skin. He scrunched his brows at her explanation just as Duncan said with amusement, "That is exactly what I already said."

She turned a narrow-eyed glare at him. "Yes, but you made it sound like you and I spent the night together which absolutely isn't true." She turned an embarrassed smile at her dad. "The truth is—"

Reagan held up his hands to stop whatever else she was about to say.

Duncan, however, wasn't inclined to stop teasing her. He raised one eyebrow at her and gave her a killer smile. "And here I thought that was exactly what happened."

Reagan fought a wide smile at Sylvie's hot glare across the table at Duncan, who slid into a chair smoothly. When Sylvie turned to him as though prepared for a full explanation, he shook his head and rushed out quickly, "You are both adults and I'm not altogether sure I want to hear exactly what did or did not take place in your bedroom last night." He softened his smile as Sylvie's mouth snapped closed and she turned bright red.

"Nothing is going on. That is exactly what I have been trying to say." She gave Duncan another scathing look. "Whether or not you want it to." Then she realized she had just added more fuel to the fire. She groaned and stared down at her hands in irritation. "You have nothing to worry about, Daddy. There is nothing going on between me and Duncan."

Reagan did smile then. He turned and reached for the coffee pot to pour a fresh cup as he said calmly, "That's a real shame. I'd have liked it if there was something going on."

Both Duncan and Sylvie turned to stare at him in surprise, but he just kept pouring coffee. Finally, he looked up and met Sylvie's wide-eyed gaze.

She looked like he had betrayed her somehow, and a small surge of guilt tightened his stomach, then relaxed as he once again thought about how she seemed off balance for the first time in years. She sounded accusing and said grumpily, "I am so confused right now. Every time I've ever told you about the men I'm sleeping with, you don't approve." She shook her head in frustration. "Now I tell you I'm not sleeping with Duncan, and you are disappointed?"

She looked to Duncan for help. Surely, he could see how nonsensical all this was. He was watching her with his piercing gaze, so she ignored him, and turned back to her father who calmly took a sip of coffee. Then he shrugged and met her confused stare. "I like Duncan. I didn't like all those other boys. No man should be okay with you dating more than one person at a time like that. That shit just isn't normal." He turned to Duncan who was nodding in agreement. That brought another wide smile to his lips, and he generously handed the coffee pot over to him.

Sylvie's mouth dropped open again and she stared perplexed at her father, who had been blunter about the men in her life this morning, than he had ever been before. She had always sensed his disapproval, but he had never actually said it out loud. Feeling a little unsure of herself, she squared her shoulders. "There are plenty of people that have open relationships, Daddy."

He reached for one of the loaded breakfast burritos with fresh hash browns, eggs, cheddar, and ham all mixed together inside the freshly rolled tortillas. Duncan had promised they were one of his favorite recipes, and Reagan groaned in appreciation as the flavors burst into his mouth. He looked between the two of them and took a swig of coffee. Then he met his daughter's offended look head on. "Yes, and I have no problem with that. But how many of those people do you know who are actually settled down and having a family?"

Sylvie opened her mouth to argue and then it snapped closed again since she couldn't remember actually knowing anyone living the family life, that had an open relationship. A little desperately she blurted, "Well even if Duncan and I were to have sex, it wouldn't be more than that. I have open sexual relationships with several men, and it just wouldn't work out to have anything more."

Duncan grinned smugly and Reagan choked on his burrito. She watched in embarrassed horror as Duncan stood to quickly go around and pound on his shoulders as what she had said sunk into her brain. She turned a crimson red and reached for the coffee pot that had been stingily kept from her. With a sinking feeling that she had somehow lost this battle, she announced, "I apologize for what I said, Daddy. I like Duncan too, but I have already decided that I don't want a relationship with him." The last she said in a determined voice.

Neither of the men responded, though she noticed a long look passed between them. Unwilling to add fuel to the fire, Sylvie added cream and sugar to her coffee and then said politely, "Daddy would you mind passing the food down here. I'm starving."

Reagan nodded and slid the glass tray down toward her. Sylvie reached for a gigantic, overstuffed burrito and smiled at her father. "This looks amazing, Dad. I didn't realize you had learned to cook."

Reagan laughed aloud and happily informed his daughter, "Duncan made breakfast, dear."

Sylvie wouldn't look at the irresistibly sexy male across from her. Instead, she gave a little nod. "Thanks," she said sounding extremely ungrateful.

Duncan didn't take it personally. Though he'd been surprised when Reagan gave them his blessing, he also appreciated it. It was one more excuse that Sylvie couldn't use, when he managed to convince her that they were going to be great together.

The silence was uncomfortable to Sylvie as they ate, though the men appeared to be completely unfazed by it. After several minutes she set down her coffee cup and announced, "I'm going to join the two of you today with the files. If there is anyone who might understand who might hate me enough to shoot at me, it's me, after all."

Reagan disagreed but Sylvie's chin jutted out stubbornly. She wasn't going to sit around and wait for the big strong men to keep her safe. She listened to all the arguments her father made without budging. To her surprise, Duncan spoke up. “Sylvie is right, sir. She would be able to tell us just by the names who might have residual anger without having to read completely through each file.”

Chapter 15

Though Sylvie had agreed to help the men, after five long hours of combing through names and files, she was ready to call a halt to the process. Both her father and Duncan searched stubbornly, unwilling to leave any stone unturned.

Exhausted, with a shoulder throbbing from the weight of her arm, even with the sling, she turned impatient eyes to Duncan. "This is no use, you guys. I haven't heard of a single person yet who hated me enough to want me dead or that gained something as a result. Let's take a break."

Duncan looked up only momentarily. He could see the exhaustion in her pale cheeks, so he nodded. "Why don't you go out and relax for a bit? If I see anything I have a question about, I will come out and ask you."

She frowned unhappily at him and her dad. "I'm starting to think this is all just a waste of time. I wonder if it really was a hunter that wasn't paying attention."

Duncan gave her a small smile. His gut had been screaming at him for days that she wasn't safe and that someone was after her, but he didn't want her worried and scared, so he kept his mouth shut.

Reagan had no such qualms. "I don't think so, dear. I have worked on enough murder cases in my time to realize that the chance is pretty slim. For one thing, you were indoors. What earthly reason would a hunter have to be this close to the house? And wasn't it dark as well? How could they not have realized they were pointing their scope at a lit-up window? I think this is someone who wants you dead."

Sylvie groaned and rubbed at her temples. "I am so sick of all this. I honestly can't think of a single person who I've tangled with on a case that might hate me enough to go to the lengths of following me out here and taking a pot shot at me," she said tiredly.

Something she'd said struck Duncan as odd and he set down the file he was browsing to walk over to her. She stiffened as he put his hands on her shoulders and then relaxed, as he began to gently knead the sore muscles with his strong fingertips. He leaned down and asked, "Does that help any?"

She sighed and leaned into the tips of his fingers, nodding and closing her aching eyes for a brief moment.

"You just said you can't think of a single person from a case that might want you dead. But what about in your personal life? Is there someone you can think of that might be this angry at you? A jilted lover maybe?" Duncan asked quietly.

Sylvie's eyes flew open, and she turned to stare up at him with wide eyes. He was watching her every expression as though he thought she might lie, which she was considering doing, so she opted for the truth. She hadn't wanted to offer Zack's name as a suspect either to the police or to her family because she didn't believe he'd have done this. Unable to hide it any longer, she shrugged. "There was this one guy that I dated a couple of years ago just out of college, but I really don't think he would do something like this."

Duncan's expression turned hard, and Sylvie tried not to wince. Zachary McDaniels had been a handsome blond with compelling blue eyes and a tennis player's body. She had met him at a friend's party, and he had immediately taken to flirting with her. At the time, she was already seeing a couple of other guys casually, so she hadn't thought too much of going out with him. After the third email he'd sent, practically begging her to give him a chance, she'd finally agreed to a date.

The date had been enjoyable, she remembered. A friendly dinner at a nice restaurant downtown. Then he had asked her if she wanted to go for an evening stroll. She had agreed only because the street was well lit, and people lined the sidewalks outside the shops, boutiques and restaurants in the mood of celebration. As they walked, he talked about his family and how he was feeling like he was ready to settle down. He'd leaned in for a kiss at one point next to a lamp-lit patio where a few couples sat at tables enjoying the refreshing evening air. The kiss had been pleasant, so Sylvie asked if he'd like to take her to his place for coffee.

He had readily agreed, and they'd had sex on the couch in his front room. Afterward, he'd told her that he was blown away by her beauty and intelligence and asked her if she wanted a family. Sylvie felt like the casual relationship she imagined for them was a far cry from what it seemed he was starting to believe, and so had told him she was seeing other people as well and only wanted something casual.

That hadn't seemed to bother him at first, until the texts and phone calls had started coming in. He asked her out again and she agreed. On their second date, however, both of the other

guys she was seeing had tried calling at different points and she had sent them to voicemail. When the texts started coming in shortly after, Zack had stopped in the middle of a funny story about him and a friend from college, to give her an annoyed look. "Is that work or something important you need to handle?"

Sylvie had shaken her head and apologized. "No, I'm sorry, it's just some friends that want to get together sometime."

Her phone dinged again as though on cue and Zack had bent over to stare angrily at the screen. A dark-haired man's face was on her screen with a text that said: *Dinner this weekend? I miss you.* Zacks expression had gone cold and hard, and he'd stood up, nearly knocking over the table as he did.

He'd glared hard at her and asked, "Is that a boyfriend of yours?"

Sylvie forced a small smile and nodded. "It is. I told you; I am very casual about these things."

He had then tried to insist that she end all of her other relationships at once. She was getting embarrassed at that point since people were beginning to watch them and shook her head. "I'm sorry, Zack, I thought you were okay with this. I was very clear from the start."

He'd given her an angry frown. "I thought you were letting me know that you wanted to take things a little slow, not that you would be actively dating a bunch of guys while we're going out. I like you a lot and I want things to work out with us. Don't you like me too?" He had flashed a charming grin at her then as though to add to his appeal. "Come on, Sylvie, just end it with those other guys and give us a real shot."

Sylvie, frustrated now, reached for her purse, glad that she hadn't invited him to her own apartment yet. She always waited for a while before giving her address to men she'd dated; in case something went wrong. Now, she flashed a warm smile in his direction and then met his eyes as he looked down at her. "I'm sorry, I really am, but I'm just not willing to do that at this point, Zack." She didn't say she wouldn't ever feel that way, but right now it just didn't feel right.

He'd gotten down on his knees then as she'd backed toward the door slinging her purse over her shoulder. "Please, Sylvie, I think I am already in love with you, and I feel like you might love me too." As though he needed something to keep her from leaving, he begged, "Marry me. I'm serious, baby. Let all those other guys go and we will get married as soon as you want. Or if you want to take a while so you can plan a big affair, even better."

Afraid she had finally run out of luck when it came to reasonable men in her life, Sylvie shivered as she stared at his handsome face. She shook her head. "I'm really sorry about all of this, but I'm not ready for that. Not now, and maybe never."

Tears had filled his eyes then and he stood. Before things could get any worse, Sylvie quickly opened the door. "I really am so sorry. Goodbye, Zack."

He'd rushed to the door as she opened it. "Please don't say that! We can work this out, I just know it!" he stated with childlike enthusiasm. Another customer picked that moment to come walking past and Sylvie had used it to her advantage. She hurriedly rushed outside before Zack could follow her. Back on the street, she had hurried up three blocks before casually stepping into a coffee shop while she waited for her ride share to come pick her up. She hadn't breathed easy until she was talking to the middle-aged woman that was giving her a ride and making polite small talk.

Sylvie had put the incident behind her and that weekend she'd called Steven, one of her other lovers, and gone out with him. She'd had the phone company block Zack's calls and moved on. It wasn't until the following weekend that she had truly been worried.

She'd spent the night with Steven again at her apartment. He was a good-looking guy from New York she'd met through a client. He was a new lawyer like herself and didn't have much time for a social life and was thus content with the casual affair they had going on. That morning they had planned to drive to work together and share a ride but he seemed impatient so she finally suggested he go ahead, and they could meet up later for lunch. He'd been relieved since he had a client meeting scheduled that morning and wanted to get to work early to prep.

When Sylvie exited her building an hour later and was waiting on the sidewalk for her ride, she'd seen someone walking toward her and lowered her phone out of curiosity. To her very genuine surprise, it was Zack. He gave her a smile that she knew was meant to be charming as he walked up and took her arm. She shivered and tried to shake him off. "My ride is here now, Zack. Let me go. I'm running late already."

His grip on her arm tightened painfully and he looked down at her, his smile slipping a little. "I just need a minute Sylvie, and then I'll let you go for now."

She gave a very pointed look at his hand on her arm and said, "You're hurting me, Zack. And I'm pretty sure I just told you that I don't have a free minute. Let go of me."

He loosened his grip, but only marginally. "You have time for what could turn out to be the best thing in your life. I know you do, and you won't regret it."

Knowing that he wasn't going to let go of her until she heard him out, she nodded. "Fine, you have two minutes, so say what you came to say."

He'd given a wounded frown at her curt tone and wheedled. "I'm sorry about our last date. I made a huge mistake. I pushed you way too hard. Please, just give me another chance. I won't push you until you are ready, I promise."

Sylvie pitied him at that moment and didn't bother to hide it. Trying to gentle her impatient tone she told him, "I had fun Zack, but I don't want to hang out with you any more. I'm sorry, I know that's hard to hear but it's the truth. Good luck, finding what you are looking for."

She'd seen her car pull up and pulled her arm from his abruptly and hurried forward to climb inside. As she closed the door, she heard him say, "Please, please give me another chance, Sylvie."

She hadn't responded, but on her lunch break, she'd canceled with Steven and taken the time to walk down and file a restraining order against Zack. She had only seen him one other time after he had been served with the restraining order. He'd waited outside her building again and when she came out, he'd rushed over to her, trying to explain that she didn't need to have a restraining order against him. He'd never hurt her; he assured her earnestly.

Sylvie looked him in the eye then and said, "Good, I'm glad to hear that. I do have a restraining order against you, however, and you are currently in violation of it now. Please move back to fifty yards and I won't call the police."

He'd thrown his hands into the air angrily as he backed away. "Fine, but when you realize how much you love me too, don't expect me to just take you back and forgive all of this."

She'd fought a laugh because she didn't want to see what he would do if he was angry, and said calmly, "You have nothing to worry about. I won't be calling you anytime. I deleted your contact."

Once again, she'd made her escape into the car that waited at the curb. He'd watched her as she climbed inside and then the car until it was out of sight. For two weeks she had been on edge and watched for him everywhere she went but she never saw him again.

She'd relaxed then and had truly believed that he had finally gotten over whatever obsession he'd had with her. Until she had been shot. He had been the first one who came to mind in the hospital but since she hadn't seen him in the last two years, she hadn't believed it warranted repeating. Now, she stared at Duncan thoughtfully. He still stared hard as if trying to read her mind.

"Who are you thinking of Sylvie?" he asked quietly.

She shook her head. "There was this guy I dated a couple of times a few years ago but I haven't seen him in years. I really don't see why he would care after all this time but maybe…" Her voice trailed off.

Duncan gave her an impatient look. "What is his name?"

She looked at him and then turned toward her dad, who was also watching her with his full attention now. "His name was Zachary McDaniels, but I really don't think he is the guy. He fancied himself in love with me and asked me to marry him."

Duncan strode over to the laptop he'd set on the desktop. He looked up with one eyebrow in the air at that tidbit of information. He started typing quickly, "How was his name spelled?"

Sylvie gave him a blank look and then shook her head. "I don't know. I only went out with him a couple of times."

Duncan typed some more and then after a minute or so turned the laptop toward her. "This the guy?"

Sylvie's eyes widened in surprise. There on his screen was a large photo of Zack looking charming with a wide smile and a sparkle in his blue eyes. She nodded and started toward Duncan. "Yeah, that's him. How on earth did you find him so fast?"

Duncan shrugged. "Just looked for a Zack McDaniels and you. It pulled him right up on Facebook." He pulled his phone out of his pocket and dialed. He paced the room as he listened to whomever was on the other end for a minute. Sylvie watched as he ran an agitated hand through his dark hair. Finally, he said, "Yeah this is Duncan Jamison. I'm just calling because I think I may know who is after Sylvianna Duncan. His name is

Zachary McDaniels and they went out a while ago, but it ended badly."

He listened for a long minute. "I hear ya. Yeah okay. I will be here with her but let me know if you figure anything out." He said goodbye and hung up, still pacing the length of the room. He glanced down at his watch and then walked out only to return a moment later with a handful of ibuprofen and a bottle of water. He handed them to Sylvie. "Sorry, I totally lost track of the time. Your shoulder is probably killing you."

Sylvie swallowed the pills gratefully. "Yes it is. I still don't think this would be Zack though."

He didn't argue with her but took her by the shoulders and gently pushed her out the door and down onto the couch. "Sit down and rest for a bit," he commanded.

Sylvie took immediate offense but swallowed it. She hated being bossed around, particularly by men, but the throbbing in her shoulder was already beginning to ease so she didn't fight him. Instead, she leaned her head back against the soft back of the tan leather and closed her eyes. What was her world coming to? She was sitting here wondering if some guy she'd gone out with a couple times, had followed her over two thousand miles and then tried to kill her. She felt his weight as Duncan sat down next to her and took her hand in his own and squeezed it gently. "Are you going to be okay?" he asked quietly.

In the past few days there had been so much sexual tension between them that she had almost forgotten how gentle he could be. Before she'd made the everlasting mistake to kiss him on that stupid horse ride, things had been different between them. He had hugged her when she seemed sad, stroked her hair out of her face when he was talking to her, and generally been a very sweet guy. Now all the sexual tension between them had her thinking twice about being within three feet of him. Having his warm strong thigh against her own now as he held her hand, made her feel like maybe the old Duncan was back here with her. She opened her eyes to meet his and nodded while forcing a smile. "I'll live. Thanks to you."

One side of his mouth turned up in a wry grin at her dry amusement.

"I'd like to help you if there is anything I can do for you."

The offer hung there in the air between them. They both knew what he was suggesting. She glanced over at the door to the den where her father hadn't yet emerged from. She turned to glare hotly at him. "You have *no* shame," she accused. Then, because she was still a little piqued at him about this morning, she said, "You have to quit talking to my dad about us. There is nothing going on here and I don't want him to get his hopes up."

He stared down at her with an unreadable expression. He was frustrated as hell by her stubborn refusal to admit she was every bit as hot for him as he was for her. Then he bent toward her neck as though to kiss her there. She froze, holding herself perfectly still. He didn't touch her, however, but stopped within a hair's distance and she could feel his warm breath against her neck and ear. She couldn't stop the shiver of pleasure as he whispered, "Not for lack of trying on my part. I'd happily take you to bed, so that you can quit saying there isn't anything going on here. I am extremely hot for you, Sylvianna Dunlap."

She swallowed as another shiver ran across her neck and through her shoulders. She turned her head a fraction of an inch to meet his eyes. His firm sensual lips were there in her eyeline, and she couldn't help staring at them for a minute before her gaze swung up to his. "I can't do complicated Duncan."

He didn't blink but held her gaze frozen there as he murmured,

"Can't or won't?"

She pulled back suddenly to put distance between them. She looked at her hands and then back at him. "I can't do it, okay?"

His gaze was steady on her face as he said softly, "And what if I'm willing to do casual?"

She tried to pull her gaze away but couldn't. There was something dark and hot and promising in the blue depths of his eyes. Something she wanted more than anything here at this moment. She felt herself begin to mourn the loss of what she was missing out on, even as she made up her mind and shook her head. "I don't think it's a good idea."

He swore softly under his breath and for the first time she saw something spark in his eyes. Anger? Or was it impatience? She watched as he leaned back and away from her. "Christ, you are infuriating. I'm a patient man Sylvie, but even I have my limits," he said, and it sounded like a warning to her.

"Jackie just called to say that she is bringing dinner over in a bit,"

Reagan said from the doorway behind them.

Sylvie jumped back guiltily before she remembered that Duncan had already put some distance between them. She glanced back to see a knowing smile on her dad's face and a warm blush stained her neck. He had been trying for the last year to talk to her about settling down and getting married. Ever since her mother had died, he'd been talking more frequently about it. She didn't want him to believe that was what was happening, so she jumped up and went into the kitchen to put some space between herself and Duncan. As inspiration hit, she poured a glass of scotch for her father, a glass of white wine for herself and grabbed a beer for Duncan. She returned to the front room where her father and Duncan were discussing the likelihood that Zack McDaniels was the guy the police were looking for. She gave them each a drink and then settled herself casually into a large, overstuffed chair.

No way for Duncan to get up close to her now.

Both men thanked her as they noticed her very casual attempt to distance herself but didn't comment. When she stepped out a few minutes later to use the restroom, Reagan turned a smile to Duncan. "Son, I can see that you really care for Sylvie. I can tell you are getting under her skin and that is a good thing. Please don't give up on her. She hasn't let anyone close to her since before Elaine died."

Duncan gave the older man a smile and a nod. "I intend to marry her, you know?" he challenged in a firm tone.

Reagan let out a little chuckle and then said seriously, "You won't get any arguments from me."

Duncan nodded. "It might take a while to wear her down to the idea." Their eyes met and they both held it steadily until Duncan held his beer toward Sylvie's dad. "To stubborn women and the men willing to wait them out."

Both men were grinning when Sylvie walked back into the room. She hesitated uncertainly, feeling somehow that she had missed something important. She could ask them but given how awkward things had been happening all day, she opted not to. Instead, she hurried back to the chair and settled down into it in silence.

Chapter 16

He watched the house for days. He waited patiently for any sign that the people inside were beginning to relax and believe the shooting had simply been a fluke chance. He reached for yet another chocolate bar and tore it open as he washed it down with stale coffee from the large Thermos, he'd packed this morning.

That old white house appeared to be a central hub for all her family and friends to hang out. His eyes narrowed on the burgundy pickup truck that remained there in the driveway. He tried not to think about why that damned man and his truck seemed to be there day and night. Those thoughts that crept in made him feel uncomfortable because they shone a light on the sexual things that he was also feeling stronger about day by day.

Though his initial plan here had started as simply erasing Sylvianna Dunlap and all she knew from this world, watching her for hours had given him a strong desire to have her body, before she was gone. She was, after all, beautiful, mouth wateringly curvaceous, and full of sex appeal. He remembered years ago when he'd first began to notice just how pretty she was, but even back then she had been that taunting young woman who flirted and teased but never actually followed through with the sensual promises that had emanated from her deep brown eyes.

He was going crazy now. He hadn't been able to see her out here for days. The blinds and window coverings were all drawn and had been since her return from the hospital. He'd considered slipping into her bedroom and surprising her late at night. He had a key he'd gotten from her purse when he'd snuck into the unsecured Jamison ranch house. He wasn't sure if that damned Jamison guy was actually sleeping with her or just sleeping somewhere in the house. Her father was a cop but a little sloppy at his age. It was well known that Reagan Dunlap drank too much and fell into bed each night in a drunken stupor. That only aided his mission, however, so he didn't much mind. It was just that damned Duncan, that had him hesitating to slip in and finish what he'd started years before.

He was going to do all this perfectly, however. He would not put his mission at risk. He could not stomach weak bastards who didn't have the stamina or patience to do a job right. He gulped more coffee and then slid out of his truck to take a piss. He had already disabled the interior lights but shut the door again quickly just in case.

The police around these parts were fumbling fools but he still wouldn't take a chance on someone noticing lights on the hill in the darkening dusk. He'd had a good laugh when he'd gotten back here from the hospital and saw that the stupid cops hadn't even checked out the spot where he'd taken the shot from. He'd been worried about whether or not to pick up his shells and the cops couldn't even be bothered to come look for them.

He chuckled low and took another bite of the Snicker's bar in one hand as he zipped his jeans with the other. He saw a shadow move across the kitchen window looking curvy and he smiled. He could almost see her there inside, all that dark streaked hair flowing down her back and around her face making wispy shadows on her cheeks, her dark lashes fluttering softly as they made shadows just below. He grinned when he remembered her naked, curvy, long-legged body.

She was delectably delicious and as he well knew a man could get addicted to such things. He swallowed the dry lump in his throat and climbed back into the seat of his truck, slapping his leg in frustration. He swore viciously because now he was hard and needed a release. He hadn't had a real release in weeks and now here he was, in the middle of nowhere Idaho, hours away from an easy woman to take the pressure off.

He studied the house with consideration. He could drive out to the nearest city and find a whore to help him out, but it really wasn't what he wanted. He wanted her. Her body. Her eyes staring up at him as he choked the life force from her. His erection grew painfully hard, and he muttered another curse as he started his truck, careful not to turn on the headlights until his front end was turned well away from the house.

He made his way down the winding road off the hilltop and pulled onto the main road. He was halfway to the highway when he spotted the silver minivan making its way toward him. He wanted to pull over and pull his hat low, but that would only make him seem suspicious. Instead, he held his head high and gave a friendly wave as Jackie Jamison drove by. She gave him a friendly smile and waved as she passed him.

Breathing a sigh of relief, he pulled up to the stop sign next to the highway. He had once again avoided disaster. Suddenly a nervous thought crept in. Unless she happened to mention seeing him and what he was driving. Then he would have a real problem. He couldn't worry about that now. He didn't want to take all of them out but if he had to, he would. He pulled out onto the highway and drove toward the nearest city.

He drove for about forty minutes before an idea occurred to him. Excited, now that the plan began to take shape in his head, he gave a high-pitched laugh. He watched the road for signs to indicate what he was looking for. When the blue sign finally appeared ahead, he smiled happily. This would work just fine. He was sure of it. He wondered now why he hadn't thought of it before. It was actually quite genius.

He made the turn at the rest area and pulled carefully around the building. Just as he'd hoped, there weren't any truckers parked here tonight. There was one small SUV and he watched from the opposite side of the parking lot, where he'd stopped out of the light of the lamps that covered most of the paved area. A couple got out and he watched as they opened the back door and helped out a small child. He thought about taking the woman, but the man would call in the cavalry right away, so he'd have to take the whole family which was a problem since he generally drew the line at killing kids.

He'd done it once out of necessity, but it really hadn't given him the same high as the mother had. That memory in mind he decided to wait. The city was still another forty minutes away and rather than drive all that way only to have to drive right back he could be patient here. Surely, he could find what he needed from here. He tucked his truck back into the brush at the back side of the tan concrete building that was barely large enough to house two bathrooms.

He watched as the couple emerged from inside, toddler in tow, and climbed back into their car after carefully buckling their child into the back seat. He smiled. Good responsible parents were hard to come by and he appreciated those who were. Glad that he had decided to wait, instead of taking them he reached for the Thermos and took another slug of bitter, cool, coffee. He had to stay alert and on top of his game.

Minutes passed before another car pulled into the lot. He sat up straighter in his seat but then slumped again as an old man climbed out and walked around to help his even older looking companion across the lot to the restrooms. Impatience set in and he once again considered driving to the city. Headlights rolled over his windshield, and he turned to watch as a grey colored Ford Focus made its way down the road toward the lit-up rest area.

He watched with heightened awareness as the car pulled to a stop under one of the bright streetlamps. He saw a woman inside and his mouth began watering. There was still the matter of the old couple inside the restroom, but he could prepare and wait for them to leave. He stilled as the passenger seat slowly lifted to reveal another woman about the same age as the driver. She looked around dazedly and then smiled and nodded at her friend's words.

He watched as they unbuckled their seat belts at the same time and slid out of the car in unison. He smiled when he didn't hear the horn that would come with the locking of the car door. He reached for the backpack he always carried with him and slid quickly out of his truck walking slowly around outside the lit area.

Once he was as close to the car as he could get in the dark, he hurried forward and casually slipped into the back seat of the car, then waited patiently. He watched from his position as the old couple made their way outside and slowly began climbing into their car. He held his breath, mentally urging them to hurry. He wanted this clean and easy, didn't want a huge mess to clean up afterward. Messy turned into sirens, and flashing lights, and policemen asking questions that were hard to answer. He liked to keep things clean and unnoticed.

He smiled as one of the women walked out of the building alone. She stopped to stretch her arms over her head as the older couple gave a little wave and drove off. Her sweater lifted to hug the bottom of her full breasts and his throat went dry. Yes, she would do quite nicely. He crouched down in the back seat as she came and climbed inside the passenger seat and closed the door. He'd planned to wait until her friend joined her to make his presence known, but she turned just then and looked into the back seat reaching for a bottle of water, from the case situated on the floor in the center of the car. "What in the hell—" she blurted and then she reached for the door handle as though to run.

The gun in his right hand pressed against the back of her head and he said softly, "Don't move or I will blow your brains out." He didn't bother telling her that she would die tonight either way, since he'd rather take his sweet time with her.

She froze and her hand dropped numbly to her side. She tried to turn and look back at him as she asked, "What do you want from me. Here, you can take my wallet."

"Uh, uh, uh," he murmured as she started to turn toward him. The last thing he needed was for her friend to notice something was wrong and call for help. "Look forward or I swear to God I will pull the trigger."

She started shaking but did as he told her. From the corner of his eye, he saw the other girl coming from inside, so he adjusted his arm to make sure it was out of sight. Apparently, she had seen her friend coming as well because she whimpered, "Please, whatever you are going to do just leave Lizzie alone."

He smiled. She was very brave and considerate and for that he would show her mercy. "How very kind of you, my dear. Unfortunately, that isn't something I can do."

She whimpered again and he could see her hand inching toward the door again and he realized she was calculating her chances of warning her friend before he could shoot her. In a low deadly voice he said, "Drop your hand or I will shoot your friend right now. I am a great shot and would have no problem putting a bullet straight into her heart."

Deidre Halloway dropped her hand to her side. Maybe just maybe, she could still think of some way out of this terrifying situation, without it ending with her and her sister dead. A tear slid down one cheek as she watched her younger sister open the door and slide inside. Something in the man's voice told her that she wouldn't survive the night and she vowed to escape now or die trying. She swung her head to her sister, and yelled, "Run! Lizzie Run!" At the same time, she reached for her own door handle and yanked it open. She never even heard the gunshot as her head exploded in pain, and darkness engulfed her.

Elizabeth Halloway heard her sister yell but was slow to react. She had just slid into the car when she heard a sickening, 'pop' and then blood sprayed the side of her face and body. She turned to stare at her sister in stunned horror and saw the gun turn to aim directly at her face. She froze, as a scream welled up inside her throat. The low voice in the back seat actually calmed her. "Now, Lizzie, your friend here was valiantly trying to save your life which is why I showed her mercy. Would you have done the same thing? I wonder."

She swallowed hard, fighting the urge to correct him and tell him that 'her friend' was actually her sister. She nodded and then realized in appalled horror what showing Deidre 'mercy' had meant and shook her head.

She tried to turn to see if her sister was dead, but the gun moved closer again.

"Close the door and start the car. You and I are going to go for a nice little drive."

Her head shook as she reached to pull the door closed. It felt like a death sentence but there were no other cars at the rest area so running for help seemed useless as well. Unless… her mind searched frantically, as grief for her sister who she was sure was dead, swelled, and tears began spilling over her dark mascara marked eyes. If she could run inside and get into one of the restrooms… she had noticed the large bolt locks inside.

Her phone was in her pocket, and she could call the police. She hesitated. If Deidre wasn't dead, then she would surely be sealing her fate by leaving her alone out here. She dared a quick glance over at the passenger side. The air swooshed from her lungs as a low moan escaped her throat. "Oh god, Deidre, no! Oh god." Blood and brain matter was sprayed across the window, door, and dash, as well as her own face and body. Unable to stop the bile that rose into her throat she opened her door and threw up on the sidewalk. As soon as she did, the thought that it wouldn't have mattered if she threw up all over the car at this point had her throwing up all over again until her stomach was empty.

The calm voice behind her said, "Now that you got that out of your system, close the door and drive." Self-preservation kicked in and she quickly did as she was told. Once the motor was running, she asked in a voice devoid of emotion, "Where do you want me to go?"

He directed her out of the parking lot and then told her to turn right onto a small dirt road. Wondering if this was indeed the end, she drove in terrified silence. She couldn't get herself to look at her sister again, but tears ran silently down her cheeks. Tears, for her sister's lost life. Tears, for what was probably going to be her own end. As soon as that thought occurred, she realized she had nothing to lose, and without a moment's second thought she slammed on her brakes and opened her door, diving out headfirst. She heard the man swear even as sagebrush scraped her legs and arms, leaving cuts and bruises behind. She turned to watch as the car slid slowly to a halt.

Frozen, she watched as it finally stopped merely two hundred yards away. Her brain was numb with shock, but when she saw the door open, and the man climb out, she scrambled to her feet and began trying to run away. If she could only get back to the rest area, she could lock herself inside until the police came. She reached for the phone in her back pocket, but it was gone. She cursed and ran toward the lit building a mere half mile away. She didn't see the man hurry around and turn off the engine and headlights before he came after her. She ran blindly as tears streamed out and down, falling onto the dry dusty ground. Her shoulder throbbed and she lifted her other arm up to support it.

She risked a quick glance behind her, but it was too dark to see if the man was there. Suddenly, realizing that not only would she be alone in the rest area but if anyone else came in before the man could get to her, they would likely end up dead as well, she turned toward the trees she could see across the field of brush she was currently in. The trees would give her some protection and even maybe help her lose the guy.

Unfortunately, he had already realized she would come to that eventually and had curved around to cut her off. She tried to swerve as she saw his shadow come running toward her, but it was no use. His weight threw her onto the ground as her head hit a large rock and blood gushed out. It didn't really matter to him, he thought, as he watched the blood begin to pool in the dirt by her hair. He undid his jeans and then yanked her skirt up and ripped off her underwear and drove into her as his fingers found their mark on her throat. He groaned as she regained consciousness, though only for a few seconds before her eyes rounded, as she was denied oxygen. He leaned close and listened in excitement as she tried futilely once more to take a breath. Her throat gurgled and he screamed as he came in her, and her body went limp.

Sated and happy now, he curled up to her body there and imagined he was there in Sylvie's room, and this was her body next to him. A wide smile curled his lips up and he breathed in deeply, willing his thundering heart to calm. There was still work to be done and it needed doing soon, before anyone came out this way or morning dawned. Feeling the euphoria of a job well executed, he stood and zipped his jeans again before reaching for his pack.

There were several pouches at the bottom with plastic emergency blankets that could be purchased at any army supply store, and he pulled one out and unfolded it. He had found them to be very useful in his missions, and he always kept several on hand. With a little kiss to her forehead, he rolled her body onto the plastic sheet and threw his pack over one shoulder before carefully wrapping and then lifting her body over his other shoulder. He walked back to the car slowly, as she was heavier than she'd first looked.

He was a strong physical man and it showed as he laid her at the foot of the trunk. Then he reached for another blanket and pulled the other girl from the front to wrap her as well. He found the button to release the trunk and quickly loaded them both inside and closed it with a quick snap.

The light in the trunk might be seen by anyone driving by and he didn't take chances. Except with Sylvie. She was the only chance he had ever taken, and he realized now that he should never have let her live. Back then he had been naïve and stupid and since then, had learned all he could about covering his tracks.

He looked thoughtfully around the brush-covered field. He would have to come out tomorrow in the light of day to make sure he hadn't left any evidence behind but for now he needed to dispose of the bodies. He threw yet another blanket over the driver's seat and slid inside, turning the car around and driving slowly back to his truck. Once there he made sure no one was parked around the building and then carefully loaded the bodies into the back of his truck and closed the gate.

Whistling a happy tune, he climbed back into the car and drove away from the building. He had picked this spot because he knew there was a small lake not more than a mile away. Once there, he found a rock and used it to weigh the pedal down enough to drive the car into the lake after rolling the windows down to ensure the car would fill with water. The DNA in the car would be washed away after hours in the lake. Satisfied that it was done when the car disappeared and didn't resurface for another fifteen minutes he turned and jogged quickly back to his truck.

He looked at his watch. It was eleven o'clock p.m. and he was anxious to get back to Sylvie in case there was a chance she was alone. He still had to bury the bodies though and sighed as he drove twenty miles back toward her family's old home, before pulling off on a long dirt road he was familiar with. At the end of the road was a large lot that had once been an old gravel pit before the family who owned it had decided to move away to the city.

He drove around the side of a rather large hill and backed up to the dirt. He unloaded the girls and pulled a tank of bleach with a sprayer out. Carefully he sprayed down the bodies until they were wet and dripping, taking care to hold the strangled girl's legs apart and spraying there between them. Then he pulled a shovel out to quickly cave down the steep side of the dirt effectively burying their bodies under five feet of gravel.

He'd bought the lot from the family when he'd first begun wondering if he was going to lure Sylvie out here. He needed somewhere private and no one ever came here. It had turned out to be quite useful as of late.

With a satisfied smile he picked up the tank of bleach from the truck and carefully sprayed the entire area down and then removed all of his clothing to place in a black garbage bag from his pack. He used bleach wipes to quickly wipe his hands and arms and face. He would shower off good as well, but this was a simple precaution until he had that chance. He tossed the wipes in the bag with his clothes. He pulled out a fresh pair of jeans and then a shirt and buttoned it up after he tossed the bag inside the passenger side of his truck. He took an extra minute to carefully spray the entire bed of the truck before climbing back inside and driving back to Sylvie's parents' old home.

Chapter 17

Dinner was a lively and enjoyable two hours, after the awkward day Sylvie had spent with her dad and Duncan practically acting like best friends. It was unnatural, and she didn't like it one bit. She wouldn't, however, dignify the way they were acting by telling them that. Instead, she held first one twin and then the other on her lap as she listened to them chatting happily about something to do with their babies and a toy dinosaur.

At one point Jackie had apologized and suggested the twins go into the other room to play, but Sylvie had only shaken her head and smiled. "I love listening to them. They are so darling, and it reminds me of all of us back then." She'd given Jackie a small impish grin. "Do you remember when we were trying to haul all of our dolls out to the loft in your barn and we tried to beg Duncan to let us use his wagon?"

Jackie laughed and leaned back in her chair. "My god, I forgot all about that. Me and Elaine begged and begged but he wouldn't budge until *you* went over to him and looked up at him with tears in those huge brown eyes of yours and begged him to help us. He finally caved."

Duncan watched them with a face devoid of emotion save for the small, amused half grin. "You were playing the opposite sex even back then, Miss up-and-coming lawyer."

Jackie laughed again and reached for the glass of water. "We had so much fun together, didn't we? There was always us girls, and then Duncan would end up enrolled into helping us save whatever needed saving."

Sylvie smiled wide and met Duncan's amused indigo gaze. "I wasn't playing anybody Duncan. It just seemed really important that all the dolls who we'd decided were a ranch family, could live in the barn."

He grinned unabashedly at her, remembering her teary bright eyes and how his heart had been beating out of his young chest. It was that feeling that had made him finally cave and haul all their dolls up to the loft that day. He hadn't wanted anyone to notice that he had a soft spot for little Sylvie. Now he leaned back as he watched her lazily. "I'm sure it's all been perfectly innocent," he said in an amused voice that sounded like he believed anything but that.

She didn't waste energy responding, only turned back to smile down at Olivia who was once again talking about how the dinosaur had been trying to get their babies.

Reagan got up from the table to set his plate in the sink and then poured himself a drink before returning to the table again. Sylvie saw the shimmer of tears there in his brown eyes as he sat down heavily. She reached across the space between their chairs and squeezed his hand. "I miss them too, Daddy."

He only nodded and took a long drink of his scotch. Duncan and Jackie watched the exchange and then exchanged a long look themselves. Since that day they had all lost their mothers, and then there was Elaine. Sweet, pretty Elaine. Elaine who had played havoc with his hormones all through high school. One moment she would be all in and the next she would tell him she was breaking up with him to be with some other kid from school, who'd asked her out.

After he'd graduated, he had agreed with his mother to take online courses for the first two years before going off to school. He and Elaine had been going out again at the time so it seemed like it would make things easier. But after the first six months she had broken things off with him, hinting once again at the fact that she was dating someone else. When he'd pressed her for more information, more out of brotherly concern to make sure she was being careful, than resentment at her once again ending things, she'd balked.

He hadn't really been all that invested emotionally by then anyway. His hormones were of course healthily engaged by the pretty girl, but even he knew that any girl would have been as good as another, and his long-lived friendship with the Dunlaps meant more to him than getting to third base by then. When he asked her who the guy she was dating was, she'd batted her lashes at him and asked, "Why? You aren't feeling jealous are you, Duncan?"

He'd shook his head to reassure her, but it had only pissed her off. "Why don't you ever care when I break up with you?" she'd asked bitterly. Duncan, taken by surprise at the bitterness there in her voice, met and held her gaze. "We were friends first, Elaine, and I wouldn't let anything get in the way of that. Not ever. Are you okay?"

She'd teared up for a moment then before brushing them away quickly, and then throwing him a cagey look. "Well, it's all whatever anyway because I am finally dating someone older and more mature." At Duncan's raised eyebrow she had plastered a sexy smile on her face and said with pointed vinegar, "And *he* doesn't want me to date anyone else, so I guess it's the real deal."

That jab had hurt, but Duncan hadn't let it show. Instead, he had reached for her hand and squeezed it. "As long as you are happy, that is what's important Elaine." He'd held her gaze for a long moment then and asked quietly, "Does he make you happy?"

She beamed a wide smile at him, and her face lit with excitement. "He does. He spoils me so much. And he wants me to move to the city as soon as I turn eighteen to be with him there."

That had raised the hair on the back of Duncan's neck. "This man lives in the city?"

She'd only shrugged nonchalantly and then given him a little smile and a wink. "See you around, Duncan."

He sat in his old truck watching her open the door and reach for her tie-dyed book bag as she slid out. Something had propelled him to say her name and when she turned to look back at him, she'd almost looked excited that he'd called out, or maybe just hopeful that he'd care. Either way her face had gone pale a moment later when he'd said firmly, "We are done this time. Don't call me when things fall apart with this new boyfriend. Not unless it's to be your friend."

Thinking about it now and all the guilt he'd put himself through in the years after her death, wondering if things would have been different if he hadn't said that to her, he sighed. After that day they had only hung out as a group of four friends and had never done anything together with just the two of them. Duncan had focused on his courses and put her out of his mind.

That is until April, another girl he knew from school had called to tell him she had just moved back and wanted to catch up. They had gone out for the next year, and he had been making out with her on her parents' couch when he got the call about his mom.

Months later, he'd been at dinner with her yet again, when Sylvie had called to tell him Elaine was missing, and they were trying to get a search party started. He'd dropped everything with April to help Sylvie and her parents as they first searched for Elaine, and then, after finding her body, dealt with the police and the investigation that followed.

Between the time spent with the Dunlaps and the time he had to spend trying to keep the ranch on its feet after his mother's funeral, he didn't have much left for April. She'd understood at first, but after several months of being blown off, she'd eventually accused him of still having feelings for Elaine, who'd been her nemesis in high school. No amount of talking could persuade her otherwise, and she had moved back to the city with her dad.

Now, the memories seemed to all be little puzzle pieces to a bigger picture, but Duncan didn't feel as though he had all the pieces he needed, to put it all together. Brows drawn together in a frown, he turned to Sylvie suddenly. "Hey, did Elaine tell you who she was dating that last year before she died?"

Sylvie blinked in surprise. "Elaine wasn't dating. I remember because she was still really bitter that you had dumped her for good."

Duncan looked surprised at that accusation. Then he looked around the table at all the adults who were giving him the same coldly interested look. He held up his hands. "Hold on, I didn't break up with Elaine. She broke up with me because she was dating another guy who wanted her to go to the city with him." At Sylvie's disbelieving expression he added, "I did tell her not to call me if things went bad again, but not until she had already broken up with me."

In an explanation brought on by years of guilt, he said quietly, "I know I shouldn't have said it to her but at the time I was so tired of her breaking up with me for other guys, only to call and try getting back together when it didn't work out."

That seemed to pacify Sylvie, who gave him a smile. "Mom and Dad were always warning her that if she kept doing that to you, you would eventually get sick of it."

Reagan nodded, but his eyes were beginning to cloud over. "I always liked when she was dating you, Duncan, because we knew where you were going and knew you'd get her home by curfew."

Duncan stared across the room for a long moment. "I've felt bad about that for years, wondering if I hadn't said that, if she would have called me again and things would have turned out differently."

Jackie jumped into the conversation with that admission. "I wondered if you felt that way, but she was still dating someone else. She never would tell me who, only that he was older and more mature, and she threatened to tell Mom and Dad all the bad things I'd done with her, if I told anyone about him before she was ready."

Everyone was watching her now and Jackie shrugged. "Sorry, that's all I know. I had slept with Billy Hanson that summer and I really didn't want Mom and Dad to blow a gasket, so I left it alone."

Sylvie exchanged a long look with her dad. "Did you know she was seeing someone, Daddy?"

He shook his head and then nodded. "I couldn't get her to tell me, but I kept feeling like she was sneaking out to be with some guy." He threw an apologetic look at Duncan. "I figured the two of you were probably sneaking off to do some neckin' so I didn't push it as hard as I should have."
"Was there anyone who came forward after her death or came to the funeral that seemed unusual?" Duncan asked, the wheels spinning in his mind.

Sylvie's face scrunched as she tried to remember. All she felt was a heavy fog in her mind, like every time she thought about that year. Her head began to ache again, and she rubbed at her temples. "That whole time is a bit of a blur, but I don't remember anyone strange." She met Duncan's eyes and said, "You're wondering if she wasn't on the mountain alone when she died, aren't you?"

He nodded and stood to pace the length of the room. He turned back and paused. "You're sure she never said anything about a boyfriend, Sylvie? She told you everything. It seems strange that she wouldn't have told you this."

Sylvie shook her head, which was now throbbing, and then turned to her father. "Do you remember anyone unusual coming around after she died Daddy?"

Reagan thought about it for a long time and then met Sylvie's eyes looking like he felt guilty. "No, I'm sorry. I remember all our friends came to pay their respects and then there were all the kids from the school that came to the services. There could have been someone, but I would have just thought they went to school with her." He sounded apologetic.

Duncan watched and thought about it as he said, "Elaine *was* popular at school and there were tons of people who came." Then as though offering comfort to the older man he said, "There was no way you could have known someone was out of place or even that you should be wondering that. Everything in the investigation had led to it being an accident."

Sylvie's voice was hoarse when she asked softly, "You think Elaine was killed?" She sounded so horrified that Duncan immediately walked around to squeeze her neck and shoulders.

She leaned her head back to stare up at him with pain in the brown depths. He wanted to wrap her in his arms and comfort her, but he wasn't sure she would let him. Instead, he offered the truth. "I think it's possible, don't you?"

She looked away as tears shimmered in her eyes. Finally, she nodded. "Given what you are saying about an unknown boyfriend and the fact that someone shot at me." She hesitated and then said firmly, "If this was *my* case, I would definitely think there is more going on."

Duncan rubbed gently at the back of her neck. At first it was relaxing but then heat began seeping down into her belly, so she stood up and walked her plate to the sink. Her father and Jackie sat, looking dazed at the table. She couldn't think any more. Her head hurt and her emotions were all over the place. Without another thought she walked to the liquor cabinet and poured a good two fingers of her father's scotch into a glass and shot it back. She jumped when Duncan said from directly behind her, "Can I have one of those too?"

She nodded absent-mindedly and poured two fingers into the same glass, handing it to him. He smiled and nodded and then tossed it back himself. From across the kitchen, Reagan said quietly, "Could you bring the bottle over here, dear? I need another drink."

Sylvie turned on her heel and walked over to set it next to him. In a small voice Jackie said, "It doesn't feel fair, because I would like a drink myself." She rubbed at her very round belly. Everyone gave her small smiles of sympathy.

Duncan followed Sylvie back to the table and they both sat down heavily. There was a quiet knock at the door and then they heard Ren as he came in. "Hello? It's just me." He stopped just inside the kitchen to take in the somber looks of everyone at the table. Even Olivia and Ariana sat quietly watching each other. His gut tightened inexorably. "What's wrong, hon?" He rushed around the table in his fresh button down and jeans. He put a tender hand on Jackie's shoulder and ruffled Ariana's and Olivia's hair with the other. "I'm sorry I'm so late, the job went much later than I expected. Now, what did I miss?"

In a quiet subdued voice Jackie quickly explained what they had been talking about. Duncan stood and grabbed a clean plate and silverware to hand to him. "The leftover chicken, vegetables, and rice are on the stove, Ren. You might as well eat."

Ren ate in silence as everyone sat, unable to make small talk. Reagan was on the bottom end of his third consecutive generous pour of scotch when his cell phone began ringing. He jumped in surprise and reached for it out of habit. Duncan walked around, looking down at the screen in curiosity, not even trying to hide the fact that he was obviously snooping. On the screen it said, 'Wilmington PD'. He looked down at Reagan's cloudy eyes and spoke firmly, "Give it to me. I'll talk to them and fill you in after."

Chapter 18

Duncan hit the green button with his thumb to connect the call as he stepped into the front room and said in a strong voice, "Hello."

Sylvie wanted to follow him, but her dad looked like he might fall off his chair at any minute, so she didn't want to leave him, to embarrass himself in front of Jackie and Ren.

Jackie ran her hand gently down Ren's arm and smiled at him as he sat next to her and settled Olivia on one knee. There was blood near his eye and her eyes narrowed. "Are you okay, babe? You are bleeding!"

She reached up to touch the spot, but Ren leaned back and away with a charming smile. "It's nothing, I just bumped my head at work."

She accepted his explanation without hesitation. "I'll clean it and bandage it for you as soon as we get home."

He gave her a nervous smile. "You most certainly won't. I'm wise to your ways."

Sylvie raised one eyebrow at his odd reaction. He picked up on it immediately and turned a wide grin at her. "Jackie is hell when it comes to nursing. She causes more pain in the 'fixing' then the injury itself."

Jackie gave a little pout. "Now, that just isn't true."

Reagan laughed a little too loudly at the joke. "That sounds like my wife," he said, managing to only slur the 'my wife'.

Sylvie offered Ren a wan smile and then tried to hear what Duncan was saying. She heard the undertones of the timbre in his low voice as he said, "I understand, sir. No, I won't leave her side. Keep me updated and I will talk to Mr Dunlap as soon as I'm off. Okay, you take care too. Yes. The Dunlaps are good friends of my family as well, sir. Good night."

Unable to sit still any longer, Sylvie stood as Duncan walked back into the kitchen. Unable to curb her impatience she asked abruptly, "What did they say?"

Duncan glanced around at the four faces that were now watching him intently and sat down with a sigh. "So it appears that maybe we are imagining things best left alone," he said quietly. When Sylvie looked like she wanted to shake him, he explained. "That was a Detective Hanlan from the Wilmington Police Department." He watched as Sylvie reacted to the name. He looked at Jackie and Ren. "Detective Hanlan says he's a good family friend to Sylvie and Reagan."

When she and her father both nodded, he continued. "He got word that we were looking into Zachary McDaniels for the shooting. He has been following the case since he heard about Sylvie being shot. Anyway, he says the investigation turned up evidence that McDaniels had recently flown out here and was somewhere in Idaho when the shooting took place. That gave them enough for a search warrant and when they searched his apartment, they found thousands of photos of Sylvie there."

"Apparently, he has been stalking her and taking photos dating back two years. He wasn't home but they found a receipt for a return flight tonight, and they plan to capture him before he boards the plane. In the meantime, he says not to leave you alone." He looked at Sylvie's stricken face and stood to go to her. She didn't resist as he pulled her gently into his arms and held her for a long moment.

After several minutes she pulled back and looked up at him. "Wait, Zack doesn't even know how to shoot."

He met her eyes briefly and then looked away as he said softly, "Detective Hanlan says he joined a shooting range five years ago and then two years ago joined a shooting club out on the east coast. He is definitely capable of shooting a rifle."

Something about this all didn't make sense to Sylvie, but her head hurt so badly now that she could hardly focus. "I still don't understand. It would take a skilled gunman to take a shot from that far away and actually hit me. Especially because I tried to duck."

Everyone in the room quit breathing and went perfectly still. Duncan reached out and lifted her chin, forcing her gaze to his own. "You saw the shooter?" he asked in a low, barely controlled voice.

She shook her head. "No, but I looked out the window and saw a flash of light. Instinctively, I tried to duck but then I remember hearing glass crack and fire blossomed in my chest. I don't remember much after that until I woke up in the hospital."

"You never told the police about that Sylvie." He sounded angry as though she was hiding something, and she turned to stare up at his tense jawline.

"I didn't even think about it until just now. I swear. I wouldn't have kept something like this from them." When he didn't look like he believed her she said pleadingly, "What possible reason could I have for not telling them this, Duncan? I'm the one who almost died."

Until that moment he hadn't heard her actually acknowledge that fact and he sighed as he hugged her again. "Don't remind me. I lost a few years that night."

"The police haven't been able to narrow down where the shots were taken so they haven't found any evidence, but if Sylvie has an even vague idea of the direction that the shooter was, they might be able to uncover some evidence." It was Ren who said what everyone else was thinking out loud.

Sylvie turned and nodded. “If there is evidence still out there anyway.”

“Any evidence that might tie McDaniels to the crime, might help get him convicted,” Jackie added with an apologetic smile at Sylvie. “I can’t even imagine how terrifying it must have been having a creep follow you around.” She shivered.

Sylvie smiled in self-directed amusement. “I had no idea he was following me. Or that he might want me dead.” Something about the whole case seemed off somehow, but she couldn’t concentrate enough to know why. She looked around at her friends and said numbly, “What does that say about my instincts or intelligence?”

Duncan slid his arm back around her shoulder and gave her a squeeze. “According to your dad, you have well-honed instincts that have broken open several cases. If anything, it speaks to your kindness since you didn’t want to believe that McDaniels would become a demented stalker and attempt to kill you.”

Sylvie shrugged and slid away from him to sit at the table again. “I’ll call the police in the morning.” At Duncan’s narrowed gaze she said, “They won’t be able to find anything out there tonight anyway and might actually wreck any evidence that was preserved by the mud that night if they try.”

He didn’t argue but gave her one quick nod and began clearing the dirty dishes from the table. Jackie stood to help, but he motioned her back to her chair. “You made dinner. The least I can do is clean up.”

She nodded but came to stand next to him. “Are you okay, Duncan?

This is all a lot and I know how bad it was when mom and Elaine died.” She held his gaze for a long minute.

He nodded but shrugged. “I’m just glad she isn’t dead.” He pointed a thumb over his shoulder.

Jackie smiled brightly at his words. “I’m glad she is okay too.” Then in a quiet tone so the others wouldn’t overhear her she asked, “Is there something going on between you two?”

He didn’t answer, just looked at her sideways and shrugged. Jackie laughed softly. “I’ll take that as a yes.”

She turned away but his next words stopped her. “I gotta run home for a bit to get a few things.” He looked at his watch. “I don’t trust her alone here with just her dad. I know it’s late, but would you mind staying until I get back?”

She smiled up at him. “I’d be happy to.” She turned and waddled her way back to the others. With a bright smile she asked, “Who’s up for a movie?”

Ren and Sylvie both turned surprised faces to her, but she just smiled in return. Neither of them was stupid enough to try to deny an eight-month-along mother any comfort. Ren stood and walked his now empty plate to

Duncan as he said, "Lead the way, honey." He wasn't sure why she was angling for a movie in the middle of the night, but it really didn't matter.

Sylvie offered to help Duncan with the dishes, but he refused her, and she ambled slowly in to sit on one of the overstuffed chairs. Jackie was acting excited as she put a DVD in the blue ray and sat back pulling the girls' diaper bag toward her on the coffee table. The twins looked like they were about to fall to sleep and Sylvie bit her tongue. She didn't want to offend her friends by mothering their children. To her relief she saw Jackie pull two pairs of purple pajamas from the bag. Ren reached for Ariana and began dressing her as the opening credits rolled across the screen.

Reagan stood in the doorway for a long moment and then announced loudly, "I think I will head up to bed and leave the movie to you young'uns."

Sylvie stood and hurried over to hug her father and say good night. "I love you, Daddy."

He gave her a kiss on her cheek and held her a little longer than normal as he said, "Night, baby. You stay close to Duncan until they catch that bastard, okay?"

She nodded and watched as he made his way slowly up the stairs. When he was gone from view she turned back to her friends. They kindly didn't mention him or his drinking. Instead, Jackie grinned and pulled a box of chocolates from her bag. "I brought dessert," she joked, and tore open the box.

The movie was about ten minutes in when Duncan walked past. He looked at her for a quick moment consideringly and then said, "I'll be right back."

She smiled and he slipped out the door locking it before he went. Since she was doomed to try to watch the movie with her friends, she took the offered piece of chocolate and focused on Tom Cruise in his leather pilot jacket. It would be a shame not to enjoy such a classic after all.

Duncan slid into his truck. He backed around Ren's shiny black truck in the driveway and turned around. He hadn't left Sylvie since the day she'd come back from the hospital, and he didn't want to leave her now, but he had to have a few things from the ranch house. Plus, he hadn't seen the ranch or how it was doing in days. He had been solely responsible for everything there until a week ago and now he found himself worried about it. He intended to check in with the foreman while he was getting a few things.

The house was lit up when he got home. He smiled as he looked up at the brightly lit front porch. He was a little surprised. His father rarely turned on the lights unless he was out there. When they were kids, they had always kept it on until everyone was home, but since his mother's untimely death the porch had been dark unless he turned it on himself. Something he had tried to do for Jackie until she had gone away to college.

With a little smile he walked to the barn. He looked around with a critical eye. Everything seemed to be in place, so he turned and made his way to the bunkhouse. There was one light on inside, and he felt a little guilty for what he was about to do. Waking a cowboy who had to be up at dawn really was inconsiderate, but he didn't know when he would have another chance. He opened the screen door and rapped his knuckles quietly against the whitewashed oak door. He heard footsteps a moment later and a man who looked to be around forty-five opened the door and peered out at him. The man obviously recognized Duncan, as he swung the door wide and motioned him inside. "Come on in, boss."

Duncan smiled and stepped inside. "Sorry to bother you so late, I just wanted to check in since I have been so busy the past few days, I haven't gotten the chance."

The man glanced at the coffee pot and then at Duncan. "You want coffee or a drink, boss?"

Duncan smiled pleasantly but shook his head. "Thanks, but I gotta drive tonight. I'm Duncan Jamison by the way." He held out his hand to the ranch hand.

It was taken in a strong solid grip without hesitation. "Frank Lesley. I really appreciate the work."

He seemed genuine so Duncan nodded. "I'm glad you can do it. How is everything going?"

Frank Lesley grinned. "It's been busy but good. I have been meaning to ask you if there is a truck, we can use to haul more hay out to the north pasture. We're running a little low out there and I only have the SUV. The others have cars, but we could really use a truck. Other than that, everything has been smooth sailing."

Duncan nodded. "I'll have a new truck brought out right away for the ranch. In the meantime, you can use my truck. Can you give me a ride tonight, though?" He hated to ask the man to handle business this late but if he left the truck here, he had no way back to Sylvie. He could ask his dad but assumed his old man was already gone to bed.

Frank nodded without hesitation. "No problem, boss, let me grab my boots and hat and I'll meet you out there."

Duncan nodded. "Thanks. I gotta grab a few things from the house and I'll be ready." He turned and strode out the door.

At the house he let himself in the door and stopped as he saw his father sitting in the old rocking chair in front of the fireplace. He nodded.

Arthur smiled and nodded back. "Hello, son."

Duncan noticed the empty beer in his hand and smiled. "Want me to grab you another?"

"No, I'm about to head up to bed but thank you." He looked up at Duncan with an amused grin. "I'm surprised to see you here. I haven't hardly seen you since the Dunlap girl got hurt. I was starting to wonder if you moved in."

Feeling a little awkward Duncan shrugged. "Not exactly. I just want to make sure she stays safe."

Arthur nodded and a serious frown creased his brow. "It's a good thing you were there, son. Have the police found out anything new about the case?"

Duncan shook his head. "Not much. They have a lead they are chasing down now but we will know more tomorrow." He smiled and nodded at his father. "Night," he said as he turned and took the stairs two at a time.

He heard his father come up and the bedroom door close as he loaded more clothes and body wash into a bag. He eyed the box of condoms in his top drawer but then shook his head. A woman that dated several men at once was certainly on birth control. He grabbed more ammo from his closet shelf, just in case, and headed back out to his truck. The lights were out in the house as he made his way silently down and out the front door.

Frank stood there by his truck, and he smiled and nodded. "I appreciate the ride, Frank."

The ranch hand grinned and chewed on a toothpick. "You're the boss and it will sure be nice to have the truck tomorrow. I been loading what I can in the back of my SUV, but it's time consuming and takes several trips."

Duncan felt guilty. "I'm sorry, I haven't been around to help more."

Frank gave a quick wave of his hand. "Nonsense, that's why you pay me the big bucks. So I'll handle things for you."

Duncan laughed as he climbed into the truck. "I'll have to talk to Jackie if we are paying you *that* much," he joked.

The ranch hand laughed and drove down the driveway. Duncan gave him directions, and fifteen minutes later, they pulled into the driveway at the Dunlaps'. He waved and thanked Frank once again before letting himself back inside with the key he'd found in the kitchen. The movie was almost over when he returned, and a wide grin spread across his face at the spectacle in front of him.

Jackie lay back against Ren's shoulder asleep. Olivia was on the couch next to her with her knees and feet propped on her mom's lap. Ren had his head back on the couch and was quietly snoring with a sleeping Ariana sprawled across his lap.

Sylvie was the only one who was still awake, and she was glaring up at him. "It took you long enough," she complained as she eyed the wide bag slung over his shoulder. "Are you moving in, or what?"

He grinned and answered, "Not exactly, I'm just tired of wearing the same two shirts every day."

She smiled at the couple on the couch. "They went out as soon as the movie started. I didn't want to wake them, and I assumed you must have asked Jackie to stay when you didn't come right back."

He smiled at her. She was beautiful and intelligent, and he couldn't get a single thing past her sharp mind. He wanted to lift her into his arms and haul her to bed, but he wasn't sure she would go for that. She must have sensed his change in thoughts as she stood up suddenly and reached for the remote. As soon as she turned off the television, both Jackie and Ren woke up. Apparently, it was too quiet for them to sleep. Jackie apologized and Ren grinned at her and Duncan. "I think we had better get the girls home, babe."

He carefully hauled Ariana out to the van and came right back for Olivia before Jackie could attempt to haul her. He held her arm as she lifted the bag and apologized once again for sleeping through the movie. Sylvie graciously hugged her and urged her to go get some rest.

As the door closed behind them, she carefully locked it and then turned to Duncan. He was watching her with his serious, hungry gaze and she fixed an impersonal smile on her face. "I'm going to head to bed. Do you mind turning out the lights before you come up?"

He grinned at her knowingly. "I'm coming up now too."

She nodded and turned to go up the stairs as he reached for the light switch. He thought he saw a slight movement of light across one of the windows and froze. Then he dropped the bag from his shoulder and ran to the kitchen window to pull the curtain aside and look out. There was nothing but darkness though he watched for a long moment. Finally, he shrugged and closed the curtain carefully again. It had probably been Ren leaving in his truck after Jackie and the kids.

He hurried up the stairs though. He didn't want to leave Sylvie alone for a second. He could hear the shower running as he made his way down the hall to her room. He smiled and hurried into the second bathroom for a shower of his own. He was dressed and clean with his hair still damp when Sylvie came in from her shower. She stared at him and then shook her head. She didn't have the energy to deal with him tonight. She was both mentally and emotionally exhausted due to the roller coaster of events from the past week. All she wanted to do was slide into the bed and close her eyes to shut out the world that she really didn't much like tonight. She did just that, without a word to Duncan, who slowly began undressing like he always did. She refused to look at him as she reached for the lamp and turned it off.

Tears threatened and she blinked rapidly.

Somehow, she had made Zack hate her so much after two dates that he had tried to kill her. She swallowed the lump of emotion in her throat as she heard Duncan move next to the bed. Angrier than she intended to sound, she demanded, "What in the hell do *you* want?"

She felt his surprise through the darkness. He held one hand out to her, and she saw with humiliation, the bottle of water and painkillers there in his palm. "I thought you might need these."

Feeling a little embarrassed she sat up. "Thank you. I'm sorry I snapped at you."

He shrugged his wide muscled shoulders as her eyes adjusted to the dark. "I have thick skin. I'll survive."

She didn't respond as tears that refused to be stopped ran down her cheeks. He started to turn away but then turned back to her when he heard her in-drawn breath. He stepped closer with all that warm sexy appeal and her shoulders shook as she tried but failed to hold her emotions in check.

He zoned in on her then. "Are you crying Sylvie?" he asked gently.

She took a sobbing breath. "No."

He sat next to her and lifted her gently into his lap wrapping her in all that strength and heat. "Liar. Now tell me what has you so tied up tonight."

She shook her head stubbornly as her shoulders trembled again. She felt his mouth on the top of her head and she gulped again as the sobbing took hold.

He held her there in the dark, silently giving her comfort through his own strength. "It's okay to cry sweetheart. Just let it all out. I have you."

Sylvie wanted to stop but for some unknown reason his words made the crying worse, and she lay there shaking and crying all over his naked chest. After several minutes she lifted her head and sniffled. "I'm sorry, I don't know what's wrong with me. I *never* cry." She hiccupped and with a little giggle covered her mouth with the back of her hand.

He ran a warm hand up and down her back soothingly. "We all need to cry sometimes, Sylvie."

She tried to peer up at him through the dark. Something about the way he'd said it had her wondering what he was thinking. "Do you want to cry too?" she asked suspiciously.

He let out a low chuckle at her surprised tone. "No, but I did cry when I thought you were dying in my arms."

That gave her pause and she held extremely still, unsure of what to say to his honesty. She had never met another man like Duncan, and he confused her. He didn't follow all the same rules as the rest of the men she dated. She reached a hand up to touch his shoulder as another hiccup found its way out of her mouth. With a little smile she swore,

"Dammit, now I have the hiccups. I *hate* crying."

He didn't say anything, just bent his head toward hers. "Would you like me to get rid of them for you?"

His tone was warm and suggestive, and Sylvie shivered even as her body jerked with the next hiccup. She started shaking her head, even as his mouth came down over hers, warm and soft. She leaned into the longing she had been feeling since the first day she got here and kissed him back. He groaned as she deepened the kiss and pressed back against the heat of his skin. Her hand ran up his chest across what felt like perfectly molded velvet covered iron. Her good hand tangled in the hair above his neck pulling him into the kiss.

She began to feel disoriented as though she was sliding into a euphoria-based fog. The telephone ringing down the hall brought her back to reality and she pulled back. "I think that it's Daddy's phone, Duncan," she said, but he was already sliding her off his lap and he stood and walked hurriedly out the door.

She heard the door to a room down the hall open and he came back a moment later talking on the phone. He sat in the dark, in the chair by the window. "Thank God. Yes, I will let them know. Thanks for letting us know, detective." He clicked off the call and bent over, taking a deep breath.

Sylvie reached for the lamp and switched it on. Before he could shutter his expression, she saw the raw anguish and relief there. There was a shimmer of tears in his eyes when he turned to meet her own. "Well, what did he say?" she demanded.

He smiled and she watched as it reached his eyes. "They caught the bastard, Sylvie. He was trying to board a plane a few minutes ago. They took McDaniels into custody and he admitted that he'd followed you out here." He held her gaze as relief once again washed through him. "He admitted he has a rifle, but they still have to check the ballistics to make sure the bullet they pulled from the drywall matches. They will know for sure in the next couple of days."

She was so taken by the raw emotion on his face that she wasn't listening to the rest of what he said. In that moment, she felt as if she knew every detail simply by looking at his face and eyes. Her heart shuddered and she groaned inwardly. So, what if he cared and was happy that she was safe? It didn't mean anything. She stared hard at him as she took in his nearly naked body, and her heart began pounding. He met her eyes and the explanation died on his lips. He stood and walked toward her. She slid back on the bed until she was against the headboard. She felt as though he was stalking her, and she swallowed hard.

He held her gaze as he moved around to sit next to her. He lifted a hand to gently tuck a strand of wavy hair behind her ear. "They are saying you are safe now. Hanlan is pretty convinced that they have your guy."

She didn't say anything, but he noticed she was breathing hard. He raised an eyebrow. "He says you should be safe now." She still didn't say anything. Unable to hold back his impatience any longer, he asked softly, "Do you want me to go, Sylvie?"

She nodded her head and then shook it. Finally, she groaned and dropped her head in her hands and attempted to speak over the loud pounding of her heart. "I don't know. I think so, but you are so damned sexy."

His eyes darkened and a slow smile spread across his face as he leaned toward her. Her next words made him pause. “I need you to say that you understand that this is only a casual sex thing, Jamison.”

He held her gaze and shook his head. “I don’t think that’s all there is to this.”

She nodded her head vigorously as panic swirled around inside her chest. “It is, I swear, and I need you to say that you are going to be okay when I go back home.”

He gave her a ghost of a smile. “I promise I’ll survive making love to you, Sylvie,” he said sounding amused.

She frowned and then laughed. “I know, that sounded pretty arrogant, but I mean it Duncan.”

He grinned as the prize at the end of his very long tunnel came within grasping reach. He bent over her and took her mouth in a hungry demanding kiss that stole what little air she had. She wrapped her good arm around his neck and leaned into him.

He groaned and rolled into a sitting position before carefully lifting her onto his lap again. He didn’t want to hurt her shoulder. She rubbed appreciatively over his steel erection, and he swallowed, making his Adam’s apple bob in his throat. She took advantage and leaned up to nibble her way down his throat and then to his chest.

He rubbed his arms gently up and down her sides and then softly he ran one hand across the side of her breast. Just the slightest hint of pressure there before moving on to rub down her arms and back up. She arched into him but when he didn’t touch her breast the way she wanted him to, she forced her eyes open and asked, “What’s the matter Jamison? Afraid you might get to third base?”

He ran his hands down her side again, barely touching the sides of her breasts. Just enough to make her arch again. He waited until she looked at him again and then he promised. “I fully intend on taking my very sweet time touching, arousing, and loving every inch of your very delectable body, Sylvianna Dunlap. Do you think *you* can handle *that?*” She swallowed even as he forced another arch out of her as he brushed his knuckle over her hardened nipple. He smiled, as he turned her on his lap and began kissing his way down the side of her neck and then her shoulder. He kissed his way down her arm and took each finger into his hot mouth with a hard suck, before lifting her arm and working his way down her side.

The anticipation was killing her, and she held her breath as his mouth hovered over the side mound of her breast. She held perfectly still, taut on his lap as he took gentle nibbles up the side and then finally, gloriously took her nipple between his teeth for a little scrape through the cotton fabric of her pajama shirt. Sylvie groaned and shoved against his mouth even as he moved across the valley between her breasts and finally bit gently at the other forlorn breast.

Feeling hotter than she'd ever felt in her life, Sylvie forced her heavy eyelids open and stared down as he gave her nipple yet another quick scrape with his teeth. There was a wet spot on her shirt where her nipple shone through slightly and she bucked against him as he finally slid his rough hot hands under her shirt and ever so slowly kissed his way up her navel until he met the undersides of her creamy full breasts.

She bucked against him again and the heat that surged at her core had her insides clenching so tightly she felt like she was almost to come undone. She tried to pull back, as some edge that she didn't understand seemed to surge ever closer. She'd had lots of sex. Sex with good looking men that knew what they were doing. She'd even tried it once with a girl in college. She knew sex. She understood sex, and yet this desperate need to be devoured by Duncan and his very sexy mouth was something new. Something terrifyingly devastatingly new.

The problem was that Duncan seemed to sense her trying to pull back and he took one of her pert nipples into his mouth and gave a hard suck even as his hand found her other breast and squeezed the nipple at the same time. She screamed and rubbed against his hard member as she felt that edge creep ever closer again.

Terrified, she opened her eyes and ran a hand down his sexy chest. When he finally looked up at her she panted the only thing that came to mind. "Too slow," she murmured very seriously and tried to get his shorts over his tip for access.

To her disbelief, he laughed and bent back to her nipples, but at least he had the decency to completely remove her top first. Just when she thought she might scream at him or punch him since he wouldn't give her what she wanted, she felt the lightest brush of his other hand against her center through her lacy underwear. She moaned and arched into him as he sucked hard at her other nipple and rubbed a knuckle there against her core at the same time. Sylvie bucked wildly and felt liquid heat between her legs, as his hand started the gentle back and forth sway there.

The liquid fire seeped through her clothes, and he smiled as he lifted his hand and sucked off his moist finger. His head arched back then as he nearly yanked off their clothes and finished it. "You taste so damn good," he sounded tortured and yet he licked his finger yet again.

Sylvie couldn't focus as she was off balance, teetering on the edge of a precipice of something she couldn't quite define. Orgasm yes, but something more as well. She gritted her teeth as she watched him lick each of his damn fingers as though it was dessert. He wasn't even touching her now and yet still she hung there over that void. She reached for his boxers again, trying desperately to get a hold of him. He moved out of reach and shook his head as his eyes opened and she stared into the dark tortured depths. "Not yet sweetheart. I want this to last a while," he said as he lifted her off him and then stood as he slid her shorts and black lacy panties off in one motion. Then he bent his head to hers and took her mouth again even as his thumb and forefinger took one nipple and his fingers brushed gently between her legs. More fiery liquid erupted and she screamed into his kiss.

Just when she was almost to find that edge again, he stilled his fingers. She cried out in mourning for the loss of the pressure there. She arched, and to her undoing, he plunged one finger into her hot wet folds there. He groaned as his cock surged hard against the restriction of his own shorts. The wet heat on his fingers was nearly his undoing. Sylvie bucked again and he lowered his head to her mouth as he moved his finger inside her slick, tight folds. She came undone, bucking hard against him and his fingers as she flew out over that all- consuming edge. She screamed, and he took it into his own mouth with a kiss as her body began clenching around his finger as spasm after spasm shook her core.

He stilled and let her float for a few long seconds even as his own body strained for release. He was going to replace every other man she had ever slept with in her memory, until all she wanted was him, even if it killed him in the process. She moaned as he bent his head and gently sucked at her breast. She opened her eyes and looked up at him, looking a little unsteady. He grinned even as he moved his finger there inside her again. "This is not a fair game Jamison."

His rock-hard cock agreed with her and yet he grinned. "I didn't realize you were under the misconception that this was a game," he said as he slowly lowered his head and took a lick at her clit.

She bucked and her fingers threaded through his hair to hold him in place there even as she said breathlessly. "That isn't a good idea, Duncan." He only chuckled and then dipped his tongue deep to taste the intoxicatingly sweet liquid that was Sylvie. He groaned as she bucked under the gentle onslaught of his mouth. His tongue delved deep again and again, and he lifted his thumb to rub erotically at her clit. She bucked hard and came again, her tight body clenching there against his tongue. He gave her a moment as he kissed his way gently up her thigh and then across her flat stomach working his way back to kiss the undersides of her breasts. "God, you are beautiful," he murmured as he took her nipple gently between his teeth.

She opened her eyes and arched into his mouth. He slid his boxers down even as his teeth and fingers built a gentle rhythm there sucking and pulling at her nipples. He reached a hand between her legs and was happy when she widened them to give him better access. "You are so responsive and sexy this way."

She moaned and arched her back again, even as he took her mouth in a long, sensuous kiss. He delved one finger inside her again and then pulled it out to replace it with two. He felt her body stretch to accept the second finger and he pulled them back out to take another addictive lick even as their eyes met and held. He was painfully erect, and he smiled at the vague look in her brown eyes. "Are you ready for me yet, Sylvie?" he asked, praying that she wouldn't say no. An incredulous look flashed across her face as though she was just now realizing that he hadn't actually penetrated her yet. He stood up in front of her and her eyes widened as she caught her first real glimpse of his erection.

He smiled and lowered himself between her legs levering his upper body onto his arms so he wouldn't hurt her shoulder. She tried to touch him, knew something was wrong because she hadn't even touched him yet. He captured her hand in his and lifted it above her head before she could grasp onto him. "Not yet, Sylvie. I'm strong but not that strong, I'll go off in your hand."

That only made her more determined to pull her hand free. He shook his head and gritted his own teeth. "Not yet. Trust me baby. You want this."

She squirmed beneath him, and he bent his head to take her nipple into his mouth even as he butted his head up against her most intimate entry. She bucked against the pressure of him there between her legs and he pushed into her tight folds one inch at a time waiting for her to adjust to his size. She felt so hot and tight he had to throw his head back, to hold himself from plunging into the wet heat. She cried his name and began bucking hard against him.

He buried himself in her and groaned as he fought for control. She was trying to ride him even as he pulled slowly back out and then buried himself again. He looked down at her and said gently, "Look at me, sweetheart." She opened her wonderful eyes and held his as he began a slow steady rhythm stroking her most sensitive spots with his tip, even as he pushed in again and again. Lost there in her eyes, he slowly sped up the rhythm as she met him stroke for stroke.

He felt her body begin to spasm around him and as he sensed himself about to go up over the edge, he sped the rhythm once again pushing into her with long hard strokes now. He watched her eyes flutter closed even as her body clamped down on him like a vice. He groaned and lost control, burying himself to the hilt over and over as he began to shake. He exploded into her hot heat, and then went spiraling out, out over a sparkling void of pleasure so deep that he couldn't even pull out of her. She came with him, screaming over the void and together they lay tangled and damp with sweat. He moved his hips and she suddenly moaned and lifted her hips to ride him hard as, yet another orgasm washed through her.

It sent him over the edge again and he groaned as his body impossibly emptied into her yet again. His arms were shaking, and he was unable to hold himself leveraged over her any longer, so he rolled to his side bringing her with him. He made sure it was her good shoulder she landed on, as he wrapped her there in his arms and promptly fell to sleep. It was a couple hours later when he woke up to Sylvie poking him in the chest. "*That,* Duncan Jamison, was *not* sex," she sounded disgruntled, and he opened one eye to look at her frowning face.

He grinned, "That, my dear, is sex the Jamison way." He sounded cocky but he didn't care.

She moved back out of his embrace a few inches to trace a hand down his hair softened chest. "I got robbed. I didn't even get to touch you yet."

He rolled over onto his back with a wide grin. "Touch away." She gave his body a long look and grinned as his penis jumped to attention.

She began rubbing her hands all over him and then stopped to stare down at him suspiciously. "Wait, how come I can touch you now?"

He opened one eye to look at her and then grinned. "Because now I can let you touch me and still give you multiple orgasms."

She stared down at him in wide eyed wonder. "Is this like a pride thing with you or something?"

He lifted his lips to within an inch of her own. "Or something," he whispered, and took her mouth again in a kiss.

She straddled his hips and began the slow teasing payback that he so deserved.

Chapter 19

Duncan awoke suddenly, on alert, and glanced toward the still dark windows. After their second long torturous round of lovemaking he had fallen asleep again with Sylvie's head on his shoulder and his arms holding her close. She had told him to go away even as she'd snuggled close. He'd chosen not to listen.

He tried to gently move from under her as he reached for his shorts. She moaned and rolled over onto her back, and he slid his boxers onto his hips even as he heard a creak down the hall. He froze as another creak in the old floorboard sounded. He slid silently out of bed and reached for the gun on the nightstand, carefully holding it away from the bed as he took three careful steps to the door to see who was in the hallway. He heard a light thud and a weird gurgling sound and stopped to zone in on the noise.

Reagan must be up and doing God only knew what. He wasn't about to leave Sylvie alone, even though he'd been reassured that Zack was probably the shooter. Something about the way Sylvie had seemed so at a loss about the man had kept nagging at him. For all apparent purposes everyone kept telling him about her gut instincts that seemed to constantly lead to breaks in whatever case she was prosecuting, and the fact that she hadn't seemed to believe Zack was capable had bothered him immensely.

She had after all slept with the man a couple of times. His gut clenched at that image of the good-looking blond guy in her bed and so he took the long years of experience and forced the image out of his mind.

He heard yet another creak against the carpeted hall floor and reached for the doorknob. He didn't want to leave Sylvie alone, but his gut was now screaming at him that he'd better go out to check on Reagan. He'd been a little more drunk than usual when he'd gone up to bed and Duncan would feel a lot better knowing that it was Sylvie's father creeping around the house. He felt only mildly interested as he wondered if the fifty- five-year-old man had heard him and Sylvie making love. Reagan had, after all, given Duncan his surprisingly easy blessing.

The doorknob moved silently under his hand as he turned it, careful not to make it too obvious just in case there was someone else out there. He shook his head, trying to convince himself that Sylvie was safe. Zack was the most likely shooter, and he was in the custody of the Boise police department. Besides, why would anyone come back tonight? Duncan had been here every night since Sylvie had first been shot and no one had attempted to come after her. He swore inwardly, as he suddenly remembered having had Frank drop him off.

His mind went into a fury of thinking. If the shooter hadn't been watching when he got a ride back, it would make sense that they would come tonight when they thought that they would find Sylvie alone. Still, there was Reagan, who was a police officer, and they had to expect a fight from him.

A sick feeling in his gut made him swallow the bile rising in his throat as the next thought came. What if the killer knew Sylvie's dad well enough to know that he'd most likely have fallen into a drunken stupor each night leaving her unprotected. He shook his head again. He was no detective and the detectives on the case were certain that Zack was their guy. Still… he was greatly concerned.

The knob stopped its silent movement with a click, and he began slowly edging the door open with the gun pointed at the floor in one hand. A few more inches and he had a slivering view of the dark hallway outside the room. If Reagan was up and at it, then why hadn't he turned on the light? More so than anything else, that fact bothered him. He took one careful step forward for a better view. If there *was* an intruder, he wasn't about to alert the guy that he was here. He could see a little better into the dark hallway but needed to see around the corner. He took another step forward spreading his feet to mitigate his weight on the old floor and came face to face with a tall, dark hooded man. Duncan reacted on instinct, pulling the gun up to aim it at the guy's chest, but the intruder responded just as quickly jerking his own arm up and knocking Duncan's arm back and nearly making him drop the gun.

In that split second, Duncan wondered if he'd just made a deadly mistake. The only reason he hadn't already had the gun up was because he was concerned that he might run into Reagan. He hadn't wanted to ruin whatever chance he might have with Sylvie by accidentally shooting her father. He fought at the guy's arm trying to pull the gun back up into position just as he took a heavy hit to his solar plexus. He would have stumbled back from the blow, but Sylvie was there behind him and there was no goddamn way he was letting this fight get to her.

He lowered his head and shoulder and charged, ramming into the attacker and driving him back into the wall across the hall from Sylvie's door. There was a loud grunt from under the dark hood and the next solid hit on his jaw took him by surprise, making stars dance momentarily around his head. He landed one hit himself, but it was with his left arm since his gun hand was still fighting to get the weapon into place. The guy had to be pretty fucking strong since Duncan couldn't seem to pull his arm loose long enough to shoot the bastard. He growled as the attacker got his legs underneath himself and shoved, sending Duncan and himself flying to the opposite wall just above the stairs.

For just a moment Duncan felt one leg lose its grip on the floor and thought he was going to go down, down, down the stairs. He grabbed traction with the toes of his one solid foot and pulled himself back up even as his gun arm slammed against the wall and the gun came loose, flying downward toward the stairs below. He took advantage of the momentary distraction and swung both arms forward taking several punches and driving the man back, even as one hit slid through his arms and hit him squarely in the eye.

He growled and saw red, pushing, shoving, and driving forward. He heard the swoosh of air from lungs, as he landed a good hit and turned slightly to angle toward the man's head. If he could only get a good head hit, he was sure he could knock the man out cold. Changing angles was a mistake and he knew it the instant the man ducked under his arm and slipped to the side of him. Duncan swerved and reached out, grasping for the man's arm but it slipped out of reach. He surged forward but the guy was running at a quick pace toward the stairs. Duncan chased him, knowing that if he had that gun in his hands he could simply turn around and shoot him.

To his surprise he watched the guy take the stairs at breakneck speed and disappear from sight. He was halfway down the staircase and could see his gun now perched at the edge of a stair tread when he heard Sylvie say sleepily, "What in god's name is going on?"

He swiveled, heart in his throat. "Go back inside and lock the door, Sylvie. Now!" He saw her retreat as he reached for the gun and ran down the remaining stairs. The front door was open, and he could see a dark form going down the front steps. He raised the gun, running after him.

Duncan wouldn't make the same mistake twice. If he got another shot, he would take it. He thundered out onto the front porch and got one dark glimpse off to the right side. He pulled the trigger twice. The loud bang stung his ears, even as the shadow disappeared.

He heard someone behind him and swung the gun around instinctively. Sylvie stood in the doorway clutching a knife in her hand, and he lowered the gun. "Jesus fucking Christ, Sylvie, I almost shot you. Get back in the house now."

She shook her head stubbornly. "And let you take a bullet for me? I d-don't think so D-Duncan." Her voice shook, and because he suddenly realized he cared more about keeping her safe than whether he actually shot the bastard that was escaping, he hurried toward her, lifting her with one arm by her waist and hauled her inside. He set her down and carefully closed the door behind them. In a still shaky voice, she asked, "Who was that?"

He swore and ran the fingers of his left hand through his hair. "How the fuck should I know." His words were harsh, and he immediately felt bad when she backed up a step. He set the gun on the back of the couch and stepped forward pulling her into his arms. "I'm sorry sweetheart, but goddamn, you scared the living hell out of me. This guy wants you dead, Sylvie, and here you are running into the fight. At this rate I'll be dead when I'm thirty."

She gave him a wan smile. "Aren't you thirty now?" she asked unhelpfully.

He groaned and pulled her tight into his embrace. "Exactly, and I've nearly died twice already this year. Once when I thought you were bleeding out on the floor, and again when you decided to come join the gunfight with a knife." After a quick kiss on her mouth, he reached for his phone and realized he wasn't dressed, and it was still likely upstairs. "Come on. Let's go up and call the police."

She didn't argue and wasn't surprised when he reached for the gun before ushering her up the stairs in front of him. When they got to the top of the stairs, he noticed Reagan's bedroom door was open. His gut clenched again, and he shoved Sylvie toward her bedroom. "Go call the police, I'll be back in a second."

She obeyed him and he stalked quickly down the hall to the open door. He hadn't seen it opened during the struggle and wondered idly if the fight had actually woken Reagan up and he'd come out.

Duncan looked at the empty rumpled bed and frowned as he turned to check the hallway for the man. A dark hump on the floor caught his eye and without thinking he flipped on the light switch. There was blood everywhere. There was a puddle on the floor and a wide arched spray across the bed and the wall. He saw Reagan there on the floor, still as death, his throat slit, blood oozing out from that long cut just under his chin and several gash marks on his chest. Duncan swallowed bile and rushed forward. His first thought was to put pressure on the throat wound. He stopped himself suddenly and bent to check for a pulse. There was too much blood everywhere for the man to be alive. He backed up toward the door as emotion clogged his throat. It seemed as though everyone he knew was destined to die tragically. Now, all he could think was that he didn't want to contaminate the scene in case the police could possibly get DNA.

He heard Sylvie coming down the hall. "Duncan? Are you in my dad's room?"

He swung around and ran toward her voice. He reached her just as she neared the bedroom door and he threw his arms around her dragging her down the hall and away from the bloody, gory, mess that had been her father. In a voice hoarse and raw, he said, "You don't want to see that sweetheart." She began struggling suddenly. "I don't want to see what?" Duncan held her tight, not budging even as she began pounding at his arms and chest trying to get free. "Duncan let me go, now! Did something happen to

Daddy?"

He turned her in his arms and pulled her back to his chest effectively wrapping her in his warmth. She struggled helplessly against his strong hold. "I swear, Jamison, if you don't let me go now, I will never forgive you!"

With tears in his eyes, he held onto her even as she began to shake and then cry. "Did you call the police, baby?" he asked calmly.

She nodded, bumping her head against his chin. "Is… he… dead?" she asked hesitantly.

Duncan tightened his arms and whispered softly, "I'm so sorry, Sylvie. God, I'm sorry. I didn't wake up soon enough, sweetheart. I'm so, so sorry."

Chapter 20

Duncan held her there in his arms while they waited for the police to come. They stood in the long hallway for several minutes as Sylvie sobbed uncontrollably, before Duncan said gently, "Let's go downstairs so we can let the police in when they get here."

She didn't argue. Only let him lead her toward the stairs. She hesitated there at the top and he simply slid the gun into his waistband and lifted her under her knees and hauled her down. Once downstairs he sat her carefully on the plush leather sofa and checked to make sure the front door was still locked. Then he pulled the gun out and set it within reach before sliding his warmth over and leaning her into his arms, with her head on his shoulder. He didn't know what to say so he simply held her there in silence. After a long while, she turned to look up at him. "Are you sure he was dead, Duncan? Should we be up there trying to save him?" Her voice broke as fresh tears slid down her cheeks to drip on his chest.

As his own throat constricted, Duncan nodded and then shook his head. "I'm sure. God, I really wish I wasn't, but there is no way he'd still be alive." Tears shone in his eyes as he admitted with self- loathing, "Maybe if I'd been ready and shot the intruder right away and then gotten to him sooner…" his voice trailed off.

Sylvie squeezed his hand. "No, don't do that Duncan. You don't get to blame yourself for this. If anyone is to blame, it's me. That fucking moron is after me." Her shoulders shook and she lay against him again.

He squeezed her and said gently, "He wouldn't have suffered much. It was over pretty quickly. I'm sure of that."

He'd killed plenty of cattle and knew that a nice deep cut to the neck was one of the fastest ways to kill them. Gunshots could take a while, unless you hit them in the exact right place in their brain. Bile rose in his throat as he realized he was likening slaughtering a cow, to the horrific way Sylvie's dad had died. He swallowed.

Screaming sirens permeated the air and he rose after a minute, intending to meet the police at the door. Sylvie tried to stand, but he shook his head and reached for a blanket to cover her revealing pajamas. "You stay here. I'll let them in."

Once again, she didn't argue, but leaned her head back against the couch and closed her eyes as she tried to force her emotions under control. Duncan was shouldering most of the weight and yet there he stood tall and strong. Her eyes snapped open. "Duncan you're still only in those boxers."

He turned and looked at her, then gave a curt nod. "I fought with the killer like this. They might be able to get DNA off of me."

She knew that made sense, after all she was a prosecutor and knew that sometimes it was good techs going the extra mile to collect DNA that made the case stick. She eyed Duncan, wondering why he was so clear-headed about all of this.

They heard gravel crunching and Duncan swung the door wide as two police cruisers skidded to a stop and four officers jumped out, automatically drawing their guns. He nodded to the middle-aged cop that was the first one up the steps. "Mr Dunlap's body is inside but the perp ran that way." He lifted an arm and pointed the direction he had shot his own weapon.

The cop nodded and turned to his companions. "Janko and Ortiz, you guys go that way and look for the intruder. Be careful and watch your six," he ordered, then turned to the female cop behind him. "Ward, stay with me." He turned back to Duncan. "Where is the body?"

Duncan swung the door wide and followed the two officers back inside.

He lifted an arm to point to the stairs. "Up there. Last door on the left."

Officer Ward zeroed in on the handgun on the coffee table. "Is that your weapon, Mr Jamison?"

Duncan nodded and picked it up, letting it hang from one finger as he pointed it down and held it out to her. "It is."

She nodded and stepped forward to take it and slid it into her coat pocket. "We will have to fingerprint and test it sir, do you understand?"

He nodded. "I do. Do whatever you need to. I did discharge it twice outside when the guy was running away."

She looked taken aback and then nodded. "Noted. Don't wash your hands until we can also test for gunshot residue, sir."

He nodded and hid a grin. It was kind of a no duh thing, but he watched as the two of them began clearing the house one room at a time before finally going carefully up the stairs. He understood it was all protocol, but it still irritated him that they wouldn't take his word for it. Unable to do anything else, he walked back over to where Sylvie sat staring silently at him. He sat down with a loud sigh, and she instantly slid close to him. She lay her head on his shoulder and asked softly, "How do you know so much about all of this, Duncan?"

He shrugged. "It's been an interest of mine for a long time."

When he didn't add more, she turned her face up to his. He met her eyes, and she could see the pain and the sympathy there in the blue depths. She looked away. She hated sympathy. She also hated when people all crowded up to give hugs and offer condolences when all she really wanted was to be alone. Another tear rolled down one cheek and she said softly, "He died because of me."

Duncan sat up so fast he bumped her chin with his shoulder. "No," he said angrily. "He died because there is some bloody, fucking bastard out there who killed him. That's it." He reached for her chin and forced her head up to meet her tear-filled eyes. "Tell me you know that, Sylvie." He stared hard at her with his jaw taut and with tension in every part of his features. "Say it."

She shrugged. "I know all of that. I just meant that if someone wasn't trying to get to me…" she trailed off.

He shook her shoulder gently. "No. If anyone is to blame here, it's me. I should have been more prepared and on the ball. Dammit, I should have had my truck outside. In all likelihood that is the reason he's gone."

Sylvie met his angry eyes. "What on earth does your truck have to do with anything?" But she knew as soon as the words came out. "Oh god," she choked. "He thought you were gone… and he killed Daddy so he wouldn't have a chance to protect me." She gagged and jumped to her feet rushing to the sink in the kitchen just in time to empty her stomach.

She felt his arms on her shoulder as she gagged again. When the heaving finally stopped, she rinsed her face and mouth and accepted the clean towel that he handed her. She turned and leaned back against the counter feeling weak kneed. Suddenly she turned to stare at him. "He would have to have known that Daddy was a drunk." She swallowed the lump as tears threatened again. "I'm a-awful, aren't I? His b-body isn't even cold, and I already called h-him a drunk."

She covered her face in her hands as Duncan moved over to once again wrap her in a hug. "It's going to be all right, Sylvie. I'll make sure it is."

His voice was filled with steely determination and somehow it calmed her. She looked up at him through her tears. "You know I'm right though,

don't you." It was more of a statement than a question, but he nodded anyway.

"For what it's worth, yes I agree." He held her gaze then as he said softly, "And Sylvie?" When she nodded, he said, "I am going to kill this bastard and keep you safe."

She shuddered at the magnitude of his promise even as she tucked herself into the warmth and comfort his strong body offered to her.

When the other two officers came inside after searching futilely and only finding boot tracks in the dirt, Duncan pointed them upstairs.

In the following hours several more policemen arrived including a chief and a couple of detectives. The crime scene unit showed up and swabbed not only Duncan's hand, but several places where he insisted that the killer had made contact with his skin. He was sporting two broken ribs along with a shiner and a large bruise that was beginning to take shape on his jaw beneath the rubble of his two-day old shadow. They took both Sylvie's statement, as well as Duncan's several times as though they thought that they would suddenly remember some detail that they hadn't thought of before.

After the first few hours Duncan asked if it would be okay if he took a shower and got a variety of reactions. Some acted as though he must have something to hide, others looked guilty for not having offered it sooner. He was a confident man, but after parading around a bunch of overdressed police officers he was beginning to feel slightly under dressed. The officer cleared it with the detectives and Duncan stood to go upstairs.

Sylvie gripped his hand, unwilling to let go. He looked down and gave her a gentle smile. "I won't be gone long."

She stood and clutched at him, and he wondered if she intended to follow him into the shower. He turned as a detective walked into the room. "Would it be okay if Miss Dunlap joined me?"

There was a volley of raised eyebrows and strange smiles that went around the room. Sylvie's soft voice cut in. "For god's sake, it's not like I'm going to go in the bathroom and mess around, while my father's dead body is in the other room." Most of the officers had the decency to look ashamed. "I'm very cold and I need to get dressed myself and a hot shower might help."

After a long thoughtful silence, Detective Lane nodded. "It should be fine. Both of you need to remove your clothes and bag them for evidence anyway." She snapped her fingers, and an officer came rushing forward with two lined plastic bags.

Duncan took them and without another word took Sylvie's arm to help her up the stairs. She froze when the doorway to her father's room came into view. Duncan squeezed her arm. "Sit here for a minute and we'll go to the ranch for this." He disappeared inside her room and returned a couple minutes later with his bag slung over his shoulder. "Come on."

In the front room he pulled away and walked over to the detective and said something low that Sylvie couldn't hear. The detective nodded and then spoke into her radio as Duncan came to put his arm around her shoulders. "Let's go," he said gently and held the front door for her to go out first.

An officer waited near a squad car and Duncan ushered her through the cold morning air. The officer nodded and opened his door. Duncan helped her inside and then walked around to slide in next to her. She was barely responding to anything and he frowned as he reached for her hand. "Are you going to be okay, Sylvie?"

The officer climbed in and adjusted his rear view to meet Duncan's eyes. "Where to, sir?"

Duncan quickly gave instructions to the ranch and then turned back to Sylvie. "I'm worried about you. Do I need to take you into the hospital to get you checked out?"

Sylvie quickly shook her head. In a clipped voice she said, “I’m fine.” Unsure of what else to do, he slid across the seat and wrapped one arm around her shoulder and reached for her hand with his other. He remembered when his mom had died, everyone had wanted to talk about it to him and console him, but all he’d wanted was time to think and blessed, blessed silence.

In the front seat, the officer decided to try his hand at small talk.

“So have you guys lived clear out here all your—”

Duncan gave him a look that was fierce enough to shut the man up. Sylvie smiled at him. She was alert enough to know what was happening and that made him more confident. He leaned down and smiled at her and then gave her a light kiss on the forehead, before pushing her head down on his still naked shoulder.

She allowed it but only because it was where she wanted to be anyway.

Chapter 21

Because she stood there numbly as he started the shower and then undressed, he undressed her too, then helped her under the steaming spray. Then he pulled out some soft sweatpants and a T-shirt that he had obviously brought from her room at her parents' place. She slid into the clothes and then watched as he toweled himself off and pulled on a pair of running shorts and a soft black T-shirt. The shirt was snug and showed off his muscular build. She was so ashamed that she'd noticed that fact under the circumstances that she began crying again.

He didn't say anything but took her shoulders and pushed her out the bathroom door gently. He urged her onto his bed, reached into the bag again and pulled out her hairbrush. While she cried softly, he gently brushed her freshly shampooed hair. The tenderness touched her, and she cried some more. After a while he urged her to lay back on the pillow and he rubbed gently at her temples and then her shoulders. Her hands felt cold against his, so he pulled a blanket up over her and she turned over to give him better access to her back.

He rubbed up and down and then began carefully kneading out the kinks. Still, she cried.

Duncan felt helpless and his heart ached as he considered everything that had happened up to now. Sensibly, he knew that he wasn't to blame for Reagan's death, but he couldn't help playing out the scenario where he kept his truck at the house, or where he'd had his gun up and shot the bastard on the spot. Or even the one where he'd seen that bedroom door open before he'd wasted precious time chasing the killer outside. Any one of those things might possibly have saved Reagan Dunlap's life and it weighed heavily on him.

After a long while he heard her breathing even out and he knew she had fallen asleep. Unable to sit still, he stood and headed out and down the stairs. Sylvie wouldn't sleep long. He was sure of that fact, and she really needed something to eat. He pulled out some fresh bread and sliced a couple of pieces and popped them in the toaster. He turned and started the coffee pot and then came back to butter the toast and put a small dish of the preserves on the plate. He filled a Thermos with coffee so it would stay hot and then grabbed a couple of mugs and a bottle of water before heading back upstairs. He met his father at the top and Arthur looked surprised. "Well, hello, son. I didn't realize you were home."

Duncan forced a small smile. He'd have to tell his old man about his friend at some point, but he didn't want to do it now. "Morning Dad." He started to move around him.

"I thought you would still be over at the Dunlaps' with Sylvie," Arthur said gently.

Duncan turned back in surprise. "Jackie called you already? I figured she'd wait until a little later." He shrugged, making a mental note to thank his sister for breaking the news to their dad so he didn't have to. Back before the Dunlaps' had moved away, the two men had seemed close. "I'm sorry, Dad. I know it must be hard."

Arthur nodded and looked at the floor. "Yeah, it really is such a shame. Reagan was a good man."

Duncan gave him another small smile. "I wish I could stay and talk but I need to get back up to Sylvie."

Arthur's eyes widened in surprise. "Sylvie is here now? Poor girl. She has lost everyone close to her, hasn't she?" He saw Duncan nod and looked at the tray in his hands and said gently, "I assume that is for her? Would you mind if I took it up to her? I'd like to give her my condolences."

Duncan shook his head. "There will be time later, but she just fell asleep, and I don't want to wake her before she's ready."

His father nodded in understanding. "Well, if you need time to take care of yourself son, I'm happy to help where I can."

"Thanks. I appreciate it, Dad." And then because it was so good to see yet another glimpse of the man his father had once been he added, "It means a lot that you care."

Arthur met his eyes for a brief moment and then finally nodded and hurried down the stairs. Duncan watched him go before turning back to walk up through the open living area and finally into the hallway where his bedroom was. Sylvie was still out cold, so he set the tray on the rough wood nightstand and gently laid on the bed next to her. He stretched his arms above his head and leaned back, watching her while she slept.

Her face was peaceful in the deep blissful ignorance of sleep, and he smiled. She had lost everyone now. Her sister, her mother, and now her father, he thought, even as a calm peaceful determination settled inside his heart. He would be there for her. He would do whatever it took to show up. He loved her. Maybe he had always loved her. He'd always felt the need to give her time and space, but he'd always hoped somewhere deep down that she would remember him and come back.

He smiled bitterly; she had come back, though not for him. She'd come back to settle her grief for Elaine, and he was simply still here because, though he'd always meant to leave and do something else with his life, he hadn't.

At first it had been the ranch and putting Jackie through school and then eventually Jackie and the kids. Now, he took an honest look at his life as it was. If Sylvie left tomorrow, there really wouldn't be anything left here for him. Was it finally time to live out his own dream? He sighed, and noticed from the corner of his eye that the door was still open a small crack.

He stood and walked over to close it tightly and then, because he was sick of worrying, he locked it and then hung an old pair of cowbells over the knob. It was an old set Jackie had given him as a joke when he'd bought the first ten of his own heifers. It was the first and only time they'd ever been used. He slid carefully back down on the bed and laid back. Sylvie rolled over and curled against his side and within minutes he was out.

He sat up straight two hours later to the sound of a blood-curdling scream that had his heart in his throat and his stomach tied in knots. Sylvie tossed and turned as she fought an unknown demon in her dreams. She let out another scream and swung her arms out in an effort to protect herself. Duncan who had just turned and was about to wrap his arms around her, caught one fist in his good eye. Blinking as his eye began to water, he swore under his breath and wrapped her body in a tight embrace. "You're okay, sweetheart, it's just a dream," he crooned as he rocked her gently back and forth.

He felt the exact moment she started waking up even as she turned and looked up at him through sleep clouded eyes. "Did you say something?" she asked groggily.

He stared hard at her, unable to believe she had recovered so quickly.

"You were having a bad dream. What were you dreaming about?"

She gave him a blank look and shook her head. "I haven't had nightmares in years."

He sat up against the log headboard and stared at her intently.

"Well, I'm fairly certain you were having one just now."

She shook her head again and sat up. "I swear I don't remember dreaming."

"How long was I out?" she asked rubbing at her swollen eyes groggily.

He gave her a wan smile. "A couple hours. No one would blame you if you did have them, you know."

She ignored his patronizing tone. "Have you heard from the police?

Have they found anything new out?"

He shook his head. He had purposely taken her from the house so she wouldn't have to watch them haul her father's body out in a bag. "Not yet. Hungry?" He looked at the dried-out toast. "I did make some toast, but I don't know if it's edible and this point."

He reached for the coffee and opened the top. Steam seeped out and he smiled. "The coffee is still warm though."

She nodded gratefully and reached for the toast, spreading a generous amount of preserves on top. He poured the coffee and then offered the white mug to her, and she gave him a small smile. "Thank you." She closed her eyes and leaned back after she took a sip. "God, I needed this."

He didn't say anything, only poured himself some coffee and then took a sip. He eyed her as she ate the toast in four bites and downed the coffee. She turned to him. "Can I get a warmup? Also were you going to eat that other piece?"

She pointed to the plate, and he shook his head and handed it to her. "Knock yourself out." She seemed unnervingly calm now that she had slept for a bit. He waited, wondering if she had forgotten about her father. She downed the toast and the second cup of coffee he poured and groaned as she leaned back again. Without thinking he reached for the aspirin on the side table and poured a few into his hand before holding them and the water out to her.

She smiled and took them like a child reaching for candy. "You really do think of everything don't you, Duncan?"

He didn't respond. He wasn't sure what she was expecting from him. He felt guilty as hell about spending the night making love to her and then falling asleep while her father lay in the other room taking his last gasping breaths as he was murdered.

It was irrational, he knew, and yet it still bothered him. She reached for his hand and squeezed it. He turned and offered her a small smile. Without hesitation she leaned forward and planted a kiss on his lips. With a little brush of her breasts against his chest, his manhood jumped to attention, but he held back. He leaned back and away from her embrace. "Not like this, Sylvie."

She frowned in irritation. "Like what?"

"I won't be your distraction from reality," he said grumpily.

She glared hotly at him. "Sometimes sex is the only thing that makes me feel better."

He shrugged. "Maybe so, but not like this. Not between us."

She didn't like the way his voice sounded and let him know. "I was very clear that sex was all this is. Judgmental isn't a good look on you."

He looked down at her sensual curvy body and cursed his own code. "I do care about you though and I don't want what is between us tainted by using sex to fill that void."

Tears filled her eyes and she said hotly, "Damn you, Jamison, can't you just leave it alone?"

He shook his head regretfully. "I really wish I could, because you look fucking hot and beautiful and I am already regretting my decision, but I can't."

She turned away angrily and slid out of the bed. "Well, what the hell else are we supposed to do while we wait to find out if they know who killed my dad?" She turned suddenly as a thought occurred. "How did he die,

Duncan?"

He had been hoping she never asked him that. He shrugged, looking clueless. "The usual way I suppose."

Her gaze narrowed and she walked around the bed as though she might attack him. "Duncan Jamison, I know that look well, and while Elaine may have fallen for it a time or two, I am no fool." She plopped herself onto his lap which he imagined was supposed to inspire him to tell the truth. He swallowed as he felt himself grow harder. She smiled too, knowing that she had gotten to him.

Feeling beaten he tried to shift his body from underneath her, but she wrapped her arms around his neck. He met her gaze and asked softly, "Are you sure you want to know?"

She held his gaze unwavering, and he took a deep breath. "God, this is harder than I thought." He looked into her warm brown eyes that deserved a world of happiness and destroyed whatever last innocence she may have had about her father's death. "His throat was… slit." His voice was hoarse, and it cracked in the middle of the sentence.

Tears filled her eyes again and he reached for her hand and squeezed it. She watched him for a long moment and then asked, "Wait, a cut throat is a flesh wound so why were you so sure he was dead when you got in there?"

Duncan couldn't look at her as he answered. "There was blood everywhere. Too much blood." His voice caught. "There were several deep cuts on his chest as well and when I didn't get a pulse, I knew."

It was as though it finally dawned on her that they were talking about her father as she gagged and then said, "Oh god. Duncan I'm so sorry you had to see all that."

He shrugged and met her gaze then, held it there in his own. His tone was steely as he said firmly, "I'm not. What I couldn't have lived with is if you found him that way."

He shuddered and wrapped his arms around her. She leaned into it and then kissed him softly, sweetly. He couldn't resist the tender promise in that kiss. He cursed himself even as he growled and deepened the kiss, and his hand began its gentle teasing foray under her shirt just shy of the curve of her breast.

She groaned. "Don't start that again, Duncan. Just have rough wild sex like a normal man."

He grinned against her mouth as his tongue dipped playfully inside, tasting the sweetness of the preserves and a hint of coffee. His thumb brushed across her nipple once, playfully. "I don't know how 'normal' men do it, sweetheart, but I'd be happy to show you how a 'real' man does it." He pulled back suddenly. "Or would you rather we just stop altogether?"

She glared at him and then smiled. "Bastard." Then she leaned into him and said, "I guess I'll take my chances with surviving your ego."

He didn't agree with her sentiment, but he did take the next hour showing her exactly how a 'real' man made love to his woman. To his great satisfaction he even managed to predict and take each of her screams into his mouth with kisses.

Chapter 22

A loud knock on his door had Duncan sitting upright and reaching for the weapon in the top drawer by the bed. He turned and met Sylvie's wide sleepy eyes as she said, "I thought the police took your gun."

He grinned dryly. "You think I didn't plan for that possible contingency?"

She shook her head in amused stupefaction. "Who are you? And where is the po'dunk cowboy that I grew up with?"

He gave her a sideways look and made his way to the door, opening it to a wide crack. Arthur stood on the other side and Duncan lowered his weapon and swung it wide. "Sorry, I just have to play it safe." He raised a curious eyebrow at his father.

Arthur nodded. "I understand son. There is a man on the front porch demanding to see Sylvie." He glanced behind Duncan at Sylvie on the bed and offered a sympathetic smile. "How are you dear?"

Sylvie sat up and forced a smile even as her heart thundered in her ears. She wasn't ready to face the sympathy yet. "I'm fine, thank you Mr Jamison."

He nodded and turned back to Duncan. "I can stay here with Sylvie, if you want to go down and talk to the guy."

Duncan turned and met Sylvie's gaze. She gave a small shake of her head and stood. "I'll come down. Who did you say was down there?"

Arthur Jamison shook his head, "I don't remember his name. A detective Mike or something like that."

Sylvie's brows came together as she met Duncan's questioning look.

She shrugged. "Maybe it's a new detective on the case or something?"

She ran her fingers lightly through her hair as they went down the stairs. She noticed Duncan was walking a little slower than usual and leaning toward the right with each step. Mildly concerned, she asked,

"Are you okay there, Jamison?"

He threw a look over his shoulder at her. "I think I broke a couple of ribs is all."

Sylvie gasped. "My god. I had no idea." She grasped onto his shoulders forcing him to look back at her. The dark smudges around his eyes were beginning to turn purple and blue. She swallowed hard and muttered, "I didn't realize you had *two* black eyes."

He nodded and abruptly moved past her and toward the front door, not wanting her to realize the second black eye was from her nightmares. A tall dark-haired man who looked to be about thirty-five stood just inside the door wearing a pair of snug, faded blue jeans, with worn brown leather loafers and a black leather jacket. Duncan lifted the gun as he watched the guy study the painting on the wall above the dining room table.

He turned as the bottom stair creaked from Arthur who had come down directly behind Sylvie. His eyes widened and Duncan had the distinct impression the man was itching to reach for a gun that he wasn't wearing. He held his own weapon steady even as the guy lifted his hands in the air with an amused smile. "Well, I see that Sylvie is in good hands," he said in a low drawl.

Duncan's hands were steady. "Who the hell are you?"

Sylvie answered that question as she stepped around Duncan and then with a squeal of delight rushed forward to throw her arms around the man. "Nick!" she exclaimed excitedly. He met her hug and lifted her up, spinning her around even as he planted a long hard kiss on her lips. Duncan scowled. "Sylvie step back. Who the hell are you?" he repeated coldly, trying to keep Sylvie out of his line of fire.

Sensing that a fight was in the air she suddenly stepped back and away, turning to Duncan whose gaze was narrowed on the man she'd just kissed. She stepped forward quickly. "It's okay. Duncan, this is Nick Hanlan from back home. He worked with my dad, remember?"

The name was familiar, but Duncan wasn't quite ready to lower his weapon. He had half a mind to shoot the asshole in the leg for manhandling Sylvie that way.

Nick held his hands up again as a knowing smile broke over his face making his crooked nose turn slightly to the right. "I talked to you on the phone before. Detective Hanlan," he said with a distinctive southern drawl. He held out a hand toward Duncan, then when he still didn't lower the gun said slowly, "I'm going to reach in my back pocket now and pull out my badge, okay man?"

Duncan's lip twitched on one side at the nervous smile that was beginning to show.

Good. He wanted the bastard to be afraid of him. He nodded abruptly and watched without blinking, as Nick Hanlan pulled his wallet out and let it fall open, revealing a gold badge.

Sylvie had reached his side again and started pleading softly, which only pissed him off. "Please, put the gun down Duncan. Nick is an old family friend."

He ignored her and studied the badge for a long moment before finally, reluctantly lowering the gun. "So, what are you doing here then, Detective Hanlan?"

Nick shrugged. "I got the message that Sylvie had been attacked again and since we just had Zachary McDaniel's transferred out to Wilmington, there is no way it was him. I needed to make sure she was safe, so I jumped on the first flight out here." He looked at Duncan for a moment and then flashed an easy grin. "It looks like you might have taken the brunt of it, though."

Duncan didn't smile, only gave a curt nod as he turned and met Sylvie's sad eyes. He wasn't sure, but it sounded like the detective hadn't yet heard the news about her dad. She gave him a pleading nod and he turned back to Nick.

Nick saw the exchange and his gaze narrowed as he glanced around the room. "Where is Reagan?"

The room was silent for a long heartbeat before Duncan stepped forward and said quietly, "I assumed you had heard..." He paused and watched as the man in front of him came to the obvious conclusion.

Nick let out a long string of black curses and turned to stare at Sylvie. "Are you trying to tell me that he's dead?"

Sylvie couldn't meet his eyes. Nick Hanlan had been her father's partner since he'd passed his detectives exam six years before. She felt Duncan move closer as he slid his arm around her shoulders and pulled her head to his chest. He cleared his throat. "I don't know how much you've heard..." he began.

Nick sat on the plush cushioned wooden rocking chair near the door that he had rudely *not* been invited to sit in. Where he came from, his mother would have been in a tiff had he not immediately offered their guest a seat and a glass of sweet tea.

He saw Duncan Jamison shift as Sylvie turned into his light embrace. He looked up and met cold blue eyes with his own tortured hazel ones and denied what he knew in his gut was true. "No, it can't be. I talked to Reagan last night. He was fine." In answer to Duncan's prompt, he said quietly, "All I know is that an officer from the front desk called me in the middle of the night because I was the detective on the case, to inform me that there was an incident and Sylvie Dunlap had been attacked again."

He looked at his hands and then back at Duncan, who looked only slightly warmer now with a sympathetic nod. "I jumped on the first flight out. I was going nuts anyway and feeling like I was useless from so far away..." His voice trailed off as he recalled the scene at the Dunlap house when he'd gotten there. He hadn't even made his way inside since he'd run into an officer in the driveway, who'd informed him that Sylvianna Dunlap and Duncan Jamison had gone to a ranch nearby. He'd gotten back in his rental car and driven straight here.

Duncan cleared his throat as he saw the man in front of him age five years. He urged Sylvie to the sofa and sat down next to her. "Detective Hanlan," he began.

Nick waved a hand. "Call me Nick."

Duncan gave a polite nod. "Nick then, we all ate dinner together last night at the Dunlaps' house." When the detective raised a curious eyebrow, Duncan expanded, "Me, Sylvie, Mr Dunlap, my sister and her twin three-year-old daughters." He breathed in deeply. "Oh yeah, and my brother-in-law, Ren Bradley. Anyway, after dinner everyone watched a movie except for Mr Dunlap who went to bed, and myself, as I had to come home for a few things." Duncan didn't feel the need to explain his personal business to the man.

He wouldn't hold back any details that might lead to a breakthrough in the case, however, so he said quietly, "My ranch hand needed my truck here at the ranch, so I had him drop me back off at the Dunlaps'." He told the story as it had happened because he was curious if the detective would come to the same conclusion that he had. "When I got back to the Dunlaps' my sister and her family were asleep on the couch and they woke up and went home. Me and Sylvie went up to bed." He watched the detective closely for any reaction and wasn't disappointed when his golden gaze narrowed.

He smiled. "A couple of hours later, something woke me, and I went to the door with my gun, of course." Duncan paused and looked away for the first time in embarrassment. "I thought it might be Mr Dunlap up walking around so I kept my weapon lowered as I opened the door." His jaw clenched and he turned guilt ridden eyes back to Nick's. "It was a mistake because I couldn't get my gun up in time and we struggled around for about five minutes before he finally knocked the gun out of my hands. It tumbled down the stairs, but I managed to get him cornered and was about to give him a knockout blow when he slipped away. It surprised me when he ran down the stairs and away.

Sylvie came to the door then and I told her to go back inside as I ran after him. I grabbed the gun from the stairs where it had fallen and ran outside where I'd seen him go. I got one shot off before he disappeared into the brush."

He turned to give Sylvie a hard look. "Sylvie came running out with a boot knife and I was worried for her safety, so I rushed her back inside. Our phones were still up in her bedroom, so we went up there and I told her to call nine-one-one. I noticed Mr Dunlap's bedroom door open then, so I went to check on him." Duncan looked down at the floor as Sylvie took a deep breath. His voice wavered as he said quietly, "Well, Reagan, was dead by then."

Sylvie squeezed his hand and turned finally to her father's partner. "I had called the police and they were on their way when I went looking for Duncan. He heard me and came rushing out of Daddy's room." Tears filled her eyes even as she held Nick's gaze. He deserved that much from her at the very least. Her voice shook as she finished. "He wouldn't let me go in there, and I knew why. God, I knew why."

Nick was in shock as she stood, walking quickly over to him to put a gentle hand on his arm. "I'm so sorry, I planned to call you but then I was just so cold, and Duncan brought me here to shower and then I fell asleep." She looked away as she left out some of the details.

His stricken gaze took in her hollowed-out eyes and pale cheeks. He nodded acceptance. "I understand, Sylvie, but Christ! I wish I could have been here. Maybe it would have made the difference."

Duncan smiled bitterly. "There were a million things that could have made a difference. If I had only—"

Nick's hand in the air stopped him. "Don't do that, man. Trust me, you did everything you could have done. I only meant that if I were here, I might have been able to help." When Duncan looked like he was about to argue, Nick asked quietly, "Had Reagan been drinking again?"

Both Duncan and Sylvie nodded at the same time and Nick sighed and dropped his head into his hands. "Dammit! I knew that was going to get him into trouble one of these days." He lifted his head and met Sylvie's brown tear-streaked eyes. "You are lucky Mr Jamison was here, Sylvie." He turned to Duncan, "Thank you for saving her."

The closeness between the two of them was getting under his very thick skin and Duncan didn't like the feeling but so far 'Nick' had been playing nice and he figured he may as well man up. He gave the detective a nod and asked, "Would anyone like some coffee or tea?"

He'd added tea for the detective's benefit. He remembered hearing or reading something about southerners and their tea. Sylvie gave him an odd questioning look and he hedged, "We might have some tea around here somewhere."

Nick's mouth turned up in an amused grin. "Coffee would be appreciated."

Duncan nodded and walked into the kitchen. He noticed his father had been sitting at the table listening to the conversation and shivered. Sometimes the old man was strange. He hadn't said a word since they had come downstairs. As Duncan put in a new filter and poured water and grounds into the coffee pot he wondered idly if Arthur was actually taking in the conversation, or just watching it as ornithologists watched birds.

His father opened the paper and looked intently at it and Duncan smiled in relief as he noticed it was, at the very least, today's paper. He looked at the bizarre stack of old newspapers that he wasn't allowed to touch and wondered if his father would let him throw them all out, now that he seemed to be feeling more like himself. He put it off. He'd ask tomorrow. No reason to make a big deal of it right now with the stranger that seemed all too cozy with Sylvie sitting in the nearby rocker.

He heard Sylvie and Nick talking quietly as he got a tray and put a small thing of half and half as well as sugar and four mugs on it. He doubted his father would actually join them, but it seemed the polite thing to do. He opened a cupboard that was mostly empty since he hadn't done any shopping all week. There was a pack of snicker doodles still inside, so he set them on the tray with a shrug. He wasn't sure exactly how far this hospitality shit was supposed to go but he drew the line there. The coffee was done so he took the pot and the tray and headed back into the front room just as Sylvie said, "I've missed you, Nick."

He frowned and considered taking his hospitality back to the kitchen. Nick saw him hesitate and grinned knowingly. "I'm here to take care of you now," he said for the benefit of the narrow-eyed beast of a man who'd finally found his manners. He watched Duncan's eyes go cold as his suspicions were confirmed.

He swore inwardly, wondering if this man was the reason Sylvie had never really been willing to give any of the men from North Carolina a chance? For as long as he'd known her, she always had men she was dating but never took any one of them seriously. He'd been hoping for the past year, that he would be the one to change that, but given the possessive way that Duncan Jamison was acting, he'd bet his left nut that they'd been sleeping together. He stared thoughtfully at the man. Good looking enough, he supposed, but a rancher? Was the rancher sort what did it for Sylvie?

He nodded his gratitude as the man poured what turned out to be a pretty decent cup of coffee. He smiled; Duncan Jamison might be all right after all. Nick grinned as he wondered idly if the man could also cook grits. That thought had him grinning widely and Duncan frowning just as severely.

Nick thought of his partner and sobered instantly as his gut clenched. Reagan Dunlap had been a damn fine officer, and in his book a damn fine partner. He lifted his cup in a toast. "To Reagan, a damn fine partner."

Duncan eyed him and then miraculously cracked a grin and raised his own. "The best indeed."

Sylvie stared dubiously between them before saying a bit hoarsely, "If I'm going to toast to Daddy, I need something a bit stronger."

Duncan stood before she finished her sentence and strode out. He returned ten seconds later with a bottle of whiskey. He poured a finger in Sylvie's coffee, then when she stared up at him with a pouty smile he shrugged and filled her mug.

He poured a small splash into his own and then held it toward Nick in question. Nick shook his head and then changed his mind. "Why not. I'm technically off duty anyway."

Together they all lifted their glasses and Duncan watched with a droll expression as Sylvie nearly drained her glass. She held it out to him, and he reached for the coffee pot knowing she wanted more whiskey. She glared but he filled it up and added a little cream and sugar. "Drink this instead. The sugar will be good for energy." She took it but continued to glare up at him. Finally, he sighed. "The detectives want to come over and interview us one more time in a little bit."

His explanation relaxed her stance, and she nodded as she sipped at the coffee. She looked through her dark lashes over the rim of the mug at first Duncan and then Nick and back again as silence stretched over the room. She opened her mouth and asked brightly, "So Nick, what's new back at home?"

Both men turned to stare at her, and she shivered. Though she often dated several men at once, she didn't normally have them in the same room together. Nick was a gentleman through and through. He would follow her lead and smooth out the tension at her invitation. It was Duncan who made her nervous. Dark, sexy, broody, Duncan.

Duncan, who was as steady as the mountains around them and nearly as strong. Duncan, who she knew had been raised with old- fashioned notions of two people meeting and falling in love, then getting married, and settling down to raise a family together. Duncan, who was so like what her parents had been wanting for her these past years. The steady, settled man who could kiss her goodbye in the morning and walk her kids to the school bus, or give her a ride to work before going to work himself.

The pleasant image startled her, and she shook her head as she realized Nick was talking and she hadn't heard a word of what he'd said. She fastened a bright smile on her face and tried to remember what he was talking about. She got nothing. Both Duncan and Nick were staring at her, waiting. She swallowed some coffee and then very bravely said, "I'm sorry, Nick, I didn't hear what you said."

Duncan grinned and turned back to the very smooth, very confident Nick, smugly. Nick looked at the blush creeping up Sylvie's neck in surprise. He'd never seen her lose her cool. He smiled gently. "I was just saying how my family has been asking when you are going to come to our Sunday night barbecue again."

Sylvie gave him a bright smile. "I love those things!"

She turned to Duncan. "Nick's family does these huge barbecues where practically the whole neighborhood is invited. There is a fire pit, and they always roast a pig, and everyone cooks delicious sides." Duncan watched her neutrally and she hesitated. "Anyway, they're great. So much fun."

He gave a curt nod. "It sounds like it."

Nick was beginning to like Duncan Jamison. He hadn't wanted to like the man, given that he was obviously the competition, but something about him said, *what you see is what you get*.

In the south everyone was friendly and fun but often left you wondering where you stood. Since he'd first seen the man, Duncan had been pretty straightforward and obvious about where Nick stood with him, and Nick couldn't help but respect that fact. Though he had started the conversation to get under the man's skin, where Sylvie was concerned, he had to admit it was refreshing to see someone who wasn't afraid to be honest about what he felt.

Sylvie stood suddenly. "I need the restroom. I'll be right back." Duncan stood as if to follow her, but she gave him an exasperated look.

"I'll be fine to go alone, Duncan."

He didn't look like he bought it but he nodded and then held the gun out to her. "Take this with you at least."

Nick raised an eyebrow at that. He couldn't imagine Sylvie shooting anyone. To his surprise, she nodded and took it and even looked like she knew how to use it. He blinked. "Do you even know how to handle that thing? Don't shoot yourself."

She laughed softly and gave him a cagey little smile. "I think I can handle it." Then she turned on her heel and strode up the stairs.

Duncan paced the room once impatiently before coming to a stop in front of Nick's chair. Idly, Nick wondered if he was expecting him to stand and fight. He settled deeper in the chair. The man in front of him was not only tall but broad and he looked strong. Between that and the fact that he had fought off a killer who had opted to run away instead of stay and face him, Nick was feeling un- inclined to take him on. He struck a purposely casual smile and looked up at Duncan.

Duncan Jamison watched him intently. He looked as though he was trying to make up his mind about something and then, finally, he sighed and took a deep breath. "I am just going to assume that you are one of the many men that Sylvie has been stringing along." When Nick didn't disagree, he nodded. "I prefer honesty over games so I'm just going to give it to you straight. I intend to marry her and build a home with her." He gave Nick a challenging look as though he thought he might get an argument out of him.

Nick gave him a sly grin and shrugged. "Whatever Sylvie wants is fine with me."

Duncan scowled, and said in a hard voice, "Sylvie, doesn't know what she wants. In the meantime, I do. Keep your hands off her and we won't have a problem."

Nick laughed softly. "You're the straight shooter type, aren't you?" He knew it didn't escape Duncan's notice that he hadn't actually agreed with him. Even if Nick had been inclined to agree with him, which he wasn't, he wouldn't have agreed for the mere fact that he was having too much fun getting under Jamison's skin. He donned a cocky grin. "I suspected as much, but man you really just laid down the law," Nick drawled lazily.

Duncan didn't smile, or grin. He relaxed his pose intentionally, to give anyone watching him the idea that he was harmless. His blue eyes went cold and serious as he nodded. "Call it an old safety habit of mine but I prefer to know that everyone around me understands exactly how I feel about them at any given time." He paused just long enough for effect. "It makes things easier when I break down their doors for payment." He shrugged easily and a chilly smile turned his mouth up. "If you know what I mean."

Nick actually felt his pulse jump a little and he laughed. "You're good, man. You had my attention from the minute you walked up." He held his hands in the air in compromise and said seriously, "I'll honor whatever Sylvie chooses."

Duncan watched him for a long moment and then, realizing it was the best he was going to get, nodded. Then he paced back toward the stairs to look upward as though he couldn't stand being away from Sylvie for another moment.

Feeling pity for him Nick said quietly, "You have it bad for her, don't you?"

Duncan only gave him a cold smile.

Nick was unperturbed. "I can't believe I'm going to say this, but I hope you get to her, man." When Duncan turned a disbelieving look at him, he said seriously, "I have seen many a man fall head first for her over the years and then go through heartache when they realize she isn't ever going to take them seriously. Now, I'm wondering if you aren't a big part of that reason." When Duncan looked only mildly interested, Nick laughed softly. "For both of our sakes I hope you aren't another one of those."

Duncan turned a scathing look at him. "Do you actually expect me to believe that you are hoping she picks me instead of you?"

"Not at all. Sylvie has never made any promises to me though I'll admit I'd settle down with her in a hurry if she wanted that. But you seem like you might have a real shot with her, and I do want to see her happy." He shivered feeling slightly unnerved. "It ain't natural for a woman to go through men the way she does."

That startled a chuckle out of Duncan. He met the hazel gaze of his competition and with an amused grin agreed. "Right! She has been doing that since her sister Elaine went missing in high school. It's almost like she is constantly trying to fill that void with sex but then gets bored, so she looks for her next fix."

Nick stared at Duncan. For not having seen her in so many years he seemed to have a pretty good handle on Sylvie. He nodded. "I think you might be right."

Duncan turned away then and asked in a neutral tone, "You hungry man?"

Nick smiled at his back. "I could use a sandwich or two."

Duncan turned to look at him with one eyebrow raised. "Is that so?"

Nick nodded; the man had offered after all. Duncan gave him an amused grin. "In this house if you want to eat you have to help out," he lied, knowing his mother was likely turning over in her grave at his treatment of their 'guest'.

Nick laughed and stood. "Touché." Then he stuck his hands in his jean pockets and said in a friendly drawl, "Show me the way, Jamison."

Chapter 23

Sylvie needed a moment of quiet. Reliving last night and the reminder that her father was gone was hard, and she spent much longer closed in the bathroom than she'd first intended. Feeling a little guilty she washed her hands quickly and then headed back out. She remembered the gun only when she stepped out of Duncan's bedroom door. Swearing under her breath she hurried back and grasped the weapon in her hand the way Duncan had taught her so many years ago. She nearly ran into Duncan's dad as she came back out. His eyes narrowed in on the gun and then he smiled warmly. "Is there anything I can do for you, dear?"

She shook her head uneasily. Then she smiled. "Thanks, but no. I gotta get back downstairs before the men start a fight."

He gave her a sympathetic nod and rushed around her. She turned and watched him go. As the door closed behind him, she turned back to the stairs with a little shiver. She didn't know if it was because Duncan had told her his father had been strange lately or the fact that she was jumpy, but Arthur made her feel uneasy which in turn made her feel judgmental. She was chiding herself for her unkind thoughts when she got to the empty front room. Her first thought was that they had gone outside to fight, and she smiled at the irrational thought.

This wasn't a western in the eighties. She turned to the sound of deep laughter and her mouth gaped open in surprise. Nick stood next to Duncan at the counter grinning. His jacket was off, and the sleeves of his pink and white striped button down were rolled up to just below his elbows. Duncan handed him a slice of bread and Nick spread mustard and mayo on it before handing it back and switching it for the next as Duncan plopped cheese and thick slices of roast beef, turkey, and ham on top. They worked in absolute synchronicity as though they'd done this every day for the last several years.

Sylvie started moving toward them but then hesitated. She wasn't sure what she had expected, but this was definitely not it. Duncan said something funny to Nick and he threw back his head and laughed even as he spread sauce on another piece of bread and passed it back. It wasn't until Duncan turned a warm grin at the detective that it truly unnerved her. For some reason that she wasn't ready to examine, the fact that he seemed perfectly fine with one of her 'boyfriends', in his house, and was even now apparently okay with his eating with them, had her wondering if she hadn't been reading way too much into his attitude toward her. She swallowed uneasily and cleared her throat.

Both men turned in unison with matching easy grins. Her own forced smile faltered as Nick asked in a cheerful drawl, "Hungry darlin'?"

She nodded her head uneasily as Duncan said quietly, "We're almost done here. If you want to take a seat at the table, we'll be right over."

Sylvie nodded and turned toward the table, but Nick's sarcastic tone had her turning back curiously. "I thought that you have to help if you want to eat in this house."

Sylvie gave him a blank look and Duncan hid a grin. "Right. Hey Sylvie, would you mind setting the table?"

She gave them both a worried look as though they might be insane but nodded and turned toward the kitchen where she knew the plates and silverware resided.

Lunch was bizarrely civil, and Sylvie looked between the two men suspiciously. Duncan gave her a wan smile. "You look like you are expecting the two of us to get in a fight over you, sweetheart."

Sylvie glared at him. "Not at all."

"Good," Nick said drolly from her other side. "Because I like to think that us men are a little more mature than fighting over a friend with benefits."

That really seemed to throw her off her game and Duncan watched as she set her sandwich back down and then moved it around on her plate as though she'd lost her appetite. Irritation crept up unwanted. Had she been hoping that him and Nick would fight over her? He hoped that she wasn't that shallow even though he knew it wouldn't matter if she was. It wouldn't change his mind or what he planned to do.

He noticed she'd set the gun between them on the table and reached over to casually move it to the holster he'd put on his belt. He eyed Nick for a long moment, making up his mind. "If you're going to stay here for a bit, Nick, I might go out and check on a few things. I haven't had a lot of time for the ranch since Sylvie got back."

Nick nodded helpfully. "Sure man, I don't have anywhere to be. Say do y'all have a motel anywhere nearby?"

"Not a chance. Nearest place is about fifty miles out and I wouldn't recommend it," Duncan answered as Sylvie shook her head. He gave himself a pat on the back for being a true gentleman and said with a somewhat genuine smile, "You're welcome to stay here."

That seemed to amuse Nick whose lips twitched, and eyes twinkled as he asked, "What, out in the bunkhouse?"

Duncan laughed and it sounded so warm that Sylvie actually felt heat between her legs. She turned to stare at him imploringly but he either didn't notice or didn't care. "My sister, Jackie, doesn't stay here any more and her room is empty."

Sylvie's stomach sank. Trying not to sound too bitchy she asked,

"Where am I going to stay if he stays in there?"

Duncan put his arm around her shoulders and pulled her into a casual hug. His tone was deliberately light. "With me. Just like last night and the night before and—"

"We get the idea, Jamison," Nick cut in, but he was smiling which confused the hell out of Sylvie.

She stared between them as her mouth gaped open in surprise. "You can't possibly expect me to do, err, ya know…" Her face turned pink with embarrassment as she realized that she'd once again backed herself into a very uncomfortable corner. She glanced at Nick who was grinning in amusement and waiting to see if she would finish her sentence.

Duncan fixed a very studious and concerned smile on her. "Err, ya know, what sweetheart?"

She shrugged uncomfortably. "Never mind."

Both men chortled and Sylvie found for the first time in her life that she wished she had stuck to dating one man at a time. Duncan bent his head and gave her a deep long kiss that she thought she probably should fight. "I love seeing you speechless," he murmured softly and stood, reaching for his hat on a hook behind his head. "You two don't get into any trouble while I'm out." He fixed a rather casual look on Nick and then smiled at Sylvie. "I'll be back in no time at all." He walked into the kitchen and grabbed a bag full of extra sandwiches they'd made before he turned to go.

He stopped at the door and turned back. "Did you bring your service weapon?" he asked Nick.

Nick shook his head. "They sort of frown on that at airports these days." Duncan walked across the room to a door and disappeared inside. He returned a moment later carrying a brown handled revolver. "It's a little old but it'll do the job," he said as he held it out handle first to Nick.

Nick grinned and palmed it. "Thanks cowboy, now I really feel like I'm in the wild, wild, west."

Duncan gave him a dry smile and turned on his heel and walked out the door.

Nick turned to Sylvie who was eyeing him with interest now that Duncan was gone. "What happened while I was in the bathroom? When I left the tension was so thick it could have been cut with a knife and now he's sharing his guns with you?"

Nick gave her his famously charming grin. "You know us boys from the south. We can sweet talk anyone."

Sylvie couldn't help smiling. "I know it. You've done your fair share of sweet talking with me." She almost looked disappointed when she said, "I didn't figure Duncan as the type to go for it though."

Nick turned serious and said very softly, "You're different around him."

She looked baffled and then embarrassed and shook her head. "No, I'm not."

He didn't argue with her as he popped the last of his second sandwich into his mouth and chewed. She was staring at him looking irritated and he chuckled softly. "I think he might be good for you."

Sylvie wasn't about to sit around having a nonsensical conversation with an idiot, so she stood and began clearing the dishes from the table. Nick came over to help her wash them and she found herself having the exact conversation she'd already decided she wasn't going to have. "If I seem different around Duncan. it's probably just because I haven't seen him in so long."

"Right," he said, not sounding at all convinced. He was actually beginning to wonder how he had ever thought that she might one day regard him as more than a friend with certain benefits. His heart hurt a little as he faced the truth. If he'd continued sleeping with her for the next couple of years, he would have only been more hurt when she eventually tired of him, and things would have become strained and awkward with Reagan. He sighed and turned to offer her a small smile. "It's been fun hanging out with you, Sylvie."

She raised one eyebrow. "It sounds like you're breaking up with me, Nick."

He shook his head. "We'll always be family. You know that."

Sylvie turned to face him. "But?"

He shook his head and then gave her a grin to soften his words. "I don't want to be another of your side pieces any more."

She looked offended. "Side pieces?" She held his gaze. "Nick, you must know that you're more to me than that."

He smiled again. "I know, like I said we'll always be family." Confused, and a little hurt she asked, "Is this because I slept with Duncan?"

He shook his head. "I'm not a fool, Sylvie. You told me you didn't do exclusive, and I was okay with it, at first." He hesitated. "When I thought that I had an equal shot with anyone else you might be dating."

Sylvie's eyes shone with tears. "I'm sorry, I didn't realize you were hurting."

Nick chuckled softly. "That's just it, I *was* hurting but not like I should have been as I watched you walk away, knowing that you would be with someone else the next day."

She was completely baffled and getting more impatient by the moment. "Then what exactly *is* the problem?"

He grinned and took the dripping plate from her hand to dry it. "I saw the way you are with *him.* I've always thought that someday maybe you would decide you wanted more than casual, and I could give it to you, but seeing how uncomfortable Jamison makes you feel, I realize that isn't going to happen."

Het sounded impossibly insensible. She groaned. "I don't understand. You're saying that because Duncan makes me uncomfortable you and I shouldn't be together any more? I would think that would give us all the *more* reason to hang out. And I have been perfectly clear with Duncan about my position and he's obviously good with it."

Nick snorted loudly. "Right." Then because he genuinely cared about her and wanted to remain friends, he said gently, "This has nothing to do with Jamison. I'd like to stay friends."

She nodded without hesitation. "Of course."

He breathed easier. "Is my staying here going to cramp your style?"

She gave him a scathing glare and said, "Too soon Nick, too soon." He gave a throaty laugh and Sylvie couldn't help joining in.

After the dishes were clean and dry, he challenged her to a few rounds of poker to try to take her mind off everything that was going on. She agreed but only if they played for bets. Luckily for him the detectives showed up an hour later as she'd already won eighty bucks off him. He pretended grand disappointment as he let them in after checking their badges.

They went over everything in detail, once again verifying Sylvie's original statement. Then they let her know that they were doing an autopsy on her father, and that they would let her know the results.

Nick asked the detectives nearly as many questions as they did. By the time he ushered them out two hours and a pot of coffee later, he had a whole list of questions he intended to discuss with Duncan.

Earlier when they'd told him what had happened, he had still been in shock and now that he was beginning to adjust somewhat, he'd realized that there were a whole lot of unlikely coincidences that he wanted to ask Jamison about.

Chapter 24

Duncan took sandwiches to all three of the hands Jackie had hired. They each in turn thanked him and then proceeded to bite into them as he walked around with them asking about each part of the ranch and how things were going. He saddled up the stallion and took him for a ride. He wasn't confident that the other cowboys could handle him and had warned them not to try. He didn't plan to be gone long, just long enough to give the horse a good workout and then check on the largest of the cattle herds in the south pasture.

He didn't want to leave Sylvie alone too long with Nick Hanlan for several reasons, but the one that bothered him the most was that he was afraid she was going to jump right into bed with the good-looking bastard.

Sure, he'd been taking good care of her in the sexual department, and he tried to be confident about that. The problem was that Sylvie was a wild card. She had always been a wild card. It was what had drawn his very steady and very sensible attention to her from the very beginning.

That last year after Elaine had broken up with him, Sylvie had thrown herself at him. She had worn tight jeans and shorts and added shirts that showed off her midriff and slender waist and had even upon occasion given him winning, even inviting smiles. He had been too well aware of the age gap between him and a daring seventeen-year-old girl that constantly flaunted her sensuality around him. He realized now that that had been the primary reason, he had taken April up on her offer to go out and then later eventually to go to bed.

Sylvie had seemed irritated at him at first when he'd told the three of them that he was seeing April, and now as he thought about it he realized he'd secretly been pleased by her jealousy. She had countered by going out with not one but two of his high school friends that were a couple of grades below him. She had invited them on their hikes, taken them to what had previously been his, Elaine's, Jackie's, and Sylvie's special swimming lake and in general irritated the crap out of him. He remembered that he'd considered crashing one of her swimming dates with Isaac Burnett one day when Jackie had let it slip that Sylvie had taken him to the lake.

Duncan had thought long and hard about showing up at the lake that day. Now, as he looked back, he realized the true reason he hadn't, wasn't because he had not wanted to catch Sylvie in the act of skinny dipping with another guy but had in fact been because he was afraid of what he would have done after he'd sent his old friend packing. Instead, he had called up April and gone to a movie two hours away, just to give himself plenty of time for Sylvie to make it away from the lake.

After that day, she had quit dating again and Duncan wondered if she had only done it with the hope that he would come crash it. He shook his head. The mere thought that she might have liked him that much was egotistical and smug of him, even if he wished it were true. She had gotten quiet after that, saying only that boys were lame and that she didn't want the drama of immature boy romance in her life.

Then his mother had her terrible accident, and everything had changed. For some reason when he'd been at the hospital waiting to hear if she had survived surgery he kept wondering where Sylvie was. She had always shown up for things like that and hung around long after everyone else was gone. She was built like that. Strong. Sensible. She had a will of iron when it came to what she had to give to any situation or friend.

Even when she finally had come to the hospital, it was with her mom and then she had only stayed long enough to give him a tight, teary, hug and tell him to call if he needed anything. He hadn't called her; pride hadn't allowed it in the beginning and then it was his fear that he might give in and take a taste of the light and joy in life that she seemed to exude without even trying.

She was still only seventeen and he had just turned twenty-two. Then her eighteenth birthday came, and right along with that, Elaine had disappeared. He had joined the search parties whenever he could. Times had been busy for him as his father's debilitating mental health had already started to plunge and he was doing most of the ranch work as well as trying to clean up the mess of the financials that had suffered since his own mother's death.

He had seen Sylvie nearly every day during that time, but never for long. People had been coming and going from the Dunlaps' day and night and it seemed that he couldn't buy a moment of quiet to really ask her how she was doing. By the time Elaine's body had been found, school was back in swing, and Sylvie had begun dating again.

She dated nearly every good-looking boy in their school at one time or another, even poor Guy John Ringer who everyone had picked on up to that point. Three dates with the beautiful if a bit detached Sylvie Dunlap had fixed his reputation and Duncan found himself wondering if that was why she had done it.

As her graduation neared, things with him and April had become strained, and she began to accuse him of still having a thing for poor, dead Elaine. It was so far from the truth that he had actually sneered at her comment, instead of taking the time to reassure her.

Then Sylvie and Jackie started hanging out again, something they hadn't done much since Elaine's death and he had once again found himself getting up while it was still dark to get his work done so that he could join them from time to time. Sylvie was different, however. Where she had once smiled brightly in hopes for all the great things their futures had to offer, she had become withdrawn and quiet. She was still her usual intelligent and competitive, witty self but underneath it all was a serious girl who didn't really look at the world the same way.

He'd been sad when she left without saying goodbye. And then shortly after he'd been happy for her. He'd hoped she was off somewhere having the time of her life and finding that deep, deep light that she'd lost. Over the years he had considered getting her number and calling, but what would he say? Hey Sylvie, it's Duncan Jamison, yeah you know the one, the one who never kissed you, or held you or went skinny dipping with you.

Needless to say, he'd talked himself out of it and focused on the success of the ranch. It had thrived and other women had come and gone throughout the process. He'd looked for love, wanted what Jackie and Ren had. Something stable and steady. Something a man could really count on.

Then Sylvie had called to say she was coming home. He'd been surprised at first, shocked even that she had called him and not one of the other many boy toys she'd had through high school or even Jackie who had kept in touch, if only through email and social media. But she had called him, and he had begun thinking of all the things he'd wanted from her back then. He had begun to consider if maybe he could get her into his bed and then somehow maybe even more.

Then she had shown up looking sophisticated and so obviously attached to her new life that he had let it go, nearly as soon as she'd climbed in his truck. She'd sashayed from the airport in white silk, a hand-sewn blouse, and grey slacks, with shoes that looked like a million bucks and showed off her very sexy ankles. She was warm and bright, and she seemed like she was happy. When he'd asked if she had someone special, she'd hedged before finally admitting she occasionally dated but nothing serious. He had immediately thought of high school and those months of watching her flit from boy to boy.

Then she had come on to him, and like the foolish lovesick kid he had once been, he had given in to the temptation to kiss her and hold her. She'd smelled like fresh rain and flowers, and he began envisioning a lifetime of having her there with him, until the cold reality sunk in that she merely wanted a quick meaningless fling that would be over as soon as he dropped her back at the airport.

His body had demanded he accept whatever she offered, but his heart and head told another story. One of spending long months, years even trying to forget her taste and smell and light. It was then that he realized he loved her, maybe had always loved her. He wondered idly if even Elaine had sensed that. She had constantly accused him of not being invested enough in her even as she was the one who broke up to be with someone else.

When he'd been at Jackie's that night, watching Sylvie laugh and talk, with her brown eyes shining brightly as though she knew every secret you had before you might possibly discover that secret yourself, he'd known it was too late. There was nothing he could do about it but hope that somehow, some way, she might miraculously realize that she felt the same way. So, he'd kissed her there, had intended to take her home to his bed until she'd insisted on going back to her own damned house.

When she'd been shot and he thought she might die, he'd wanted to hold her hand and go into the dark oblivion right alongside her. But there was the ranch, and Jackie and the twins and he couldn't afford to think that way. So, he'd manned up and dealt with the situation as best he could.

Now, as he stared out over the herd of cattle, at his tremendous financial success, he felt nothing. Nothing but numbness. There was nothing here for him now, he realized. There really had never been anything here for him except the fact that no one else had seemed inclined to pick up the pieces and find a way to put Jackie through college. His father had been around of course, though never fully present and now he, Duncan Rayne Jamison, had one of the largest, most successful and sought-after ranches in the state of Idaho, when he'd never even wanted to be a rancher. He laughed coldly at the irony of that realization.

Then he thought of Jackie. Jackie who had always loved these mountains. Jackie who had always dreamed of someday running the Jamison brand.

A wide smile filled his face. He bent and scratched the stallion's head between his ears. "What do you think, huh?" he asked, though he didn't really expect an answer. The horse shifted beneath him anxiously, and Duncan laughed again even as he reached for his cell phone. This pasture was high enough that he got okay service here. He patted the stallion again. "Me too buddy. Me too."

Lifting the phone, he hit one of his speed dials. When she picked up on the other end he said cheerfully, "Good morning, sis. How would you like to take over running the ranch for good?"

Chapter 25

Sylvie found herself beginning to worry about Duncan when he didn't come back until well after dark. She was disgusted with herself for even noticing but admitted that now that Nick had been clear that all he wanted was to be friends, Duncan was the only man focus she could really have.

She was still a bit baffled by Nick's rather odd reaction to her, since coming here. She wasn't angry at him; she had always genuinely liked him and his naturally charming, good looks. He was, in fact, one of her favorite hangs back in North Carolina, which was the only reason she had tried to talk him out of his decision.

She wondered if he had met someone he wanted to be exclusive with, and that thought brought a warm smile to her lips. He deserved someone who could give him love, joy and a house full of babies. His family was one of the warmest, most fun-loving groups of people she'd ever had the pleasure of meeting, and when she thought of him years into the future it was always him with a house full of kids, cherished and loved by all.

She herself had long ago realized *that* life wasn't for her. She had wanted it at one time, even ached for it, long ago. She'd wanted that kind of obsessed connection that two people seemed to have when they were willing to let go of everything else and embrace only each other. Her sensible streak had finally helped her to realize that she would never have that. She had tried to give that kind of devotion to a couple of guys, but in the end, they had been frustrated and angry with her and accused her of always holding back, which she'd felt was unjust since she had tried to give everything to the relationship.

After the second one ended bitterly with an old school mate, Mark Whittaker, telling her that she was a cold bitch who obviously didn't have a heart, she'd sensibly taken to casual.

Casual worked for her. It was simple, so long as she was clear and upfront with them that she was also seeing other men. They could hang when it worked, have sex when the mood struck and then Monday morning when her busy schedule rolled back around, she would walk out their door feeling ready to take on the world. With most it worked well, even with Nick it had been easy. Yet now here he was, obviously ready for something more and she couldn't blame him, he deserved that more.

Her heart ached for an instant, as yet another one of her 'friends' found something they wanted with enough intensity to say no to all the other options. She tipped her chin onto her hand against the table as she wondered idly if she would ever find that. With a loud sigh, she let the thought go. She had already been down that road and it hadn't turned out well at all. The best thing she could do for herself, and others, was to know her limits and be clear about them.

"Fifty for your thoughts," Nick said in a quiet amused tone and Sylvie knew it was his naturally irritated instinct, that had made him use that particular number, since she'd been winning most of their hands since they'd sat at the table earlier.

She smiled. "Only fifty?" she asked with one eyebrow up.

He cocked a carefully crafted look of self-disgust and said, "Fifty is all I've got left after what you've taken off me today."

Sylvie laughed and the warm sound of it washed over the room, making him wonder if he'd made a mistake by ending things between them. She pulled a stash of twenties from her pocket and held it out. "We could always just play for candy or something."

His southern upbringing would never have allowed him to go back on the deal and she knew it. Still, she couldn't resist teasing him. Besides it wasn't as though he couldn't afford it. Though a good many of his family, including two of his brothers, three of his cousins, one uncle, and an aunt were all cops, they also all had an uncanny knack of opening side businesses that were lucrative enough to more than make up the difference of their modest salaries.

He gave a dramatic groan as he glared at the thick wad of cash in her long slender fingers. "As you well know a deal, is a deal, is a deal," he complained. He really didn't care about the money; it was more of a pride thing at this point.

"Maybe if Duncan ever comes back in then you can win some of his hard-earned money." She tried to reassure him under her fluttering lashes.

He cocked one eyebrow at her third mention of Duncan Jamison.

"You worried about him?" he asked in a neutral tone.

Sylvie shook her head. "No, it just seems strange. Since I've been here, he hasn't hardly left my side and yet now that you're here then he takes off for…" she turned to the clock on the wall to estimate the time. "Eight hours now." She didn't really need Duncan here, it was just that she was starting to suspect that maybe now that Nick had come here, Duncan was no longer feeling it necessary to take care of her. The darker side of her brain worried about the way bodies seemed to be dropping around her if something had happened to him too. She bit her lip.

"I'm sure something just came up and he'll come walking in, with that hat of his ready to sweep you away." His tone was wry, and she turned to stare at him in curiosity. It was a side of him she hadn't seen. He almost sounded jealous.

She shook her head. Nick had broken up with her, not the other way around. Her mind turned back to Duncan, and she bit her lip again. "It's just that the killer could be out there," she said softly. "It could be anyone. Since we now know it wasn't Zack, there is no telling what kind of creep is out there—" she broke off as a shiver ran down her spine.

Frustration seeped in as she wondered who was systematically trying to hunt her. Her head throbbed again, and she lifted a hand to massage her temples. She was normally so quick when it came to such things and yet now that someone was here and after *her*, she couldn't seem to come up with a single decent idea of who might want her dead.

Nick reached out a hand and grasped hers. "It's going to be okay, Sylvie."

She nodded and fought off the tears that once again threatened her eyelids. She hadn't shed a single tear in two years, since her mother's funeral, and yet since she had come back to Idaho it seemed that she couldn't get her emotions in check. She nodded and leaned her head on his shoulder so he wouldn't see the tears that were threatening to well over.

The front door opened, and Duncan walked in with a wide happy smile on his ruggedly handsome face. He turned toward the kitchen and saw them there sitting at the table. Sylvie blinked as the warm smile that had taken five years off his age turned cold and slowly disappeared. Something undefinable flashed there in his eyes and he turned on his heel and headed up the stairs without a word.

She stared after him looking worried and bit her bottom lip. Then she turned to Nick. "Do you think he has a problem with poker?"

Nick offered her a wide gentle smile and shook his head. "I don't think he even realized we were *playing* poker," he said quietly.

Sylvie stared at him for a moment and then stood. "What else could it have been?"

Nick hid his amused grin. "I wonder the same thing."

Duncan was in the shower when Sylvie got upstairs and rather than wait to talk to him until he got out, Sylvie let herself inside. "Duncan? Are you in here?" she called, just on the off chance it might be someone else.

She heard him swear low and under his breath before he said roughly,

"Go away and come back later."

Worried as well as completely baffled by his unusual attitude, she asked gently, "Is everything okay, someone else didn't get hurt, did they?"

He snorted. "Would you really care?"

She felt like he'd slapped her, but she held her ground. "What the hell kind of question is that? Of course, I care," she said more bitterly than she'd intended.

He poked his soapy head out of the shower and gave her a small smile. "It's nothing. Go downstairs and I'll be down in a bit." He almost sounded apologetic, but his voice was so casual that she couldn't really tell.

More determined than ever to get to the bottom of what was obviously bothering him, she plunked down on the toilet seat. "I can wait."

She thought she might have heard another swear word but the water running over his face muffled the sound. He took several more minutes and Sylvie was beginning to wonder if he was trying to wait her out when he finally turned off the shower and shoved the curtain aside. His naked skin was slick and wet, and she could see drops of water running down his Adonis body. She swallowed as her stomach clenched and wet heat surged to her core. She followed the line of his dark hair down his chest to the downward vee at his hips and then shivered as she watched his manhood surge and grow with surprising speed as she stared at him.

He swore savagely and reached for a towel knotting it around his waist and covering his erection. "What the hell is wrong with you?" he spat, giving her a look of such disgust as he walked past, that Sylvie actually began wondering if she'd done something she shouldn't have. She couldn't think of anything, but there was obviously something very, very wrong since she had never in all her years known Duncan Jamison to act this way. She offered him a weak trembling smile. "I'm sorry," she began in a voice carefully devoid of emotion. "Have I done something that bothered you?"

He turned to stare at her coldly. "I imagine not, in your playbook."

She wasn't sure where to take that, so she squared her shoulders and followed him out and into the bedroom. "At the risk of making whatever transgression I've made, worse, would you mind telling me what I've done that has so obviously pissed you off?"

He stomped toward the closet, and she watched the muscles in his back contract. At the door he turned back and bit out, "Do you honestly expect me to fall into bed with you only hours after you have left Nick Hanlan's bed?"

A small laugh escaped her lips before she could stop it and Sylvie slapped a hand over her mouth. His brows went up and his blue eyes went from angry to icy cold. He looked her up and down critically and then in a very soft, very cold voice said, "You're a great lay sweetheart, but even I know the risk of getting an STD from someone who loves to play musical beds."

She felt as though he'd stripped her naked and then gave her a sound spanking on her bare ass. Anger spiked but she swallowed it even as tears filled her eyes and to her great mortification began falling down her cheeks. She wrapped her arms around her middle and turned her face down to say, "I'm sorry you feel that way. I won't bother you any more." Then she squared her shoulders before she could lose her nerve and walked quickly to the doorway out of the bedroom.

He caught her three steps later. Wrapping his arms around her from behind he bent down and in a hoarse voice he whispered, "I'm sorry." Then he leaned his head down and kissed her neck. "That was unkind, uncalled for and certainly not fair."

She swallowed the lump of emotion in her throat even as a shiver of anticipation at his kiss on her neck had her shoulders trembling. She turned to look up at him and another shiver washed over her at the look in his eyes. Unsure why she felt obliged to share with him, since he had been a complete ass to her, she said quietly, "I didn't sleep with Nick, Duncan."

At his disbelieving and challenging look, she amended. "At least not today."

That seemed to pacify him, and he lowered his head to take her mouth in a deep hungry kiss. He had missed her today and now he felt like he was

drowning in the sweetness that was her. He closed his eyes and arched his head back. "I think you just might be the death of me, Sylvie Dunlap."

She wiggled against his erection, and he groaned and leaned down to take her mouth in his again. She sidestepped the kiss and stared up at him. "I'm not sure how you thought *I* would have the energy to have sex with Nick after how many times you have had me this morning. Good god, Duncan, I'm not Aphrodite."

He gave her a reluctant grin. "Well, sue me if it seems like having all those boyfriends might sort of make you exactly like the freakin' goddess of sex. All those horny, needy men given the tincture of life by one very sexy, very beautiful, and very intelligent woman." He shook his head in exasperation.

Sylvie's next words had his heart thumping wildly and his cock jumping to attention. "To be honest, all *I* want right now is one very specific, very erotic, and very talented man in my bed."

He took her into his arms and began the slow tormenting process of winning her over. She complained, of course, trying to urge him to take things a bit faster, but he retaliated by moving his mouth from its moist target to nibble and bite gently at the tingling skin of her inner thigh. With a moan she gave herself over to the pleasure of his torturous lovemaking.

Chapter 26

Nick was fully engrossed in the files the detectives had dropped off as per his lieutenant's request when Sylvie and Duncan finally came down. He noticed Duncan's possessive hand on her waist as they made their way to the table where he was. It was obvious that they had made up by the shine in Sylvie's cheeks and Duncan's easy relaxed smile. He looked up and gave them both a friendly smirk. "Is all well in paradise, again?"

Sylvie blushed and turned toward the kitchen. She was starving. Duncan had taken his sweet time making her beg for what she was now beginning to crave. He made her crazy with wanting him. It was a whole new experience for her. This cathartic, needy desire that lasted forever, in which she felt like she was being taken on a roller coaster of need and lust that sapped all of her energy. It also made her stomach rumble. "Are you guys hungry?" she asked as she rounded the corner into the kitchen.

Both men nodded but she didn't see them. She peeked around the pile of newspapers to peer at them. "Uh, hello?"

Both Duncan and Nick looked up at her with matching irritated looks.

"Do you guys want something to eat?" she persisted.

They both nodded silently again, and Sylvie turned to the refrigerator. She had a sneaking suspicion that she had just been nominated to make their dinner. She looked through the fridge and the cupboards, but they were looking a little sparse. There were no potatoes and the only vegetables that she saw were a large tub of mixed greens and some grape tomatoes. There were also steaks in the fridge. Making the executive decision, she pulled out a cast iron griddle and set it on the gas stove top. She seared three steaks to make some version of a sliced steak salad with a creamy garlic dressing that would taste delicious with a side of thick garlic toast and a piece of apple pie, which she'd found in the freezer ready to bake.

Nick and Duncan sat at the table looking through what the police had found so far, which wasn't much. They still hadn't found the initial spot where the shooter had been, nor had they found any evidence in the house that wasn't expected. Both Duncan and Sylvie had given them a list of all the fingerprints that would have likely been found at the house and they hadn't found any other fingerprints or for that matter DNA

Duncan groaned in frustration. "Something has got to give," he told Nick in frustration. "I swear, if I had the skills, I would do the DNA tests and fingerprints myself."

Nick laughed quietly. "I hear you, but these things take time. It really is just a matter of patience." He gave Duncan a small smile but at his intense frown, Nick sighed. "It's really only a matter of one tiny mistake and we'll get the guy."

Duncan nodded even as he went over every tiny piece of evidence in the files once more. Frustrated, he raked fingers through his wavy dark hair. He was about to start at the beginning again when Sylvie informed them that dinner was ready.

His basic instincts for manners overcame his need to search the files yet again for anything he may have missed. He smiled and nodded at her and then rose to set the table. His eyebrows went up as Sylvie hauled in plates loaded with greens and fresh veggies with a perfectly sliced medium steak fanned across the top and a wide chunk of garlic bread on the side.

He sniffed in appreciation taking in the garlic and herb seasoned steak even as Nick followed her in with an apple pie that was still steaming from the oven. She disappeared again but returned a moment later with two beers and an opened bottle of wine. "This looks great, Sylvie, thank you," he said and meant it. One brow in the air sardonically, he asked, "When did you learn to cook?"

She laughed softly but then shrugged, giving him a cagey grin,

"Probably right around the time that you did."

That was a fair point, and he chuckled under his breath. "Touché." Last time he'd seen her cook it was mac and cheese from a box and even that had only been barely edible. He took a tentative bite of steak with greens, and in complete surprise, the flavors burst into his mouth making him lean back and close his eyes. "Damn, that really is good, sweetheart."

Silence greeted his comment, and he opened his eyes to find Sylvie staring at him, obviously a little offended by his lack of trust. Nick Hanlan was giving him a knowing, amused smile. It was apparent that he was now in trouble with Sylvie.

She tossed her hair over one shoulder and picked up her own fork.

"Don't sound so surprised, Jamison. I could cook you some of the tastiest dishes you've ever had. And don't even get me started on my own best fried chicken recipe."

Because he must have a death wish he raised one brow. "I have never really cared much for frie—" He cut off at Nick's warning shake of his head. "What I meant to say is that I would love to try it sometime."

Her eyes had narrowed but as he finished, she smiled. "I'll make it sometime for you."

Feeling like he had just barely avoided walking through a field of land mines he gave Nick an appreciative smile and a nod. Sylvie saw it, but to Nick's credit, he was busy taking a cold swig of beer by the time Sylvie looked at him.

Duncan speared another bite of steak and salad with a dark spicy sauce drizzled over the top before he could say anything else stupid. He bit into the garlic toast which was crispy and warm and had some sort of white cheese melted on top. Yes, he thought with a small grin, Sylvie Dunlap had definitely learned to cook.

For a man who had done the majority of the cooking in his house for his father and sister over the last several years, it was a nice change to have someone else cook a decent meal. Jackie had, of course, learned to cook though not until after she had left home, but Arthur Jamison was a terrible cook on the rare occasions he had actually tried. Determined not to say anything more, Duncan bit into another hot tender bite of steak.

When dinner was done and cleaned up, Sylvie poured yet another glass of wine and sat on the sofa. Duncan and Nick came in as they finished the dishes. As Nick walked past the bar he asked quietly, "What is all this about?"

Duncan shrugged and made his way to sit beside Sylvie, putting his arm around her shoulders and pulling her close. "It's my dad's stuff. He doesn't like me to touch it."

Nick stared at the stacks and stacks of newspapers thoughtfully. Then he sat across from the sofa, a beer in hand. "What does he do with them?" he asked conversationally.

Duncan looked a little uncomfortable, but he answered, "Nothing, as far as I can tell."

Sensing Duncan's discomfort, Nick let it go. Sylvie leaned back against Duncan's shoulder and then finally ready to cope, asked quietly, "What did they find out about my dad?"

Duncan squeezed her shoulders. "Nothing much yet."

Sylvie sat up straight. "No DNA? Or fingerprints? Or boot prints?" She looked incredulously at Nick and then Duncan. "How is that even possible?"

Nick leaned forward wanting to comfort her even as he realized it was no longer his job. "This happens sometimes Sylvie, you know that," he said gently. "How many cases have you tried that were thrown out or you couldn't prosecute because of lack of evidence?"

She looked stricken and Duncan pulled her close and held her. In a lethal murmur of conviction he promised, "I will find the bastard and handle it, you have my word."

With tears in her eyes, Sylvie looked up at him feeling worried. "I think you need to stay out of this Duncan. Look what could have happened to you last night. You could have died." She swallowed and took a deep breath before continuing. "If that man had gotten the gun…" Her voice wobbled and she shook her head. "I don't want you dead because of me."

Duncan took her chin gently and turned her face up to meet those deep blue eyes of his. "I can handle it." His voice was hard and unrelenting. She started to shake her head again. "I *will* handle it," he vowed with quiet finality. Then he lowered his head to kiss the tears on each of her cheeks.

Nick cleared his throat and Duncan turned to stare at him with a pleased masculine smile. Nick smiled right back. "The thing I've been wondering," he said in a thoughtful tone, "is how a small-town cowboy like yourself seems to be taking all of this death and intrigue, not to mention physical attacks and gunfire, in stride." His gaze hardened a little as he held Duncan's steady gaze. He saw a flash of irritation combined with admiration before the man holding Sylvie hid it.

With a casual shrug of nonchalance Duncan replied softly, "I was hunting by the time I was eight with my dad and I care about Sylvie." As though that explained it all.

Nick nodded. "I get that, but we all know that dealing with death when it comes to people versus animal is a whole different story."

Sylvie nodded but Duncan gave him a silent warning look that only made Nick's curiosity grow. He didn't think Duncan wanted to harm Sylvie of course. It would have been obvious to a blind man that Duncan Jamison had a bad case of the feeleys when it came to her. It was just that something about the man and the way he handled himself seemed off somehow for a cowboy from the sparsely populated mountains of Idaho.

Chapter 27

Patience was not his strong suit. He had to keep reminding himself to take a breath and wait it out. He watched them from a distance, ate, pissed, and watched them some more. He watched for a chance. Any chance. He was beginning to be seriously worried that Sylvie was going to compromise him and his position.

Once, he had seen her walk upstairs alone at the Jamison house and had considered trying to get to her there. It was risky with all the men in the house with her though and he'd hesitated. Then the moment was gone, and he vowed that next time he would be ready.

He reached for his mug and took another hot slug of black coffee. Acid burned through his stomach, and he reached automatically for the antacid tablets he always kept nearby. He'd needed them more and more often this past year. Even as the acid settled a little, he watched as impatience had him splitting his top lip in a grimace.

He'd hoped since that fucker Nick Hanlan had come, that he might have a better shot at her. Hanlan had obviously had a thing with her, and Duncan couldn't possibly intend to bed her even as her boyfriend slept nearby, could he?

His lips curled in a dirty grin. If Duncan Jamison actually had the balls to do that, then he had to admit that he had sorely underestimated him.

His loins tightened as Sylvie leaned into Duncan on the couch and he imagined her skin touching his, with his hands on her throat, tightening, tightening ever tighter. He closed his eyes and swallowed.

Then he remembered the girls from the rest stop and felt the familiar stirrings. It would have to hold him over until he could have her. After all, he'd already had her sister, years ago, but still the memory was sweet. He'd been naive back then and hadn't killed her right away. Even as he'd reveled in taking Elaine there on the mountain, he'd squeezed her throat. Elaine had fought and then eventually blacked out. He'd thought she was dead until she came back to him kicking and screaming as she fought for the life that she now knew was slipping away moment by moment.

The cliff had been an accident of sorts. He had wanted to take her with his hands, but she had landed a rather solid kick against his groin, and he'd seen red. There was a cliff looming out there behind her and he had smiled gently at her and shoved her off. He could still hear the sound of her long-lived scream as he'd rushed to the edge watching as her body tumbled like a rag doll and then finally splintered down at the bottom.

He'd hiked down afterward, grateful that he'd used a condom when he had considered not doing so at first. He wiped her body and cleaned her nails taking extra care not to disturb her more than necessary. It would only rouse suspicion about the way she'd died. Then he'd prayed for rain. Rain to wash away any potential DNA that he might have missed. His prayers had been answered months later when the case went cold for lack of evidence. And even though one detective had suspected foul play due to slight bruising on the collar bone, they had eventually closed the case and officially declared it an accident. Sylvianna Dunlap was the only loose end. He opened his eyes. Dark, empty eyes. Now, there was only Sylvie.

Sylvie who had seen him, and even now could blow everything up in his face if she wanted to. *If she dared to*, his mind taunted. He'd warned her back then. Told her to never look back. He'd thought she must have listened until she came back home and hiked up that damned mountain again.

Back then, he hadn't realized just how thrilling the kill could be or he'd never have waited. In truth, the only reason he hadn't gone after her these past years was because he had been busy. Very, very busy. He hadn't wanted to take the time away from his work to go hunt her down. Since she hadn't spoken up, he assumed she wasn't going to and left her, and the possible can of worms going after her could open, alone.

Chapter 28

Jackie rubbed a hand across her aching back even as she bent over the tub again to finish scrubbing Olivia's hair. "That's it baby, just let me finish rinsing it and we'll get you out," she murmured to her daughter who was crying in outrage at having her hair washed. It'd had peas and rice from dinner smeared through it and Jackie didn't have the luxury of waiting until the following morning.

She finished and helped Olivia out, gently wrapping a white towel with a rainbow unicorn on the hood around her daughter who was slowly starting to calm. She took one hand in hers and led her out of the bathroom snagging Ariana's hand in her other as they walked past. Ariana had a pink and black Minnie mouse towel with big ears on the hoodie and her grinning face made Olivia pucker up again.

Jackie was exhausted more than normal tonight. She was still a few weeks away from her due date but each day taking care of the girls, coupled with her worry for Sylvie and Duncan, ended with exhaustion. To make matters worse, Ren had called to let her know he was going to be late nearly every night this week.

He'd also had a couple of emergency calls from his crew that had taken him out in the middle of the night for several hours at a time. He had apologized, of course; he knew how hard it was on her. She tried to let that be enough as she fought to get pajamas on the girls. Her phone rang and she reached for it automatically, though she paused to take a deep breath before answering. It seemed like lately every time the thing rang there was more bad news. She smiled as the picture of Ren came up. "Hi, baby."

Ren sounded washed out even as he tried to talk with enthusiasm.

"How are all my ladies?"

Jackie smiled happily; he could have that effect on her. Even after five years together she melted inside at the love and tenderness there in his deep voice. She teared up unexpectedly. "We are all good."

He was quiet for a moment, then said, "You sound tired and emotional sweetheart. Are you sure you're okay?"

Jackie tucked the phone under her ear and reached for Ariana pulling a long pink sleep shirt over her head. "I'm okay, I promise. Just a little wrung out."
"I was calling to say that I might be working late again but if you need me home, I'll come right now."

"Don't do that Ren, I know how hard you have been working to get this job done so that you can take time to be with us when the baby comes. Keep working, I'll be fine."

Ren hesitated for a long minute in indecision. Finally, he said, "Can I say goodnight to the girls? I'll try to finish up here by ten, maybe eleven." Then he said softly, "If you need me before then just text or call and I'll be on my way." She agreed and put the phone on speaker and set it between the girls.

As Ren talked to them, Olivia told her father all about how mean her mother had been. Jackie took the opportunity to put away dirty clothes, hang the damp towels on the rack and get their toothbrushes ready for them. When she returned, they were just saying goodbye to their dad, so she said goodbye as well and hung up. She had some important things to talk to him about and so she was determined to wait until he got home to go to sleep.

The girls went down surprisingly easy after only two storybooks. She turned on the small rotating nightscape light and gave them each a kiss on their rosy sleeping cheeks. She made her way to the kitchen and put away what was left of dinner after putting a plate together for Ren. At nine thirty she cleaned the kitchen and swept up the peas and rice that the girls had ended up throwing at each other. Then she walked through the house quietly picking up stray blocks and toys, that were just a side product of having toddlers in the house.

Just after ten she went to their shared bedroom and took a soothing shower with the door open so she could hear if one of the twins woke up. She took a few extra minutes to rub cream into her tight belly and the rest of her body because it was nearly eleven and Ren still wasn't home. At eleven a text came in that he was still going to be a while. She sighed and gave in to the temptation to slide under the thick silver pleated duvet onto the thick pillow top mattress. She tried to stay awake and just rest her tired body but finally drifted off at twelve with the bedside lamp still on.

She didn't even know how late it was when Ren finally climbed into bed with her. When he did, she rolled over to snuggle against his hard, warm body and with a contented sigh was back out.

Chapter 29

After dinner and a night cap, Nick began questioning Duncan. He asked about the gun left on the stairs. He thought that was a strange reaction for someone who'd wanted Sylvie dead bad enough to break in with a cop in the house and kill him in order to get to her. Duncan agreed with Nick, and Sylvie chimed in but only to remind them that Duncan had beat him up and maybe, just maybe he hadn't wanted to take another beating.

She was right of course, but Duncan's gut said something different, and he could tell as he met Nick's hazel gaze that the cop agreed. They talked about the likelihood that it was someone from Sylvie's past in North Carolina. Nick assured him that they were looking into every person who had flown from N.C. to Idaho since Sylvie had and whether or not they had any link to her. It was Sylvie that finally voiced another option. Duncan noticed she rubbed at her temples even as she said it. "What if it's someone who was here already?"

His gaze sharpened and everyone in the room heard the sharp intake of breath as he sucked it in. "Is there something that happened that you haven't told us?"

She shook her head and he rubbed his fingers into the back of her neck. Duncan went automatically to the cupboard and returned with a handful of aspirin and a bottle of water. She took them gratefully and laid her head back against the seat, closing her eyes to wield off the spots of color and lights that made her vision splotchy. "I swear to God, I don't know who is doing this!"

Duncan took her hand in his own. "What about these headaches? How long have you been getting high grade migraines?" He sounded worried,

Sylvie opened one eye to look at him through the dark lashes. "I don't know. I guess since I got here. I used to get them a lot after Elaine died and then for a couple of years after I took off to school but eventually, they quit bothering me so much. The doctor said it was probably unbalanced hormones or something I lacked in my diet," she added unhelpfully.

Duncan frowned and squeezed her hand. "I'm worried about you. I think maybe we should take you into town to see the doc tomorrow and make sure it isn't a bad side effect of being shot."

Sylvie sat up and forced her eyes open. "No, it isn't, remember? I got one when we were hiking before I ever even got shot."

Duncan remembered Sylvie screaming and tackling him to the ground as though he was in grave danger. His first instinct then had been to roll on top, to protect her beneath his body. He nodded. Then as the desperation began to fill him that they wouldn't be able to stop the killer in time to save her, he stood abruptly. "I need to make a phone call. I'll be right back," he said tightly.

Both Nick and Sylvie watched his back as he left the room. She turned back and met Nick's curious look with her own raised eyebrow. "What's up with him?" Nick asked.

As if she had any clue how or what Duncan Jamison was thinking. She gave him a glare. "How should I know? Maybe he's tired of feeling like it's his job to keep me alive." She chuckled desperately at the end.

She had been doing everything she could to show everyone that she was strong, and that it didn't really matter that someone was systematically trying to kill her. Her hands shook a little, so she folded them together and laid them in her lap.

Nick raised a brow but didn't smile. "Are you doing okay?" he asked gently.

She nodded and blinked back the tired, overwhelmed, tears that threatened to spill over. For a week now, she had gone from feeling the pressure of coming home to facing secrets and demons she hadn't been ready to face. Then being shot and living through that only to have her father killed because he'd been seen as a protector to her. Duncan was the only reason she was still sane at all, and she looked back toward the stairs where he had disappeared.

Suddenly Nick was there next to her, and he pulled her into his strong arms. The words he murmured against her hair made her heart ache. "Just because we aren't sleeping together any more doesn't mean we aren't friends."

She swallowed and leaned against his warm chest, nodding. She lay that way for several long minutes before she got control of the tears and pulled back. Then she squared her shoulders and faced him. "Okay,

Detective. Let's do this. I think it's about time for me to get my head in the game and figure out who this bastard is."

He nodded and grinned at her. "There's that famous grit that I remember.."

Chapter 30

Duncan pulled his phone from his pocket and stabbed at the screen as he closed the bedroom door behind him. When the voice on the other end picked up sounding frustrated, he grinned. "Hello Jon. I need you to do something for me."

The other end of the line was quiet for a long time before a man's deep voice sighed and asked, "Jamison?"

Duncan chuckled softly. "Yeah. It's me."

Agent Jonathan Graham sucked in a breath. "Why are you calling me?"

"I need a favor."

There was another hesitation. "And you believe that I am just going to throw a bone your way?"

Duncan grinned. "That is exactly what I believe." "Fine. What is this favor you need?"

"I have a list of people that I need profiles done on. Someone close to me is in danger and one of the names on the list has to be the murderer."

"What's in it for me?"

Duncan laughed. "The case could be big news afterward and you could get involved and make the FBI look good."

"How many names are we talking about?" Agent Graham asked.

"There are fifty-two prominent names and five that I'm fairly sure aren't involved but I'd like a profile done just to make sure."

"Jesus, Jamison that will take a whole team of profilers. You know I can't use department resources for personal use."

Duncan shrugged. "Then don't. Open a case file. Hell, I don't care how you make it work, Jon. Just do it."

Another long pause. "Who is the target?"

Duncan played his ace. "Assistant District Attorney Sylvianna Dunlap from Wilmington, North Carolina."

An indrawn breath. "And you said that the perp has already attempted to kill her?"

"Twice. Also, he murdered her father last night and tried to take me out in the process." Having a body on the perp already would go a long way with the agent and Duncan knew it.

"Are you telling me that this could turn into a high-profile case with multiple murders?" Jon asked suddenly, sounding shrewd.

Duncan swore. "No Jon. I'm telling you to fucking help me out with this *before* it turns into a high-profile case with multiple deaths."

The FBI agent sounded properly chastised and in a quiet voice said,

"Fine, send them to me. I'll take a look."

"I already emailed the list while we spoke. Don't wait on this. He won't wait long to come after her again. I can feel it in my gut."

"Sure. I'll get right on it. I just closed a case, so I have some time."
"Thanks Jon. I really do appreciate it."

"Okay, but Duncan…" He let the word trail off.

"Yeah?"

"Why don't you just do them yourself?"

Duncan swore low and then said through his teeth, "Because, *I* have been very busy doing everything I can to keep the damn girl alive."

"Got it. You'll hear from me as soon as I have anything. You need me to see about sending some agents out to babysit her?"

"No." Duncan clicked off the call without another word and walked silently back downstairs. He froze at the bottom and watched with teeth clenched as Nick fucking Hanlan held Sylvie in his arms.

He stepped forward as she finally pulled away and barely heard what she said with quiet conviction. In spite of the red haze that was coursing through his veins, he smiled. Here was the powerful, edgy, determined, prosecutor that he had read so much about over the years. He cleared his throat but only Hanlan backed up a foot.

Sylvie turned to stare up at him. "Where did you go?"

He walked around and gave Nick a cold look as he inserted himself between them on the sofa. Nick held his hands in the air and grinned.

Duncan turned instead to Sylvie. "I just had to make a phone call."

Sylvie nodded. "I've been thinking about it, and I think maybe I should go back home to Wilmington." She watched Duncan's face, fully expecting a fight.

He shrugged. "What good would that do?"

She stared at him feeling a little disappointed. She had expected him to

feel at least a little upset that she was going to leave him. She carefully smoothed out her tone. "I was just thinking that both Nick and I have much better resources there that we can use. The police department here doesn't want to divulge all the information about the case, and I could get it all through higher channels back home. Not to mention that I have other detectives there that I can use to help us out." She watched his thoughtful face for any sign of an argument.

He thought about it for a minute, then said, "I think that it's a good idea. You also might be safer there if the killer really is from around here. Do you know when you will go?"

She swallowed the speech that she had prepared for his argument. Then she looked at Nick who was watching Duncan with an unreadable expression. She shrugged. "As soon as the doctor clears me, but I suspect that he'll do that as soon as I go in." She rolled her shoulder slowly, carefully. "A lot of the pain is beginning to ease."

Nick stood and went for another beer. He held it up in question to Duncan who shook his head. He popped the top and took a swig as he walked back to them. He looked at Jamison and then Sylvie. "I'll fly back with her to make sure she is safe," he offered with a helpful grin.

Duncan nodded curtly. "I think that would be good."

A small look of surprise knitted Nick's forehead. He had fully expected Duncan Jamison to insist on accompanying her himself. He frowned.

Maybe he had misread the man's intentions after all. A tiny surge of hope seeped in. Maybe, just maybe, there was still a chance for him and Sylvie after this mess was cleared up.

Sylvie turned away with a hurt expression at Duncan's quick agreement only to cover it with a small smile at him. Nick swore inwardly because the bastard had hurt her. He gave her a wide comforting grin.

Duncan walked over to his pack and pulled out a laptop. "I guess we'd better get your flights booked."

Sylvie rose and followed slowly behind as he sat at the dining table.

Nick watched for a long minute before rising and going after them.

Five minutes later Duncan looked up and met his eyes. "Flights are all set." He held Nick's gaze with a hard look. "You will keep her safe, won't you?"

Nick nodded and gave him a small grin. There was obviously something that Jamison wasn't telling them. He put it away. He'd ask later when he was alone with him.

Soon afterward, Duncan showed him up to a room that had obviously been attached to a teenage girl. There was a bathroom up the hall that Duncan showed him and then left Nick at the door.

Sylvie was in Duncan's room when he finished showing Nick to Jackie's room and he slipped inside silently, watching her quietly as she fumbled with her bag. His gaze narrowed as he realized she was loading her clothes inside. "What do you think you're doing?" he asked harshly, wondering if she was planning to go join Hanlan in his room. His jaw tightened.

She jumped at his hard tone and then turned to him. She had a very carefully constructed look of nonchalance. "You seemed like you were done with me, so I thought I might stay in one of the other rooms or on the couch."

His throat constricted painfully. "Don't even think about going to Nick's bed." His tone was harder than he'd intended, and he saw anger blaze in her eyes before she looked away.

She squared her shoulders. "I can sleep wherever I damn well please." She picked up a pile of clothes and plopped them into her suitcase with a swift glare at him.

His eyes narrowed dangerously. "Don't try me, Sylvie," he warned coldly.

She turned to him then, her own eyes blazing. "Don't try *you?"* she countered, feeling reckless now that she realized that Duncan didn't really care about her. "My god, do you even hear yourself?" She stomped across the room to get the jacket she'd laid across the chair in the corner. "I told you that I-I'm going back home, and you don't even care." To her horror a tear slid out the corner of one eye and down her cheek.

Duncan's hard expression softened as he caught sight of that tear. He moved to her and took her into his arms. He hadn't dared to hope that she might care what he thought at all yet. This reaction was a very, very good sign. He smiled with his lips against her hair and kissed her cheek. "Of course I care, sweetheart. I've loved having you here." He turned his face down and forced hers up to his to meet his solemn gaze. "I will miss you for every moment until I see you again." He took her mouth in a deep tender kiss. When they were both breathing hard, he pulled back. "But I need you to be safe first and foremost."

That made her smile a little but then a small crease appeared in her forehead. "You will come see me sometime?"

He gave her a pinch on her ass and smiled down at her. "I promise."

She relaxed completely into his arms then and he held her close for a long moment before he began nibbling at her ear and then lower at her neck. A minute later the heaped suitcase and all that was in it tumbled to the floor with a quiet thud as he swiped it aside and lifted Sylvie by her hips to set her gently on the bed. He knelt between her legs and tenderly used his body to show her exactly how he felt because he wasn't ready to say the words yet, and he knew with absolute certainty that she wasn't ready to hear them either.

After their long lovemaking they lay tangled in bed together. He adjusted his angle to rub her shoulders gently as she talked about her life two and a half thousand miles away. He listened and responded with questions or just the quiet uh hmms, that it seemed kept her talking. When she was finally worn out and began dozing, he turned and adjusted so that he could wrap his arm around her slim waist. She curled into him with a sigh, and he murmured quietly just before she dozed off. "I am really going to miss you, Sylvie Dunlap."

Chapter 31

Sylvie woke to an empty bed and the sound of the shower running in the bathroom. She stretched out languorously and rolled over. Then because it was her last day here and she was also going to miss Duncan terribly, though she hadn't told him that, she rose and walked to the bathroom to join him for a shower. He was already soapy, and she stopped just inside the door to watch through the see-through curtain as he turned to smile at her. "Morning sleepy head," he said teasingly and smiled.

Sylvie smiled right back. "Morning. Mind if I join you?"

She had already removed her nightshirt and underwear just in case he needed convincing. He eyed her lithe body and his eyes darkened slightly. "Come on in."

She didn't need a second invite. She stepped inside without another thought and then found herself enfolded against his warm hard, soap slicked body. She sighed and leaned into the embrace. He held her that way for a long while. Even long after his body had lengthened and hardened there against her belly. After a while she started sliding her hands up and down his arms and then his chest. He groaned and turned her under the spray of hot water. She responded by reaching down to wrap her hand around his erection. He jerked and took her mouth in a stormy kiss that had both of them gasping for air a long moment later.

By the time they both emerged together and made their way downstairs, Nick already had breakfast nearly done. He turned and surveyed them both with a wide grin. "Nice of you two to finally come down," he said dryly.

A pink blush worked its way up Sylvie's tanned neckline. She smiled and nodded, "Good morning, Nick."

Duncan swept a look at him but gave only a polite smile and a nod. "Mornin'."

Nick motioned to the coffee pot. "There is fresh coffee." He turned over some hash browns in the frying pan and joked. "I was beginning to worry that all you Idahoans eat was beef and potatoes, but I finally found some bacon and ham at the bottom of the freezer."

Duncan gave him a curt nod. He hadn't come right out and asked Sylvie if she and Nick had kissed last night because he'd been afraid of what he would do if she said yes. Instead, he had done his damnedest to drive her out of her ever-loving mind both last night and this morning, in hopes that whatever steamy kiss they might have shared would be erased from her memory.

The thought of Nick sitting next to her on the long flight home and then possibly staying the night at her place, had his jaw taut and his hand squeezing the coffee mug so tight that the handle cracked right off. He caught the mug before it slipped from his hand, though a bit sloshed over and burned him. He swore under his breath and walked to the sink to run cold water over it.

Nick chuckled dryly. "Something got you out of sorts with yourself this mornin', Jamison?" he asked but he had an idea about exactly what the man was thinking of. He was a bit curious to see just how Duncan would respond.

Duncan gave him a cold look and poured another cup of coffee.

"I'm good. Now, what was this about breakfast?"

Sylvie mixed milk and sugar into her coffee. "Yes, Nick, what *is* for breakfast. I'm starving!" she exclaimed.

Nick raised a brow at that. Then he gave Duncan an amused grin.

"I'll bet you are."

She looked confused, but Duncan gave him a warning scowl. Nick laughed softly. "I fried some ham and bacon, and hash browns and toast. I would have fried some eggs but those seem to be nonexistent even though we're on a farm," he said as though Duncan should be ashamed of himself for that fact.

Duncan ground his teeth together and said in a low warning voice, "*I* have been extremely busy these past few days and haven't had a chance to restock groceries."

"Right," Nick said, sounding as though that was no excuse. He was having extreme fun teasing the uptight Duncan who it seemed, was all tied into knots over Sylvie Dunlap.

"Well, I for one, am grateful, Nick. Let's eat." Sylvie reached into a cabinet for a stack of plates.

Duncan nodded tersely and took them from her even as he reached for silverware. He marched past the two of them and left the kitchen.

Sylvie turned to watch him stalk off with a frown. "Nick," she complained. "I think you broke him. He was perfectly fine until you accused him of not having eggs." In a low almost whisper she said, "I think showing hospitality must mean a lot to him."

From the dining room Duncan heard Nick's peal of laughter and the scowl on his face deepened. The bastard was going to get his teeth knocked in if he wasn't careful. He knew what he was feeling was absurd, but it rankled inside that Nick, and not he would be accompanying Sylvie on the long flight home. He briefly considered changing his plans, but the most important thing was that she was safe, and he had things he needed to get done.

With an effort worthy of a saint, he relaxed his jaw and plastered a friendly smile on his face. He was going to have to play nice with the damn detective for Sylvie's sake. For that reason, when Nick brought two heaped platters of food to the dining table he said simply, "Thanks for making breakfast, man."

Nick gave a wide grin as though he could see right through the pleasant smile on Duncan's face. Then he cast a look at Sylvie as she carried a third plate of stacked buttered toast. "No problem. I was under the impression that cooking was required if I wanted to eat."

Duncan gave him a sharp warning look. "Don't tempt me, Hanlan." Nick backed up a step though he grinned and held up his hands.

"Okay." Then, because he couldn't resist, he turned to Sylvie. "Are you all ready for our flight out tonight?"

Duncan sucked in air and forced his legs to sit in a chair across the table. Sylvie plopped the plate and a jar of Mrs Ginny's preserves in front of him. "Yep, I'm all packed up and ready to go after breakfast."

They ate in relative silence, only interrupted when Sylvie sat up straight suddenly and turned to Duncan. "You will come out for Daddy's services, won't you?"

He nodded briskly. "I'll be there."

She relaxed and picked up her toast to take a bite. "He would want you there, you know."

He smiled gently at her and put his hand on her knee. "Don't worry sweetheart. I'll make sure I'm there."

Nick's smile slipped a little and Duncan didn't miss his shaking hand as he lifted a piece of bacon to his lips and took a bite. His anger abated a bit. Nick Hanlan had not only been Sylvie's lover but had been a partner to her dad and it was obvious that he cared about Sylvie. He was the right choice to send her with now.

Since Duncan was, after all, a man who gave credit where it was due, he looked at him. "I appreciate you coming out here and now going back with her to keep her safe, Detective."

Nick gave a slight nod and a smile. "Sylvie is family, like I said. I would have come sooner if Reagan had filled me in, instead of calling the station to tell them that he wouldn't be in and that he was jumping on a plane out here."

Sylvie teared up again. "It's my fault he's dead, isn't it?" she asked angrily.

Duncan threw a harsh frown toward Nick and took her hand, squeezing it as he said firmly. "It is no one's fault but the bloody perp, Sylvie, and we'll catch him."

Nick's brow went up at that statement. "Don't you mean the *police* will catch him, Jamison?"

Duncan smiled then and it was a cold, menacing thing and suddenly Nick was very, very glad that he hadn't kissed Sylvie again. He watched as clear blue eyes settled on his unblinkingly. "Sure. However, it all works out."

An hour later, Duncan pulled Sylvie to him and squeezed her tightly in his arms. He looked over her blonde streaked brown hair to Nick Hanlan. "Take care of her. Don't let your guard down and when you arrive at her place there make sure you eliminate any chances this bastard has of taking another shot at her."

Nick nodded but he looked amused as Duncan held onto her. He kissed the top of her hair and then finally tilted her face up to his. "You..." he said gently. "Stay safe and keep me informed, okay?"

Sylvie nodded and he bent his head to give her a hard kiss on her lips. Then he opened the passenger door of Nick's rental and helped her slide inside. He bent down to meet her dark eyes. "Don't take any bloody chances, okay sweetheart?"

Sylvie nodded again, then said softly, "I'll miss you." And it surprised her just how much she meant it. She blinked as Nick shook Duncan's hand before he walked around and slid inside the car with her. Without a word he put the car in gear and drove away. She looked in her rear-view mirror until she could no longer see Duncan standing on the porch, and then she watched until the roof of the large cabin style house was completely gone from view.

When she finally looked away, Nick was smiling. "See," he said quietly.

"You're different."

Sylvie shook her head and changed the subject. "If the doctor doesn't clear me for the flight, I'll need you to drive me, Nick."

He shook his head. "No way, Sylvie. I'm not taking you on a thirty-nine-hour drive across the country." She lifted her chin stubbornly. He sighed, "Let's just see what the doctor says and go from there okay?"

She felt like picking a fight, but she was also a little tired, so she only nodded. An hour up the road they noticed two police cars off the right side near a rest area looking around and Nick slowed automatically. "Wonder what that's all about," he mused quietly.

Sylvie stared at the policeman who were walking around the building as though looking for something. She shrugged with a grin and joked" Maybe someone lost their potatoes and are now out looking for them."

Nick laughed just as she knew he would, and she turned and smiled at him. Then she cautioned, "I can say stuff like that because I'm from Idaho, but don't ever try it yourself or you'll find yourself dropped miles into the desert with no friends around."

He nodded. "Thanks for the warning, friend."

It was two hours before their flight when Sylvie and Nick made their way through customs at the airport. The doctor's visit had been quick, and Sylvie had promised to check in with her own doctor once she was home, which relaxed the doctor tremendously.

She noticed Nick was watching every person who passed them carefully and she had even looked behind them so often that her own neck was starting to feel kinked. "Do you think he's here somewhere?" she asked softly, as they stood in line waiting to show their IDs and tickets to the officers behind the small desk.

Nick shrugged. "No way of knowing that, but if he hangs around, I'll recognize him. We should be okay since we didn't tell anyone we were leaving except Jamison. It's more likely that it will take the killer a bit to realize that we are gone and come after us."

That gave her only a bit of comfort, but she nodded. "Hopefully he doesn't want me dead bad enough to follow us across the country."

Nick nodded and smiled but it didn't quite reach his eyes. "Hopefully," he agreed.

It took Duncan exactly thirty minutes to pack his bags, fill a Thermos with coffee, and throw both in his truck. It took him another twenty minutes to hook onto a trailer and take the rest of what he needed. He made one last quick stop in the house to use the restroom. He ran into his dad who was just coming down for the day. He nodded and then because his father had been a little better lately and might actually care, he told him that he was taking off for a bit.

Arthur looked surprised. "Where are you going, son?"

Duncan smiled gently at his old man. "I have a few things I need to do. I'll keep Jackie updated and she can update you."

Arthur smiled and nodded. "Thanks, I 'preciate it," he said sounding uncertain. Then he looked up at Duncan. "Where is Sylvie? Is she staying here with that detective?"

Duncan shook his head. "Nope. She's already on her way to the airport."

Arthur's brows went up. "She's heading home so soon?"

"I know, but she felt like she could do more with all the case information on that end." Duncan smiled again. "Don't worry about her though, she'll be okay."

Arthur looked even more worried after Duncan's explanation but didn't argue. "I guess we'll have to trust that detective to keep her safe."

Duncan nodded. "Bye."

"Bye," his father echoed.

He climbed into his truck and called Special Agent Jon Graham who was the assistant special agent in charge of the Chicago FBI field office.

"Any information yet?" he asked when the agent answered.

"Hello to you too," Jon said wryly. "And yes, a little." He took a long pause.

"What?" Duncan asked impatiently.

"I have three profilers working on the files you sent. They haven't turned up anything overly concerning yet, but I have another guy who says it just came over the wire that there are a couple of girls missing somewhere around that area. I don't know if it's connected or not, but he heard me say Idaho and told me about the girls. Anyway, most of the names in the files have come back clean but there is one that I'm looking into. I'll let you know if anything turns up."

Duncan frowned. "That sounds like a whole lot of nothing, Jon."

"I know how it sounds but we are making progress that could help later on."

"I don't want help for later on. I want info that will help me nail this bastard, now!" Duncan was practically shouting at the end. He took a deep breath and ran agitated fingers through his hair. "She's out there, man. She's about to climb on an airplane with three hundred and fifty other unknown people. I need to fucking find this creep and take him out before he gets to her again."

The other end of the line was silent for a long minute. Then Jon said, "I've been meaning to ask you, Jamison, who is Sylvie Dunlap?" His tone was cool and calculating.

"An old family friend," Duncan bit out.

"How old? Because I've looked back seven years so far and I haven't found a single thread tying her to anything to do with you."

"I knew her in high school before she left for college. She left for North Carolina in 2011 if I remember right. Why does any of this matter, Agent?"

There was another hesitation. "Just wondering how you got involved in all of this. Last I knew, you were determined to stay away from the law and chase cows around on the mountain."

Duncan reminded himself that he needed Jon and forced an even tone. He needed Jon's connection to the FBI. Quietly, truthfully, he said, "Sylvie and I were old friends. She came back home because she wanted to have a memorial for her sister, Elaine, who died when she was eighteen. It was on my watch that she was shot." His tone was hard now.

"It's not your fault that someone is after her," Jon said and for the first time sounded human.

"I know that." Duncan ran a hand across his face. "She was shot on my watch and now her dad is dead, and I'll be goddamned if I will let that asshole get to her again, so find me something, Jon."

He hung up and took a deep breath before calling his sister to let her know where he was going. He glanced down at his GPS. It was going to take him thirty-nine hours and twenty-two minutes to drive to Wilmington. He had a long drive ahead of him and too many things to get done on the way. With a little sigh he pulled out of the driveway of his childhood home and began the long trek toward North Carolina.

An hour later, another pickup pulled out onto the highway behind him unnoticed, heading for North Carolina as well. The driver just simply couldn't take the chance that part of Sylvie's plan was to spill everything she knew, once she believed she was safely away from him. He couldn't fly out there or people would be suspicious. It meant that he was in for a long drive but the thought of that thrilled him. With a little luck, he would be able to make a couple of fun stops along the way.

Chapter 32

Sylvie and Nick arrived in Atlanta, Georgia at four thirty a.m. eastern time. They had a layover there because the Wilmington airport wasn't open around the clock. They had to wait until six thirty to finally board their connecting flight. She talked him into a drink at one of the only open airport bars while they waited. Nick hesitated because he didn't want to take any chances with her safety, but Sylvie persisted, "Come on Nick, it's just one drink and I can use it." She pointed to her shoulder to guilt him into it.

Since he hadn't seen anything out of the ordinary as of yet, he finally nodded. It would be well worn off before they descended at ILM. He nodded but only ordered a beer to go with her dry martini.

She finally fell asleep minutes before their flight was announced over the loudspeakers and he had to nudge her awake. She started, as though she'd been dreaming, but after staring wide eyed at him for a long moment, she sat up. "They just announced our flight," he said soothingly.

"Thank God, I can't wait to get home and climb into my own bed." She smiled as she stood, and they made their way toward the boarding ramp. "I miss my bed."

"I miss your bed too," he said before he could think better of it.

She laughed softly. "Then maybe you should come home with me."

He already regretted what he'd said, and it showed in his eyes. He looked away. It would be so easy… But then he remembered the way Sylvie had looked at Duncan. It was that look that had told him that Jamison had in a few days, managed to do what he'd been trying to do with Sylvie for two years. He turned a gentle smile on her. "I do plan on staying at your place, just not in your bed."

She sighed and turned to show her ticket to the flight attendant on deck. "I suppose you haven't changed your mind, then?"

He laughed softly. God how he wished he could change his mind. Even rumpled and tired from being awake all night, she was appealing. He reminded himself that it was self-preservation. "Unfortunately, not."

She laughed at his hesitant reply. They boarded the plane together and made their way to their seats. Nick urged her in front of him and then took a long moment to look around at each of the other passengers nearby before taking a seat in the middle between her and anyone else who might come by.

The Wilmington airport was small, and it only took ten minutes to get their bags and make their way outside. The balmy morning air hit them like a warm sauna as soon as they stepped through the double sliding doors. Within minutes, their uber pulled up to the curb and Nick loaded their bags into the trunk before opening the door for her. Sylvie had a place out on Wrightsville beach that she had bought a year ago. It was only twenty minutes from the airport, and though they hadn't had any trouble, Nick was happy to finally be back where they could relax a little, even if it was only marginally.

As they crossed over the first bridge, he looked out over the edge at the hundreds of boats docked in the water and smiled. This was one of the prettiest places out here. Boats of every size, from small sail boats and speed boats to long yachts made their way through the waterway. Buildings and homes dotted nearly every space along the shores of each side. There were restaurants offering seafood caught locally and tourists who paid way too much but ate it happily because they were here on vacation. There were bike and surf shops catering to those who wanted a little more adventure than a day lazing on the beach or swimming in the water that was just beginning to warm up from the cold winter months.

As they made their way up the island toward her house, she gazed out, hoping to catch a glimpse of the ocean. *Her* ocean. That was how she saw it. She loved it here. Had loved it here so much when she'd come to visit during school breaks from Raleigh, that she had been thrilled when the New Hanover's District Attorney's office had called to offer her an internship. She had applied, of course, but hadn't really believed she would or could beat the other fifty-three applicants for the same position. She had worked through her last two summers of law school here in this town that was growing faster than the locals were ready for.

When finals were done and she was prepping for the bar, she had been working here again for the summer. She had gotten to know District Attorney Lemonte well that summer. She had in fact taken him to bed without any qualms of repercussions. She was dating three other guys at

the time and had been clear that all that was between them were a few weeks of sex.

It had actually been good for their work relationship as all the sexual tension in the workplace was taken away, filled by the knowledge of how each other worked in every part of their lives.

It had only lasted a couple of months because he had met a woman who he'd ended up marrying later that year. But he and Sylvie had found a kinship. A comfortable space where they worked well together. He'd been a huge help to her passing the bars and then, after she passed, he'd taken her and the rest of the office out to celebrate.

A week later, a formal offer for a job was on her desk. Sylvie had accepted it happily. They worked well together, and she loved this place.

This happy, friendly town where people swarmed downtown to the water walkways and shops to celebrate and drink during the week and then to the nearby beaches on the weekends.

Benjamin Lemonte had proven to be a loyal man with a finesse at handling the media and the public with respect and honesty. Sylvie was proud to work with him and was forever indebted to his tutelage and kindness as a human being. Together they had solved and tried many cases that might have been neglected or overlooked by others and the public seemed to like them both.

A year into the job he had bumped her pay up considerably and given her an investigative team. Still, she always took the time to go to his office and update him because she felt that he deserved to know what was happening in his building and he appreciated her for it.

She'd been at his wedding and then again, the first one to the hospital when his son, James, was born. She was, in fact, the godmother of James Lemonte, though she'd never understood what had propelled the man to choose her. She was as far from stable and sturdy as anyone could be, but she'd felt honored and accepted graciously.

She watched as they drove past neighbors' houses and rental homes and units that were rented out by vacation realters. Some even rented by neighbors who had a little extra money and wanted to own a second place to rent out nearby. The taxi slowed and she sat up straight as her own house came into view.

Chapter 33

The house was a warm beacon of light to an exhausted Sylvie, as the cab slowed and pulled into the drive. It was a three-story, white rectangular house with white wooden siding and big full windows on the ocean side. The entire house was on stilts making the bottom floor two long garages with sliding doors on the front facing the road. There was barely enough room in the driveway for the driver to pull in sideways at an angle. She handed him some money before Nick could reach for his wallet and told him to keep the twenty-dollar tip.

She smiled as they walked up the wide long staircase between the two garages that led up to the main level of her place. The main level had one spare bedroom with an adjacent bathroom tucked off to the side of the open kitchen. The kitchen was bright, with light silver cabinets that were topped with dark grey granite counters and back dropped with gorgeous assorted red, aqua, grey and white small rectangular tiles. There was a huge wide bar with a wide deep sink. It was the only thing that separated the large roomy kitchen from the wide-open front room with long sweeping windows that showed off a fabulous view of the ocean. On one side of the room was a large gas fireplace and directly across from that was a long dining table set to the side and just down from the kitchen.

Her furniture was rustic and chic and gave the whole house a charming country feel even with the tile and granite and beautifully hand-finished moldings. Through the windows and ocean facing double glass doors was a huge cherry wood deck complete with a fire table and surrounded by a sofa and comfortable chairs. On the other side was a covered grill and a shimmering glass table with eight cushioned chairs tucked around it. Right down the middle at the ocean end was a stairway that led to the planked walkway below that gave her direct beach access.

There was a gate at the edge of her small green planted yard, with a security pad to enter or exit from the beach. Sylvie drank her coffee out on the deck most mornings as she looked through her files and listened to the ebb and flow of the ocean waves.

Tucked between the kitchen and fireplace were the stairs up to what she viewed as the loft. The top floor was where the other two bedrooms were. The master bedroom was set directly above the front room facing the ocean with big open windows up here as well. There was another deck out the front, though this one was much smaller and didn't lead to the beach but there were two white wooden rockers that were cozy and the view from up here was spectacular. The long extravagant bathroom ran down one side of the room with a wide walk-in shower, double sinks and a huge corner bathtub. The entire room was tiled in gorgeous tan and aqua blue glass tiles giving it that feel as though you'd somehow stepped into the sea.

The other bedroom and bath were at the other end. It was a smaller room though it also had a small deck outside. This deck, however, looked out over the bustling beach street with its restaurants, tourists and locals all out enjoying the weather. All in all, she loved her place, and she threw herself down on her bed as soon as she'd trekked up both flights of stairs. Nick was eyeing her even as he plunked her bags down at the foot of her king-size bed.

She hadn't needed a king bed but had found that the men she slept with often preferred the extra space. It had a grey tufted and padded headboard and was covered in a purple and grey patterned duvet with a soft down filling. She had no sooner closed her eyes in ecstasy than her doorbell rang. She sat up and looked toward the stairs, sadly. Unable to do anything about it, she rose and took the stairs down, careful not to jar her overtired, sore, shoulder. Nick paced down quickly behind her. "Let me get it, Sylvie.

We need to be careful."

She shrugged. "Like you said, the shooter probably hasn't had a chance to get here yet." She reached for the doorknob even as Nick's hand shot out and clasped her own pulling her back behind him as he stepped forward and reached for the doorknob himself.

DA Benjamin Lemonte stood impatiently on the landing at the top of the stairs. Nick widened the door, and he pushed in and past, his eyes on

Sylvie. "Good god, are you okay?" he asked quietly even as he wrapped her in a gentle hug, careful not to jostle her shoulder.

Sylvie stepped back and stared at him with a bemused expression.

"How did you know I was home?"

He waved a hand in the air. "Never mind that. I have been following the case closely since Ricardo first told me about it." He fixed her with a chastising look. "What I'm wondering, Miss Dunlap, is why you didn't bother calling me yourself?" He stared her down waiting for her to give him an explanation.

Sylvie sighed and turned toward the coffee pot. "Would either of you like some coffee? If I'm going to do this right now, I need a gallon of coffee first."

Both Nick and Ben nodded, and she noticed Nick carefully locking the door before they followed her into the kitchen. She motioned to the bar. "You may as well take a seat, sir."

District Attorney Lemonte nodded gratefully and sat in one of the wide grey cushioned bar stools. Nick walked over to the windows with a frown as he thought about Duncan's warning. *Make sure you eliminate any chances this bastard has of getting to her as soon as possible*. He looked up and located rolling wooden shades and began systematically unrolling each one, window by window.

Sylvie turned to stare at him. She was sure it was the first time the shades had actually been used. With a shaky smile she asked, "I guess taking a run on the beach in the morning is out now, huh?"

Neither man laughed and she lifted a shaking hand to smooth back her hair. Ben watched Nick for a moment and then turned back to her. "Tell me what happened. And start from the beginning." He fixed her with a stern look. "Leave nothing out."

Sylvie looked to Nick for help, but he only shrugged as he lowered the last of the shades and then began flicking on lights to make up the difference. She took a deep breath and turned to her boss. "As I'm sure you know, I went back to Idaho to take a little time for a memorial for my sister Elaine, who died eight years ago…" she began nervously.

Two hours and a million questions later she sat back on the sofa where they had moved after they'd had coffee. Nick had nearly as many questions for her as Ben did and she'd felt put on the spot. Each time she had attempted to skim the most relevant details only, one or both of them had zoned in on her and started throwing questions at her. When she'd briefly mentioned tackling Duncan on the hike, Nick had narrowed his gaze. "I don't remember you telling me anything about that. Why did you tackle him?" Then when she admitted what she'd thought she saw he asked, "Are you sure there was no one there hiding among the rocks?" And: "Did you and Duncan actually look around to verify that you were indeed alone?"

Sylvie, who had already gone over all these questions countless times in her own head since she'd been shot, shook her head. "You don't understand. There wasn't anywhere out of sight that someone could have hidden around there. There definitely wasn't anyone there on the mountain with us." She reached a hand to her aching head and wished Duncan would suddenly appear with a handful of painkillers. He didn't, of course, so she sighed and tipped her head back for a moment. "It was almost like it was in my head," she mumbled softly.

Nick pounced on her. "What the hell does that mean?" He sounded grumpy and Sylvie wondered if the exhaustion was getting to him too.

She straightened up and shrugged. "I don't know, Nick." She turned to look at her boss who was quiet and thoughtful. Exhaustion was setting in again and she tried to stifle a yawn. "I don't know. I'm so tired now that I can't think very good," she hedged.

District Attorney Benjamin Lemonte narrowed his gaze on her face. She looked away and he frowned. Suddenly, he turned to Nick. "You ought to go get some sleep, detective. You can't very well keep her safe if you're so tired that you aren't prepared for anything that comes."

Though Ben wasn't his commanding officer, he was higher ranked than Nick, and their departments worked closely together. Nick really didn't want to make an enemy of him. Still, he opened his mouth to argue, but Ben held up a hand. "I'll stay here and keep a watch out until you've slept for a few hours, detective." Then to Nick's pleasant surprise he reached into his jacket and pulled out a handgun. "I came prepared."

Not wanting to incur his anger, Nick nodded and gave Sylvie a smile before turning toward the spare room. "I'll be just in here so if you need me all you need to do is holler."

Sylvie's mouth went dry as she turned and met Ben's direct look. She swallowed and looked away, searching uncomfortably for something to say. Her mind went blank.

His low quiet tone was meant to unnerve her, she knew. "I have worked with you for a long time now, Sylvie. We have worked on cases through the night, focused on cases where you got no more than a couple hours of sleep for weeks at a time, and I have never, *never,*" he enunciated the last, "heard you say that you weren't thinking straight because of being tired." His gaze was hard and unyielding as she forced her own up to meet it.

She shrugged. "I'm sorry, sir. I don't know what to say." In a scared voice that was a mere whisper she said, "I'm a little afraid that I might be losing my mind."

His warm deep laughter at the admission had her gaze jerking back to his. She looked offended so he leaned close to her and smiled gently. "I have dealt with a lot of people over the years dear, criminals, lawyers, judges, including my fair share of those on the mentally challenged scale, and I can honestly tell you that I don't believe that you are anywhere on that scale."

She looked a little relieved and then hesitant. "I just keep feeling like there is something floating around inside my head, but I can't seem to focus on what it is. It makes my head hurt," she admitted quietly.

"I don't have a degree in psychology, but I have to say that it sounds like you are overworked, tired and exhausted, all of which is a given, considering what you have been through." As though it suddenly occurred to him that her father was dead, he added gently, "Reagan Dunlap was a damn fine cop. In the past few days, you have been shot and barely survived death, lost your father, and watched someone you care about get beaten up. Those are all things that are bound to exhaust you both mentally and physically. Why don't you go upstairs and get some rest and we will talk about this some more when you wake up."

Sylvie mentally added and *slept with possibly the sexiest yet infuriating man I've ever known.* But she didn't say it aloud. Instead, she nodded and said, “Thank you, sir.” She rose. “There isn’t much in the refrigerator as I emptied it before I left but help yourself to anything there is.”

He nodded and pulled out his phone to check his messages. He didn’t look up even as she turned and tiredly climbed the stairs. She wanted sleep like it was a drug and she was an addict, but she turned instead to the bathroom.

Flying always left her feeling greasy and dusted over and she knew she would sleep better if she had a fresh shower first. After washing and shampooing her hair she wrapped herself in a towel and then quickly brushed her teeth. She was so tired that she reached for an oversized T-shirt and slipped it over her damp hair and collapsed onto the bed. The sun was shining but not so brightly that she couldn’t sleep through it with her bed tucked back far enough from the wall that the direct sunlight didn’t touch it.

The problem was that she kept picturing Duncan here, and she knew that he would have been over there closing all the shades long before now. She groaned and snuggled deeper into her mattress in denial. After several long minutes of not being able to sleep, she swore and threw the blanket off of her. “Damn you, Duncan Jamison,” she muttered as she marched to the windows and pulled the white with purple and rose- colored flowery privacy panels closed. That done, she marched back to bed and plopped back in, yanking the blanket up to her chin and fell asleep instantly.

Chapter 34

Duncan drove his truck and trailer straight through the night, gulping coffee like it might somehow fill the void inside him, that was left by Sylvie's absence. It didn't. But it did keep him alert and awake as he drove across the flat eastern side of Wyoming, with only occasional hills and plateaus off in the distance to break the monotony. He was on a major freeway and was making good time as he cut across the border and into Nebraska. It took him half the day to drive across Nebraska's long flat country. He stopped to fuel at a truck stop and took a few minutes to buy a shower, a large bag of jerky, some potato chips, and a jumbo pack of licorice. All were good driving snacks that would keep him alert and on the road for longer.

He'd spent several hours on his phone by the time he finished with the police department in Idaho, then Agent Graham of the FBI, then his sister, his bank, and then finally a real estate agent that his sister had given him the number for. Then, he'd started over with the police department and Agent Graham. All of the phone calls served a dual purpose. They both kept him awake and they were helping to give him a clearer picture of everything that had happened so far.

The only thing that didn't seem to fit into the big picture was Sylvie tackling him on that mountain. He couldn't stop wondering if she had suspected that she was in danger even then. Had she seen someone or something on the mountain that day, that he had missed? Worse, he had to wonder, was she telling him everything, or was she holding some major detail back that would ultimately break open the case and save her life?

All of these questions ate at him even as he trekked across the plains of Iowa. He stopped again for fuel and a bathroom break, refilled his coffee Thermos and grabbed a couple of five-hour energy drinks just in case.

Duncan finally maxed out somewhere on the Iowa side of the Iowa/Illinois border. He pulled off at a roadside store and fuel station and took a minute to check on the cargo in the trailer. He'd been driving fast and wanted to verify that all was good. Then he backed the trailer up to a rear fence behind the building and laid his seat back to sleep. The sleep was fitful, but he managed to get around four hours before he finally lifted his seat upright again. He went inside for fresh coffee and took a minute to splash cool water on his face and neck before pulling back onto the freeway.

Two hundred miles behind him, a hooker at a truck stop met her fateful end, under the pressure of a man's strong weathered hands. She was sprayed with bleach and buried in a shallow grave before he removed all his clothing and dumped it into a dumpster a hundred miles up the road.

When Duncan neared the Illinois border, he changed routes heading north-east toward Chicago. Three hours later he stopped in Naperville at another truck stop, just off the freeway. He took the time to shower again, brushed his teeth and took off his hat and combed his hair. Instead of the casual button up and jeans that he normally wore, he slipped into a blue dress shirt and black slacks with a blue, black and red tie. He slipped into matching loafers and made his way back out to his truck. He did another quick survey of the trailer before sliding behind the wheel and driving straight into the heart of Chicago.

He parked in the parking garage on one side of Roosevelt Road and strode across the street to make his way quickly inside the ten-story rectangular building. He stopped as he walked over the insignia painted on the floor in the center of the huge open room. It read Department of Justice, Federal Bureau of Investigation. He grinned and walked to the first desk he saw. A rather broad looking woman in a guard uniform looked up as he strolled up. "What can I do for you today, sir?"

Duncan gave her his most pleasant grin and held out his hand.

"Duncan Jamison, ma'am. I'm here to see Agent Graham."

She ignored his outstretched hand and plunked at the computer for a moment. Then she raised her deep-set green eyes that were at odds with her complexion to his for just a moment. "What is this about, Mr Jamison? Agent Graham doesn't have an appointment."

He offered another charming smile. "Agent Graham will know. She typed some more and then she picked up the phone receiver.

"Yes, sir, there is a Mr Jamison here to see you." She listened for a long moment, then she lowered the phone. "Agent Graham will be right down, sir. You are welcome to wait over there." She pointed to a long row of uncomfortable looking office chairs that Duncan was sure were normally relegated to criminals who had just been brought in.

He offered her another unaffected warm smile. "I think I'd rather wait here," he drawled in amusement. She gave him a long look through her dark lashes, and he thought he saw amusement in her gaze. "I'm wondering…" He paused. "Does the job require you to be dour and unapproachable, or is that just a personal preference?" he asked in droll amusement.

He did see amusement then as one side of her dark mouth turned up slightly. He gave her yet another toothy smile. "I see. So, what reception do I get if I'm say an agent or a profiler?"

She quit pretending to ignore him and turned fully to meet his gaze. "*Who* are you, anyway?" she asked curiously.

He smiled and held out his hand again as he got the full impact of her brilliant green eyes in contrast to her dark skin. "Duncan Jamison, at your service, ma'am."

She took his hand this time and shook it. "Agent Graham doesn't take many visitors, so you must be important," she mused quietly.

He chuckled and shook his head. "Unfortunately, not. I'm a simple cattle rancher from Idaho. By the way, has anyone ever told you that you have stunning eyes, ma'am?"

She blinked at the swift shift in the conversation and then looked a little uncomfortable as she began to blush lightly.

That was the picture that Jonathan Graham saw as he came through the doors behind the desk and held out his hand. "I'd say it's a pleasure but it's really more of an unpleasant surprise," he said with a grin as he shook Duncan's hand. He turned to look at the female guard, "He wasn't giving you any trouble was he, Connie?"

The guard gave him a reassuring smile. "Not at all, sir."

"Good," he said as he held out a visitor badge hanging from a dark blue lanyard toward Duncan. "You'll need this," he said briskly, as he turned and motioned for Duncan to follow him. They walked past a long line of metal detectors inside the next set of doors. "He's good, he's with me," Agent Graham said to the guard who pushed a button and let them through a small side gate.

They made their way down a wide hallway and then finally, about ten doors down, they ducked into an office that was completely empty except for a large metal desk, the chair behind it and two hard-backed folding chairs that faced it. Duncan looked around the room with an amused smile but sat at the agent's signal. "What can I do for you, Mr Jamison?" Jon Graham asked with a serious expression. It was well practiced, Duncan knew, and it made his own face widen into a grin.

"What is this? The closest unused office to the exit?" he asked in a challenging tone.

Graham held his serious look. "I'm not sure what you mean."

Duncan laughed at his carefully maintained expression. "Look, you know why I'm here so cut the shit and either take me up or tell me that you aren't going to. Don't waste my time, Agent. Sylvie is still in danger and if you aren't going to let me help, tell me now so that I can spend my time on more productive things."

Jon let a small smile crack his face at Duncan's directness. "That is one of the things I always liked about you, Duncan. That ability to cut straight through any bullshit in the room." He watched Duncan for a long moment as though considering his options. Finally, he stood. "I suppose I could use your insight anyway; we are at a bit of a loss at the moment on where to look next and you drove all this way."

Duncan raised an eyebrow at that observation. "How do you know I didn't fly?"

Agent Graham laughed. "I have given the airlines strict instructions to call me if anyone on my list of people of interest in this case gets on any flight."

He'd figured as much, but Duncan wanted to pick the man's brain at every opportunity. He nodded. "What are we waiting for."

At his impatient nudging, Jon stepped out into the hallway and led them down and around a corner where there were four large elevators lining either side of the hall. "I assume that Sylvie made it to Wilmington, okay?" Duncan asked in a conversational tone. He already knew she had, since he'd threatened Nick heavily if he didn't give him regular updates.

Agent Graham smiled. "I can't confirm that on the record, but I assume that she did."

This was going to be fun, Duncan thought with a grin, as he resisted the urge to rub his hands together in excitement.

"You look like the cat that got the cream Jamison… It's not a good look for you," Jon drawled dryly.

Duncan grinned. "I've never given much care to what I look like to others, but thanks for the advice, I suppose."

"What am I going to get out of all this?" the agent asked as he fixed Duncan with a steady look.

"Nothing," Duncan answered honestly. "Except whatever you get for the positive media when you catch the bad guy here. And the knowledge that you're doing your job."

Agent Jonathan Graham sighed heavily. He was a large man, though next to Duncan he imagined he looked like an ordinary size. He was six one and had wide shoulders, dark hair and grey eyes, and what many had told him was a charming smile. He didn't care a whole lot what he looked like unless it gave him an edge when he was interrogating suspects or witnesses.

He did notice, however, that Duncan Jamison was much more intimidating in person than he looked in the profile Jon had studied so well he knew it like the back of his hand. It was the reason that even though it made perfect sense that Duncan Jamison might be involved with whomever was threatening Assistant District Attorney Sylvianna Dunlap, he knew Jamison wasn't. It was more than a gut instinct. It was years of practice of looking through every detail of a man's life and feeling afterward like you knew that man as well as you might know your brother, or the best friend you'd grown up with.

For that reason alone, Jon had hesitated to take Duncan upstairs, to where his team was working on what had been dubbed 'The ADA Dunlap' case, for show. He'd wanted Jamison to feel as though he was doing him a huge favor because he was planning to ask for something in return, and he didn't want him to feel like he could turn him down.

It took two hours to show Duncan all the evidence they had so far and get his opinion on it. Graham's team was treating Duncan like an outsider, which he was, until Duncan slowly won each of them over in admiration as he continued to see threads and get their points, before they'd had a chance to actually give them to him. They sorted through files of information they'd managed to collect from hours of hounding the police, the airlines, and now, even the one man who seemed to be involved the deepest in a case that was beginning to look like it had a much more sinister history, than any of them could have ever imagined from the jump.

Chapter 35

Sylvie slept straight through the afternoon and into the night. She didn't wake until the following morning around five thirty. She rose and slipped into some jeans and a T-shirt and brushed her hair before pulling it back into a ponytail. She didn't bother with make-up. At this point she wanted a hot cup of coffee and some real breakfast.

She made her way downstairs quietly not wanting to wake Nick as she walked to the kitchen. She started coffee and picked up her phone. She glanced at her screen. No missed calls or texts from Duncan. She sighed, not knowing why she even cared. He hadn't told her he would call. But somewhere between all his worry about keeping her alive and his lovemaking while protecting her, she had come to believe that he would follow through to make sure she was safe.

Now, it seemed he had dumped her off onto Nick Hanlan, who had broken up with her and didn't want to see her again, except as friends. Sylvie suddenly felt utterly alone. She considered calling one of the other men she'd been hanging out with from time to time, but it didn't feel right, so instead, she sat perched on a bar stool while she waited for the coffee to percolate.

She nearly jumped when Nick said from the hallway, "I thought I heard you up. How are you feeling?"

She cast him a quick smile. "I'm a lot better, now that I slept. I'm sorry, I slept straight through the night."

He shook his head and moved into the kitchen. He was wearing black joggers and a grey T-shirt that looked good on him. She looked away. "I'm glad you slept," he said in answer.

Sylvie faked a smile and moved around to the coffee that was just about done. "I made coffee. Want some?"

He nodded and moved over to sit on the bar stool next to the one she'd vacated. "I'd appreciate it."

"Did you sleep much?" she asked conversationally as she filled a blue mug and handed it to him.

He nodded as he took it and inhaled the fresh scent. "I slept a few hours yesterday and then I was up for a bit before I finally crashed again around ten last night."

She turned with another full mug and added a dollop of cream and sugar. Then she asked quietly, "DA Lemonte left, I assume?"

He looked hard at her then for a long minute. Then he nodded. "He did. Murmured something about his wife being *very* charitable but not so charitable that she would be okay with him spending the night here." He watched her face for any nuance of expression.

Sylvie smiled. "Good, there isn't any reason for him to stay here and lose sleep."

Unable to squelch his curiosity any longer, Nick asked, "So, when did you two have a thing?"

She fought the grin that threatened and instead she raised her brows daintily. "A thing?" she asked, as though looking for great clarity.

Nick ran a hand through his hair. "You know what I mean. When did the two of you have an affair."

Sylvie shrugged. "I wouldn't call it an affair really; it was more like convenient sex between two people who were overworked and didn't have enough of a social life to go out with anyone else."

Realizing she'd left out the main answer to his question Nick frowned. "Don't be vague. *When* did you have an affair?"

She turned an annoyed frown at him. "A long time ago, okay?"

"Before or after he was married?" Nick persisted.

Sylvie plunked her glass on the counter with a loud sigh. "Don't you think..." she started in an irritated voice. "That question is a little personal given that you have let me know in no uncertain terms that you no longer want to see me?"

He had the decency to look a little guilty. "Sorry. I'm just wondering what kind of a man the DA is."

She stared into her coffee. "Ben is a great man. He has taught me so much over the years. He's kind, loyal, and fair to a fault."

Nick gave a wry smile. "Glad to see you're not carrying a torch for him."

She gave a shout of laughter. "For Ben?" she sounded incredulous. "Not even a little. Ben is like a big brother or a close friend to me." She leveled a cool look at him. "Why do you care anyway?"

He shrugged. "Just because I can't have you, doesn't mean I don't care."

She wasn't sure where to go with that, so she took a long sip of coffee. "I think I might just be done with men," she said half seriously.

Nick gave a shout of laughter. "Right," he said sarcastically. He'd almost sounded insulted, and Sylvie turned to stare at him through her lashes. He had been acting strange ever since they got back from Idaho. She was about to ask him what that was all about when the doorbell rang. She gave him a questioning look, but he only shrugged.

Wordlessly she slid down from her perch to answer it, but Nick shook his head. "I'll get it. Stay here."

She followed him to the door. After a quick look with his service weapon in the air that he must have had dropped off last night, Nick opened the door wide. Her boss slipped silently inside and closed and locked the door behind himself before turning to her. He was in a freshly pressed grey suit with a light pink shirt and a blue and pink square patterned tie.

"It's a little early for a social call," Sylvie said dryly.

When he didn't smile, she began to get nervous. He walked into her kitchen and poured himself a cup of coffee without a word. She followed him, dragging her feet, and dreading what he was going to say. He took a couple of sips and turned back to face her. "I came to check on you. Were you able to get some rest last night?"

She nodded tersely. "Tell me what you came here to say."

He sighed, took another sip of coffee and said, "Sit down."

With dread in every step, she walked around and perched on the stool and reached for her coffee, more for the warmth of the mug than the coffee itself. "What is it?"

He took a deep breath and looked at Nick. "There are a couple of young girls that have gone missing in Idaho. They haven't found anything to tie to this case yet, but I'm not willing to take the gamble that it isn't, given that there has been very little crime in that area in the past twenty years. Now, suddenly women are going missing, and someone is trying to kill you." He ran fingers through his hair. "Shit, sorry," he apologized automatically. "The FBI are going to try to come in and take over."

Sylvie raised her eyebrows. "Why are the FBI interested in this case at all?"

"Beats me, but your dad's office has been fielding calls from them since yesterday morning, and now they have been calling my office, asking if we have any more information to add to the case."

Nick frowned. He hated it when the FBI came and stuck their noses in the middle of his cases. "We aren't cooperating with them, are we?"

"I'm afraid so. Apparently, they got the judge to sign a warrant for any information related to the case."

Sylvie ran an unsteady hand over her hair, smoothing a loose strand back. She wanted to scream. She was used to feeling in control of the cases she worked on, and now here she was the very target of an insane person and yet it felt like everything was fraying all over the place, completely out of her control. "Damn,," she muttered as she gulped the rest of her lukewarm coffee. "What am I going to do?" It was a rhetorical question so when Nick started answering in a hard tone her head jerked toward him.

"I'll tell you what we are going to do. We are going to tell those fucking FBI bas—" he cut off at a warning glance from the district attorney. Then muttered determinedly, "We are going to solve this case and bag this guy before this case gets any messier," he finished in a less angry tone.

"Now that, sounds like a real plan," Ben said, and he reached up and loosened his tie. "I'm going to work from here today." He pulled out his phone and called the office. Five minutes later he turned back to Nick and Sylvie. "My secretary is going to have all the files brought over that we need."

Sylvie looked uncertainly between the two men. "If it's easier we could just go back to the office," she offered lamely.

Both men adamantly shook their heads. "The risk of exposure is too high there." It was Nick who pointed this out.

Sylvie sighed. She guessed that for the time being she was just going to have to get used to feeling out of control. She settled onto the sofa. "Are you guys hungry? I think I might order delivery for breakfast."

Both men nodded agreement and she called in a breakfast order at one of the local restaurants that had a delivery service. As the men sat down and started going over everything that had happened so far for the millionth time, she went upstairs to put on her make-up and comb her hair. She found a bottle of aspirin and popped a few.

That made her think of Duncan, and she sat down and stared at her phone for a while again. She wanted to call him. Wanted to tell him what she was feeling, but knew it wasn't smart or kind. She wasn't interested in a long-term relationship with anyone, and he'd been clear that was exactly what he wanted. She found herself wishing she had never dared him to kiss her that first time.

Maybe then they could have had a simple friendship and she would be able to talk to him today without the awkwardness. For a friend that she had gotten along without fine, for so many years, it was increasingly evident that was no longer how she felt. It must be the need she felt to pay him back because he had saved her life. Yes, she thought, that must be it.

She took as much time as she dared and then reluctantly went back down to join the men in trying to figure out who hated her so much that they wanted her dead. The whole ordeal gave her a constant headache, and some small insignificant part of herself wished she could just forget about it all and fall into a blissful, uncomplicated life again.

The files had been delivered as well as the food when she returned, and she listened with one ear only as the men droned on and on about all the pertinent details.

Breakfast turned into lunch and then into dinner. Around five p.m. another detective from her father's precinct who'd worked with Nick showed up to help. Sylvie knew the thirty-two-year-old blonde, blue-eyed Mason Cornwall a little better than she wanted to admit to anyone. It had been a while since they'd seen each other, but there had been a few months two summers ago when they met and had a lot of fun together before Mason had moved on.

At six, a woman from her own investigative team, Detective Linda Shelley, showed up for a bit to see if there was anything she could do. She took one look at Sylvie's man club and shook her head. "Oh, hell no," she'd murmured to Sylvie, who only laughed in understanding. In a low voice meant for her ears alone Linda said, "Call me if you need a little women's intuition but otherwise, I'm outta here. It looks like Wyatt Earp and the whole gang is here."

Sylvie thanked her for coming and showed her out. She offered to order food again and was just about desperate enough to beg to go for a grocery run, when the doorbell rang yet again. Feeling a little peevish after dealing with the grumpy single-minded men all day, she stomped to the door and threw it open before any of them could stop her or rush ahead. "Who is it now?" she asked grumpily.

Her hand went to her throat, and she stared in astonishment at a very cool, very sexy, and very tired-looking Duncan. Her mouth gaped open even as Mason rushed up behind her. "My god, Sylvie, are you *trying* to get shot?"

She shook her head even as Duncan's grin turned dark as he got his first good look at the man inside with Sylvie. He put his hand possessively on her back. "Do you know this guy?" Mason asked quickly.

Sylvie nodded. "Duncan this is Mason Langdon. Mason, Duncan Jamison."

Mason held out a hand and relaxed. "Ah, you're Sylvie's Duncan. It seems we all owe you one for saving her life."

Duncan gave a curt nod, but his gaze was on Sylvie. He was drinking in the dark circles under her eyes and the way her shoulders seemed to droop with exhaustion. He stepped forward and pulled her into his arms. She came willingly which surprised him, though only a little. He kissed the top of her head and smelled the fresh scent of jasmine shampoo. "I missed you," he said simply.

Sylvie let him hold her even as he backed her into the house and secured the door behind his back. "I didn't know you were coming," she choked softly. Then to her absolute horror, tears filled her eyes and began brimming over, and getting his nice dress shirt dirty. That thought had her leaning back. "You look nice. I don't think I've ever seen you in a tie."

He grinned. "Does prom count?" He had taken Elaine to prom his senior year. She laughed softly and lifted her face to meet his kiss. Mason had already taken his cue and left them alone in the hall, but the overwhelming pressure of having three men she'd slept with comparing notes all day had worn her down, and she didn't want to deal with more fallout, so she pulled back.

"You really should have told me you were flying in. I would have picked you up from the airport."

He offered another tired grin. “I didn’t fly, sweetheart.”

She had just started toward the kitchen but turned back at his comment. Her eyes widened. “Are you saying that you drove all the way out here?”

He nodded.

“Why on earth would you do that?” she asked, sounding unintentionally rude.

He shrugged. “I had things I needed to bring with me that can’t fly.”

She rolled her eyes. How like the man to want his own truck bad enough to make a trek across the United States. She turned back suddenly. “Wait, if you’re here, who is taking care of the ranch?”

He held her gaze in his own. “Jackie will handle things. She has been dying for her chance at ranching and now that we have some good hands to help her out, it’s the perfect opportunity.”

Not sure what to say to that, Sylvie led the way into the front room where she introduced him to DA Lemonte and then she made an executive decision and ordered three large pizzas. After the introductions were done, Duncan disappeared outside again, returning with a large travel suitcase and several bags of groceries. He set them on the bar. “I figured you might need these,” he said quietly, as all three men turned to stare at him in unison.

Sylvie teared up again. “Thanks. I don’t even have the basics and it was beginning to drive me crazy.”

He shrugged and looked around. “Nice place.” She smiled. “I like it here.”

He took in her cheeks, now flushed with warmth and excitement and said gently, “So do I.” Then he drank in her long legs, sexy curved ass, and full breasts and added, “The view is amazing.”

She blushed crimson. For a woman who’d had a healthy sexual appetite, and slept her way through the college dorm, it was a bit of a shock to realize she was embarrassed. All four men were grinning at her as she turned and offered to show him upstairs.

Nick called out behind them, “Don’t forget that we are down here.”

Duncan grinned all the way up behind her. She showed him around and he was properly impressed. He immediately began telling her in distinct detail everything he’d like to do to her, to make use of such finery. She laughed and backed away from him. “I have guests’ downstairs. I’d better get back down there.”

He gave her a warm, lazy smile. “That’s okay, sweetheart, I can wait.”

That was when she noticed that he had blatantly brought his suitcase up and it was now taking up a chunk of space on the floor by her bed. She fled. He followed at a more leisurely pace.

The pizza arrived and everyone helped themselves to slices of deep dish supreme, a thin crusted vegetarian and a Hawaiian with ham, pineapple, and bacon. That was Sylvie’s favorite, though everyone but

Duncan turned down the pineapple pizza. She didn't mind, it meant all the more for her.

Over pizza, the men kept going over the evidence. Duncan looked exhausted, though he jumped into the discussion without hesitation. He made himself at home and seemed so comfortable at the table with the two detectives and the DA that Sylvie actually began to feel ungrounded. He didn't fit into her world; she'd told herself over and over and yet there he sat talking cop with some of the best in their city.

After the men quit going to the kitchen for more pizza, Sylvie boxed it up and slid it into the now full refrigerator. She glanced at the men who seemed to be deeply engaged in their conversation and decided to go up to bed. Not wanting to interrupt, she took a bottle of water and slipped quietly up the stairs. She walked into her bedroom with a sigh and turned on the shower. She squealed and jumped when she turned and saw Duncan in the mirror. He was watching her intently with a rather dark scowl.

Not sure what she had done wrong this time, she sighed and asked quietly, "Is everything okay?"

He took a threatening step toward her and forced a small smile. She backed up to the base of the tub and he followed, stalking her. She put up her hands in a small attempt to hold him off. "Duncan, you're scaring me!"

He grinned. "You should be scared, sweetheart."

Her eyebrows went up. "Did I do something wrong?"

The laugh that came out was harsh and low as he bent and took her mouth in a deep desperate kiss. She leaned into it, melted. To her surprise, he pulled back suddenly, staring down at her with accusation in his blue gaze. "Tell me, Sylvie, is there any man in this city that you haven't slept with?"

Sylvie, who had always been confident about her life choices and what she wanted sexually, blushed. Apparently, he *had* been aware of the subtle closeness with each of the men downstairs. She nodded. "I haven't slept with the pizza guy, there are a couple of guys I work with, that I haven't slept with; I haven't slept with most of the detectives at my dad's old precinct…" She paused and turned to frown up at him. "Come to think of it, it would actually be easier if I tell you who I *have* slept with." She was a little angry now, that he thought he could come into her home and basically call her a slut. She was even angrier that she felt shame at his accusation.

He groaned and wrapped her in his arms, taking her breath away even as his hands came up to cup the side of her face and neck and his tongue

slid into her mouth tasting the delicate texture of her. He pulled back to look down at her for a moment. "What am I going to do with you?" he asked a little hoarsely, and desperately.

She smiled. "Take me to bed?"

His harsh shout of laughter warmed her heart even as he lifted her hips and ground her pelvis against his own hard, erect one. That shut her up, and she wrapped her arms around his neck and pulled his head back to hers for a hungry mind-numbing kiss. He reached behind her after a long moment and ran hot water in the bathtub. Then he walked over to turn off the shower. "Bathe with me?" he asked somberly.

She nodded and beamed a smile at him. "I'm really glad you're here, Jamison."

She saw something dark cross his face and stared at him. He took a frustrated breath and turned desperate eyes to hers. "If I wasn't here…" he hesitated. Then with more power behind his voice asked, "Would you be up here with one of the other readily available males downstairs?"

Sylvie considered his question for a moment, wanting to be honest with him. Apparently, she took too long, because he ran aggravated hands through his dark hair and over his eyes. "Fuck!" he growled under his breath.

She put a soothing hand on his arm. "No, I wouldn't."

His eyes snapped open. "You wouldn't what?" he demanded.

She shrugged. "I wouldn't be in bed with any of the men down there." She carefully left out the other two men that she might have called if she were alone and wanting company.

He eyed her, knowing there was something cagey about her response. He couldn't take the thought of her in another man's arms giving herself— He cut the thought off. "Why not?" he asked, hating himself for both pushing the issue, and also now potentially having to hear the answer that he was sure he wouldn't like.

She shrugged. "I dated Ben a long time ago, before he was married. Mason and I ended things last year because it wasn't really working any more, and Nick said he wanted to just be friends when we were in Idaho."

That seemed to stop him short. He considered that last tidbit. The man had some scruples after all, he thought with an inward smile. He raised a brow. "Hanlan actually said that in Idaho?"

She nodded. "Yes, the day he came."

Duncan grinned, remembering how jealous he'd been when he'd come home and thought they might have had sex while he was gone. He bent down and pulled her shirt over her head. "In that case, sweetheart allow me to take you to bed."

She let him undress her, slowly, torturously as he always insisted on doing. He kissed his way up her belly giving a flick of his tongue in her belly button as he moved upward. She sighed and leaned back, closing her eyes. He lapped at the undersides of both of her breasts before finally reaching around her to unhook the lacy blue bra she wore. Then he began slowly working his way back down as he reached for the button on her jeans.

Sylvie leaned into the teasing touches and didn't know what propelled her to say it, but she needed to know that he was clear where they stood. "This is only casual sex, Duncan."

His tongue darted into her belly button again. "Uh huh," was his only response.

She pulled away and looked down at him. "I'm serious, Jamison. If you weren't here right now, I wouldn't be sleeping with the guys downstairs but if I got lonely, I would have called someone else I'm seeing." She needed him to understand.

His jaw hardened and just when she thought he would pull back, he lifted his hands to cup her breasts and to tease at the nipples, turning them into hard peaks. He held her gaze in his own and asked calmly, "What are their names?"

That took her by surprise, and she sat up. "Why do you want to know?" she asked suspiciously.

She had hot need coursing through her and wanted, no, needed, him to finish what he had started. His hands moved down and rubbed her sides grasping her small waist and then lightly skimming down to the undone band of her jeans, slipping just underneath and making her buck.

He grinned. "I'd like to have a little talk with them." His thumb was drawing distracting little circles under her waistband going lower, lower, lower…

She sat up straight suddenly as his words sunk in. "You will do no such thing, you idiot."

He shrugged. "Don't you like what I do to you, sweetheart?"

She gasped as his thumb delved into the triangle between her thighs and found its gentle, quick mark. She'd forgotten what he asked. She looked up at him as his thumb circled back up and out working toward her navel again. "What did you ask?" she murmured through the haze of passion.

He chuckled low in his throat as his thumb delved below her waistband again. "Don't you like what I do to you? Am I not thorough enough? Do I need to take more time?" She thrust against his thumb, and he got sweet, sweet moisture. Deliberately, he lifted it to his mouth and licked it off. She bucked against the hand that was settled on the side of her waist, urging him to touch her again.

He obliged. "I'm just wondering what you need all those other guys for, sweetheart." He circled her clit and watched as she lifted her beautiful curvy hips up, trying to take his thumb inside herself. "I'm happy to take care of you any time you need it. So, what else is there that you need? What else do you want from me?" he asked softly.

Sylvie bucked as his thumb hovered there over her entrance. Then she panted, "I need you to goddamn fuck me, Duncan. *That* is what I need." She opened hazy eyes to stare up at him pleadingly. "You make me lose my fucking mind every time before you give me what I want. *Not* cool."

He yanked her jeans down and pulled them off even as his finger slipped inside. She threw her head back and bucked. "Is this what you want?" he asked as he watched her intently. He slid his finger back out and then pushed two inside her.

She bucked, nodded, and then shook her head as she realized what he'd asked. "Fuck me, please!" she gasped desperately.

He nodded. "Just a second, sweetheart." Then he used his fingers to push in and out once more. She tightened and surged and came on his hand squeezing and pulsing against his fingers.

He groaned and yanked off his own clothes leaning down to kiss her belly even as she began to settle again. Then he lifted her hips and shoved inside. Her eyes flew open, and she gasped as her body convulsed and started coming again. He didn't let her relax this time. Instead, he rode her hard, instinctively needing to possess her.

She wrapped her legs around his waist and surged up with every thrust. She screamed and he swallowed it even as his own shout tore through his lips in a loving curse. He felt like he was blinded by the light and colors that blossomed as he soared out over the edge. He held her as together they flew on the warm breeze of wonder.

When they began to slowly settle back toward the ground, he lifted her gently and stepped into the hot steamy bath, settling her on his lap, curving his arms around her. He kissed her hair, her eyes, and then gave her a firm kiss on the lips.

She opened her eyes, her deep, intelligent brown eyes and smiled. "Who knew you could be such a tease and yet so damned good in bed?" she asked breathlessly.

He watched her with his deep lazy blue eyes unblinkingly. Quietly, somberly, he said, "I love you, Sylvie."

Chapter 36

Sylvie sucked in a breath even as her face twisted in alarm. "No, no, no. Jamison, take it back!"

He watched a volley of emotions flit across her face as one side of his mouth turned up in a half grin. "No," he said stubbornly.

She slid away from him and turned to face him across the tub. He watched as anger slowly settled over her delicate smooth face. "I told you from the start that I don't do anything serious."

He didn't move a muscle, only watched as she tried to stare him down. Finally, he shrugged. "I guess I don't follow orders as well as the rest of your harem."

The comment stung and she looked away. Finally, she reached a shaky hand out for her body wash and a foamy looking scrubber. She began very efficiently cleaning herself, systematically beginning to scrub every remnant of their lovemaking off her body. "That isn't fair," she said softly. He watched her for a long moment in silence, then he rose up on his knees over her and took the soapy sponge. "Let me," he said quietly. She shook her head and turned to glare at him but there were tears in her eyes.

His gut clenched. "Please, Sylvie, let me."

She relinquished it, but only because she didn't want to fight with him. Tears seeped out as he began brushing gently at her shoulders. She couldn't speak through the emotion clogging her throat. Anger spiked again, as even now she felt herself responding to his touch.

He dropped the sponge and groaned as he lifted her onto his lap and settled back, wrapping her in his warm embrace. In a voice tight with regret he said, "I'm sorry, sweetheart, I know you aren't ready to hear that yet." He tilted her face up to meet his gaze. "It was unfair of me to tell you that I love you, but it *is* true. The harem comment however was an asshole thing to say." His jaw tightened noticeably. "But I'm not sorry I said it." When she raised an eyebrow, he explained quietly. "I have spent eight long years wondering how you were doing and trying to give you space."

She gave him an incredulous look. "Do you actually expect me to believe that you cared about me that way before I left Idaho?"

He shrugged again. "I don't expect you to believe anything you don't want to." He took her hand and curled his fingers through her own. "I liked you a lot. Even back then, but I was…" He looked away as guilt crossed his face. "I was way too old to be looking at you that way."

She stared hard at him, looking for any sign of deceit in his handsome face. "I chased *you*," she stated flatly.

A hard grin twisted his lips. "I know. And it nearly drove me mad. You were still too young for what I felt around you and I knew it." He held her gaze, imploring her to believe him. "Then you left and even though I wanted to run after you, I told myself it would be wrong. That I should let you live your life and grow up." He shrugged. "After five years, I considered looking you up, but by then I didn't know enough about you to know if you would even want me to come, so I left it alone."

"If that's true, then why are you only telling me all of this now, when I've been crystal clear about my casual policy?" she challenged with feeling.

His jaw tightened again. "I wasn't planning on telling you how I felt any time soon." He gave a self-mocking grin. "It just slipped out."

She could see by his serious expression and clear eyes that he was telling the truth. She covered her face in her hands. "What do you expect me to do about this, Duncan?"

"Nothing. Not really." His jaw went taut, and his eyes darkened. "If you want me out of your bed, I'll go. But I won't leave you alone until I know you're safe." He hesitated, looking for the words to say what he felt. "I'm hoping that you like me in your bed as much as I have enjoyed having you in mine, and that you are willing to let me stay for a bit longer. I won't ask for more than you are willing to give, and I will keep my feelings to myself if that helps."

Then because he couldn't help himself, he added in a low voice, "And I'm hoping that even though you don't care about me the same way, that you won't sleep with anyone else until I go." He closed his eyes and ran a tired hand over his tight expression. In a low tortured voice he admitted, "I honestly don't know if I can handle another man's hands on you without causing a fight."

She smiled at that. Then she reached out a hand to lay against the side of his face. "I do care about you, Duncan. I care a great deal, which is why

I should have kept my distance in Idaho, and not let sex get in the way of our friendship."

When his eyes opened to look across at her, she smiled.

"Is that supposed to make me feel better?" he demanded. "Are you seriously telling me that you regret this?" He rubbed long fingers up her side and grazed the edge of her breast.

Her nipples puckered and she moved back and away. "Of course not! I would never regret having these nights with you. I just wonder if it wouldn't be better for the sake of our friendship if we keep it strictly platonic from now on."

Duncan eyed her like a predator looking for any sign of weakness before he pounced. Then he nodded as though to agree with her. She blinked; she hadn't expected him to cave so easily. He picked up a pink bar of soap. Began lathering up his own hard muscular form. "I can do that."

She stared at him nervously. He kept scrubbing. She reached for her own sponge again. Something deep inside was screaming at her that something was wrong. She didn't take her eyes off him as she scrubbed her neck and arms. Suddenly, he turned his gaze back to her and there was heat, and rigid determination in his dark blue gaze.

He ran a hand over her calf casually and squeezed it before running it up her thigh. "Since we've already been together today, I don't see that it would hurt for one last time…" He let the words trail off. Watched her eyes close as she swallowed and tilted her head back looking for strength. His hand stilled and rested there a few inches above her knee on the inside of her thigh.

Her voice trembled. "God, you are so exasperating!" Then she arched her hips, trying to edge those fingers ever closer to her core. He laughed softly and rose up over her to take her mouth in a deep desperate kiss. She met him there, arching into him even as he plunged one long finger into her. It took her by surprise. She had expected another slow tortured building that he so seemed to enjoy. Instead, he worked her high and then held her as she flew out over the edge, her body holding onto his gentle fingers. As soon as she began to float back down his fingers moved again and she was tight again and searching for that peak.

A half hour later she looked up at him through hazy passion-glazed eyes. "Please," she whimpered. She had lost track of how many times she had come. She had been carefully urged up toward that cliff of ecstasy and

then flung over the side again and again. He grinned. "Please what, Sylvie?"

She threw a desperate look at him. She'd had so many orgasms she'd literally lost count now. She was getting high again, but she couldn't handle the thought of going over that edge once again without him there with her. He stroked her clit with his thumb, delved deep with a well-honed finesse, rubbing against her ever so sensitive core. "Do you want me to take you over again, sweetheart?"

She shook her head even as she moaned and arched into his hand. She gasped for air. "Please, Duncan, I need *you!"* she gasped brokenly. He bit at her chin and surged up over her dipping into her tight welcoming heat. She screamed and he rode her hard taking her up and over two more times even as he emptied himself into her. He collapsed and rolled slightly to the side. With a little contented laugh he said, "I think we might need to go back into the bathtub again."

She shook her head. "No fucking way, Jamison. I don't think I'll be able to stand up straight for a week as it is."

He opened one eye to look at her. "I wonder what your guests will think about that."

She gasped suddenly and turned bright red. She had completely forgotten the three men downstairs in her front room. She rolled over to curl up to his body, but he pushed up and away from her. He gave a polite little bow. "I guess that's my cue, huh?"

She stared up at him in confusion. "What?"

"I told you that I would honor your wishes," he said, as he buttoned his shirt up and pulled on his jeans. "Okay if I take the other guest room?"

She was still reeling from the lovemaking as he turned, picked up his suitcase, and strode out.

Tears filled her eyes, and she rolled over to curl up against a feather pillow. As though in a trance she whispered, "I love you too, Duncan Jamison." But he was long gone and would never hear the broken admission.

Chapter 37

As Nick looked through yet another case Sylvie had been involved in at the DA's office, he turned to look up at the stairs where both her and Duncan had disappeared. He turned and caught Mason with a look of interest on his tanned face. Mason's brow went up in question. Nick shrugged. Then he sighed and tossed the file on the stack that was designated 'no interest' in the case.

The room was quiet as the three men worked. Pulling files and going over them closely before adding them to the stack 'of interest' or the other 'no interest' stack. Picking up his fourth file since the couple had gone upstairs Ben turned to Nick. "Are they…" His voice trailed off. It was none of his business.

Nick laughed harshly. "I'm going to guess yes." At Ben's frown he said in understanding, "I know man."

Mason lifted both eyebrows. "Sylvie's different with him, isn't she?"

All three men nodded at once. Ben broke the silence. "She deserves to be happy." He had long since hoped that Sylvie would find someone that made her want to actually try for a long-term relationship. Long ago he'd wondered at that possibility being him, but things hadn't gone that way. And then he'd met his Laura. So full of life, steady, grounded, and ready to build a future. Sylvie hadn't even balked when he'd broken things off.

"I noticed it first thing when I got out there." Nick grinned in amusement. "And that was before Jamison laid down the law and told me he plans to marry her."

Mason gave a loud guffaw. "Did she actually agree to that?"

Nick laughed. "I don't think he's told her anything about it yet." Admiration lit his face up. "He has stones though." His brow wrinkled suddenly, and he turned to the others. "Is there something about him that strikes y'all as odd or off somehow?"

Mason lifted a brow. "Anything specifically?"

Nick shook his head. "It's just that he's supposedly a rancher from the sticks in Idaho but he handles himself… well…" he hesitated. Then he shook his head. "I don't know, almost like a cop?"

Ben's eyes narrowed in on him. "Have you checked him out?" He reached for his phone. Entered his password.

"Are you thinking that maybe he's more involved in all this mess than he's letting on?" Mason asked.

Nick shook his head, "No. He isn't involved. That man has it bad for Sylvie. If he thought he could help find whoever is doing this, he would tell us."

Ben eyed him for a long moment. "What makes you so sure about that, Detective?"

"It was the way he looked at her and me." He shrugged. Both Mason and Ben were watching him now, waiting for an explanation. He sighed. "There was this moment, after he'd more or less told me to keep my hands off her or else, where he left for a bit. While he was gone, Sylvie got emotional and me being a gentleman, well, I went and sat by her and gave her a hug. That was when he came back in." He looked at his hands thoughtfully. "The way he looked at me was well, cold. But her..." he paused. "I think he's in love with her. It was like he couldn't stomach the thought that *she* might have wanted someone else."

Ben leaned forward. "What did he do?"

Nick grinned suddenly. "Absolutely nothing." At their raised brows he shrugged. "He turned and stalked up the stairs."

"So, he was jealous," Mason noted. "We've all been there though."

Nick shook his head. "It wasn't just jealousy, man. He looked like he might throttle me, then her and then go upstairs and throw up." He stood and walked over to grab a beer that Jamison had been thoughtful enough to bring. He held it up in question and then grabbed two more as he walked back to them. He tipped the bottle back and took a swig. He glanced at the other two men and said, "the weird thing, was the way Sylvie reacted."

The other men popped the tops and took a drink. Finally, Ben asked,

"How did she react?"

Nick smiled. "She jumped up and chased him upstairs." "Then what happened?" Mason asked curiously.

Nick's eyes narrowed and he stared at his beer. Not coming up with a pleasant way to say what he meant, he looked up. "What do ya *think* happened?"

They all laughed and took another drink. Then all three of them turned to look at the stairs where Sylvie had gone, and Duncan Jamison who had been in the middle of explaining something had suddenly stood and followed her, leaving the men to stare on.

"Were they a thing before she left Idaho to come here?" Ben wanted to know.

"Not according to Sylvie," was all Nick could say.

"We weren't," said a hard voice behind them.

They all turned to see Duncan, who was standing by the bar. He turned and grabbed his own beer. Then he walked over to sit on a chair across from Nick. "She was too young for me."

The men didn't say anything. Duncan lifted his own beer to his lips.

Nick took a long chug for courage. "And now?"

His cold blue gaze turned to Nick in irritation. Suddenly, intentionally, his jaw relaxed, and his eyes softened. "Now, I think it might be too late."

They all sat in silence and drank for several minutes. Then Duncan reached for another file. The rest of them followed suit. Ten minutes later, Nick said, "You look like hell, Jamison, when was the last time you slept?"

Duncan looked up at him and then glanced at his watch. "I can handle a few more hours," he said with a determined tone.

Ben, ever the voice of reason, said quietly, "Sylvie might need you at some point and it seems to me like maybe you ought to be rested for that." Mason and Nick nodded. "It wouldn't hurt anything to be rested, man.

I'll be here on the sofa too, in case anyone tries to come at her," Mason said quietly.

"I'm already set up in the guest room," Nick added.

Ben stood. "Why don't we all get some rest and then we'll hit it hard again tomorrow." He looked at his own watch. "Laura will be wishing I was home right about now anyway." He turned to go but then turned back. He couldn't get what Nick had said earlier out of his head. "Are you on the up and up, Jamison?"

Duncan looked amused. "What in the hell does that mean?"

The three men all turned to him in unison, but it was Nick who explained. "What he's wondering, Jamison, is if you have something you aren't telling us that will come back and bite us in the ass later on."

Duncan laughed. "Not exactly, gentlemen." He lifted his beer to his lips. "Haven't I told you that I'm a small-town rancher from Idaho?"

Not a single one of the other men smiled. He stubbornly nursed his beer, having given them the only answer he was going to.

Ben said goodbye and left. Nick headed off to take a shower. Duncan picked up the next file and began to read. Interest piqued; he studied the face of a low-level cartel drug runner. Could what Sylvie had gotten involved with be as simple as a case like this one? His gut said no, but his head had run out of other ideas.

He'd forgotten about the other detective until Mason cleared his throat. "Look man, I'm planning on sleeping on that sofa so if you don't mind..." He let the impatient tone peter off.

Duncan looked up in surprise. "Oh yeah. Sorry about that." He stood and reached for a stack of files. "I'll just take these upstairs with me."

Mason gave him a pointed look. "Won't that keep Sylvie awake?"

Duncan turned a cold unwavering stare at him. "I'll be taking them to the extra room upstairs." He gave a polite nod and turned to stride away.

He paused at Sylvie's door. She was curled up with her back to the door, wrapping herself around a long pillow. His heart caught in his throat. He wanted to go to her but knew that would take away from all of his carefully laid plans. He opened the door wide without a sound before turning to walk into the other bedroom.

He closed his door before he picked up his phone to make his next call. Jon Graham sounded groggy when he rasped, "What do you want, Jamison?"

"I need an update on the case," he said without hesitation.

Jon groaned and Duncan could hear the rustle of fabric before he said, "It's eleven thirty. Can't this wait until morning."

Duncan had forgotten the time difference. It didn't matter. "Not if it means the difference of her life."

There was a loud sigh and then, "Fine. We've been digging around more in Idaho." Jon hesitated. "It looks like there have actually been a number of missing cases in the surrounding area that are unsolved. I'm starting to think that there is much more at play here than one victim…"

An hour later Duncan hung up the phone. His eyes burned, his shoulders ached, and he had the beginnings of a migraine. He hadn't slept more than a few hours in the past three days and was running on fumes. Everything the FBI agent had told him wasn't adding up. Even if there was someone in Idaho strategically taking women for some unknown reason, how had Sylvie become involved?

He couldn't think straight any more. He sighed and leaned back against the black leather headboard. "What have you gotten mixed up in, sweetheart?" he wondered aloud.

When the words in the files began to blur in front of his eyes, he laid them down. He pulled off his clothes, leaving only his customary boxer briefs on and walked over to open the door. He wanted to make sure he could hear Sylvie if she needed him. Because he was weak, he walked silently to her doorway. Her breathing was deep and easy, so he walked in and quietly turned off the lamp on her bedside table before turning determinedly toward his own bed and room. His last thought before he drifted off was that somehow Sylvie had gotten tangled in a decade old case that had just recently come to the attention of the FBI.

Chapter 38

Duncan sat up and reached for the handgun on the nightstand glancing at the alarm clock. It was three thirty. When the second scream sounded from Sylvie's room, he was up and bounding silently from the extra bedroom, carefully checking that no one was there in the hall above the wide staircase. He heard a choking sob and quickly made his way into her room.

Through the dark he could see her silhouette there, laying or rather tossing about on the bed. He didn't see anyone else in the room, so he lowered the gun and rushed to her side. She cried out again and kicked at the covers. He set the gun down on the tabletop and climbed into the bed at her back, wrapping his arms around her shaking, sweat slicked body. "Shhh. It's just a dream, sweetheart," he murmured softly against her ear.

She settled instantly. Then she moved against him as she snuggled closer into his arms. Since this went directly against what she'd told him she wanted, he wasn't sure if he should stay. His body, hard now as she snuggled her ass there against him, jerked, stabbing into the curve of her back. He tried to pull away, but she grasped onto his arm and settled back in. He hated that he was weak, but he couldn't make himself leave her to deal with the nightmares alone.

Instead, he lay there for long tortured minutes willing his body to relax and his mind to shut off, so he could sleep again. His body ached from lack of sleep, and he really needed the rest so he could stay focused. He planned to lay with her for only a bit until she was good and settled again, but having her there, safe in his arms, helped him relax and he dozed off.

He woke up to the sound of Sylvie's confused tone. "What are you doing in here, Jamison?" Her voice was hoarse from sleep, and she sounded grumpy.

Duncan rolled over and opened one eye to look at her. Memories from the night before flooded in and he sat up scrubbing his hands over the rough stubble on his face. "I'm sorry, I must have fallen asleep."

She eyed his mostly naked frame. "Why were you in here at all?" she asked pointedly.

He turned to look at her then. Her eyes were a little red and puffy and he wondered if she had been crying before she went to sleep. He wanted to take her into his arms and hold her. Maybe even kiss her sleep softened mouth. He knew she wouldn't welcome it though, so he scooted off the bed. "You were having nightmares again."

She stared hard at his back. "I was not."

He turned and eyed her stubborn frown. "You don't remember?"

She shook her head. "I don't have those any more. I told you that before."

His patience was wearing thin. "You were crying out, so I came in here to check on you." He grinned sideways at her. "You held on when I tried to go, so I stayed for a bit, but I must have fallen asleep."

She looked like she didn't believe him.

He sighed. "Why would I make something like this up, Sylvie?"

She shrugged. "How should I know. We really don't know each other that well any more."

His temper flared, eyes narrowed, and he stared hard across at her.

"Don't do that."

"Do what?" she asked, her own temper going off.

He advanced. "Don't try to diminish our friendship just because you are afraid of what I said last night."

He half expected her to ask what he'd said in denial but instead she turned away and walked toward the bathroom door. He strode around and cut off her exit. "Come on Sylvie, sweetheart, talk to me."

Her brown eyes sparked. "There is nothing to say. I don't do anything but casual, Duncan, and you are obviously too old fashioned to do that."

His gaze narrowed. "You want easy breezy, huh?" She nodded.

He advanced on her. Without any warning he grasped her to him and took her mouth in a hungry kiss with just a little bit of anger on top. She tried to pull back, but his tongue darted out and teased at her lips until she finally moaned and gave in. He kissed her until she thought she might topple over if he let go. Then he stepped back and away from her. "Were you crying again last night, Sylvie?"

She nodded her head before she could think not to. The moment she did, she knew she had fallen into a trap he had laid for her.

He grinned,. "Why were you crying?"

She tossed her ruffled hair over her shoulders and stared belligerently across at him. "That is none of your business and has nothing to do with this conversation."

He knew she was lying but didn't call her out. Instead, he turned and walked away. He reached for his gun and took it with him as he said over his shoulder, "I see. Well, I'll just get out of your way then."

She wanted to call out to him, but she didn't. She watched the proud lift in his shoulders and his incredibly sexy backside as he walked away. He turned and gave her a small polite nod before he closed his bedroom door abruptly.

Sylvie slipped into the bathroom as tears welled up in her eyes. Why couldn't he just make things easy? She wondered to herself. She didn't want a complicated relationship with anyone, but she did enjoy having sex with Duncan. It was in fact, what had been keeping her sane through everything that had happened over the past weeks. She started the shower, unwilling to allow herself to feel sorry about the fact that he wanted more from her than she could give. If he didn't want the lovemaking it was his loss, she decided angrily as she stepped under the hot spray. She spent half an hour in the shower and then brushed and blow dried her hair, and then took the time to carefully apply her make-up.

They were putting her dad's body on the plane home today. Ben had informed her last night that two officers had flown to Idaho and were accompanying the body home since the autopsy had been completed. She was supposed to meet them at the airport to sign for him today, so she wanted to look her best.

By the time she finally made it downstairs the smell of fresh brewed coffee and something sweet permeated the air. She sniffed pleasantly and made her way down, dragging her feet. She had noticed

Duncan's door was open wide and assumed he had already gone down, and she wasn't ready for any kind of confrontation.

Duncan wasn't downstairs, however, only Nick. There was indeed a fresh pot of coffee and a stack of golden Belgian waffles with another plate of bacon on the counter. She smiled at Nick. "Good morning."

He grinned. "Mornin'."

She eyed the coffee and breakfast. "Are these up for grabs?"

Nick smiled around a bite of waffle. "I assume. Jamison made it all before he left."

Sylvie paused mid pour. She turned to Nick in surprise. "Duncan left?"

He watched her carefully. "Yep. He came down and made breakfast and then asked me to tell you that he had some things to take care of, but he would be back later on."

She nodded and tried to keep her face expressionless. She offered a wan smile toward Nick as she added cream and sugar to her coffee. Cream and sugar that Duncan had been thoughtful enough to bring. She turned away with the excuse of getting a plate from the cupboard to hide her emotion and then reached for a waffle. A waffle that Duncan had made for her, despite the fact that he was obviously upset. She sat down next to Nick at the bar and took a sip of coffee.

He cleared his throat and she turned to look at him. "Is everything okay, Sylvie?"

She nodded and forced a bite of waffle down. "Of course."

He watched her with a doubtful expression, then he sighed and set his own fork down. "I couldn't help noticing that Jamison was a little, well, out of sorts this morning. We are still friends, you know. It seems pretty obvious that you aren't feeling so hot yourself..." He let the words trail off.

She shrugged and blinked away the emotion. "I'm fine. It's just that Duncan doesn't want to do the casual thing and I really wanted that with him." Her mouth opened in alarm as she realized how Nick might feel about her admission.

He gave her a small smile. "Did he tell you that?" he asked in a mild tone.

She looked away and then forced herself to meet his eyes again.

"Yes. Well, not exactly that, but more or less."

He read a lot in the carefully worded response. "What exactly, did he say?"

She blinked. She hadn't expected him to ask that. In fact, she'd expected Nick to shy away from the subject since it would have been uncomfortable for him, given the situation. She pushed a piece of waffle around in the puddle of syrup. "Well, he said he loves me."

Nick's eyebrows shot up and a grin turned his lips up. "And that was how he told you that he doesn't want to be casual?"

Sylvie nodded and turned toward him. "Don't give me that look. I told him that it wasn't fair to say that to me, since I have been very clear from the start that I'm only open to casual dating."

Nick nodded. "What did he say to that?"

She sighed and dropped her fork, all pretense of eating gone. "He said that he wants me in his bed regardless, and that just because he said he loves me doesn't mean anything has to change."

Nick grinned. "I don't see the problem then, honey."

Sylvie turned her eyes to him. "It's just that he also said that he doesn't like the idea of other guys touching me or…" She trailed off as a blush crept up her neck.

Nick laughed suddenly. "I hate to break it to you, Sylvie, but I'm pretty sure all of us felt that way."

Her eyes widened in surprise. "You didn't like that I slept with other men?"

He shook his head with a definitive jerk. "God, no."

That made her laugh, but then she studied him with open curiosity.

"Then why did you agree to it?"

He grinned and shrugged. "Partly because you are a lot of fun and I wanted you. Partly because I thought that's what it would take to maybe…" He hesitated. "Work towards something more."

She frowned. "I'm sorry, Nick. I didn't realize you felt that way."

He shrugged. "I knew what I was getting into. You were very clear with me from the start. And," he added with a smile, "it was fun."

She stared hard at him with a frown. "Are you trying to tell me that it's okay that Duncan feels that way and that I should still be with him anyway?"

He shook his head but smiled. "I'm not telling you how to live, Sylvie.

All I'm saying is that it's pretty normal for us guys to want to have a woman all to ourselves. It makes us feel strong and macho." He watched her digest that information. Then because curiosity won out, he asked, "Are you wanting to have another boyfriend over, Sylvie?"

She blinked and shook her head. "Not really, no. Why?"

He chuckled. "Why didn't you just tell Duncan *that* then?"

She opened her mouth to reply but then shut it again. He watched as she took a long drink of coffee. Finally, she turned back to him. "I think it's different for him," she admitted quietly.

"How so?"

"I don't know exactly; it just feels like he wants so much from me, and I already have so much going on with all this…" She raised a hand in a wide arc. "But it feels like he wants some altruistic promise from me not to sleep with anyone else."

"If you don't want to sleep with anyone else right now then what is the problem?" he asked quietly.

She sighed. "I don't want to hurt him."

"Then why sleep with him at all?" Nick asked and reminded himself to tell Duncan about all he had sacrificed in an effort to help him. Jamison would surely owe him a favor for this.

Her sharp gaze flew to his face. Then she swallowed hard and reached for her coffee, holding its warmth there in her hands. "I don't know. I was curious, I guess." She studied his easy smile. "Why are you being so cool about all of this, Nick?"

He shrugged. "I try to be a good person, and I want to see you happy. Was it everything you imagined it could be?" he pressed on.

She gulped coffee and squirmed in her chair. "Making love with Duncan is like this deliciously torturous excursion that you want to go on forever, and yet you crave the heightened high of the main attraction, if you know what I mean."

Nick watched her, with a carefully blank expression. If he didn't know Sylvie so well, he'd have sworn she was already in love with Jamison with the way she talked about him. He shook his head. "Not exactly. It sounds rather trying."

She shook her head and blushed all the way up her neck and into her cheeks. "It's a completely new experience but so addictive." She slapped a hand over her mouth as the words slipped out. Then she turned an even darker shade of red. "Oh god, Nick, I'm sorry. That sounded like things weren't good with us, but that's not how I feel." She noticed his eyes narrowing a little more with each explanation and faltered.

He chuckled softly. "I thought things were pretty darn good." She nodded. "Absolutely."

He wondered if he should have been offended but the concern there in her brown eyes coupled with the fact that he was pretty sure the main difference with Jamison's skill was that Sylvie cared for him more than she was willing to admit, salved the wound. "All I can say is that it sounds to me like you and Duncan might actually be a lot closer to wanting the same thing than you realize."

She gave him a small smile. "I'm beginning to wonder that myself."

She took a small bite of waffle, buying time while trying to think of a blasé way to ask her next question. "So… Did Duncan happen to tell you where he was going?"

He grinned. "No, he didn't, but he did tell me that he had his phone on him if we needed anything."

She nodded, looking disappointed. "Do you think I should call him?"

With a wide grin he shook his head. "I have a better idea."

Chapter 39

Sylvie stared down at the GPS on her dash in disbelief. She was sure it was sending her in circles since she had looped around to the right at least five times. She was out in the country, somewhere outside the city of Wilmington. She had followed the highway around town and then crossed Cape Fear Memorial bridge and before getting off an exit that soon had her driving through green foliage with trees and plants that reached out around her as though trying to grow over the road. She had been driving on the country road for several miles, curving and turning only to curve and turn once again. Out here most of what she passed were small homes or trailers on little plots of land where the forest had been cleared back just enough for a yard and home.

What on earth was Duncan doing out here? She glanced down in irritation as her GPS told her to once again turn right. She slowed and stared at the green growth that seemed to take over any space that wasn't constantly kept up with. Old oak trees with moss hanging down from the branches, overhung bushes and vines dotted with ferns, and small sapling pines that were just starting. She stared hard, looking for any sign of a road or anywhere to turn right.

Finally, she saw what was a small dirt road that wound off through the trees and foliage. She hesitated. There was no telling what was up in there and the road was narrow enough that she would have to back out if it came to that. There was also the concern of mud. Though it hadn't rained the last couple of days, her small silver BMW wasn't likely to handle any leftover mud very well. The only good thing about being this far from anything was that she was absolutely certain that no one was following her. She'd had her eyes on the rear-view mirror constantly, watching. She had also made all the loops and turns exactly as Nick had told her to do just to be safe. If anyone had been following her, they would have caught up by now.

She hadn't driven all the way out here for nothing, however. She made up her mind and turned the car onto the tracks. She pulled through the trees and brush, wincing as a branch scraped noisily along one side of the car as she pulled up over the small hill.. Suddenly, the road opened up and with relief she saw that it turned into a wide paved lane that led down a long driveway. Still wondering what Duncan was doing all the way out here, she breathed in the freshness and the beauty around her. Something about the place felt surreal and untouched.

The road curved ahead, and she stared in wonder as the land opened up in front of her car. There was a wide-open field of grass on the left side of the road with two horses nibbling lazily in the sun. She smiled and found herself wanting to ride again. Maybe that was why he was out here, she thought. Suddenly her brain registered the stallion. She slammed on her brakes and cranked her head back to stare.

One of the horses bore a remarkable similarity to the stallion she'd ridden at the Jamison Ranch. She pulled forward as the land opened up even more. A wide stretch of mowed and trimmed grass sloped out and up to a gorgeous white and brick home with a barn off to one side and large detached garage. She pulled up to the house, feeling like an intruder until she saw Duncan's truck parked there off to one side. She frowned.

There was a rather familiar looking horse trailer backed up to the barn and her eyes narrowed as she parked and slid out of the car. She stared at the insignia on the side of the trailer. It was too far to see well, but she lifted a hand to shade her eyes as she tried to make out the words on the side. The hair prickled on the back of her neck, and she swung around to see Duncan watching her.

He had one shoulder propped against a solid pillar on one side of the wide brick stairs that led up to a gorgeous covered front porch that spanned the width of the house. He watched her idly for a moment before straightening up and taking the stairs down two at a time. He stood there in front of her, not saying anything, only watching her face for any reaction.

She glanced around and then looked up at him. Her conversation with Nick had given her a new perspective on things and she searched for the words to tell him what she was feeling. When she couldn't think of anything that felt right, she finally moved the last few feet to him. "I'm sorry for being so bitchy, Duncan."

He studied her for a long moment, then he opened his arms. She ran into him as though her life depended on it. He held her close. "I'm sorry too, sweetheart. I really didn't plan on telling you that I'm in love with you for a long time yet."

She wanted to ask for clarification on his comment but didn't want to start another fight. "I care about you too and I really do like being with you." She searched his expression for anything to indicate what he was feeling. "I can't promise anything more than casual, but I do want to be with you." Suddenly, she looked around again. "Where are we? And what are you doing all the way out here?"

He grinned. "It's my new place."

She turned back to stare at him, stunned. "You rented this place because you felt like you couldn't stay with me?"

He shook his head. "No. I bought this place, sweetheart." He eyed her curiously. "Didn't you see my horses out in the front pasture?"

She turned to stare back the way she'd come from and nodded. "I thought that was your stallion." Stunned and very curious she turned back to him. "You don't seem all that surprised to see me here."

He held her gaze and shrugged. "Nick called. He wanted to make sure you got here okay."

"I don't understand, Duncan…" She hesitated. "Why would you want a place out here? What about the ranch?"

He took her hand in his and squeezed. "Why don't you come in. You want some coffee or sweet tea? I hear that is the big thing out here," he grinned lightly.

She followed him up the brick stairs and onto the porch. It was wide and clean and freshly painted with a cushioned porch swing on one side and a table with chairs on the opposite side of the stairs. She turned and looked out in wonder. From here she could see the horses frolicking in the long grass and the entire open thirty acres that spread out and were finally edged on each side with thick forest. The sky beyond looked out toward the east to where she knew the ocean was.

She breathed in the scent of pines and all the greenery around. "This place is beautiful, Duncan."

He only nodded and held the deep red, painted front door open for her. She stepped inside and looked around. It was old. She estimated 1940s or 1950s. Everything had been refinished, from the lightly textured sheet rocked twelve-foot ceilings with six-inch wooden planks every couple of feet, all the way down the cream-colored walls to the refinished hardwood floors. The only thing missing was the decor. All the walls were bare except for a big rooster clock using the belly for the round part of the clock. The room was obviously intended to be a front room but had no furniture yet. On the right side was another long space with a wooden bench and coat racks with six feet of open hardwood floors.

She stepped forward and saw a long, heavy dining table with the capacity to seat at least fourteen. She whistled at the table which looked to be two huge chunks of a log that had been cut lengthwise, three inches thick, and was completely finished with black, grey and white streaks down the center where the two chunks came together and was smoothly finished with resin epoxy. The wide brown leather chairs that circled the table looked cozy and fit.

"That is gorgeous," she gushed as she moved over to run a hand across the smooth tabletop.

Duncan grinned. "I like it too. It was one of the selling points of the house."

She glanced uneasily at him, still not sure why he had bought a house in North Carolina. "This came with the house?" she asked, then she caught sight of the open kitchen straight ahead.

He gave a small laugh. "The sellers said they couldn't fit it through the door since he had built it right here in the dining room."

The kitchen was a mixture of gorgeous dark walnut cabinets and creamy white walls. The countertops were all cream-colored granite and there was modern cream, grey and black tiles on the walls behind them. The appliances were all shiny stainless steel and huge. The stove was a six-burner gas unit that looked like it could handle a party. The wide bar that jutted out from the right side was all that separated the dining room from the kitchen and was complete with a second wide sink on the end. Floor to ceiling carved walnut cabinetry ran the length of the wall to the left. No need for a pantry with all those gorgeous cabinets, Sylvie thought. There was an arch off to the left side of the bar and she looked over curiously.

Duncan smiled. "There are two bedrooms with a bathroom between them over there." The kitchen was so roomy there was also an island in the center adding charm to the cozy space. Once again it was devoid of decor and the only thing on the counter at all was a fancy-looking stainless steel coffee machine. She noticed there was fresh coffee inside.

"What's back there?" she asked, looking at a four-foot archway on either side of the back corners of the kitchen.

Duncan looked where she pointed. "There's a huge open room that I was thinking I might turn into a home gym, or it could be used for a more formal purpose. The other side leads to the stairs."

Sylvie glanced in that direction and said, "That's right. I remember noticing there was another level. Why do you need so much space?"

He grinned. "I plan to have a family someday, sweetheart."

That made her squirm, and she avoided his gaze as she asked quietly, "What's upstairs?"

He took her hand and pulled her with him. "Come on, I'll show you." The wide hardwood staircase started just on the other side of the arch coming from the kitchen. The stairs ran up one side of the ten- foot-wide space with ornately carved railings for support. The other side led down a wide hall that ended with wide sliding glass doors going outside to what appeared to be a large deck.

She followed him up and stared out over the railing at the top. The small loft at the top of the stairs looked out over the room below that Duncan had mentioned could be used as a gym. She turned and followed him through the wide-open curved archway. There was a short hallway and then the space opened into a large rectangular room with several wooden doorways off each wall.

Duncan smiled again as she looked around curiously and he said, "There are two more bedrooms there and another bath between them. An office there." He pointed to a set of double doors. "And this." He pulled her toward a wide single door going toward the front of the house. "This is my favorite room."

She stepped into a lushly carpeted room that was about twenty feet wide and had to stretch nearly the full width of the house. There was a huge log post bed with a couple of nightstands on either side of the bed. The rest of the space was empty. She smiled happily as she spotted the round stone fireplace that sat several feet from the foot of the bed. He pointed to the right side. "Over there are the walk-in closets." He paused, "And over there is what I think is supposed to be a bathroom."

At his strange explanation she turned toward the bathroom. Warm grey tiles covered the floor and stretched out in each direction. She glanced around the wide room. She saw a small room with a toilet and a sliding door

on one side. The outside wall led to the ten-foot-long mirrored wall with a long granite sink top and two glass top bowl sinks. Underneath were warm natural cherry wood cabinets with a variety of drawers and cupboards. She followed the wall around to the huge square spa feature that sat directly in front of the door with black marble rolling down the wall and all around the tub. She knew instantly it was a waterfall feature that ran to fill the giant tub. She turned to the right where it was walled off with only a tile pathway forward. She stepped around and gasped. The floor turned into small ornate colored tile that shimmered but gave good traction. The path curved all the way around the wall before ending in a huge open, floor to ceiling tiled ten feet, by ten foot, shower with multiple shower heads at different angles throughout. On one side was a small, tiled bench that was wide enough for two to sit if they wanted. "It's gorgeous, Duncan," she breathed.

His hands were tucked in his pockets as he looked around. "It really is," he agreed. Then he turned with a shrug. "Coffee? Or tea?"

She nodded and he led the way back toward the stairs but not before she saw the open door of the floor to ceiling cedar built walk-in closets with bright shimmering lights placed around two tall mirrors. He poured coffee for himself and lifted a brow in question at her. She smiled. "Coffee please."

Together they walked to sit at the wide bar. She took her time sipping at the dark steaming liquid. Finally, she couldn't hold it back any longer. "Why on earth would you buy a place like this, Duncan?"

He grinned over his mug. "I told you; I plan to have a family someday."

She glared hotly at him. "You know that's not what I mean. Why would you buy a place like this clear across the country in North Carolina?"

He shrugged. "I like it here."

She groaned and set her coffee down. "Don't be obtuse, Jamison."

He met her gaze, held it there in his own. "Are you sure you want to do this Sylvie?" he asked very quietly.

She blinked and looked away. Then she reached for her coffee and took another sip for courage. She lifted her eyes back to his and nodded.

"Someday, not now I know, but someday, when you realize that you love me too, I plan on raising a family here with you."

"I have the beach house," she argued even as the ridiculousness of her response had her shaking her head. "God, that doesn't even matter. The point here is that I may never be ready to have a family, Duncan."

He held her gaze. "The beach house is great for weekends and summer vacations, but our kids will need room to run and play and ride."

She looked away as tears welled up. "Please don't," she pleaded quietly. He sighed and walked over to take her into his arms. "I love you, Sylvie. I *need* you." He bent and kissed a tear on her cheek. "I know you aren't ready to hear that yet, but I already said it and now I need to keep saying it."

Her eyes flashed angrily, and he held up a hand. "I don't expect anything in return. I will take whatever I can. I'm very patient and I can wait until you're ready. If all you want now is sex, I'll give you that and do my damnedest to drive you out of your mind with pleasure."

She swallowed the lump of emotion that was stuck in her throat and tried to pull away. He clasped her tightly to him. "I don't need anything in return right now. Just let me love you." He bent his head slowly, giving her a chance to back away even as his mouth closed hungrily over her own. "Please Sylvie, just let me love you."

His hoarsely whispered words were as balming to the pain she felt inside, as his lips were, and she moved against him restlessly, unable to deny him what he so badly wanted. She nodded against his chest, and he lifted her into his arms and walked toward the stairs even as his mouth took hers again

Chapter 40

It took him five days to get to his destination. He could have been there sooner but had spent each night in a new city, searching for, and finding himself some good company. Because of the pit stops in Denver, Kansas City, and Nashville he was feeling more patient today. The sightseeing as it was, had lent some relief to the pressure he felt for not having already handled Sylvie.

Each of the bodies of the companions, he'd hauled until safely ensconced in a rural place where no one would stumble onto him as he dug their shallow graves. He was very careful with DNA, using bleach on the bodies, and always throwing away his own clothing as well as carefully cleaning his own body and truck afterward.

He cursed as he pulled past the beach house. It was going to be tough keeping an eye on the place when there wasn't anywhere, he could easily park. He drove past several times looking all around and trying to come up with a working plan to get to her.

He noticed a small unit across the street a few houses down that said it was available to rent and called the number. The place was a dump, which worked for him as he figured it was the only reason it was available in what was the busy tourist season in full swing. He paid for a month, just to give himself plenty of time to get to her. Maybe if he waited for a couple of weeks everyone would decide she was safe and leave her alone.

The real estate guy with long greasy hair met him at the apartment and gave him a key as soon as he pulled out a large stack of cash. He paid a little extra to keep the guy quiet and slipped inside the raggedly furnished space. There was one bedroom with a sagging mattress and a small table near the bed, one bathroom, a small kitchenette with a round table between it, and the front room that had one old ratty brown suede couch in front of a box television. The couch was stained and lumpy. He didn't care. He walked over to the door that opened out onto a tiny balcony that faced the street across from her house and supposedly the ocean. He couldn't see the ocean, as the four-story modern house directly across the small street blocked whatever view this run-down building might have once had. He could see her place from here, so he sat on the one worn and faded white rocking chair and pulled out his binoculars and cell phone.

He watched the front of the house for several hours before finally taking off his boots and strolling out across the street and toward the beach.

He would have to find a better place to watch her from there.

All of the windows were covered in shades as he'd feared so he began to make a plan. A plan where he could slip in and take care of her without any of her neighbors being aware.

Chapter 41

While Duncan was happy to see Sylvie, he had come out here because he also had some things to handle on the down low. Unlike Nick, he wasn't willing to stick her in her car and send her driving across town alone, however. He sighed as he slipped out from under her head and climbed out of the big log bed. She turned over and stared up at him. "What is it?" she asked quietly.

He gave her a blank look. She groaned and rolled up to sit up, wrapping her arms around her knees. "I can tell that there is something bothering you, Jamison, so spill."

He shrugged into his shirt and reached for his jeans. "I just feel like I'm missing some pieces. Like there is some big part of the whole puzzle that I don't have any of the pieces to."

She eyed him. "Like what?"

He ran a hand through his dark hair combing it back. "I don't know, it's just a feeling I have," he said in a frustrated tone.

She smiled and scooted over to place a hand on his arm. "I'm going to be okay Duncan. I promise."

His gaze narrowed. "Is there something about all of this that you aren't telling me?"

Sylvie stepped back. "Why on earth would I keep anything from you that might help catch the person who wants me dead? And what reason have I given you not to trust me?"

He eyed her cautiously. "I don't know. Maybe it has something to do with one of those legendary boyfriends that you have."

She laughed. "Good god, I couldn't care less about those guys, Duncan. They are men I sleep with, nothing more. There is nothing I have to hide from you."

His gaze was steady on hers. "Then why haven't you been trying harder to help us solve this case?"

She blinked. She *had* been trying to help them. Hadn't she? A little flustered, she tipped her chin up. "I don't know what you are talking about. I have been doing everything I can to help."

He shook his head then and advanced on her. "No, you really haven't. In all the days that I spent going over the details with first your dad and then Nick, you never once stepped in and got involved. I've been talking to Lemonte, Hanlan and Mason and they all say that you are normally like a dog with a bone when it comes to a case."

"Yet all you have really done is cook, and order food, but you don't really delve into the case with us. It's almost like you're detached from it all," he accused as he watched her tight expression for any nuance of emotion.

Suddenly her eyes filled with tears, and she looked down at her clasped hands. "Do you think this isn't hard for me, Duncan? *I* am the only one that monster seems to want dead. My dad died because *he* thought it would make it easier to get to me. But he didn't want *you* dead bad enough to shoot you when he had the chance. The truth is that I am losing my effing mind over all this."

Duncan stepped forward and took her clasped hands in his own. "Then why not get involved and help us solve this?" he asked softly.

She hesitated, took a deep breath and then finally looked up to meet his gaze. "Because. I keep having this overwhelming feeling that I should already know who he is. I spend every waking moment racking my brain, going over cases and boyfriends and trying to figure out who is behind all this, but somewhere deep inside, I feel like I *know* this man. Do you have any idea how frustrating it is to feel like I can't focus well enough to figure out who the most likely person I know is?" Her eyes teared up again. "It's killing me and trying to think about it at all gives me a migraine every time."

He frowned at her. There wasn't any indication of deceit or that she was trying to hide something from him. He sighed. "I'm sorry all this is happening, sweetheart." He pulled her against him and held her tight for a long moment. "I feel like it's all my fault."

She pulled away suddenly with an incredulous look. "Why in God's name would you think that?"

"Because, you didn't have any problems with anyone before you came back home to me."

"Now that, is just plain ridiculous, Duncan. Whoever this is, most likely followed me to Idaho. There is no way this has anything to do with you."

He shrugged. "Then why now, Sylvie?"

Her eyes bulged with anger. "Why now?" she asked shrilly. "Perhaps because he finally built up the courage to come for me, or maybe because he has had other priorities that needed handled first. There are a million reasons why now might be his perfect choice. Maybe he's been following me for months, or years even, and thought that Idaho might be a nice easy place to handle it."

Duncan shook his head. "But none of that makes any sense. I have been studying every detail of your life for the past five years and he would have had a million opportunities to take you or hurt you if that was what he's been wanting all along, but he hasn't. So, what changed when you came back home?"

She reached up to hold her aching head and said tiredly, "I don't know, dammit. I don't know what changed." She was gritting her teeth in frustration.

He smiled suddenly. "What if you do know but it was something that seemed so ordinary that you never thought twice about it. It could have been anything. Slighting someone, talking over someone, putting them behind bars, or even taking someone's loved one away. Think, Sylvie, who could there be that we haven't already considered?"

"I don't know," she whispered futilely and leaned into him as sobs shook her shoulders. "I just don't know."

He held her there for a long while before stepping back. "I had to come check on the horses but I don't have many groceries here yet so we will have to get lunch somewhere else." He went into the bathroom and returned with a bottle of Tylenol. "Take a couple of these, maybe it will take the edge off."

She swallowed them dry and then looked up at him. In a freak moment of weakness, she asked, "What if I don't want to remember, Duncan?"

He lifted one eyebrow. "Are you suggesting that you might know who it is but don't want to face it?"

She nodded then groaned. "I don't know anything any more, and it is driving me mad. I just can't help wondering…" Her voice trailed off.

"What?"

She shrugged. "Every time I listen to you guys trying to figure this out,

I feel disconnected and withdrawn as though none of what you're saying means anything at all. What if it's because I know something, but I just don't know what?"

He nodded as his gut tightened. This could be the missing piece. "If that is the case, what can we do to help you remember what you know?" He was already reaching for his phone.

She clasped his hand that held the phone. "Don't. I don't want anyone else to know what I told you." When he lifted a brow she said quietly, "It makes me feel small and weak and I can't stand the thought of you all watching me any more than you already do. It's like you're all waiting for my mind to explode."

He nodded, then took her hand and pulled her in for a warm hug. "In that case why don't you go get dressed and we can go out to lunch on our way back to your place."

She smiled through her lashes and slipped into the bathroom. "I would like nothing more. I don't know if you noticed but you have been keeping my appetite at top notch." She poked her head back around to say, "Duncan?"

He looked up. "Yeah?"

She hesitated then said softly, "I have to go get daddy at the airport after lunch. Will you go with me?"

He held her gaze and nodded seriously, "Of course." "Thank you. I just don't know if I can do it alone." "I have you Sylvie."

"Well, thanks. I'm going to grab a shower."

He nodded and then waited until she'd disappeared around the corner again before reaching for his phone. He stepped out of the bedroom. "Hello, Graham," he said cheerfully into the phone as the agent answered on the other end.

"What is it now, Jamison?" came the impatient response. "I'm right in the middle of something, so make it quick."

"What are the chances that the killer doesn't have anything to do with any of Sylvie's cases or boyfriends?" he asked.

"Well, I'd say they are pretty good considering the fact that we have looked at every case since she started as an intern at the DA's office, and we haven't found anything that stands out, other than Zachary McDaniels and we all know that he didn't do it." Suspiciously Agent Graham said,

"Why are you asking though?"

Duncan grinned, how like Graham to try to turn this and get information out of him instead. "Just a hunch. I'll let you know if anything comes of it."

He hung up as Sylvie emerged looking refreshed and beautiful. She had a warm rosy glow from their lovemaking, and he smiled as he bent to kiss her and tuck her into his side as they walked together to the staircase. "So where do you want to go for lunch?" he asked cheerfully.

She smiled. "Well, there is this great place by the water downtown and not too far from here if you like seafood…" She let her words trail.

He smiled. "I may as well start getting used to eating like I live near the coast."

She swatted his arm playfully. "We have lots of options if you want something different."

More seriously, he said, "Not at all. Who knows? Maybe I'll become the king of seafood. The only thing I really need to know is do they serve beer?"

Sylvie laughed even as he walked her around the house to his truck, instead of her car. He didn't want to be rude but if he remembered correctly, she had been a terrifyingly fearless driver in their youth, and he had a specific growing desire to live. He didn't even want to imagine her driving in the nervy little sports car.

Chapter 42

"How is the ranch surviving without you, Jamison?" Sylvie asked as they drove toward the beach and her home after a very relaxing lunch followed by a teary stop at the airport where she stood with Duncan by her side, as they escorted the casket with her father's body to a hearse and then followed to the funeral home.

He glanced sideways at her. "I sold the ranch."

"You did what!" she asked incredulously as nerves began to settle in her stomach like butterflies trying to get out. "Why would you do that?"

He grinned, "Don't look so worried, sweetheart. I have been wanting to try something different for a long time. You should know that."

She nodded. "True but you have stayed there all this time. How did Jackie feel about selling your family's home?"

He chuckled and turned to look at her out the corner of his eye. "She was actually quite pleased, seeing as how she's the one that I sold my half to."

Sylvie's brows wrinkled. "Jackie bought the ranch from you?"

"I was planning to just leave it to her, but she insisted that with her half of the money I have been giving her these past years, she wanted to buy me out. She wants to give it a real go." He shrugged. "She has always wanted to run the ranch, but it just hasn't always worked out that way. Her heart is in it though, and now that we hired some hands and things are easier, I figured it's the perfect time for her to take it on." He smiled. "Plus, the girls will love it. They love the horses and are always begging to come over and ride."

Sylvie took a deep breath and asked the thing she had been worried about since the conversation started. "But why now?"

He turned to look at her as he came to a stop at a red light. Forward and straight ahead she could barely see a hint of the sand and the beach with buildings lining the road parallel the ocean. His blue gaze held hers and he didn't blink, didn't smile. "You know why Sylvie."

She looked away. "I can't do anything but casual, Duncan."

He grinned sardonically. "I know. In fact, you have drilled that into my brain so hard I'm fairly certain I have a burr hole at this point."

She didn't laugh, just looked at him feeling miserable and not knowing how to stop it. "Why can't you just let it be casual and leave all the feeley stuff out?"

He grasped her hand in his and squeezed as he turned left and drove parallel to the beach toward her home. "Maybe the issue is you," he said quietly. But when she turned to stare at him in disbelief, he smiled. "Maybe if you weren't so spunky, so beautiful, so charismatic, so sweet, so sophisticated, so very sexy…"

He let the words trail off at her smile. Then he said softly, "It really is all your fault, sweetheart." This he said with a serious tone and an unmoving expression.

She looked away again, unable to maintain eye contact with his obvious feelings for her so blatantly in the air between them. Suddenly she felt sad, and she turned to look sideways at him. "I'm sorry, Duncan. I know you deserve more," she said quietly.

He shrugged easily. "I deserve you, Sylvianna Dunlap, so if this is all you have to give right now, it's enough." He pulled his truck into her drive at an angle. Then he turned and pulled her in for a quick, light kiss. "Everything is going to be all right, okay?"

She nodded against his chin and then he released her and walked quickly around to open her door. Nick met them at the door having heard her key in the lock. When he saw them, he smiled and re- holstered his gun. "Good, you're back."

Duncan nodded and followed Sylvie inside carefully securing the door behind her. "What's up?" he asked calmly, taking in Nick's furrowed brows.

Nick motioned them toward the kitchen table where Ben and Mason were seated with files strewn across the table. Nick ran a hand through his hair and glanced at Sylvie, hesitating. Duncan wrapped an arm around her waist and said calmly, "Tell me."

The DA stood and looked between Sylvie and Duncan for a long moment. "I suppose I should just tell you what I found out." He turned as both Sylvie and Duncan nodded in agreement. He cast an apologetic look Duncan's way. "First, I should probably just admit that I've had my doubts about the kind of person, you are, so I did some digging."

Sylvie felt Duncan suck air into his lungs, and she squeezed his hand, wrongly believing it was because Ben had questioned his integrity. Duncan was nothing without integrity, however, so she wasn't worried. She missed Duncan's hard look, and the small shake of his head at Ben Lemonte.

Ben continued in spite of Duncan. "I pulled all the files I could find on you which wasn't much." He looked at Sylvie and then back to Duncan. "I was, however, a little surprised to find an attachment with a confidential seal."

Duncan cut him off with a wave of his hand. "Stop with the theatrics, Lemonte, this isn't a courtroom, and we aren't a jury you're trying to convince," he said tightly. "You know that I'm not a bad guy so move on and tell me exactly what you found." All three men stood shoulder to shoulder and watched him. Duncan's jaw hardened and his eyes turned cold. "What did you find?" he bit out each word like venom.

Sylvie tensed a little against his obvious frustration. "I don't know what is going on with y'all, but you need to get it together and talk," she said in the steel calm, determined way that she was so well known for.

Nick sighed. "You don't know, do you, Sylvie?"

Her temper spiked. "I don't know what? Quit beating around the bush and tell me what the hell is going on, Nick."

Nick looked at Duncan then, held his hard gaze. "Jamison here has been involved with the FBI for a number of years."

Sylvie pulled away just enough to bend back and look up at Duncan.

"What is he talking about?" she asked in a bewildered voice.

Duncan gave the other man a cold look. Then he turned to Sylvie and sighed. "It's nothing, sweetheart. Not a big deal." The last he said through gritted teeth as he threw another cold look at Nick.

Sylvie couldn't help it. She actually stomped her foot in frustration.

"*What* isn't a big deal, Duncan?"

Nick chimed in. "It turns out Jamison here has been helping the FBI out on some pretty serious cases for quite some time now."

Duncan looked down at Sylvie. "Listen to me, sweetheart, these guys don't know what they are talking about." He cast a dark look over his shoulder and said quietly, "Sit down and I'll tell you what really happened."

Sylvie sat on the chair Duncan slid behind her knees. She was staring at him, and remembering the moments when things hadn't quite fit. Duncan

holding that gun like he was well accustomed to it. Duncan taking all that had happened in the past two weeks in stride. Duncan calmly pulling her back, so she wouldn't see the gored bloody mess of her father. She'd always thought of him on a horse, riding in the mountains. Hiking those same mountains. But the FBI? She glared hotly at him. "You have been lying to me?"

He shook his head. "I haven't lied once. I swear."

Her incredulous look seared him. "Oh God, please don't be that guy."

He looked confused. "What guy?"

She smiled bitterly. "Let me guess, you didn't lie. You just skirted the truth and omitted anything that you didn't want me to know?"

He shook his head. Everyone was watching him, waiting for his explanation. His face carefully devoid of emotion he said quietly, calmly, "I will admit there are a couple of things I didn't tell you, but not because I cared if you knew. I honestly didn't see that it made much of a difference either way."

Her voice was scathing when she asked, "My God, were you even a rancher?"

That question hit him like a ton of bricks and his shoulders squared. "Of course, I am! I wouldn't lie to you about something like that." He looked around at the men who were all watching with avid looks of curiosity. He sighed in exasperation and lifted his hand. "Look, you guys have this all wrong. I don't know what Agent Graham told you all, but—"

"Who the hell is Agent Graham?" Mason asked and the others waited for Duncan's answer.

His patience was wearing thin. "If you will all kindly let me speak, I'll explain everything." He fixed a frustrated glare at Mason and then softened it as he turned back to face Sylvie.

"It all began two years after you left…"

Chapter 43

"You never actually worked for the FBI then?" Sylvie asked, her brows furrowed twenty minutes later.

Duncan shook his head. "Not officially no. As I said, they tried to get me to join several times over the years, but it was a busy time for me."

"Then why did Assistant Director Donahue tell me that he has known you for years and that you have worked with them on countless cases," Ben Lemonte asked calmly.

Duncan eyed him for a long moment. "*Because*," he said with heavy emphasis, "AD Donahue was the special agent in charge of the Chicago office who they sent six years ago to try to recruit me. He must have come out to the ranch ten different times with ten different offers, each one better than the last."

"If that is true, why wouldn't you have taken them up on their offer?" Nick asked calmly.

Duncan shrugged and sighed. "I wanted to at the time. I really wanted to, but the ranch was still on the verge of bankruptcy, and I was trying to pay my sister's way through university. I couldn't just take off and leave it for her to deal with."

"So then, who is Agent Graham?" Sylvie asked quietly, as Duncan still hadn't told them that yet.

He turned a smile toward her and answered easily. "Agent Graham worked directly under AD Donahue back before he was the AD. He knew about me because they had discussed it several times with their team." He hesitated, not sure how much to share.

Sylvie lifted a brow and he sighed. If he didn't open up about everything, he was afraid that she wouldn't ever trust him again. "He is also the one who first sent me a case file that they wanted me to profile. He said they were hoping that I might have some fresh perspective since they kept striking out and the man they were hunting had already killed several people." Everyone was staring at him. He smiled. Ben Lemonte raised his hand in the air. "Well, what happened?"

Duncan thought back to that time, that first case. It had been thrilling, giving him a small fleeting sense of power. Until the unsub had killed another woman. A woman who had two kids. He rubbed a hand over his eyes. "Another woman died," he said flatly.

"Because you were wrong about the profile?" Mason asked.

Duncan shook his head. “No. Because I was right, but I hadn’t sent the profile to them because I was trying to get them off my back. I knew that if I helped them, they wouldn’t stop coming back to me, and I was already overworked and tired. I’d done all the basic training at that point as well, so I was exhausted.”

“Basic training?” Sylvie asked curiously.

Duncan nodded. “Of sorts. I couldn’t take off to Quantico, but I was curious if I could handle the training so I asked Donahue to send me a list of all the basic training qualifications so I could see if it was something I wanted to do.”

Nick laughed. “And he actually sent it to you?”

“He did,” Duncan said with a grin. “I think he thought it might motivate me to join up but all I did was make copies and send them back as requested.” He waved a hand. “Apparently he’d had a hard time convincing his boss to let him send them and they wanted the file back asap.”

“Did they ever know you did the training drills?” Nick asked, looking slightly impressed.

Duncan laughed. “I’ll never forget the look on Donahue’s face when he came out a few months later. He got all serious and asked me if I’d thought any more about going to Quantico to train. Everyone was smiling now. Duncan smiled right back. “So, I told him that I had already completed all of the training drills and exercises.”

“What did he say to that?” Sylvie wanted to know.

Duncan grinned. “He didn’t believe me. I was young back then, eager to show off you know, so I took him out to the old gravel pit and did all the shooting and fighting drills for him. I even asked him to spar with me to prove myself. When I was done telling him about every interrogation technique that I’d studied, he stared hard at me for a long time before he finally said, *Well I’ll be damned.*”

“What happened with the case they gave you?” It was Sylvie again. Duncan sighed and frowned. “When Agent Donahue called to tell me that they had another victim I felt sick. I threw up, and then I logged onto my computer and sent them my thoughts.”

“Did they catch him?” Nick wanted to know.

“Yeah, the next day. Turned out he was a sicko from a large family who had disowned him at twenty for not living by all their strict standards. He was systematically finding victims who were like each of his own family in age, look, and lifestyle and killing them. I saw the connection because the first victim was an older male and the second an older woman. Each kill after that was getting younger and there was enough evidence in the kills themselves to indicate that the unsub had family trauma.

When they put all the new information in their system, they immediately got a hit based on his family. The new parameters along with the information of his next sibling in age led them to a shortlist of women who fit the possible description. They found him stalking one of them, looking for his opportunity. He confessed as soon as they picked him up."

Sylvie shivered. "How disturbing. Was that the only case you helped them with?"

Shaking his head, Duncan stood. "No, it wasn't. I'd learned my lesson that day. The next time they sent me a case file they were having a hard time with, I looked it over right away and sent it back within hours." He stretched. "I need a drink, anyone want anything?" he asked as he walked to the fridge.

Everyone was looking around the table in silence, so he grabbed five beers and five water bottles and walked back over to sit down.

"Now," he said in an implacable voice. "Tell me what you found, Nick."

Nick smiled; he'd wondered if Duncan had forgotten. "The FBI finally got back to my boss about the case. We had put in a formal request before I left for Idaho for anything the feds might have that could be related. Anyhow, the feds being feds, took their sweet time but today finally sent over a case that they're working on."

Duncan waited patiently. "And?"

Nick continued. "The case that they are working on, is a missing persons case. It turns out that someone reported two girls missing that were known to have driven through that area around the time that they disappeared. It was about a week ago while Sylvie was still there. The feds still haven't found anything except that the girls' phones were turned off somewhere in the vicinity the day before they were reported missing by their brother who they were traveling to see." He took a breath and stood, shoving a thick file toward Duncan and reaching for a beer. Sounding sick, he said quietly, "It turns out that looking into that angle got the FBI looking more closely and they have now found another eight missing girls that they think could be related to the case."

Duncan nodded; it was all the information he'd already had. "I see. Is there anything else?"

Ben and Sylvie eyed him suspiciously. "You don't look surprised."

He looked at Sylvie. "I'm not. I've been working closely with Agent Graham on this. I stopped by Chicago on my way out here."

Her brows went up. "And you didn't think that bore mentioning?" she said quietly.

He shook his head. "Not at all. We still don't have any evidence linking any of these girls to you. For instance, why would a killer who has been killing women all these years suddenly pick you as a focal point?"

Everyone thought about that for a moment. "That is a good point. Unless…" Nick hesitated.

Duncan eyed him. "Unless what?"

"Unless all of this has been about you and not Sylvie. If the killer is only focused on her because you care about her. I've had cases where someone obsessed over the family or loved ones of the person, that they are angry with."

"I can see that potential," Ben admitted with a nod.

Sylvie stared at Duncan, tears in her eyes. "Is my dad dead because of something you are involved in?"

He shook his head but then stopped. The thought had crossed his mind, though he had soon let it go when he couldn't see any connection. "I don't see how it's possible. For one thing, I was never officially FBI, and therefore no one knew I was involved in any of the cases. The other thing, is that I have always kept close track and every offender I have profiled is still behind bars."

Sylvie nodded, seeming to accept his explanation. "Could it be the family member of someone who you helped put away?"

He shook his head, "I doubt it. Even if they knew I was involved, why would they choose to hold a grudge against me? I wasn't there when they were arrested, or when they were interrogated, or really in any way that might lead them to see me as a threat."

"Maybe someone in the FBI told them they wouldn't have been able to catch them if not for you." That comment came from Mason who had been quietly nursing his beer.

Duncan thought about that for a long moment and took a swallow of his own. "I guess there is that possibility," he said quietly. He looked down into his beer for another long moment. He didn't like where all this was leading. It was something he'd already thought of and discarded several times since he didn't see any way that it could be true. His blue eyes lifted and met Sylvie's brown ones. "The only other thing I can think of is that it might be someone from Idaho that you knew before."

"Someone that had obsessed about you before you left, and then when you came back it triggered them in some way. Someone who was there killing all along in your absence." His mind reeled and his tone hardened as he continued. "It would be a male, most likely white, given that all of the missing women are white." His mind turned this way and that as he worked it all out in his mind.

Sounding surer now, he said firmly, "Someone who'd felt challenged by a female figure that he thought should respect him. Maybe he saw her as belittling, and he would want to take the women to prove his strength and virility. To prove that he was ultimately stronger than them in the end." He looked around the table feeling sick. "Fuck! It has got to be someone in Idaho!"

Everyone looked around feeling a little bit sick themselves. Sylvie turned to stare at him. His mind was sharp, and it was entrancing watching it flow and twist as he worked through the issue. She gave him a small smile. She imagined that being able to put himself in their shoes in his mind, took its toll. He looked away.

Nick eyed him thoughtfully. "How are we going to figure out who might have taken the women when we don't even know who they all are yet?" He looked down at the file. "There are a few in here that might be related but we need a way to search for all of the girls that went missing within a hundred miles of that area between then and now."

"How is it that there could be so many missing women, and no one has been looking for them all this time? It seems like someone should have put it all together by now." Sylvie said looking sad.

Duncan smiled reassuringly. "They aren't local girls though, and most of them were traveling through the area and it wasn't until I called Graham and insisted that he open a case into your shooter that they began piecing it together. The police departments where the girls were reported missing all have unsolved open cases, but they are spread all over the place, so they never knew that there were other related cases."

"We'd need to look into every missing girl and try to narrow down which ones may have traveled through there at some point before they were reported missing."

Nick ran his hands through his hair in frustration. "That could take forever."

Sylvie rose as her headache was kicking in full force again. "Unfortunately, I think Duncan is right. It would have to be someone I went to school with or someone I dated or knew pretty well back then. Or maybe someone that I didn't know, who felt scorned." She looked around the room. "I imagine you are all going to want me to write down a list of everyone I dated or knew back then?"

The men all nodded in unison. She sighed. "I'm happy to do it but not yet." She looked around the room. "I have another migraine and I'm going nuts being trapped inside all the time." She eyed the door leading to the deck and then ultimately, the warm beach.

"Don't even think about it," Duncan warned.

She turned to look at him and said quietly, "There isn't any way that I am going to be able to focus enough to remember every name from back then, with this headache. I'm sorry."

He met her gaze, held it in his hard and determined one. "I don't want you out there where he could possibly take a shot at you Sylvie."

She nodded. "I know, but think about it, Duncan. There is a big chance he didn't even follow me all the way back here. Then there is the fact that I have stayed indoors almost exclusively since the first shooting, so even if he is here somewhere, he wouldn't be planning to shoot me with a rifle. He'd have to get up close and I'd have you out there with me."

He shook his head. "I have an idea of how I could get a list of the missing girls." He sighed. "It's a long shot but I need to make a phone call."

"Maybe Nick could come with me?" she suggested calmly. She met Duncan's pained look. "Please. I need some fresh air and I will be super careful."

He caved. "Fine, but Mason goes too, and you stay away from crowds." He gave her a hard look. "I mean it, Sylvie, stay between them at all times and don't stray."

"He sounds like a fed," Nick said wryly. "Acting all bossy and telling all of us lowly cops what to do."

Duncan didn't smile. "Just keep her safe and I won't take it out of your hide."

After getting the guys to agree, Sylvie slipped upstairs to change into shorts and a sports bra. It was warm and sunny outside. She glanced in the mirror and saw the ragged round stitched scab where she'd been shot. She sighed and reached for a sheer cover up top. She didn't want to scare anyone while she was out.

When she got downstairs, Nick was also wearing shorts and a tank. Mason stood in bare feet; pants rolled to just above his ankles. She smiled at them and gave a little wave to Ben who was once again studying the file the FBI had sent him. She looked around for Duncan, but he wasn't there.

"He's upstairs making a phone call." Nick answered the question she was too stubborn to ask.

She nodded. "Thanks for agreeing to this. I really need it."

They both nodded and she watched as Nick secured his gun holster around his waist. Together they all walked out onto the deck and then down to the access gate. She quickly punched in a number as both Nick and Mason perused everything in sight, alertly watching for danger.

Chapter 44

"I don't understand what you're talking about, Duncan. Are you telling me that there is a serial killer on the loose out here?" Jackie asked as she gently rubbed Olivia's crying back.

"Yes, sis, I think there might be, but I need to find out what girls have gone missing in the area, so I can narrow it down to find the killer. I also need to know that you are safe. Is Ren there with you? I don't want you alone, sis."

Jackie walked to the front door with a shiver and carefully locked the deadbolt. "No, he had to go away for a couple of days. Work," she said quietly. "Duncan, do I need to take the girls and get out of here for a while?" Duncan swallowed hard. "Where is Ren?" He didn't mean to sound suspicious but at this point it could be anyone and he wasn't taking any chances.

"Duncan Jamison I can hear that tone. Don't speak to me that way about Ren. This isn't him. I would stake both mine and the girls' life on that."

"Please don't," he said curtly.

"He has been checking in every couple of hours Duncan. He is in the city taking some meetings, trying to finalize the new state trooper facility's plans before the baby comes."

"Be extremely cautious until I call you again, do you hear me? I can't lose you too." His voice was rough.

She sighed. "I will be careful. But I won't be keeping my distance from my husband, Duncan, and I won't tell him about this either, because I don't want to ruin the friendship that the two of you have built. He's bound to be much less kind if he thinks you believe he could be a serial killer," she said, sounding slightly bitter.

"Damn it, Jackie, that isn't what I'm saying. There is someone on the loose and women are disappearing. It feels like it's someone we might know at this point, and I'd have sworn two weeks ago that no one we know could be a killer either."

"I get the message. I'll be careful, I promise," she assured him gently.

"Good. Now, about those newspapers," he continued in a no-nonsense tone.

"That's the part I don't understand, Duncan. What do all of Dad's old newspapers have to do with a serial killer?"

"Nothing. It's just that reporters always seem to nag and get every bit of information they can, especially about anything local, so I thought maybe you could go through them and see if they referenced the missing girls. If any of them heard about girls thought to have gone missing locally, they would have printed it. I'm fairly certain Dad has kept every newspaper he's bought, since…" He hesitated. "Since Mom died."

She laughed out loud. "So not only are you asking me to take the heat with Dad if he catches me touching all of his papers, but you're telling me that after all these years, Dad's obsession with those papers might actually help solve a case?" She laughed again. "Now that, I never thought I'd see."

He ran a tired hand over his face. "Me neither. If you had any idea how many times, I've almost thrown them all in the burn pit…" He let the words trail off. "Anyway, start with the newest and work your way back. Write down the names of any of the missing girls, and sis?"

"Yeah?"

"Be careful."

"I will. What should I tell Dad when he has a freak out?" Jackie asked quietly.

"Tell him the truth. He has to want Sylvie's shooter caught as much as the rest of us. I think that will be enough." He paused. "Thank you, Jackie. Send the list to me as soon as you have it."

"I will. I love you, Duncan. Now go knock those city cops down a notch."

He chuckled. "I'll try."

He clicked off the call and then scrolled through his contacts looking for the police station in Idaho. He paused with his finger on the call button. What if it was a local cop that was doing this? He lifted his finger before it touched the screen. He thought about the ranch hands and went through the same thing. What if it had been one of them that had killed Reagan Dunlap? He sighed and looked down the road. Pedestrians strolled, some hand in hand, some alone walking dogs or going for an afternoon jog in the warm muggy air. He watched for a long moment, deep in thought. Who the hell was he supposed to trust at this point? He thought of Ren Bradley and a small smile turned his mouth up.

Jackie was smart as hell, and he was going to bet on her. He punched in the number and waited as the phone rang once, twice, a third time. He was about to hang up when his brother-in-law came on the line. "Yeah?"

"I think you need to go home and make sure Jackie is safe," he said quietly.

There was a long silence and he heard Ren say something to someone on his end of the line. "Hang on a minute, Duncan. I'm in a meeting. Let me get somewhere quiet."

Ten seconds later he came back on. "Okay now, what the fuck is going on, Duncan?"

Duncan raised an eyebrow. Ren rarely swore and he'd never heard that kind of venom behind a single word. "I think there might be a serial killer on the loose somewhere out there. I asked Jackie to go over to Dad's and look through the old newspapers, but I'm worried about her safety. Where are you anyway?"

"I'm in Boise, but I'll be there in a few hours," Ren said quietly, and Duncan could hear his footsteps down an echoing hallway.

"Don't let her or the girls out of your sight until I get this guy, Ren."

"Jesus Christ, you are scaring me right now."

Duncan nodded. "Good. You still have a handgun, right?"

"Yeah, but I haven't used it in a while."

"Well make sure you aim to kill if you end up needing to shoot. I'd jump a plane tonight if I thought Sylvie would be all right."

"I know you would. We'll be fine. You just find this bastard, Duncan."

He heard a car door slamming, and he raised his eyebrows. "What about the meeting?"

"I don't give a crap about that right now, man. Do you or the FBI have any leads on who might be doing all this?"

Duncan thought about the question as he stood on the small deck outside the extra bedroom. Down the street he watched an old lady with long stringy grey hair make her way slowly, carefully, across the road. Something about the woman had his gaze swinging back to look at her again. He studied her hair and profile carefully but there was nothing familiar. He sighed. He was beginning to lose his mind.

Ren cleared his throat and Duncan swung back toward Sylvie's house. "We don't know much yet. It has to be someone that knew Sylvie all those years ago, I think. Someone who would obsess about her enough to warrant going after her, in spite of the limelight she is in. All of the other girls we suspect might have fallen victim are all quiet cases, missing, but quietly from other places. Less likely to be missed right there in our hometown."

"Okay, well, be safe and keep us updated, now go protect your girl."

Duncan hung up feeling a little better about Jackie. Because he was still worried, he called the eldest ranch hand, Frank and asked him to watch out for Jackie and the girls to get there and stay with them until Ren arrived. Then he went back inside where Ben was still determinedly looking through files for the umpteenth time. He had to admit the man was like a hound dog when it came to the case. He nodded. "Find anything interesting?"

The DA shook his head and sat back. "Unfortunately, not. None of this makes sense. This guy would have to have a connection to Sylvie, right?"

Duncan nodded. "I think so, yeah. I think he'd likely be someone who knows her well."

Ben nodded. "That's what I thought. I have a couple of detectives finding all of the high school yearbook photos for her graduating class so that we can look over them, in case Sylvie forgets anyone that it could have been."

"Smart," Duncan said and realized he hadn't given the man enough credit. Once he'd realized the guy had slept with Sylvie, he'd chosen to dislike him. He sighed now. "How long will it take your team to get a hold of them?"

"Not long. Assuming that the high school there has evolved enough into the twenty-first century to download them onto those yearbook websites sites that most schools have now." His phone buzzed and he looked down. "Laura," he said simply and rolled his shoulders as he typed a quick response.

Duncan watched him. "How does she feel about your spending so much time with a woman you had an affair with?"

Benjamin Lemonte grinned, and his dark eyes swung up to Duncan's. "How long have you been wanting to ask that question?" He chuckled softly. "Sylvie is great. Beautiful, smart, a drive like no other. But Laura is all those things and still soft. Does that make any sense? We have a son together and don't tell anyone, because it's supposed to be a secret, but she is expecting again."

Duncan's brows went up. "Congratulations. So how does she feel about all this?"

Ben laughed again. "She likes Sylvie, and she knows that I love her, and would do anything she asked me to do and yet she hasn't asked me to come home." He smiled at Duncan. "That is the kind of woman that she is, and I think it should give you an idea of how she feels." His phone buzzed again, and he stared down at it for a long moment. Then he grinned and stood up. "They just sent the photos over."

Duncan turned to the printer they had moved onto the end of the table turning the area into a makeshift office. "Print them so Sylvie can go over them." He added another thick chunk of paper and looked at his watch. "How long are they going to be gone?"

Ben shrugged. "I don't know. They didn't say." He grinned. "Mason looked a sight in his suit with his pant legs rolled up to walk on the beach."

Duncan cracked a grin at the image, even as he reached for his phone and punched in Nick's number. "Where are you guys?" he asked impatiently as soon as Nick answered.

"On the beach. Everything is good. I haven't seen anything out of place, man. Just tourists out to catch the beach and waves and locals making the day of it. Nothing out of the ordinary."

"Don't be gone too long. Come back soon."

"Will do, sir," Nick said in a mocking voice that grated on Duncan's nerves. He hung up as the first couple of pages full of pimpled high school kids' faces fell off the printer. He snatched them and sat down, already beginning to look over each face. Most of them he remembered, though he couldn't remember all of the names. He sighed and began to make a tiny notation next to each that he remembered seeing Sylvie talking to or going out with. Ben made more coffee and Duncan thanked him as he poured over the growing stack carefully. After switching pages a few times, he looked up. "How many of these, are there?"

Ben shrugged and looked down at his phone. "Enough for four years' worth of year books I'd guess."

Duncan sighed and went back to marking each individual who might possibly be running around taking women. The creep who'd killed Sylvie's dad. He sighed and took a sip of coffee. "This is going to take all night. If you need to go home to the wife, we'll be okay here."

Ben took another drink of coffee and leaned back in his chair. "I'll go in a bit. You're good for her you know?"

Duncan looked up. "Huh?" Then he realized what the man had said and smiled. "I'd better be, since I intend to marry her."

"So, I heard," the man said with amusement. "You do know how she feels about commitment, right?"

"I do." He took another sip of coffee. "She'll change her mind." "What if she doesn't?"

Duncan didn't flinch. "She will." He sounded so sure about it that Ben almost felt sorry for the man. Almost.

Chapter 45

He had watched the house for hours that day before anyone came or went. A couple of Ubers showed up and two men went in the house. Still, he waited and watched. To anyone looking at him he was a less well-off vacationer, there on the tiny white peeling deck on the ocean side of the small apartment. He had a wide hat and was in shorts and a T-shirt with a mixed drink on the window seat that looked toward the beach. Even his binoculars seemed to fit. Someone watching the flight of seagulls or cranes as they lifted and soared only to dive back down and toward the water again. Most of the day passed with no entertainment. He'd walked out to the beach for a bit. Walked aimlessly as he casually strolled past the gate that he assumed was locked from the inside. He smiled; he could get over the fence easily enough if that was how he chose to go in. Children laughed, and he found himself watching as they ran into the swell of the waves and back out again. Such simple joy. He wondered what it would feel like to derive such joy from such a simple activity.

Since Elaine had died, he hadn't felt much of anything. Except when he had his hands on the throat of a young girl with her whole life in his hands and his dick sticking her. Here, families laughed. They built sandcastles and dipped their feet in the water. There were coolers of cold drinks and those with beer even though alcohol wasn't technically permitted on the beach. He saw one little boy eating cheesy fish crackers and then tossing them to the birds as they flocked forward fighting over each cracker he launched from his chubby fingers.

Couples sat in bright chairs under umbrellas or laid out on towels together soaking up the sun. He watched all of them playing and enjoying something so mundane as a beach, and he swallowed thirstily. For the first time in seven (or was it eight years now?) he regretted killing Elaine. She had been simple-minded enough, but she had given him joy and pleasure. She had made him feel something besides the empty weight of the failure that he had become. He'd loved her in his own way, her shining dark hair and big brown eyes so different from his own. But she had turned away from him and betrayed him and that was unforgivable.

Unable to take the joy any longer he made his way quickly back to the shoddy apartment on stilts, that he was staying in. The only good thing it offered, was an actual garage under the apartment where his truck was tucked nicely inside, and the closed door hid it from prying eyes.

He watched the house and then, to his great pleasure, found that if he stepped on the chair he could actually climb easily onto the low worn roof. From this angle, far to the right side of the house he could see about half of her deck as well as the path leading to the beach. He smiled and went back in for a towel to soften the shingles and an umbrella to shade him from the relentless sun. Even now, he knew that anyone who saw him would simply think he was enjoying the day like the rest of the people that bustled up and down the street.

He saw Duncan Jamison's familiar truck and frowned as it indeed turned into her driveway. That was an issue. Why had Duncan come all this way? His brows furrowed together in concern. He hadn't counted on him coming this far. He should have known better.

The man had an uncanny need for duty, honor and loyalty. He'd sat up straighter when Duncan had walked around the truck to help Sylvie out. Though everything else looked in place, however, a long-range rifle wouldn't go unnoticed up here, so he wasn't prepared. He watched through angry slits as the two of them spoke and then walked together into her house.

From this vantage point he'd watched as she made her way out and onto the beach with two men on either side of her and his carefully crafted plan slid front and center in his mind. He stood quickly and slid down off the roof. Then he hurried inside to get everything ready. It could work, he thought, a little giddy at the thought of finally finishing this and getting his life back on track.

Fifteen minutes later, he walked outside and made his way across the street heading to the beach. He froze, as he saw Duncan watching from the front balcony, but then he turned his head away and hurried out of sight.

Chapter 46

Sylvie laughed as the wave of cool water sloshed up her ankles, going higher than she'd anticipated. Mason swore as water sloshed up his pant legs. She turned to walk backwards, smiling up at him. "Teach you to come to the beach in a suit, buddy," she teased.

He gave her a frown and darted for her as though to tackle her. Her headache was well on its way to being gone and she dodged easily since he was only going after her half-heartedly. She veered right, moving around a group of various aged kids looking happy as they splashed around in the waves. She smiled and waved at a little girl who had her legs buried in mud and looked like she was eating as much mud as she had on her legs. The blonde-haired girl looked up at her and gave a shy little wave.

They were nearly a mile away from her house as she looked out at the glorious aqua colored ocean. The water was gorgeous today and she tipped her head back so the sun could kiss her cheeks as she sighed. "God, I needed this." She turned to look at Nick and Mason who were a couple steps behind her. "Thank you, guys, for being such great sports about this."

They both nodded and continued to look around cautiously. A couple was watching them, and she smiled as they walked past hand in hand. She let the water wash over her ankles again and turned back. "You guys are causing a scene, looking all stressed out that way."

Nick looked at Mason's suit that was soaked up to his knees. "One of us is, anyway," he said with a grin.

"I'm hungry!" she said happily. It was the most exercise she'd had since she'd left the hospital, and she felt great.

"No way," Nick spat. "Jamison already called and laid down the law once. We are not going to sit in an open restaurant. I love you Sylvie, but not enough to take that kind of heat," he joked, half seriously.

Sylvie looked at the buildings as they passed. With a happy little smile she said, "Okay no restaurants, but we could at least grab a couple of pizzas. I know this great place and it's not much farther up the strip."

Mason was looking down at his pants with sand stuck to the wet bottoms and shaking his head.

"Please. You don't even have to go inside. I'll go in and grab it and we can walk the strip back to the house and share with the other guys," she cajoled with a playful little pout.

"Fine," Nick said but he looked around them uneasily. The hair on the back of his neck was standing up. He looked behind them, but nothing looked out of order. Suddenly, he wanted to get them off the beach and onto the street.

Mason looked at him with an eyebrow up. “Everything okay, Nick?”

He shrugged and glanced behind them again. Nothing or no one you wouldn’t expect to see out here enjoying the remainder of the beautiful sunny day. He shook his head. “Let’s go get that pizza and get back inside.”

They made their way onto the busy sidewalk, weaving around a couple and a family. The street cleared and Nick saw the flashing open sign across the intersection with a pizza slice lit up next to it only a block away. Eyes looking around, he took hold of her arm and led her carefully across a side street and eased her around a cross-walk post. The street was clear, and he walked quickly toward that flashing pepperoni sign. Just before they got to the next street a crowd of tourists came rushing around the corner.

Nick scanned the group, three women in miniskirts and shorts with bikini tops and gauzy blouses. An old lady pulling a large luggage bag. Three teenagers and one woman pushing a stroller. Nick relaxed and dropped his arm to his side letting her go. They moved to the right side of the sidewalk sandwiched between the crowd and the souvenir shop on their right.

The crowd moved over and started past their trio. There was a quiet pop, pop, and all hell broke loose. Nick turned toward Sylvie at the same time that Mason did, but she was fine. Another girl screamed and Nick turned and watched in horror as a small splotch of red on her shoulder began to spread. He reacted without thinking. He rushed forward to put pressure on the wound even as another scream sounded, and he saw Mason hunch down over a teenaged boy. Sylvie was looking around stunned, and Nick turned back to put pressure on the wound even as he reached for his phone to call an ambulance.

Sylvie looked around trying to see what was happening. People were screaming and scattering away. An old woman tried to get past her and bumped into her shoulder. A door opened off to her right and a man stepped out. “What the hell is going on?” he asked loudly.

The old woman tripped on her shoe and Sylvie reached out a hand to steady her. She felt something hard ram into her back and turned to look at the woman. The very familiar looking woman. She scrunched her brows as a strong arm shoved her inside a door. She tried to turn to see who was manhandling her. Nick or Mason were most likely trying to keep her safe, but she was terrified for the people still on the street. She didn’t want to bail. She fought against the arms that held her.

She heard a low laugh and then a cold piece of wet fabric slid over her mouth. It had a funny smell and she tried to think what it was, even as she slumped noiselessly to the floor. The woman behind her smiled and lifted

Sylvie easily to her shoulder and hurried into the back of the shop. She held the gun out, fully prepared to shoot anyone who was inside on sight.

The old woman's luck prevailed as the man who'd run out was obviously the only one working the small shop today. Quickly she opened the suitcase and began tucking her prize inside. Five minutes later she ducked back out of the store and carefully rolled her suitcase past the crowd huddled around. "I called the police, they are on their way," she said in a rough cackle. Then she turned on her heel, and carefully wheeled off. This hadn't exactly been the plan, but it had been too good an opportunity to pass up.

Nick turned to look for Sylvie even as blood oozed through his fingers around the point-blank gunshot wound. Sylvie was gone. He swore and Mason looked up from where he was quickly tightening a belt around the kid's leg as blood spurted from the nicked artery. "Where the hell did Sylvie go?" Nick shouted. Mason finished the tourniquet and then spun around searching for Sylvie, but there was no sign of her.

He turned back toward Nick. "Shit, man. She's gone."

Chapter 47

Duncan was still staring at the sheets of high school photos when Ben stood.

"I guess I should go home and see my wife and son."

Duncan nodded absent-mindedly and glanced at his watch. His gaze strayed to the back door. They had been gone far too long. He stood. "I think I'll go out for a bit and stretch my legs."

Ben chuckled. "I'm sure they're fine."

Duncan's phone rang and he reached for it automatically as he slipped off his black loafers and walked toward the door. "Yeah?"

There was a whimper on the line, and he stood from where he'd crouched to remove his socks. "Hello? Are you there, Jackie?" he asked as he pulled the phone away to glance down at Jackie's face on the screen. Gaze narrowed, he asked, "Jackie are you okay?"

Another whimper and then she sobbed, "Oh God Duncan, it's him. It has to be him."

"Slow down, sis, who are you talking about?" Duncan demanded as he turned and motioned to Ben who had turned back from the door. Ben strode over quickly, even as Duncan switched the sound to speaker. There was another sob from Jackie. "Jackie, *talk* to me. Is someone there?"

He could hear her sobbing again. "It's Dad, Duncan. It has to be him.

He killed Mr Dunlap. Oh god."

Rage, unlike anything he'd ever experienced numbed his brain. He forced himself to take a breath. "Jackie, sweetheart, what do you mean? Why do you think Dad killed Reagan Dunlap? They were friends."

He heard her take a deep gulping breath. "It's him. I know it! The newspapers Duncan." He heard her gagging, and a moment later she came back on the line. "I'm sorry," she sobbed.

"Take a deep breath, sis. What did you find in the newspapers?" he asked without any feeling. In quiet detached relief he realized that he didn't feel anything at all.

"It's all in there, Duncan. All those women…" He heard her gagging again, and asked gently. "Is Ren there with you, Jackie?"

She gulped. "No, Frank is helping me, but he agrees, Duncan. Is Sylvie, okay?"

That question threw him into action. "Dad is there in Idaho, right?" he asked as he yanked off his single remaining sock.

"I'm so sorry, Duncan, but I haven't seen him in days." She sobbed again.

"Are you saying that you think he might be here?" he asked numbly.

"I'm so, so sorry, I didn't keep in touch with him like I said I would," she whimpered.

"This isn't on you, sis. I gotta go. Call Ren and lock all the doors. There is a gun in my room on the shelf in the closet. Code is the twins' birthday." He clicked off even as he and Ben dashed out the door at a dead run toward the beach.

The gate was locked but Duncan catapulted over the top and kept going. Behind him he heard Ben call out, "Wait up, Jamison, I know the code."

He didn't pause. He ran with every ounce of strength he had in his strong body because in his mind he felt Sylvie slipping away and the emptiness he felt at that realization, terrified him. He dialed Nick's number at a dead run. Voicemail. "Damn it, Nick, pick up."

He dialed again. Voicemail again. Still, he ran. The sand tugged at his heels, tried to pull him down into it. He swerved through a group of teens, closer to the water where the ground felt firmer. He picked up his pace as he got Mason's voicemail. He swore loudly and saw a young mother grab her son who looked to be about five and try to cover his ears even as she threw a dirty look his way. He didn't care. He swerved around a young couple and dialed again.

Then, he heard the sirens. Numbly, he followed the sound. He ran out onto the street like a madman. He felt glass slice into his heel and realized that someone had obviously dropped a glass bottle and shards were all over.

He didn't slow down. He turned the corner and saw the flashing lights ahead three blocks. A car narrowly missed him as he ran across a side street. He didn't slow or stop, until he saw the woman lying on the sidewalk. His feet slowed and his mind went numb, even as he tried to remember what Sylvie had been wearing.

Her hair was long and brown. Maybe too brown? he hoped. Then it hit him that he was actually hoping the woman lying on the ground bleeding all over Nick, was someone else's heartbeat, someone else's loved one, and he swore and pulled himself together. Nick looked up with a helpless searching look and Duncan's heart bottomed out again. "Is she…" He paused to gasp for air. "Dead?" He bent over at the waist, unable to get himself to look at the pale lifeless face of Sylvie.

Suddenly, Nick realized what he must think, and he moved away from the paramedic. "It's not Sylvie, Duncan. Someone opened fire on a crowd of tourists."

Duncan jerked up and the gut-wrenching torment on his face had Nick sucking in his breath. He hurried over to put a hand on Duncan's arm. "Are you okay, man? You don't look so good."

"Where is she?" he asked desperately. Nick didn't answer and Duncan turned to shake him. "Where the fuck is Sylvie, Nick?"

Mason walked over and he and Nick exchanged a look. "We don't know yet, Jamison. She was here and then someone shot into the crowd. I checked on her several times, and she was fine, but this woman and another boy that the first ambulance already took to the hospital were on the ground bleeding out and we had to help. I turned around a few seconds later and she was gone."

"There wasn't anyone here that seemed threatening," Mason added.

Duncan's knees were shaking, he wanted to wrap his hands around their necks and squeeze. He refrained, even as he lowered into a squat to keep himself from toppling over, gasping for air. His dark head fell into his hands. Sylvie was still alive. She had to be. He didn't have any reason to believe that she was dead yet. He laughed suddenly then, crazed insane laughter and then he stood up. Nick and Mason both stared hard at him as his shoulders shook. She might be dead, and he was so incredibly stupid because losing her was what he deserved. His face hardened suddenly. "Did you see an older guy?" he rasped out hoarsely.

They both stared at him as though he had two heads. He felt deranged somewhere in a deep place, where all the bright hope that he'd had left inside, died. He laughed again and aimed the next question at Nick. "Did you see my dear old dad anywhere, Hanlan?"

Ben came jogging up, out of breath. "Damn\ you're fast," he said to Duncan and then he quickly scanned the face of the woman being lifted onto the stretcher. He looked relieved and then guilt crossed his tanned face.

"Where is Sylvie?" he asked.

Duncan gave another crazed laugh. "Yes, where, indeed?"

Nick shot him an irritated look. "We lost her in all the commotion."

Ben looked worried. Duncan looked like he might start ripping his hair out any minute. Mason looked away. He couldn't stand here watching the man who had been so cool and clear-headed since they'd met, fall to pieces in front of them. His partner had recently lost her husband and it had been hell watching a good strong woman lowered to soul shaking grief.

"Why would your dad be here, Jamison?" Nick asked suddenly.

A dark look of hatred and anger crossed his eyes before he replied. "My sister Jackie says that he's our killer," he stated with another little laugh. "That's us Jamison's, keeping it in the family."

All three men stared at him for a moment before looking away from the uncomfortable truth of his words and a man who'd been leveled because he loved that same woman. He sobered suddenly. Sylvie was still alive. She had to be. He rubbed a hand across his chest where his heart thundered painfully. He would know if she was dead, wouldn't he? He would know if his father had ripped away the bright future and life that she had, wouldn't he? He should be able to feel that at least.

Coldly, feeling both numb and a jittery high at the same time, he turned to Nick and Mason who were still waiting for an explanation. "You said that there wasn't anyone here that seemed threatening," he said to Nick. "Walk me through this. Who was here?" he glanced around. There were several men around on the curb, several police officers, too many people who could have been a threat in his mind.

Mason answered for Nick because one look at his fellow detective told him that his friend was about to throw up. He pointed behind them. "We were the only ones on the street on this side. We were going to the pizza place." He pointed. It was only two buildings down from where they stood. He turned his thumb toward the corner. "A swarm of tourists came around the corner. Three teenagers, a mom pushing a stroller, three beautiful laughing women." He paused, thinking back. "And an old lady with a luggage bag."

Duncan stared at him as he continued. "They were walking past when there was a quiet pop pop. The gun was silenced, I'm sure of it. Anyway, the victims started screaming and me and Nick checked on Sylvie. She was fine so we turned and help the shot woman and boy. Then when we turned back, she was gone. Nick was on the phone with nine-one-one and the shop owner ran out to help." He paused again. "The old lady ran inside to call the cops." He shrugged as he couldn't remember anything else.

"Where are all the witnesses? I assume they were rounded up?" Duncan asked. His words were clipped.

Mason threw another thumb over his shoulder. "The cops took them all over there to give their statements."

Duncan walked stiffly toward the curb and eyed the small group there. He swore suddenly and turned back toward the men. He started running again and they watched as he jogged over to them. Then he ran right on past and tore off down the street.

"Where the hell is he going?" Nick asked even as all three of them broke into a run following on his heels. A cop shouted for him to stop as Duncan leapt over the crime scene tape he was attaching there. Duncan never even looked back.

Chapter 48

Sylvie jerked awake as a putrid stench blossomed under her nose. She tried to sit up, but she was bound at her wrists and ankles. She fell back but then caught sight of a hand as it removed the white bubble looking thing that stunk. She strained against the bindings, but they wouldn't budge.

"I wouldn't bother with all that fuss, dear. You won't get away," a light, cheerfully nasal voice said from a distance. An all-too familiar voice. Fear shivered down her spine as she lifted her head and tried to grasp who was talking. The room was dark, with only a small lamp in the far corner that was lit. She was on a bed, that much she knew, and she could see an old couch on the other side of an archway.

"Who are you? Why are you doing this?" she asked, her voice shaking with fear.

"Oh, Sylvie my dear, you can stop pretending. It's just you and me now." He stepped closer.

Her head throbbed as she squinted up at him, trying to see his face. Suddenly, she smiled in relief. "Mr Jamison? Is that you?" She sounded relieved and he looked taken aback. He nodded.

How had he found her here? she wondered through her foggy brain. She closed her eyes, trying to focus through the pain bursting in her skull. She remembered an old lady tripping, fireworks, bloody spots on the woman, Nick trying to help her, the old lady again, something hard against her back, that sweet, sweet, smell and then nothing.

Then suddenly everything came at once, overwhelmingly vivid, terrifyingly clear, she moaned and pushed against her restraints. Her eyes popped open, and she stared up at him as every broken memory wriggled and fought for its place in her damaged mind.

Mr Jamison cracking a rock against Mrs Jamison's head, then her body falling downward, tumbling down the rocks. Sylvie herself sliding back into the notch in the rock closing her eyes, hoping, praying that he wouldn't see her there. She'd barely taken a breath as he'd hefted Mary's limp body, with blood dripping from where the rock had bashed a hole in her head, over his shoulder and walking off like it was nothing.

She'd been out hiking that day. Alone. It wasn't something she was supposed to do, but she had been missing Duncan terribly since he clearly did not reciprocate her feelings, and she'd stopped trying to get him to notice her. There were other boys, she'd told herself. Then she had tried all of those other boys. Tried desperately to find anyone who made her feel alive the way Duncan Jamison did.

She was more disappointed each time and yet still she'd tried. That day, however, one of the girls at school had called her a slut in the girls' bathroom, and she had fled in tears. Looking back now, it seemed amusing, especially since she'd still been a virgin then.

She'd taken Elaine's car and drove to the mountain trail. She always felt close to Duncan here. It was *their* spot. The place where he'd gently lifted and then carried her down the mountain. The place where he'd quietly admitted that he was tired of playing games with Elaine, who had just broken up with him once again. The place where they had run so far ahead of Jackie and Elaine, he had nearly kissed her. He'd denied it, of course, but she had seen that look there in his clear blue eyes. He'd wanted that kiss as much as her. And so, she'd come here. She'd practically run up the mountainside, gut aching and wheezing for breath, as she thought about how useless her life had become.

She didn't have any real friends besides Elaine and Jackie, and they were always harassing her to leave them alone. She was popular, because all of the boys liked her, but the girls were only nice when the boys they liked were nearby. She was only seventeen and had her whole life ahead of her, but she couldn't seem to get over her stupid childish crush on Duncan Jamison. She had been desperately in love with him.

A tear slipped out the corner of her eye. Who was she kidding? She was desperately in love with him now. If only she'd had the courage to tell him… She sobbed as she looked up into Arthurs ugly, ugly, blue eyes. God, she wished she had told him when she had the chance. Now… She couldn't let herself finish that thought.

"Why ain't you never talked to anyone about me, Sylvie?" he asked, sounding a little hurt that she hadn't.

She swallowed her fear. Sensing that he would want that from her. She heard Duncan's words in her head. *It would be a male, most likely white*, he'd said. *Someone who'd felt challenged by a female figure that he thought should respect him. Maybe he saw her as belittling, and he would want to take the women to prove his strength and virility. To prove that he was ultimately stronger than them*. She smiled a little. He had been dead on. Arthur saw the smile and leaned down toward her with a frown.

"So?" he demanded. "Why ain't you told nobody?"

She looked up at him and forced pity past the fear in her stomach.

"You fool. I didn't even remember anything about you or anything that happened until now."

He looked surprised, stunned even. He shook his head in denial.

"That's not possible. I told y-you I'd kill you if you told anyone. You wouldn't have forgotten that."

The rest of her memories settled into place. “You killed your wife. I saw you do it.”

Arthur stepped back. “No, you didn’t! No one saw anything that day.”

“I did.” She laughed loudly, obnoxiously. “I was there that day. I skipped school and ran up the mountain because I was sad. I heard you yelling at Mrs… Mary, and I stopped and listened. She was calling you filthy and dirty because you are,” she said with feeling.

He slapped her hard across the mouth and she tasted blood on her lip. She refused to show the fear that rose like bile in her throat. She refused to give him anything. Instead, she smiled. A wide, beautiful, bloody, smile.

“Mrs Jamison was talking about calling the cops and turning you in for something. I didn’t know what, at first, but then she said you had ruined her friendship with my parents because she could never look them in the eye again after what you had done to my family, to Elaine. I remembered hearing Elaine talking to Jackie about a secret guy that she was dating, and I knew what you had done. I knew you were a pedophile sleeping with a young girl.”

He spit out the side of his mouth, and anger lit his eyes making them glow slightly in the lamplight. “I ain’t no pedophile, you bitch. She was of age, and I loved her. I had felt dead inside for as long as I could remember.” He looked at his feet. “I couldn’t even get it up with Mary any more. That’s what made her suspect that I was cheatin’ and she followed me. She was the one who wanted to go somewhere to talk so that the kids couldn’t hear what we were fightin’ about. Said it might damage Duncan and Jackie. So, we went up the mountain.”

“Did you plan to kill her before you hiked up?” she asked softly.

He turned and looked at her, then he grinned. “Look at you, little miss Assistant District Attorney herself, trying to get me to confess to premeditation so you can take me down.” He laughed and spittle flew out the side of his mouth. “It doesn’t matter anyhow. You ain’t gonna live through the next hour.”

He was smarter than he looked, and she would remember that. She smiled. “I figured as much.”

He blinked at her easy acceptance. “Why ain’t you sad then?”

She laughed softly. “You have managed to kill off every one of my family, at this point, Mr Jamison. It might be nice to join them.”

He eyed her with intelligent eyes. “I didn’t kill your mother.”

She shrugged. “You may as well have. The stress of losing Elaine took her out in the long run.”

Sylvie wasn’t responding to anything the way he’d expected her to, and he didn’t like it. She smiled, “So why did you kill Mary, Arthur? Was it because she was too much of a woman for you?”

He turned red with anger. “That bitch practically forced me to marry her. She chased me and wooed my mama and daddy until they were pushing me to the alter. She had them seeing rainbows and sunshine where they had thought I was a big fat disappointment. I never did like ranchin' you know? My daddy mocked me all the time, sayin' that I wasn't a real man. But Mary Jensen, she was a good girl and my daddy said if a woman like that could love me, I must be better than he thought."

"So, I married her, gave her everything my hands could work up. I worked at the ranch even though I hated it. The only time I ever took anything for myself was when I found my sweet Elaine. She started sneaking downstairs when she'd stay over with Jackie, flirtin' with me. She was pretty and she wanted me. It was the only time I ever acted selfish," he exclaimed.

She widened her eyes in challenge. "Well, not the only time, right? What about since then, Arthur?" She watched him squirm a little. "Were you selfish with those other girls?"

He stalked away and came back with water to wet his dry lips.

"You don't know what you're talking about, girlie."

She smiled brightly again. "Oh, but I do. You have been a very, very, bad man," she scolded.

She saw his fist coming this time and managed to turn her mouth away. It connected with her cheek and slid into her eye socket with a sickening pop. She bit her lip, tasted blood, bit down harder. She would not give him the satisfaction of fear.

She was placing all of her faith in Duncan and his profile even with as quickly as he'd summed it up. She had to buy herself time. Time to find an escape path. Time for Duncan to find her. Time for *anything* but death.

She tossed her hair and head lightly with a little laugh. "You really know how to play rough don't you, Mr Jamison?"

He stared at her, panting off his anger. A chilling look entered his eyes as he studied her, ran his gaze down her scantily clad body. He reached for his cock, stroked it. "You look a little like her you know?" he said almost reverently.

Sylvie didn't like the look in his eye, but she fought the surge of panic swelling her throat. She swallowed it. "Like whom, Arthur? Mary? Or Elaine? Or one of those other poor girls?"

He raised his fist but didn't slap her. "You know who I mean. She was special. She wanted to please me. Did you know that?" he asked as though he actually thought that her and Elaine had sat down and talked about how she'd pleased him sexually.

"I didn't know you were the one she was sleeping with until I heard you that day. I hid on the cliff until you were gone. I knew Mrs Jamison was dead, but I couldn't quite grasp that fact. When you went off the trail I ran ahead and left before you saw my car. I saw your truck there."

He met her eyes searching for evidence that she was lying. She met his gaze steadily even through the eye that was burning and beginning to swell shut. "I drove straight home. I'd planned to tell my parents what I saw, but Elaine was home by then. Jackie had given her a ride and she was pitching a fit to my mom and dad, because I'd taken her car. They asked me where I had been, and I told them I was having a rough day, so I left and went for a walk in the mountains. They cussed me out for an hour. Then when they were done, Elaine started in on me. She called me a spiteful little bitch. Don't you think that's funny? Elaine calling *me* spiteful?"

His gaze narrowed dangerously. "Elaine was a sweet girl."

She laughed. "Elaine was a spiteful girl who slept with you because she spent so many years lusting after Duncan who wouldn't have sex with her because she couldn't ever stay with him longer that five minutes at a time." She watched his face as she drove her point home. "She slept with you, hoping it would somehow make him jealous." She knew that it was a lie because Jackie had mentioned that Elaine had been planning a future with an older man. Sylvie couldn't stand the thought that her beautiful, bratty, sister would have given up her own future for the sick man in front of her.

"You won't talk me out of this, Sylvie. You know too much. Why didn't you tell your parents?" He was like a child on a bike who didn't know how to steer.

She sighed. "Truthfully, I tried, but they told me to be quiet and go to my room. Then a couple of hours later, Mom came up and got me. She said Mary was in a terrible accident and had fallen off a cliff. I thought maybe you had tried to save her. When I got to the hospital, I saw Jackie and Duncan and I just couldn't say anything. It was like my mind just sealed up and went away somewhere quiet.

"Later that night, when I heard she'd died, I cried, alone in my room. I felt responsible somehow. Like if I'd run right down the mountain and called the police she might have lived." She turned away from him then, unable to hide the shame she felt with those memories. She forced her head back toward him and his ever-watching eyes. "That was why I became a prosecutor. Did you know that?"

He grinned. He'd finally gotten a piece of something from her that was weak. He walked over to her, brushed her breast with his knuckle. "I wish I could make it quick for you," he licked his dry lips. "I have just been waiting too long for you, my dear."

She wasn't sure what he meant by that but swallowed the bile on her tongue at his touch. He ran a hand between her legs that were tied, spread apart. She jerked, even as she tried to will herself to stay still. She fought the panic, trying not to give him any reason to keep touching her. He laughed and delved two fingers up her shorts a couple of inches. It took every ounce of willpower she had not to cry out or show fear. He changed tactics at her lack of response. She could see it now. That deep need he had to see her afraid, wanting to feel his power over her.

He pulled her gauzy white top up to her neck. Touched her nipple there. She bit the inside of her cheek. He pushed at the shoulder wound suddenly, and she screamed in pain before she could bite her tongue.

He laughed. "I did this to you."

She blinked away tears and forced a smile. "Didn't take me out though, did you? I'm not so easy to kill." She said it casually, as though it didn't matter.

He stared at her, bent down so she felt his breath there on her neck. She shivered. His eyes saw that slight movement. He smiled gently, and she knew that she had lost. "I see you now. You are a smart girl, Sylvie, but I see it now. The fear you hide…" He sniffed her skin and then slowly began pulling her shorts and underwear off. "It's time to finish this, dear."

Sylvie began twisting and turning, as panic finally took over. He only worked her shorts just low enough to give himself room to rape her. She screamed and tried to bite his arm as it went past her mouth. He pulled it back before she could do any real damage then slapped her hard. He clucked his tongue. "Yes, dear, let's end this."

She saw him pull down his pants and her mind went blank with fear. She heard a loud crash and tried to turn to see where it had come from. Arthur reached for the gun on the bed at her feet, then turned toward the sound. "He has a gun! Don't come in!" she screamed. as she was suddenly terrified that Duncan had indeed found her and would come barreling into the room and get shot.

"I bet I'm a better shot," he said, rasping for air from his run. From the corner of her eye, she watched him step out, his gun in the air.

Arthur flinched at the barrel trained on his head. "Now, son, let's just talk about this like two sensible men."

Duncan allowed himself one tiny glance at Sylvie to make sure that she was still alive. Bile rose in his throat. She'd obviously been raped, and he was lucky she wasn't dead. He looked his father in the eye. "It's over, Dad. We saw the papers." He hadn't seen them, but he guessed that if it was bad enough that Jackie had been crying, it was something pretty telling.

Arthur raised his free hand in the air. "Look, son, I don't want to shoot you. I could have killed you countless times, but you are a good boy. Put the gun down and let's talk about this." He turned a quick glance toward Sylvie. "If you let me finish her off, we can both go together. No one ever has to know the rest."

"You're one sick bastard," Duncan ground out. "You actually think I would be okay with any of this?" He looked like he might throw up.

Sylvie tried talking some sense into him. "Just go Duncan. Please…"

she pleaded. She kept imagining him dying because of all the stupid choices she'd made. If there was truly a God, she prayed that he wouldn't ask this one thing of her.

Duncan's jaw tightened at her plea. "I'm going to count to three and if you don't drop the weapon, then I'm pulling the trigger, you asshole."

He saw his father's reaction and knew what he would do even before Arthur tried to pull the gun up to shoot him. Duncan shot him dead center in his forehead. As he watched Arthur's body crumple to the floor, he was grateful for the blessed numbness he'd felt since Jackie had called him. He heard Nick, Mason and finally Ben run into the apartment wheezing and out of breath. He strode over and laid a blanket over Sylvie's bare skin gently. Then he quickly cut the ropes, tying her to the bed. She rose up and reached for him, but he felt nothing even as her shaking body made contact with his.

He looked down at her, feeling dead inside. "I'm so sorry I didn't catch him sooner," he said quietly, as though defeated.

She stared up at his blank expression. "Are you kidding me, J-Jamison?" The name caught in her throat; she held his gaze. "I would be dead right now if you hadn't…" Her words trailed off as she saw him glance at the crumpled body on the floor.

"Jesus, Jamison are you okay?" It was Nick's voice and he turned to meet dark eyes and give one quick nod. Then he pulled out his cell phone and dialed. "Graham, you'd better get down here."

"I'm at the airport now. Jackie called me, she was worried about you."

"Good," was all Duncan said. Then he turned and stalked out. Nick and Mason held onto Sylvie and helped her outside for fresh air. They were only three houses down the street from her house, and she shivered as she realized Arthur had been watching her all along. Duncan's insistence to keep windows covered had likely saved her life once again. She could only see out one of her eyes as she looked at Nick.

"Where is Duncan?"

He shrugged but reached for her hand. "I think something broke." She tried to see him better but her good eye teared up. "What happ…" she gulped, "How did he find me?"

He shook his head. "I don't have a fucking clue. He took off running from where Mr Jamison…" He saw her flinch at the name and changed it. "From where Arthur took you and we all followed, but he was running like a demon was on his tail. He had to have run the two miles in ten minutes because it took me fourteen and he had time to do all that." He pointed inside.

Sylvie tried to smile. "I need to talk to him."

"I'm sure he just needs a minute," Nick assured her, but they had both seen the haunted look in his eyes. Neither of them thought he was okay. Nick looked away as Sylvie nodded through her tears. He turned back to ask gently, "Did he… hurt you?"

She laughed and tried to see him through her good eye. "Not a scratch, Hanlan."

He actually blushed. "I know he hurt you, Sylvie, what I'm trying to ask is…" he hesitated again.

She swallowed but shook her head. "He didn't rape me, if that's what you were wondering. He was on top of me taking off his pants when Duncan crashed through the door." A desperate giggle escaped. "I'm pretty sure he died with his pants halfway down."

Nick met her gaze and smiled. It was little comfort in a tragic moment, and they might as well take it, since he had a strong suspicion that it would be the last comfort for a long while. "I'm sorry I left your side," he said softly. Mason nodded and chimed in his apology as well.

Sylvie looked at them each in turn. "Don't ever be sorry for trying to save someone's life."

They both nodded. She stared each of them down with her good eye. "Say it," she demanded.

Nick grinned. "Yes ma'am. I made the right call."

Mason seconded that with a grin and a nod then he turned to Nick. "I'm going to hold down the scene until the crime scene unit gets here, but you should take photos and then take her home to clean up."

"You sure?" Nick asked gratefully.

Mason looked at Sylvie's swollen face and then remembered the look on Duncan's, when he'd thought she was dead. "Yes. Do it. I'll handle any slack we get for it."

They took several photos of her outside and inside. Up close of her injuries. Her shoulder wound which had been scabbed over fully earlier today, was now oozing blood again. She held her shirt up as they took photos of that area up close. Finally done, Nick walked her back to her house. Before they could walk in, however, Duncan strode out wearing his shoes and socks. He looked at them with an eyebrow up.

"We took lots of photos for evidence. I was bringing her home to clean up," Nick offered quietly.

Duncan shook his head, turning to Sylvie. "I'm sorry, but Agent Graham will be here any minute, and he wants to talk to you and see the scene himself before it gets disturbed by the CSU."

She nodded. She of all people understood the importance of tidy police work. Besides, if Duncan was going to catch any trouble over the shooting of his dad, she would do whatever she could to make up the difference. Sirens sounded in the distance, and they all turned and watched as two patrol units and a black SUV sped towards the old building across the street. The patrol cars screamed past and skidded to a halt in front of Mason, who began talking to the four officers as they jumped out. She saw him hold out his badge, even as the black SUV screeched to a halt a mere four feet away. She turned and watched as a tall lanky man with dark sunglasses and a sleek grey suit climbed out and walked around. He was somewhere in his mid-thirties she guessed, and had an air about him as if he was used to bossing people around. She smiled. She knew people like this man.

He held out his hand. "Agent Jonathan Graham, ma'am. You must be Sylvianna Dunlap." He turned to Nick and held out his hand "Detective?"

"Hanlan," Nick offered. "Nick Hanlan."

Graham nodded at Duncan and his eyes stayed on him for a long moment before he turned back to Sylvie. "Pardon my bluntness, ma'am, but you look like you have been through hell." He looked at Duncan again, who didn't offer anything. "Has anyone taken photos? Scraped your nails? That sort of thing?"

Sylvie nodded. "Detective Hanlan and Detective Langden did all of that, sir."

"All righty then, why don't you go in and get cleaned up while I mosey on over and take a look at the scene," he suggested kindly. "I'll come back in a bit, and we can debrief you then."

Sylvie thought Duncan might follow her inside, but he didn't. It wouldn't have mattered anyway, as the agent said quickly, "Walk with me, Jamison."

She wasn't the only one who saw him flinch at the name. She sighed. She would have to talk to him later. Nick helped her inside and up the stairs. "Make sure you set all your clothes here on the sink so I can bag them," he said gently and then bent to run hot water into the tub. "Take a long hot bath, it'll help with the soreness later on."

She nodded and began undressing. He left the room, closing the door gently behind himself. She watched the tub fill and then sank gratefully into the hot depths. Maybe if she took long enough, Duncan would come join her. She brushed that thought aside. He would likely be busy for weeks tying up all the loose ends.

She smiled and adopted a line from his book. She could wait. She remembered him telling her that several times and tears slid down her cheeks. She saw the empty look in his eyes replay over and over and felt as though he was slipping away from her, but there was nothing she could do.

She could be strong, she reminded herself. She could stand strong in the face of all that had happened, and maybe, just maybe, someday, somehow, she would finally feel at peace with it all.

Once Duncan came back to her, she would tell him how she felt, and she would tell him the truth about all those years ago. Then, she would lay it all to rest, and finally plan for the future.

But Duncan didn't come for several hours. When he did, he had Agent

Graham, two local detectives and Mason with him. Ben was on their tail. She tried to smile at all of them though her vision was a bit blurry. She offered them hot coffee. All but one detective took her up on it and Nick took the pot from her hand and poured it for them.

She nodded gratefully as she had been slightly worried about melting her skin off, if she misjudged how close the mugs were. She tried to go to Duncan. He wouldn't look at her, but his arm did go around her shoulder and pull her close for a moment before he leaned down to say, "I brought everyone who needs to hear this so that you'll only have to go over it all once. I'm sorry, it's the best I can do. I can't keep them away forever." His tone was gentle, but when she looked at him and tried to hold his gaze, he looked away.

She sighed and took a sip of hot coffee herself. She sat at the head of the table, and everyone found a spot around it. When there was silence for a moment, she said softly, "When Arthur first took me, he looked like an old lady. I thought I had tripped her with my foot but when I reached out to help her keep her balance, she shoved something into my back and dragged me into that little store we were by. He then shoved something under my nose, and everything went black." She lifted her eyes to Duncan's, but his gaze shifted away. She swallowed. "The next thing I remember is waking up to him waving something with a very powerful stank." She wrinkled her nose in memory.

She saw Duncan smile at that. "Did you at any time actually see Arthur Jamison's face?"

She laughed. "Oh yes, yes, I did. I remembered what Duncan said about him wanting power and I was determined not to show him fear. I talked to him, calmly asking questions about the women, my sister Elaine, and Mary Jamison," she said the last quietly, and with shame. She saw Duncan's head jerk up to stare at her and she slowly looked up.

There was curiosity there in his eyes. It wasn't love, or joy, but it was something. Duncan watched her face and asked, "Why would you ask him about *them*?"

Sylvie looked down at her hands. "Because my memories came back." She let that statement hang in the charged air for a long minute. "Do you remember how I had forgotten that your mom had died that year, Duncan?" She glanced up to see his nod. "Well, I remembered everything. I feel like this is all my fault somehow…" Her voice trailed off. "Maybe I could have stopped it before all of this happened." She took a while to explain what she'd seen, how she had felt and how she hadn't wanted to hurt Elaine by talking to her parents about it with her there.

Then later when Mrs Jamison was dead, she wasn't sure it was worth it because Arthur Jamison had scared her, and what if he could get to her? Tears rolled down her face as she lifted her eyes to his, dreading to see the condemnation there. His eyes stared back, stark, blue, tortured, unjudging. She swallowed. "I swear I had no idea that she was still alive, Duncan. I would have stayed and tried to help her. But the hole in her head was awful." She broke off. In a near whisper she said, "She was so limp, I thought she was already dead."

The room was silent but then Nick moved over to her side and wrapped his arm around her shoulders. "You know that you did nothing wrong, Sylvie. You were just a kid. None of this was your fault." He squeezed her again.

Duncan was watching them, and Nick saw one tiny flash of irritation before Duncan stood and said implacably, "Nick is right, none of this is on you. You have no blame in anything that happened." Then he turned and walked out. The gentle click of the door behind him was like an a-bomb in the silent space.

Sylvie broke, tears streamed down her face, and she rocked, lifting her knees onto the chair and wrapping her arms around them as silent sobs racked her body. After a long while she looked up at Agent Graham who was watching her with something like sympathy. She squared her shoulders. "I'm sorry, I'll finish now."

"Take your time, ma'am. He's not going to get more dead, though I'm beginning to wish I was the one to pull the trigger." All the men smiled and nodded.

Ben walked around to take up the place on the opposite side to Nick in a show of support. She looked at all the familiar faces and then those that weren't. Finally, her gaze landed on Jonathan Graham. He was the most likely to tell her the truth. "You know him, sir. Do you think he will ever forgive me for making him kill his father?"

Graham's face moved into a tight smile. "I don't think you need to worry about that, Miss Dunlap."

She stared hard at him, and her face started to crumple. "Don't you get it? I *am* worried about that, terrified in fact, that he won't ever forgive me."

Nick patted her back soothingly and Ben reached for her hand, tears evident in his own eyes. "Sylvie, Duncan isn't mad at you honey."

She stared at him. "Of course, he is! If it wasn't for my weakness all those years ago, none of this would have happened and some cop would have come and hauled that bastard off to rot in a jail cell."

"That isn't necessarily true, ma'am," the agent said with a gentle smile. She turned back to him listening avidly. "Severe memory loss like you're describing is common with kids who experience trauma. It's their brain's way of keeping them safe until they can actually handle dealing with it. You had probably already forgotten what you'd seen by the following day."

She shook her head. "That's just it. I remembered the next day because I was in the hospital waiting to see if Mrs Jamison was going to make it and I saw Duncan." She looked down at her hands clasped around her knees.

"He looked ravaged, hollowed out, and I wanted to run to him and tell him that his dad had done it, but then Mr Jamison came in all sad and teary eyed and I thought maybe everything would be okay and I wouldn't have to face it."

"That is a very natural and very common thing to feel," Agent Graham assured her.

"God, are all you feds this arrogant?" Nick asked, incredulously.

Graham smiled. "Not all of us. Just those of us that actually know what we are doing."

Nick threw a nasty look his way. He missed Ben's warning look and plunged on in. "You make me sick, man. A man is dead, two innocent people are in the hospital fighting for their lives, another man is on the verge of losing himself in the madness, and all you can do is sit here telling Sylvie what she should be feeling. Who the hell do you think you are?"

Ben opened his mouth but closed it again sending an apologetic look at the agent. "As you can imagine, Agent Graham, we have all been under immense pressure for the last couple of weeks, and tempers are flaring. You'll have to excuse the tension."

Graham nodded. "Look, I get it." He turned his cool gaze to Nick. "I understand where you are coming from, Detective Hanlan. I want you to also see this from my point of view." He waited and when Nick finally nodded, he explained. "Since Duncan first called me to look into this, shortly after Miss Dunlap was shot, I have uncovered multiple missing girls and my gut, along with Jackie Jamison's horror at what she found in her father's newspapers, is telling me that there is a whole long string of families that deserve closure for their daughters and sisters and friends."

"The calmer Miss Dunlap feels, the more relaxed she is, the more likely she is to uncover clear healthy memories." He turned back to Sylvie. "I'm guessing you've had a lot of migraines of late?"

She nodded. Then suddenly she looked up at him. "It was my brain trying to get hold of the memories, wasn't it?"

He nodded. "Another common side effect of damaged memories. We can't count on your memories holding up in a court of law, however, so we need to find ways to back up the memories with evidence wherever we can. Internal affairs and the FBI review board are going to be all over this case, and we don't want any of us, especially Duncan Jamison, going down for this."

She nodded. "I asked him about all of it. He talked to me, sir. I know I didn't record it, but I had him talking about killing his wife. He bragged about shooting me and poked at the wound until it bled." She heard Nick's indrawn breath and reached out to squeeze his hand. "The only thing I didn't get him to confess to me was killing Elaine."

"What makes you think that he killed her too?" Agent Graham asked gently.

"I don't think, I *know* he did it," she said firmly. "The week of Mary's death the whole family was busy with the hospital, then the funeral, and finally dealing with all the people that kept showing up to tell them how sorry they were and to bring them food. But then things began dying down and one night I stayed up late studying. I had a test coming up and I had decided I wanted to start getting better grades."

She looked around the room and her gaze froze on Duncan who was leaning against her bar, listening intently. She smiled a little, but he only gave her a little nod. She looked around again. "I had decided that I wanted to become a lawyer and eventually a prosecutor and that meant I needed good grades. Anyway, that night I heard Elaine sneaking in past her curfew, so I opened my door and told her to come in." She glanced at Duncan. "You see, I had a feeling she had been out with Mr Jamison again, and I wanted to warn her to stay away from him because he was dangerous."

Duncan moved over to sit again, and Sylvie continued. "She argued with me and told me that it was all a big mistake and that I was making it all up. She told me about how Mary had fallen off a cliff because her whole body was broken and not just her head."

Sylvie looked down at her hands. "I threw up then. Something about my sister talking about a dead woman as though it was normal, got to me. Anyway, she kept telling me over and over that it was an accident, that the Jamison's had been out hiking and Mary had slipped and fallen."

"She even told me that Arthur had hauled his wife's body all the way to his truck and tried to get her to the hospital as soon as possible." Shame filled her voice then. "I don't know why but after the way she sounded so sure of herself over and over, I started believing her. I thought that maybe I'd had a dream, then I started wondering if I was insane. Those two thoughts ran over and over in my head for the next two days. Then Elaine went missing and I wasn't thinking about that any more." Tears filled her eyes. "My sweet, bossy, beautiful sister had told me what happened, and I wanted to believe her. When I found out that she was dead, I was grateful it was a cliff and not something else. Then she was gone, and I knew that she must be right. It doesn't make any sense now, I know, but then it felt like everything. I don't even remember being threatened by Mr Jamison," she added thoughtfully.

"He threatened you?" Nick asked incredulously.

She shrugged. "Like I said, I don't remember, but when he had me tied up, he said something about me talking to him about what he'd done and told me that he'd threatened me. He said that if I talked to anyone, he would kill the rest of my family. Again, I don't remember that part. That's just what he said."

"After Elaine's funeral I focused on getting good grades and getting into a good school for pre-law. I had nightmares all the time and it stressed my parents out, though I never remembered the dreams when they woke me up." She finished and looked around the room. There were seven faces all looking tired and ragged and traumatized.

"I know this is all my fault and I should have come forward sooner..."

She let the words trail off as all seven heads shook in denial.

Chapter 49

Nick insisted on staying the night with Sylvie as everyone said their goodbyes. Duncan had disappeared an hour before, and she wondered where he had gone, but she didn't want to pester him after everything. An hour after everyone left, she went upstairs and looked around. There wasn't a single sign that Duncan had ever been there. She tossed all night, waiting for his familiar warmth to slide into the bed next to her, but she waited in vain.

When the morning sun shone through, she stretched and walked over to open the drapes, and the door to the beach, letting in fresh air and the calming sound of ocean waves as she dressed and combed her hair. Then she carefully did her makeup, doing the best she could to cover the black eye.

Nick was already up when she went down, and she looked at him questioningly. He only shrugged and told her that he'd made coffee. She didn't hear from Duncan until that afternoon when he texted to let her know that he was having her car dropped off to her house. She rushed out, expecting him to be the one driving but a young man slid out and handed her the keys. "Mr Duncan said to return this to you, Miss Dunlap."

She thanked the young man and went back inside. She went for a long leisurely walk on the beach and felt the sun on her bruised face and skin and the sand between her toes. Nick came out after a while, and they talked as they walked back to her house. Around four o'clock, Duncan called to let her know that the FBI task force wanted to do another interview in case they had missed anything. She agreed and asked him how he was doing. He told her he was fine and that he had to go.

He didn't get to her house until halfway through the meeting and then he poured coffee, sat next to her and didn't move a muscle when she put her hand on his. She cried inside at the aloof expression on his face. When the interview was over, he left with all the other agents.

It was Nick who told her that Duncan had flown back to Idaho with an FBI team to sort through all of the evidence there. She tried Duncan's phone but only got his voicemail. She missed him and told him that in a message.

She called Jackie who was shaken to her core. They'd both cried through the conversation. Before she'd hung up, Sylvie had said, "I'm so sorry Jackie, for my part in all of this."

The other woman had laughed and cried at the same time. "I don't know why *you* would be sorry. You lost everything because of my dad. I'm the one who's sorry."

They'd both cried again and then said their goodbyes. Though Sylvie had called to ask about Duncan, she hadn't had the courage to ask for anything from his pregnant sister, who was already reeling from the horrific truth.

It was Nick who came and held her hand as he told her about the gravel pit and the twenty-seven bodies Duncan, and the FBI found there. It was also Nick who held her as she cried for all of the lost lives of those same women. She desperately needed to talk to Duncan, but constantly having that thought circling round and round her head was beginning to drive her mad, especially since he seemed in no particular hurry to talk to her too.

He kept his word about her dad's service. He showed up for the viewing and stood by her side through the entire ordeal until all of the well-wishing cops and friends finally said their goodbyes and wandered away. He'd held her then, for one long moment where she started to feel like everything was going to be okay, but then he'd released her and walked away without a backward glance.

Ben came over to tell her that Duncan was under investigation for the shooting of his father and had been taken in for questioning. She demanded that he take her right to the precinct where Duncan was, but Ben had refused, telling her that he had already sent a lawyer that would do better than either of them could. He stayed with her throughout the day until his phone rang and the person on the other end informed him that Duncan had been released and was no longer under any suspicion of murder.

She had herself another good cry after Ben left. She cried for Duncan and the pain he was going through, and for everyone that had lost something at the hands of Arthur Jamison, a likely psychopath. Nick came over again and brought dinner. He told her that the FBI had almost finished the investigation. Though there was no way of knowing if there were other women out there who Arthur had killed as well, they saw it as best to close the case and let all of the mourning families that were being hounded by the media, heal.

Five days after the incident, Sylvie finally drove out to Duncan's house. The young man who had dropped off her car was there, and he informed her that Mr Duncan was out but that he'd told him to let Sylvie into the house if she wanted, or to let her ride, or really anything she wanted to do.

That information surprised her since she was certain that Duncan hated her for being the cause that had made him shoot his own father. She missed him so badly that she asked to ride the stallion, and the young man showed her where the tack was in the barn and helped her saddle up the beautiful horse.

She rode him for an hour around the huge property at a trot and then she urged him into a gallop. As the wind threw her hair back, she felt alive again and she could almost feel Duncan next to her side. When the horse tired, she walked him back to cool him off, and then spent another hour brushing and washing him down because it comforted her. She left with a wave to the young man, as he rode on a bright green mower trimming the huge section of grass around the house.

She went back to work on Monday morning because she couldn't stand to sit around waiting any longer. It felt good to be back in her element and she delved into a new case that DA Lemonte hand delivered to her. She knew it was meant as a distraction for all that was going on, but she enjoyed it anyway. The case was a sexual assault arrest where two girls had come forward and admitted that their boss at a fast-food joint had been forcing them to have sex with him in order to keep their jobs.

The traumatized teenagers, the asshole of a man, and the entire case had her feeling alive again and she told herself that it was good. After work she drove to Duncan's again in case he'd come back, since he still wasn't answering her phone calls.

He wasn't home, but he did have more furniture in the house, and it was beginning to feel a little lived in. She walked up to his closet and noticed that he'd had some boxes of his things shipped that were waiting for him to come put them away.

She opened the boxes and carefully sorted and folded his clothing and stacked his shoes and boots on the cedar shelves in the gorgeous closet. The young man was here again and this time she'd asked his name.

Jamal Brown, he'd told her with a grin, but then he'd told her to call him Mal. She hadn't been ready to go home to her quiet empty house, so she'd gone riding again instead. This time she'd taken the beautiful spotted mare just because she wondered if they all needed exercising.

She hadn't gotten home until eight o'clock and had found Mason waiting outside her place with takeout bag in hand. She smiled. "What? Did you and Nick decide to take turns coming to check on me?" He looked away guiltily and she laughed. "Wow, you really did, didn't you?"

He didn't respond to the question but held up the bag with a sheepish grin. "I brought food," he bribed.

She laughed and let him in. "Well, if I'm honest I don't mind the company, I have been a little lonely of late."

"Still haven't heard from him, huh?" he asked gently as he unloaded takeaway boxes with shrimp, fries and side salads.

She stared at him, wondering if he knew something she didn't. "Why do you ask that?"

He shrugged. "Nick said that you hadn't a couple of days ago, so I wasn't sure."

She let it go. After all it was Duncan that she wanted to talk to. Duncan that she wished would show up at her door with dinner and a hug. The words he'd told her were beginning to fade away in her mind, starting to seem like a figment of her imagination. She sighed and bit into a lightly battered shrimp. "Well, you can report back to Nick that I'm fine, and that you guys don't have to worry about me any more."

He grinned. "We don't like seeing you all alone after everything you've been through."

She set down her fork and reached for a fry. "I get it but I'm not alone, I'm back at work now and I have been…" her voice trailed off as she was unsure how much they knew about Duncan's place outside of town.

Mason misunderstood her hesitation for sadness and reached for her hand. "I know I said I couldn't be with you any more last year Sylvie, but I'd be willing to give it another try if you want that."

She turned to stare at his handsome face, brilliant green eyes, his wide square jawline. But he wasn't Duncan. She raised one eyebrow. "Are we talking about pity sex, Mason?"

He shook his head but grinned when he saw her smile. "I'm talking about you and me giving it another shot." His gaze was warm. "Sex was never an issue for us. We were good together, it was just, well, all the other stuff," he said quietly.

She lifted her un-bruised eyebrow at him. "Really? I seem to remember you telling me that you'd met someone that you wanted to explore a deeper relationship with."

He looked away and then back at her skeptical face. "I lied," he said simply.

She looked surprised. "What did you lie about exactly, Mason?"

He hedged for a long moment, then finally he said firmly, "I couldn't stand the thought of you running out of my bed to someone else's any more. I just… couldn't stomach it."

She stared at him as though trying to gauge the truth of his words. Then quietly, she said, "I'm sorry Mason, I didn't realize that it was an issue for you."

He laughed harshly. "Good god, Sylvie. You have to know that all the men you date feel that way. You are beautiful and smart as a whip and I'm fairly certain that any one of us would have married you in a heartbeat, if you'd given us a shot."

She looked uneasy. "Have you talked to *other* men I've slept with about this, Mason?"

He hesitated and then finally he nodded. "Of course I have. We call it being Dunlopped."

Her mouth dropped open in surprise. "You what?" she choked, horrified.

He laughed and reached for her hand to squeeze it. "We call it getting

Dunlopped. You know, because we want you so bad that we go for whatever you're willing to offer, until we finally realize we won't ever really have y—" He stopped suddenly as though realizing he'd said too much.

She laughed incredulously. "And here I was telling every new guy that I dated, that there are tons of men that are mature enough to handle casual." She shook her head in wonder. "I'm surprised you didn't all start a Dunlopped club."

He looked away and she couldn't hold back her shout of laughter. "No. You didn't, right?"

He shook his head. "No, we didn't, but there may be a few of us that get together for drinks from time to time."

She threw back her head and laughed. "Oh god, that is just too funny." The genuine laughter felt good, and she smiled at him. "Thanks, I needed that." She thought of Duncan and broke into another laugh. "I practically told Duncan to be a real man and learn to be okay with casual." She laughed again and this time Mason joined in. She stopped suddenly and looked up at him. "Does Duncan know about this whole Dunlopped thing?"

He shook his head. "No, that's why we were all so impressed with him.

He did something none of us ever thought to do."

Her eyes widened in surprise at his admission of liking Duncan.

"What did he do differently?" she asked curiously.

"He backed off all the other men without telling you about it and then he kept you so busy in bed, that you wouldn't go looking for sex somewhere else."

"He did not!" she said disbelievingly. "Who did he back off?"

It was Mason's turn to laugh. "He told all of us that he was going to marry you and that we should stay away."

Her brow furrowed even as the warmth of what he was telling her seeped into her cold lonely heart. "Nick was the only one that he knew I was sleeping with for sure and he didn't say anything to him."

Mason shook his head, "I beg to differ. He warned Nick off the day that he got to Idaho and realized that the two of you were a thing. Then when he came out here and realized that we'd all had relationships with you at one time or another, he told us all in no uncertain terms that you were his." He eyed her for a moment. "Tell me, have you heard from any of your other little sex buddies since he's been here?"

She frowned and shook her head. "No, but I haven't called them either."

"Isn't it a little unusual for them to wait three weeks to call you, Sylvie?

If not, you've slipped, since my memory is of me calling for time with you every chance I got."

"Are you suggesting that Duncan told them to back off too?" she asked in disbelief.

He smiled. "I'd bet a hundred dollars that he did." He held out his hand to shake on it.

She took it. "You're on. I never even told him their names," she laughed.

He laughed right back and said quietly, "Check your phone, Sylvie. My guess is that their contacts have been completely erased from your phone."

"No way. I would have noticed," she disagreed as she reached for her phone and opened up her contacts. She couldn't find them, however. She sighed and went to her text lines. She knew she had texted them hundreds of times. There was nothing. She looked up at him in amazement. "When would he have even had the chance to do that?"

He grinned. "That's what we all kept asking. How is this guy keeping tabs on everything with Sylvie, on zero sleep like the rest of us, while in the middle of a case? He's good, Sylvie. In fact, he's better than good."

Tears filled her eyes as she thought of Duncan. She turned to Mason.

"Thank you for telling me all of this."

He looked disappointed for a minute but then he smiled. "See, here I was thinking I was going to get another shot with you, meanwhile all I did was make you want Jamison more. Damn him," he said but there wasn't any real anger behind the words.

After Mason left, she tried to call Duncan again. His voicemail was full, so she texted him instead.

Duncan, call me, text me, come home. I don't care which, but I need to talk to you. Please.

She set the phone down, but it buzzed, and she snatched it back up to read his message.

I'm sorry. I just don't think that us talking is a good idea. Be well and be safe.

She re-read his text three times. What the hell did it mean? She wanted to ask him but didn't want to start a fight with him. How was she supposed to feel well and safe when he was gone. He had somehow taken over every thought and desire, until all she wanted was more of him. She felt the familiar fear at the thought of loving someone that she could lose but it was already too late. She sighed and reached for the phone.

I'm sorry too. That's why we need to talk. Friends first, remember?

Maybe that would get him to call her, she thought with a smile. His strong sense of loyalty and duty above all else should call out to him.

She was staring at the screen when his next message came through.

Nice try. I can't be anyone's friend right now. Call Jackie if you need someone to talk to. God knows she needs a friend right now too. Good night,

I have an early morning.

Anger and pain warred inside her as she read his dismissing words. She went upstairs to bed but after tossing about for a while, she packed an overnight bag and drove back to Duncan's house. She needed to be near something of his and he hadn't left anything of his at her place. She fell asleep on the log bed that still smelled like their lovemaking while holding a flannel button up she'd taken from his closet.

She spent the next few days in court, which kept her busy, though she still managed to find her way out to spend time with the horses. They were the only comfort to her loneliness. The attorney that was her opposing council asked her out and she refused. He was good looking, but he looked hard, and she wasn't sure she could handle rough and tough right now.

She wanted Duncan back more than anything but each day that he stayed away left her feeling less and less sure that he'd actually cared for her at all. When the same attorney asked her out a third time and offered to take her somewhere fancy, she finally agreed. Maybe it was time to move on.

She was only ten minutes into the meal when she started regretting it. By fifteen minutes she wanted to punch the guy in the face simply for not being Duncan. She excused herself and went to the restroom to cool off. When she returned, he slipped into the booth next to her and tried to kiss her.

She almost slapped him. Instead, she shoved at his chest. "I'm sorry Dean, but this was a mistake. I need to go." He reluctantly slid out and sat heavily on the other side.

"I thought we had a mutual thing going." He sounded injured but she couldn't handle his feelings when her own were threatening to choke her to death.

She stood up. "I'm really sorry. I have to go." Then she had fled with both him and the entire restaurant watching her hasty departure.

She drove without thinking and before she even realized where she was going, she was almost to his house. Jamal was there again feeding and brushing the horses. He smiled at her as she walked over in her fancy little dress to talk to the horses. "Do you think Duncan will ever come back here?" she asked him, as she reached a hand to run lightly down the stallion's forehead.

Jamal looked a little uncomfortable. "This is Mr Duncan's house isn't it, ma'am?" he stated quietly.

She laughed and nodded. "I suppose it is, though one starts wondering when the owner never shows his face." She turned and walked to the house and made her way inside. Someone had been here cleaning since everything sparkled and she didn't see dust anywhere. She groaned and put on a pot of coffee. She was hungry since she'd left the date before the food showed up, but the fridge was empty. She reached for her phone to order takeout and saw Duncan's face on her phone.

Heart beating frantically, she reached down and touched the message notification.

Sylvie, sorry to bother you, I thought you would want to know that Jackie had her baby. He is a beautiful baby boy. They are naming him Reagan after your dad. Be safe.

She stared at the bright faced, dark haired baby boy picture he'd attached, and tears slid down her cheeks. He looked like Duncan, which made sense, because Jackie was his sister after all, but somehow staring down at that beautiful little face so like his, broke her. She collapsed onto the tiled floor and wept.

Chapter 50

It took her two more weeks to finish prosecuting the rape case. When the verdict came in and the defendant was convicted and sentenced to twenty years behind bars, she did the usual hugging and hand holding with the young victims, before she finally bid them and their parents farewell and drove home. She couldn't take another night alone without any sign from Duncan, so she tried calling him again. He didn't answer her call, so she texted him. He still didn't respond.

Her frustration eased slightly with the galloping horse beneath her, and she sighed as she rode the stallion back to the barn and untacked him before giving him a good brush down. She didn't see Jamal around but noticed that the watering trough was empty, so she added a little water for them in case he wasn't coming out tonight before she went inside for a shower and some dinner.

She didn't sleep at all, too exhausted to think straight but unable to stop wondering about whether or not she was ever going to see him again. Duncan had come here and ruined her perfectly good routine of easy breezy, though if Mason was to be believed, maybe that hadn't been as successful as she'd thought either. Then he'd waltzed right back out of her life. She threw the covers off at five a.m. and picked up her phone. No amount of texting or calling was getting through to him, and she had things she needed to tell him.

An hour later she was climbing into an uber on her way to the airport.

The first flight left at seven and she would be on it.

The flight wasn't long but there were two layovers so that, combined with the time difference, it took her most of the day to get there. She pulled into the ranch at six thirty p.m. in a rental car, looking for Duncan. No one answered the door though she banged persistently for twenty minutes. She didn't see Duncan's truck anywhere, though there was a shiny new blue chevy by the barn. She groaned and rubbed a hand across her tired eyes.

"Damn it, Jamison. Where the hell are you?" she murmured as she walked back to her car. She drove to Jackie's on the chance that he might be there. It was rude she knew to show up without calling, but she didn't want to give Duncan a chance to bow out.

It was just after seven p.m. when she knocked on Jackie's door. Ren opened it a minute later. He looked surprised, but he gave her a tired smile. "Come on in, Sylvie." He held the door wide.

She stepped in with a huge gift bag in hand. "Is he here?" she asked him.

He didn't pretend not to know who she was talking about. He shook his head. "I'm sorry but no. Jackie is on the couch."

She followed his pointing finger and slipped off her shoes as she walked around him and toward a very tired, very fragile looking Jackie. Jackie forced a smile at Sylvie, though it was obvious she didn't feel it.

"I'm sorry to just show up…" Sylvie said, then she saw the bundle in her friend's lap and smiled. "Is that him? I want to see."

She handed the gift bag to Jackie and reached for the wiggling bundle. He was beautiful, with big eyes and splotchy dark hair. "You know you're always welcome," Jackie began as she held out her baby. "I'm just a little surprised is all."

Sylvie touched his tiny hand and held him close to her chest, grinning down at him. "He's perfect, Jackie. He looks like a perfect blend of you two. Are the girls down?"

Ren and Jackie exchanged a look and then shook their heads. "They are playing with their own babies," she said softly. Then she held her friend's brown gaze. "Why are you here, Sylvie?"

"Where is he?" she countered calmly.

"Duncan?" Jackie asked. Sylvie smiled. "Yes, Duncan."

"I don't actually know where he is right at this moment," Jackie hedged.

"Cut the crap, Jackie, I need to talk to him."

"I was under the impression you were angry at him." Jackie said softly.

Sylvie's brows shot up. "You're what?" she sputtered.

"Duncan told me you are upset with him and that he's not ready to talk to you about it all yet," Jackie admitted.

Sylvie offered a determined smile, "Three things brought me here, Jackie. One is that I have wanted to come see you and tell you that I'm sorry about your dad since he, er, well died. Two is that ever since Duncan sent me a picture of this little guy, I have wanted to come see him. And the third is well, that I need to talk to him."

Before Jackie could argue, Sylvie said quickly, "Contrary to what Duncan may have told you, I'm not angry with him, other than because he did a disappearing act. I just have some unfinished business that I need to handle with him." She looked down at that tiny hand curled around her finger. "He's beautiful by the way."

Both Jackie and Ren smiled. "He really is, isn't he?" she beamed. Then sadness crossed her face. "I just hope he doesn't feel the energy of everything that was going on around his birth." She shivered as she finished.

"How are you doing with it all?" Sylvie asked quietly.

"Well, I have Ren, and Duncan came for a bit so not too bad all things considered. It's just such a shock you know, to realize you come from someone or something like him. It damages your mind, and Duncan has it worse. Him being a man and then still carrying the name. I can just go with my married name, and no one is the wiser but now that the media got a hold of everything, the name Jamison will forever be tarnished."

Sylvie hadn't thought about that, and she was ashamed to admit it. "Oh god, I didn't think of it that way." She remembered Duncan flinching each time the name was used and swallowed. The agony in his eyes… She looked away from Jackie to the baby. "I'm so sorry I didn't do something sooner…" Her voice trailed off as the damn tears filled her eyes again. It seemed that she was forever crying these days.

Jackie waved a hand in the air. "We are all sorry. You for your trauma, us for ours. Tell you what, why don't we just make a deal here and now to live our lives with joy in spite of it all and quit apologizing for something that was out of our control."

Sylvie laughed and raised tear-filled eyes to Jackie's sad ones.

"Deal," she agreed. Then she held Jackie's blue gaze, so much like Duncan's. "Have you decided if you're going to tell me where he is or not?"

Ren laughed and Jackie smiled. "I'm still deciding." She eyed Sylvie with a curious look. "Why don't you tell me what you want to see him for, and I'll decide."

Ren laughed again. "I apologize, Sylvie. I'm fairly certain that Jackie is on the hunt for fresh gossip."

Sylvie tucked the baby into the curve of her arm. "That's okay. It's what friends are for." She stared at the baby in her arms. "Is it true that you named him Reagan?" she asked quietly, not quite sure how to put into words what she felt yet.

Jackie smiled and nodded. "Reagan Marion Bradley. He needs good vibes to start his life with."

"It's perfect," she said softly and touched Reagan's soft hair with a finger. "I love him, you know?"

"Me too. He's my favorite new guy," Jackie joked but she met Sylvie's gaze as she raised her brown eyes hesitantly.

"Duncan, you idiot. I love Duncan so much that I ache with it," she stated it quietly, powerfully. "How is he? I have been so worried about him since, well, since he took off without a word."

Jackie looked pleased at her admission. "I don't know, truth be told. I've never seen him this way." She hesitated. "It feels like he has demons on his tail, and he can't quite run fast enough." She smiled softly then. "I'd hoped you would tell me how you felt."

"I figured you all probably knew by now." She gave a small self-mocking smile. "Apparently, I can be a bit, well, evasive to things I don't want to face." There was honesty on her bright make-up free face when she said quietly, “I’ve loved him since we were kids. I didn’t realize that was the reason I was keeping other relationships at a distance, until a friend recently pointed it out to me. Anyway, I had convinced myself that I was better off not loving anyone than suffering another loss.”

“What changed your mind?”

“Duncan.” She said without preamble. “Well, Duncan and the fact that I finally realized it didn’t matter what my intentions were, because I already loved him anyway.”

“Love does that.”

Sylvie laughed. “I suppose it does. So, are you going to tell me where he is?”

Jackie laughed. “You always were stubborn and single minded when you got an idea into your head.”

“You were always wonderful, Jackie. How do you do that? Always be everyone’s rock?”

Jackie looked surprised, but Ren nodded even as he wiggled his way onto the sofa next to her to put an arm around her shoulders. “She has been very patient love, are you going to tell her, or should I?” Jackie laughed. “Okay, okay, he’s in Chicago.”

Sylvie groaned. “Chicago! No. I was closer to him in Wilmington. What on earth is he doing there?” But she knew the second she asked. She looked at Jackie. “He joined the FBI?”

“He did.”

“Why, after all this time?” Sylviee wondered aloud.

Jackie shrugged, then sighed “He said he couldn’t sit by any longer when there were guys like our father out there killing for sport or because they’re sick. Did you hear that dad had collected every paper that referenced any of the women he killed? He circled their names and made notations of the dates he’d raped and strangled them. Even my mom.” Her voice was shaky. “God, when I saw what he’d written I wanted to kill him with my bare hands. I tried to call Duncan, but it was already too late. He had already got to you.”

Jackie stared at the floor, “All those papers were sitting there untouched by us, all these years while more girls died, because we didn’t want to upset him. God, it makes me sick.”

Ren was gently rubbing one hand on her neck and shoulders and squeezing her hand in the other. “There was no way you could have known, love. I think you’d almost have to be as sick as he was and in the same way to wonder something like that about someone you loved.”

She turned her face up to him. “Duncan was worried that it might be you. He told me to be careful.”

Ren smiled. “I’m glad he was worried about your safety first and besides he called me to come home, remember?”

Jackie nodded. “He saw the error of his thinking. That’s why I forgave him so easily for thinking such a thing about you.”

He kissed her there in front of Sylvie. “That’s my girl.”

Sylvie cleared her throat with a little grin. “Uh, guys, I’m still here and waiting for that address.”

They all laughed together as Jackie turned to her. “New baby, lack of sleep muddled brains over here, sorry.”

“Don’t even try to pretend you aren’t slow walking me, Jackie.” She smiled to take the sting out of her words. “Also, I have another favor to ask.”

“What’s that?”

“You can’t tell him I’m coming.” Jackie looked uneasy. “I don’t know about that…”

“He’ll run away if he thinks I’m coming.”

“What makes you think that?” Ren asked.

Sylvie laughed at the question and looked down at her phone. “Let’s see, one hundred and twenty-three voicemails, fifty unanswered texts and some guy that he has looking after his place in North Carolina named Jamal.”

“I see your point,” he said with a little laugh.

“Also do you happen to have that Agent Graham’s phone number?”

Jackie raised her brows. “Why do you want that?”

Sylvie met her gaze steadily and said deadpan, “In case I need backup. I got the idea that Agent Graham both respected and cared about Duncan and his well-being.”

Ren gave an impressed little laugh. “I win the bet on this one, hon. Payup.”

Jackie planted a wet sloppy kiss on him.

“What is that supposed to mean?” Sylvie asked, pretending to be insulted.

Ren grinned, “I bet Jackie that you were going to toughen up and come after Duncan like you meant business.”

She eyed her friend. “You bet against me?”

Jackie laughed and held up her hands. “Only because I win either way.”

Chapter 51

Duncan eyed the group of analysts who were working late on their current case. The teams quarters was a large open square with several desks and computer stations all facing the front of the room where the wall was covered in flat screen televisions, along with a couple of electronic marker boards. The SEC had turned over a bunch of evidence they had on a securities investment firm. The theory was that the company was stealing their so-called clients' hard-earned savings and spending them while pretending to invest them.

The only reason they had gotten away with it thus far, was because they had been carefully purchasing just enough properties to make it look legit. The CEO would have the press involved in each purchase to give all the incoming clients the idea that they were making bank, only to turn around and quietly sell the same company, or land under the table to friends in the business at a loss. All in all, it had been a pretty good scam. The owner and CEO, James Childs, had lived well and high for the last seven years and had amassed millions in offshore accounts.

Unfortunately, the CEO had been covering his tracks pretty well and it was taking longer than he'd anticipated to bring the company down. This was due mostly to the fact that halfway through the case, Duncan began to suspect that all the 'friends' James had been selling to, were also aware of, and even involved in, the scam. However, with this being his first solo case as Agent Duncan Jamison, he was determined to get everyone that was involved. He suspected all of the companies had been helping each other dupe millions of good hard-working civilians out of their money.

He knew that the powers that be, had given him this case because it stood to be a case with high media coverage that would put his name out there and might start helping clear the Jamison name. He didn't care about that. He cared about the thousands of faces he saw in the investor portfolios. All of the old couples who were counting on the money for their retirements, or the young people who'd decided to try to start investing early on, or the young parents who were investing because they wanted to create a better life for their children. Each of those faces had a story, and a deep-seated reason that they had taken the too-good-to-be-true offer and gone for the scam. It was their faces that swam in his vision each night as he finally made his way back to his hotel room, when he was too exhausted to continue.

Well, those faces and Sylvie's. But her face was like a constant haunting vision in his mind. Her face bloody and swollen from the beating his father had given her. His fists clenched even now as he thought about it. Her legs spread out, her body half naked and on display. His father's pants undone, nearly falling off his narrow hips. He closed his eyes and scrubbed a hand across his face again.

Then he looked around the room. "Listen up everyone," he said calmly. Fifteen people stopped typing, talking, or sorting files and looked up. "It's nearly midnight. We aren't going to solve this tonight. Go home and get some rest." He looked at his watch. "Let's all meet back here at eight o'clock sharp, rested, and ready to get these bastards. Remember, these companies all know that the FBI is looking into them so the longer it takes us to solve this, the more time they have to transfer money where we can't get our hands on it, and sell companies and properties at a loss, and most importantly, flee the country.

"Go home, take a shower, and get some rest so that we can all give it our best effort tomorrow." He paused and chairs began scooting. He held up his hand. "I would just like to say… I know that you don't normally work overtime on these types of cases, and I appreciate you all doing it without complaint. These victims deserve everything we can give them."

"They will soon find out that their financial security, however they saw it, is a lie, and it will be devastating to most of them. I want to know every business, every property, and every account that we can freeze to try to get at least a small percentage of what they lost, back for them. Goodnight." There was a chorus of tired goodnights and then one by one they got their things and shuffled out of the room. He watched them go and then turned back to the wall of photos, pertinent information on the officers of the investment companies, and a list of the companies they had tied to the scam in one way or another already.

He had a list of ten more that he felt certain was involved. As soon as they tied them to it, warrants would be issued and coordinated arrests would be made across the city. He sighed and reached for his suit jacket that was laid over a black leather chair.

"What are you still doing here, Jamison?"

It was Agent Graham and Duncan turned to look at him. "I was just leaving."

Jonathan Graham grinned. "You do know that this is a fraud case that doesn't require around the clock hours, right?"

Duncan gave him a small smile. "It does if I want to secure the accounts before they all have a chance to transfer the money and disappear."

Jonathan laughed. "See, I told the A.D. you were the best guy for this." Duncan snorted and turned a wry smile at his friend. "We both know exactly why you pitched me for this, and while I appreciate it, I would give as much effort to any case, I was given."

"Exactly. Which is why this was as good a case as any for you to handle."

"You need something? I'm heading out."

"Just checking in. You need some sleep, Jamison. You look like hell warmed over."

Duncan raised a hand in mock salute. "Aye aye, skippy." Then he turned on his heel and strode toward the door. He turned back to see Agent Graham looking over the investigation and wondered bitterly if he was checking his work, just to make sure that Duncan wasn't showing any signs of the same insanity his father had. Without a word he walked away.

He couldn't blame anyone for wondering that. He himself was wondering that. Every thought, every desire he had was dissected for any sign of mania. He swore inwardly and punched the elevator button for the ground level. He had his truck across the street in the parking garage, but his hotel was only a mile away and he needed to think so he turned down the street pulling his jacket on, in the cool night air, and also covering his leather holster with his weapon.

He saw Sylvie's face again though this time it was her telling him that *she* was sorry with a split lip and one eye so swollen she couldn't use it any more. He couldn't handle the self-hatred he had. He'd seen those damned papers. He closed his eyes, his jaw taut. It had all been sitting there on his kitchen counter all these years. He couldn't forgive himself for that. He couldn't ever forget that. He'd been so trusting.

He'd known something was off with Arthur Jamison after their mom's death. He'd chosen to believe it was grief that destroyed his father and had completely missed the obvious signs. Women had died because *he* hadn't wanted to see the demented man that he saw every day. Sylvie had nearly died, had most probably been raped.

He'd seen the file. Had listened to most of her interviews, but whenever she started talking about what his dad had done to her, a loud buzzing began in his brain, and he had to shut it off.

His only choice was to focus on the light. Sylvie, laying in his bed after he'd loved her thoroughly, relaxed and sated and God so beautiful.

Sylvie running up the mountain ahead and turning to smile at him as she walked backward for several steps dangerously close to the edge of the trail, fearless.

Sylvie on that damned stallion riding away from him with his heart thundering in fear for her life. He groaned as he crossed a dark empty street. The lighter visions of her were torture, because the dark always followed. Sylvie lying bleeding out on the kitchen floor. Sylvie spread out on that dirty bed, tied down. His father actually thinking that there was a way that he, Duncan, would help him kill her and walk away.

The light inevitably led to the dark because that was where his real fear lay. He had been obsessed with Sylvie since that first kiss. He had wanted her with a deep need that made him uncomfortable, and yet that discomfort hadn't stopped him. How long before that deep love he felt turned to something else? Something darker? Something more sinister?

He crossed a wide street and slid his hands into his slack pockets. He had been on the verge of coming up with a way to have himself locked into a cage before he could hurt anyone else when Agent Graham offered him another way out. *"Come work for me, Jamison. Come work at the FBI and we'll watch you. What better place could you know that you won't do something like that, than if you have the entire FBI watching you? If I see anything to be concerned about, I won't ignore it, you have my word,"* he'd said. And Duncan had grasped for that straw because he didn't know what else he could do.

He couldn't sit around waiting for the moment that his mind became deranged. He couldn't in good conscience, hope that he would notice the change. After all, if he wanted to hurt someone, he likely wouldn't see it as wrong. He saw the hotel ahead, the bright sign looming out over the lobby. Sylvie laying spreadeagle, stripped and bloody. "Fuck! Just leave me alone," he whispered hoarsely. He thought about Sylvie smiling as she rushed into Nick's embrace. He groaned. No, no, not that image. Sylvie very obviously close to the Wilmington D.A, Lemonte as he squeezed her hand in comfort. Sylvie, giving that little personal smile to each of the men in her house. He punched a pole with a crosswalk sign on it because now he'd come full circle again. Because now he was wondering just how long a man could feel this level of jealousy, before he snapped and killed her.

The night receptionist smiled at him as he walked past. A flirty smile. He didn't smile back, only gave her a tight nod in response. He didn't want any women around him. It was too risky.

He stepped into the elevator and imagined Sylvie there with him. He imagined taking her into his arms to comfort her. Kissing her. Sylvie smiling at him with the sun on her bright cheeks, her hair shining.

The elevator dinged and a woman got on. A young pretty woman with a bright floral bag in tow. He stepped back against the far wall and then on second thought quickly stepped off, stopping the doors that were beginning to close. Better not to take any chances. He'd take the stairs. He climbed the last three floors without breaking a sweat. When he wasn't home trying to sleep, he was at the gym in the FBI building, trying to work out his demons that way.

He stepped out into the hall and walked down the long corridor. A right turn toward his room and he froze. Sylvie was sitting with her back against the door of his hotel room, her head leaned back, eyes closed, a large luggage bag standing on its wheels beside her. He was imagining it. He had to be imagining it. She couldn't be here, his exhausted mind screamed. He hated himself even as he couldn't resist stepping closer.

Her face was mostly healed now. Her eye only had the slightest hint of grey-green hue in the corner by her nose. She looked tired. Exhausted. Like she hadn't been sleeping well either. He wanted to bend down and pick her up and carry her inside to his oversize lush king-size bed. Then he wanted to curl around her and hold her while they both slept. Then he wanted to wake up and make love to her as the sun peaked inside their room.

He would make love to her and beg for her forgiveness. Then she would grant it after he pleaded with her and then they could spend weeks, months, no, years even, making up for lost time. Until he started to see her differently and killed her.

He backed up a step, turned to go. "Duncan Jamison, don't you dare walk away from me!" she said a little desperately.

He thought about running. Thought hard about it. Knew that he could outrun her if he tried. Even as he turned back, he cursed the dark weakness inside. The weakness that could someday become the demon he was bred to be. He watched as she stood slowly, careful not to move too abruptly. She watched his eyes, held them in her own. She knew he was thinking of bolting. "Don't," she pleaded softly.

He swore a long string of curses inwardly. He should have stayed at work after all, he thought. She took a small step toward him. He groaned, "I can't, Sylvie."

She stopped. Held his gaze. "Can't what? Can't talk? Can't see me? Can't stand the sight of me?" Her voice broke on the last question.

His eyes widened and he groaned again. "God no, sweetheart. I can't be alone around you or really any woman."

She stared and then gaped at him. "Is that what all this is about, you idiot?" She advanced. "Are you afraid you might do something to hurt me?" His gaze darkened, as he ran his hands through his hair, his jawline taut with tension. "I already hurt you…" The low anguished quality of his voice was something she hadn't ever heard.

She shook her head. "You saved my life, Duncan. Over and over and over." She advanced another step. She was almost within touching distance now. She smiled sweetly. "I'm exhausted, Duncan. I haven't slept well in weeks and not much at all for two days. Can I come in and we'll talk?"

He started to shake his head. She frowned, "Please, Duncan, I just need to sit for a while."

He looked down at the figment of his imagination. His heart was ripping apart at the seams, its wild rhythm pounding at his throat. This was the real test, he realized. Being able to look down at her warm smile, wildly erotic eyes, undeniably sexy form and walk away. "I'm sorry, sweetheart," he said quietly.

He pulled his room card from his inside pocket, held it out to her not even realizing he'd used the endearment. "You can rest as long as you need to, but I can't go in there with you," he breathed heavily.

She reached for the card, nodding her agreement and then she pounced, wrapping her arms around his waist as she laid her head against his pounding heart. "*I'm* sorry, but that just doesn't work for me, baby."

He stiffened and then relaxed as the floral scent of her hair teased at his nostrils. She felt so good. So warm. He closed his eyes and wrapped his arms around her, unable to pull back now. "What have you done?" he whispered hoarsely. "God, Sylvie, what have you done."

"Talk to me Duncan, just talk to me, okay?" Tears rolled down her cheeks. "I need to talk to you. It's been pure torture not talking to you all this time."

He lifted the card and opened the door reaching for her bags with one arm and pulling her against his side with the other. "Don't cry, sweetheart. Please don't cry, we can talk," he begged as he shoved the door wide. "Come on in."

Chapter 52

Sylvie watched as Duncan removed his jacket and then carefully took off his weapon harness and slid the gun into a safe on the top of a table. "You look good," she said softly. And he did. Even in his grey suit that was wrinkled from a long day at work, he looked sleek, tough and handsome. He wore the suit well and she realized, and not for the first time, that she had underestimated him.

He laughed hoarsely. "Let's keep this casual, and I look like hell."

He did look tired, but even the lines at the corners of his eyes that seemed more prominent since she'd last seen him added to his appeal. She laughed as his words sunk in. "Isn't that my line?"

He smiled as he loosened his grey and blue striped tie. "You want a drink?" He motioned to the mini bar on the side.

She nodded. "Just some water though, please." The social nature of bringing it to her might calm him down. She had begun to realize after talking to all of her friends that Duncan was judging himself for everything that had happened, but she'd never imagined the kind of self-degradation that had been evident in the hallway outside his door.

She took the bottle of water he held out and took a sip trying to think of a gentle way to broach the canyon between them. "Thanks," she said softly and watched as he poured a small bottle of scotch into a glass. "So, there have been some changes since I last saw you, huh?"

He looked around and then back at her as he threw back the scotch and then reached for another bottle. "A few," was all he said as he emptied the second bottle into the glass and took a swallow.

"I've missed you," she said quietly.

His gaze swung to her, burned her with the intensity in the indigo orbs.

"What happened to little miss casual?"

She didn't look away, even though it stung. "I deserve that I guess."

She saw a flicker of surprise in the blue depths before it was replaced by fear. "I can't be with you, Sylvie," he said flatly. "If that is why you came here, then you deserve to know that."

She swallowed her heartache. She hadn't expected this to be easy, had she? Maybe she had, since Duncan Jamison had always been gentle and easy, at least where she was concerned. Tears filled her eyes as she watched the hard man in front of her who had previously been tender, intelligent, and patient beyond words. Now he looked wound tight, like a spring that might snap at any moment. "I came to talk."

He saw the tears and tried to harden himself against them. He should say something horrible to hurt her bad enough that she would leave and never come back. He thought about that but couldn't think of anything to say. The tears rolling down her face were distracting him, so he walked over and grabbed a box of tissues, giving it to her without touching her. "Here. What did you want to talk about?" Maybe if he let her say her piece, but maintained his distance, she would go away, and leave him in the exile that was his life now.

"A lot of things. But first I want to say…" She paused and took a deep breath. "I love you, Jamison."

He flinched at the name. Stubbornly, she stood and walked to him, despite the hard look he was giving her. "Don't do that, Duncan. You are not your dad, and you own the name more than he ever could." She placed a hand on his tight jaw. "I love you and I don't care what your name is." He couldn't look away as she tempted him with her soft silky-smooth fingers. "In fact, I'd like to take Jamison as my name when we get married."

He moved away so fast she jumped. "Are you out of your fucking mind? Why in all that's holy would you believe for even a second that I would marry you?" His words cut deep but she wasn't going to bend.

"I know that you want to, Duncan. Nick, Ben and Mason, all told me what you told them." She intentionally used the present tense.

He turned his back to her and threw back his second scotch. He walked to the sliding glass doors that led out to the small balcony and stared out at the dark night. The city spread out in a light spotted view. "I wish they hadn't done that," he said honestly.

He heard her indrawn breath behind him. Hated himself for hurting her this way. But it was better than her being dead, he reminded himself as he turned back to meet her tear-filled gaze with his own hard one. "They would all be thrilled to take you to the church, Sylvie. You should run back to them and take any one of them up on it."

Her lips trembled into a shaky smile. "I think Laura might have some thoughts about that."

He narrowed his gaze at her joke. "Fine, so go back to Nick or Mason." She held out the last bottle of scotch to him. He smiled bitterly and reached for it, even knowing he shouldn't take the chance of getting tipsy, when he couldn't be sure what he might do. "If you're trying to get me drunk it won't work. I can drink a bottle and still maintain focus."

She gave him a small smile. "I'm trying to help ease the unfathomable pain I see."

He looked away. Here he was being rude and terrible to her when all he wanted to do was… He stopped his train of thought in it tracks. She was being sweet and not taking any of his challenges the way she should be. He ran a hand through his hair and threw back the third bottle. He should have run as soon as he'd seen her there at his door, he realized with a harsh laugh. The moment he paused; he'd lost the battle.

He turned back and walked stealthily toward her. Her eyes widened in surprise but there wasn't any fear. She actually stepped toward him even as he opened his arms and bent his head taking her mouth in a hard, unyielding kiss. She leaned into him, softened under his hands, and opened her mouth in surrender. His hands gentled and he drank her in like she was a drug he craved. She tasted like apricots and cherries and sweet, sweet honey. He pulled back suddenly. "If we do this, sweetheart, this is the last time. We can never do it again."

"Uh huh," she murmured against his throat, willing to say anything she needed, to keep him here in her arms this way.

His head came down on hers again with a low groan and she melted into him. With a small whimper she tried to push into him, tried to meld their bodies into one. She didn't want him to ever let her go. He responded by lifting her into his arms and walking quickly to the bedroom. He took his time drinking in every moment as he made sweet, tender love to her. Each moment was priceless, each arch, each moan etched forever in his mind, for this was the last time he would ever see her.

Afterward, they lay entwined together in the sheets. He on his back, with her head curled up on his chest, his arm holding her to his side, her hand splayed possessively over his abdomen. She lifted her head as though to speak. He shook his. "Don't ruin this moment," he pleaded softly. She smiled and curled closer to his warm strength.

They fell asleep in each other's arms. It was the best sleep either of them had gotten in weeks. She woke to the sound of the shower and a missing Duncan. She slipped out of the bed and walked silently to the bathroom door. It wasn't locked so she opened it and slipped inside to wrap her arms around him from behind. He groaned and turned, even as he hardened at her closeness. "We can't," he said desperately.

She licked his hand as he turned to her. "If this really is our last night together, it's not quite over."

He moaned and took her mouth again even as his hands slid up her sides caressing his way to her shoulders. After a few minutes he backed her out of the shower and back to the bed, where he once again tenderly took his time giving them both the drug that he craved. They fell asleep again, his leg thrown over her own, his body curved protectively around her small frame.

She woke with a start awhile later and knew instantly that he was gone. She cursed and slid out of the tangle of bed sheets to walk to the shower. Just outside the arched ceiling that led to the bed she saw the covered tray and the note. She reached for a T-shirt, slid it over her head and walked slowly over. She didn't want to read what it said but felt compelled forward, with her heart in her throat.

She lifted the cover to find a tray of fresh croissants, toast with jam and a bowl of fresh fruit. How like Duncan to make sure she was taken care of, even as he was sending her away. She set the cover back after picking up a warm croissant and taking a bite and reached for the handwritten note with a shaking hand.

Sylvie,

By the time you see this I'll be gone. I had breakfast brought up for you, so you can eat before your flight. I took the liberty of booking you an eleven o'clock flight back to Wilmington. Don't miss it! Nick Hanlan is a great guy and I think you should give him another shot. If I can't have you, he would be my second choice.

She rolled her eyes, "Of all the arrogant…" She broke off and began reading again.

I don't want you here. No, I can't have you here. I'm sorry if that hurts but it's the truth. I have no future and nothing to offer anyone any more. You deserve happiness and a sane man who can give that to you. I won't see you again after today so don't even try. If you don't board your flight, I won't come back here and I won't be weak again. I can't afford to be weak where you're concerned. Please just go. Don't make this harder than it has to be.

Duncan

She lifted the croissant to her mouth as she finished. Then she slammed the note down hard on the table. "You damn fool, Jamison," she muttered under her breath and reached for her phone.

Agent Graham answered on the first ring. "Sylvie," he said shortly.

"I need your help with something, sir."

"Stop calling me sir. I'm thirty-four, not ancient and I thought we were becoming friends at this point," he said without any real bite to his words.

"Sorry, I need your help, Agent Graham."

He sighed. "Jon, just call me Jon and I take it this means all didn't go well last night?" She had called him as soon as she landed at O'Hare yesterday. They had met at a restaurant across from Duncan's hotel to discuss Duncan.

She sighed as tears filled her eyes. "That depends on your perspective."

"Meaning?"

"He spent the night with me but left a very clear letter this morning, letting me know he expects me to be gone when he comes back, or he'll bail."

"Jesus, I'm sorry. That can't be easy, given the situation."

Her voice hardened. "Not as hard as walking away," she said flatly.

"What are you going to do?"

"Can you meet me for coffee. I have an idea."

He grinned. He was walking down the hall toward his office but turned around mid-stride. "Tell me where," he said, as he walked back toward the elevator, he'd just ridden up in.

Chapter 53

Duncan was more energized and relaxed than he'd been since he got to Chicago and his team noticed it. There were quiet murmurs as he gave them instructions on where to start for the day. His good mood had everyone bustling about with renewed energy, and because of that renewed energy they were making more progress in a few hours, than they had been all week. He praised them as he turned back and added two more suspected companies to the list of those they'd proven were involved.

He thought of Sylvie and for the first time since his father's death, saw her sprawled comfortably in his bed, instead of that dark disgusting room. Guilt surged as he realized that she had likely been hurt and angry at his note, but even that couldn't slow him down. He glanced at his watch. It was ten forty-five. She should be boarding her plane any minute. He'd give her twenty minutes and then call to make sure she had made the flight. He'd meant what he'd told her. He wouldn't go back to the hotel with her there.

Eric Dannon, a twenty-five-year-old computer genius, stood suddenly, with excitement written across his face. "Uh, sir, you might want to come look at this."

Duncan strode quickly over to look down at what the young analyst was pointing at. "What am I looking at, Eric?" he asked, glancing at a monitor with a long line of chat room dialogue scrolling down the screen.

"We got them, sir," he said in excitement. He pointed to the dialogue. "I found a private chatroom they created where they have all been communicating about every fraudulent purchase. See here." He pointed to a post by user 3miltakeabreak. "This here where he refers to the amount of rest he's had and how many minutes he needs to work out to make up the difference, he's referring to money coming in from investors and how much he needs to spend, to make it look legitimate."

Duncan read the post but wasn't seeing it yet. The analyst grinned. "Then look at this post by user cantminttakeahint1, he references a gym and how much it will cost for that particular workout. He's referring to a business he wants to get rid of that he had previously purchased. See, look here." He pulled a stack of financial papers over with the exact amounts shown on the bank statements.

Duncan stared at the list and whistled. "Tell me we can track them all down using their IP addresses."

Eric shook his head. "We can't, they have likely routed them through several servers to make it hard, but I can do you one better. Using this chat line, we can compare it with all the bank statements for the companies and see who made the transactions. Any judge would give us a warrant for this, and we can freeze all of the assets and haul them all in while we sort out the rest."

"You all hear that," Duncan asked across the room. Everyone who wasn't already watching and listening, turned to him. "This is now our new priority. Everyone is on this. Track down every single investment, purchase, and the person behind it." He turned to his assistant. "Get Judge Delaney on the line, Cameron, and let's get this handled."

Everyone quickly pulled all the bank records from their stacks and conglomerated around Eric. He went to the beginning of a very long chat dating back five years and started calling out amounts. "I have that one right here, it's the account of Linley Securities and Trust."

"Someone start typing this up as we go," Duncan called as he reached for the phone his assistant was holding out to him. "We are going to need that list for the judge."

"I need a warrant, Your Honor," he said into the black receiver. "It's going to include the officers of at least twenty large investment companies, sir." He listened for a long moment. "Yes, sir, we do. I'll be down in two hours to present it to you." He paused again. "Okay, sir, I'll do that." He hung up and turned back to the room.

"Split into three groups and each take two years, we need this handled before the judge leaves the courthouse at two." The team efficiently split up, handing correct files off to each other and then separating.

Duncan glanced at his watch. His heart throbbed; Sylvie should be gone by now. He walked out into the hall and called the airport. "Yeah, this is Agent Duncan Jamison, I just need to verify that one Sylvianna Dunlap boarded flight two-eight-nine heading for Wilmington, North Carolina." He listened for a long moment as the operator put him on hold. A moment later a woman came on. He listened and then said firmly, "Good, yeah, that's all I needed to know, thank you."

He clicked off the call and turned back to the white-collar crime unit door where he saw Jonathan Graham watching him from a few doors down. He offered a polite nod and turned back into the room without another thought.

Graham watched thoughtfully as his friend went back to work. He hoped to high heaven that Jamison was going to forgive him for what he'd done. He sighed and walked back down the hall toward the elevator. He pulled his cell phone from his pocket and typed.

He took the bait.

Jon hesitated for only a second before hitting send. He could still walk this back. Nah, he thought as the elevator dinged and he stepped in. Someone had to do something about all of this, and it might as well be him.

Chapter 54

By three o'clock all accounts had been frozen and FBI teams as well as the police, were dispatched across the city to twenty-one different investment offices. The orders were simple, take all officers of the company into custody and send everyone else outside while the FBI boxed up anything that might be applicable to the case. By four o'clock, the FBI field office holding units were overloaded with men in two thousand-dollar suits asking for their lawyers before Duncan even had a chance to interview them. He gave each in turn a cold smile. "That's all right, we already have everything we need to charge you with anyway."

He never tired of the guilty looks that then turned sly as they thought they could sell someone out and cut a deal. Within the following two hours, he verified through their help that he had indeed got every company involved. He ran a hand over his face feeling tired as the last of them gave him that sly smile. "I have valuable information and I'd like to make a deal."

He adjusted his legs and sighed. "There are no deals to be had here, but if you tell me what you know then I'd be happy to inform the prosecutor that you cooperated, provided you give me a full confession."

The guy hesitated only a moment. "Reachen's Investments are the ones who started it all."

Duncan smiled. "So, I've heard." He stood and tossed a pen and a pad of paper toward the guy. "Write it all down."

Jackson Dewitt, from Dewitt Yourself Investments stared at the pad of paper. "You don't actually expect me to confess on paper, do you?"

Duncan shook his head, hands in his pockets and turned from the two-way mirror he knew Graham and a few other agents were watching from. "No, I don't. You're welcome to ask for your attorney or decide not to cooperate." He let the words hang in the air. "However, prison is hard on men like you. All that smooth white skin…" He paused. "You get the idea, I think. So, if you'd like me to tell the prosecutor that you cooperated and possibly buy yourself some good will, to maybe cut down on your sentence, well, that would be good for both of us."

Dewitt picked up the pen. Hesitated. Set it back down.

Duncan smiled. "You know, if you'd really like to buy yourself some good will though…" He paused and waited for Dewitt to quit chewing on his lip and look up.

"What?" Dewitt asked quietly. "What can I do here?" He sounded desperate which was exactly where Duncan wanted him.

He pounced. "You don't seem as stupid as your friends after all." He waited for that tiny flash of pride and continued. "Write down every account number you transferred funds to offshore, and the prosecutor might consider giving you a break."

Dewitt reached for the pen, hesitating again. He looked up at Duncan who only looked mildly interested in his decision. "You think I will do less time if I do this?"

A quick nod and Duncan said, "Possibly."

"I guess being broke, does seem better than spending my life in a cell." He began writing. He looked up again, but Duncan still looked bored. He sighed and went back to writing.

"I'm going to step out for a sec, do you want a soda? Coffee? Anything?" Duncan asked in a friendly tone.

"Sure, I'd take a black coffee," Dewitt responded without looking up.

"Sure thing, oh and Dewitt?" Duncan paused, doorknob in hand waiting for the small man to look up. When he did, Duncan smiled pleasantly. "When you get out of prison don't even think about trying to take advantage of anyone ever again, because you and I, we don't want to see each other again, do we?" His gaze narrowed.

Dewitt shivered. "No, sir, we do not."

"Good," Duncan said as he walked out and closed the door behind him. There were two agents in the hall, and he grinned. "One of you go get him some coffee." They both grinned as he walked away.

On the other side of the glass, Graham looked at AD Donahue, "So what do you think of Jamison so far, sir?"

The AD grinned. "He's bloody brilliant. I especially liked the way he made them feel like he was giving them something in return for their confession and money." He looked thoughtful as he turned to Graham. "I've never seen anyone work an interview looking so relaxed."

"It's part of his charm. Nothing fazes the man," Jon said in honest admiration.

"Not even finding out his father was a serial murderer living under his roof?" the AD asked pointedly.

"Well, maybe that. But any normal man would be haunted by that. Besides he has an ace he doesn't know about yet."

The assistant director of the FBI looked at Agent Graham curiously. "Yeah? What's that?"

"Sylvie Dunlap," Jon said with a smile.

AD Donahue looked confused, but only nodded. "If you say so. Stay here and make sure everything gets tidied up behind Jamison, Jon. I have a meeting I have to get to."

"A meeting at six p.m.?" Jon asked in surprise. Donahue sighed. "Damn bureaucracy never sleeps."

They both laughed as the AD walked out. On the other side of the glass, the door opened, and Duncan walked in with a friendly smile and a cup of coffee. "Here you go, sir." He set the steaming cup of freshly made coffee in front of Dewitt.

Dewitt reached for it and took a sip. He closed his eyes. "Damn, that's good. I thought all feds and cops had shit coffee."

Duncan smiled pleasantly. "Not all of us," he said simply. He didn't mention that he'd sent one of the analysts out to buy a bag of expensive coffee beans to aid in his interrogations. "Are you almost done?" he asked even as he studied his nails as though he'd seen dirt there.

"Almost, I just have a couple more accounts. Thanks for helping me out here. I know you didn't have to do that." He took another sip of coffee and sighed. "Damn good coffee." Then he picked up his pen and finished writing. He studied the list for a long moment, then looked up at Duncan. "Here you go, this is all of them."

Duncan didn't reach for the list right away. Instead, he smiled. "You sure that's all of them?"

Dewitt looked over the list again looking at it like it was money that was about to walk away. "Yeah. I double checked. Twice."

"Okay." Duncan stood and held out his hand. "I won't say it was a pleasure, because we already agreed that we don't ever want to see each other again, but at least you were man enough to own up to your mistakes." He walked around the table and opened the door. "Bryan, Meg, go ahead and take him down to booking." As the agents came in with handcuffs, Duncan walked out.

Jon Graham came out of the viewing room and walked with him. "You did good here, Duncan."

Duncan shrugged. "We'll only recover a small percentage of the money they took."

"Hey." Jon reached out and grabbed his shoulders. "You gotta take the wins, man. Not every case is going to work out this good and you have to accept the wins when you can, because God knows you also have to accept the losses too."

Duncan nodded. "I get it."

Agent Graham looked frustrated. "Dammit, Jamison. If you don't take this shit seriously, I'm going to have to recommend you start seeing a therapist to help you deal."

Duncan stopped walking and turned to him. "Actually, I've been meaning to talk to you about that."

Jon's brows came together. "About a therapist?"

Duncan nodded once. "I think it would be a good idea if I see one once a week and have them send a report to you."

Agent Graham was staring at him as though he had two heads. "You actually want me to approve weekly psychiatric visits? I'm not sure I have the budget for long term…"

Duncan sighed. "I'll pay for the visits; I just think it would be good to have a professional…" he hesitated, "monitoring my mental health."

Jonathan Graham threw his head back in a bellow of laughter. "I never thought I'd see the day," he said with amusement. "That an agent actually requested for their mental health to be monitored."

Duncan didn't smile. "I can't afford any chances. You understand."

Jon turned serious then and ran a hand over his face. "No, I don't understand. I understand that your father was a psychopath and that you are concerned that he somehow passed that on to you, but Jamison…" He waited for Duncan to meet his dark eyes. "I just watched you take apart this case like the genius that you are, and I don't understand how you can have all that genius floating around in your head and not get that you aren't him."

The image of Sylvie's half naked body splayed out bloody and beaten floated behind his eyes. He sighed. "Just do this for me."

Jon nodded. "I will approve the first three weeks and have it emailed to you but only because I think it might be good for you anyway, with all this shit coloring your perspective. We'll talk after that."

Duncan nodded. "I gotta go back in there and talk to the team but thanks, Jon."

It was the first time Duncan had used his given name and Jon found himself wondering if he was being played as smoothly as each of the white-collared bastards Duncan had taken apart today. He watched Duncan walk away thoughtfully. He devoutly hoped that Jamison wasn't pissed off when he got home and realized what he'd done, because Duncan Jamison would be a terrifying choice for an enemy.

Chapter 55

It was around nine o'clock when Duncan finally left the office. Since he hadn't made it to the gym he opted to walk again. It was cool tonight and he tucked his hands into the pockets of his suit as he walked. Sylvie's memory came again, only this time he remembered her lying as she had been this morning, curled into a pillow with the sheet tangled around her naked waist. His body tightened and even as it did, he was thinking about how even this discomfort was better than the torture of seeing her over and over, tied on that filthy bed. Too late, his mind went there, and he groaned as he crossed a side street.

She was gone now. Truly gone, and the deep empty ache inside himself heightened at that realization. She would stop calling him now. She would quit sending him texts that he was tempted to answer. Eventually she would even stop thinking about him. Just like she had the first time she'd left. That thought hurt the worst, but he brushed it aside. Best to deal with knowing that he would never have her again he thought and pulled that empty aching feeling close to his heart.

Panic threatened but he pushed that aside, focused on the long empty, lonely years ahead of him. Him trying to make up for the horrendous things his blood had done. He should have let Arthur kill him then and there. But he hadn't and now he had to deal with his own selfish choice that day.

He could have waited for Mason or Nick and let them shoot his father. But he had wanted to kill him from the moment he had shot Sylvie, even before he'd known it was Arthur Jamison. When he'd seen Sylvie there in bed, he'd known he would find an excuse to do it. He'd waited, calculating even for that one moment when he knew he could justify the shot. His father had given him that much. Duncan laughed bitterly and reached for his phone. He hit the call button and waited until the deep drowsy voice said hello.

"Nick, it's Jamison. Sylvie is back in Wilmington, and I need you to go to her."

Nick sat up in bed where he'd been asleep. He had an early morning tomorrow and had gone to bed early. "Come again?"

"Go to her," Duncan said in a tortured voice. "Seduce her and then hold on even when she tries to push you away. You need to make her marry you and then make her happy."

Nick laughed softly. "I find this conversation a little bizarre given that you've told me, multiple times I might add, to stay away." He paused for a long moment. "If you want her happy and married, do it yourself, you idiot. She is in love with you."

Duncan closed his eyes, remembering Sylvie telling him that softly.

He groaned. "Damn it, Hanlan, I'm giving you an opportunity here."

Incredulously, Nick laughed again. "Uh, no. What you are suggesting is that I go to a woman you no longer want and console her into my bed and then marry her even though she is grieving her family and her lost relationship with you. No thanks, Jamison."

"I do want her," Duncan said quietly.

"I didn't think I'd be having to tell a smart guy like you this," Nick said with amusement. "Boy loves girl, girl loves him back, easy solution. They get together, get married, and grow old together. Get it Duncan?"

Duncan wasn't laughing. He gritted his teeth. This conversation wasn't going at all the way he'd thought it would. He changed tactics. "Ha, ha. I was under the impression that you had a serious thing for Sylvie, Nick. I apologize for calling since I was obviously wrong."

Nick laughed. "I have been in a few interrogation rooms you know."

Duncan blew out a frustrated breath. "Damn it, Hanlan, if you won't go to her, I'll call Mason."

There was another light laugh from Nick. "I wouldn't do that if I were you. He might actually go to her. He wasn't in Idaho to see just how different she was with you."

"Sylvie?" Duncan asked, unable to quell his curiosity. "She was different in Idaho?"

Nick laughed. "For someone who claims he doesn't want anything to do with her, you seem awfully curious. Oh, and Duncan?"

"Yeah?"

"Man up before I have to get involved." He hung up and laid back down in his bed.

Duncan stared at the dead phone, wondering what the hell Hanlan had meant? He *was* manning up, which was why he'd sent her away. Why couldn't anyone seem to understand that, he wondered, just before he realized that Nick had just used his own technique on him. Duncan was laughing as he stepped inside the lobby of the hotel. He actually smiled at the receptionist, and she beamed right back. "Have a nice night, sir!"

He thought about calling Mason on the elevator, but it was late. Feeling better than he had in a long while he pulled out his room card and swiped it. He looked around the room as he entered. Her things were all gone and conflicting feelings warred inside. He pulled his gun from the holster and put it in the safe before removing his jacket and pulling a bottle of water from the fridge. He tipped his head back and guzzled. Then he saw the note. Curiously he walked over and picked it up.

Duncan

You didn't really think I'd let you go that easily, did you? I love you, remember?

He frowned and turned it over to see if she'd written anything else. He sighed and sat down in a chair next to the small round glass table reading the words again. It didn't make sense. He ran a hand through his hair and went to the mini bar. The small scotch bottles had been replaced and with a curious smile he picked up the full bottle of Macallan scotch that was tucked nearby. He shrugged and opened it to pour a bit into a glass. He remembered Nick's refusal to go to Sylvie and threw back the first bit before pouring some more.

"Good. You found my gift, and it looks like you are almost ready," Sylvie said from behind him.

He spun around sloshing scotch over the rim. He took one look at her scantily clad creamy skin and gulped. The dark blue lingerie left little to the imagination and he groaned and threw back the last of his scotch even as a surge of anger tasted like bile in the back of his throat. He stared hard at her, trying not to look at her body. He swallowed. "Now, Sylvie, I told you to be gone when I got back."

She advanced a step, and he noticed the connecting door to the next room was open. He rubbed a hand over his face even as he backed away from her. "Don't do this, sweetheart," he said hoarsely.

She smiled. "Don't do what? Show you how much I love you?"

He held up his hands as he backed away another step. "I can't keep doing this and letting you go after," he said, sounding tortured.

"I'm counting on just that," she said softly, and her warm eyes smiled even as she walked steadily forward until his knees buckled against the bed. She laid a soft hand on his cheek. "I love you, Duncan, and I know you. I won't stop coming at you until you realize that you are the most gentle, intelligent, man I've ever met and that I can't live without you."

Tears pooled in his eyes, and he looked away. "No, don't..." he whispered even as his arms came up to pull her sleek body close.

She pulled his face up to hers and kissed him. Hard. Biting gently at his lips when he refused to open to her tender onslaught. He groaned and yanked her over him, even as he opened for the sweet, sweet taste he so craved. He couldn't keep doing this, he thought, even as his hand lifted to cup her round breast. She arched into his hand, and he lost the battle.

Afterward they lay silently together for a long while. Her trying to figure out a way to get him to let her stay. Him thinking about how his addiction to her had to end before she got hurt. He sat up suddenly. "Why did the airport think you had boarded the flight to Wilmington?"

She looked away not wanting him to be mad at Graham. "I may have told them to say that," she hedged, not wanting to flat out lie.

He studied her face for a long time. "And they just said, 'Oh yeah, sure no problem, we can do that'?"

She squirmed out from under his leg and rolled over. "Something like that." He snagged her wrist, and she turned back to look down at him in all his glorious naked wonder. "God you're hot." She hadn't meant to say it out loud and she regretted it the moment his face twisted in anger.

"Do you really think I'd be distracted by that right now?" he bit out. Sylvie bit her lip. Duncan had never been angry with her, and it was a new experience. She sighed. "I didn't mean to say that," she said honestly.

He stared at her and then relaxed his grip. "Which one of them helped you?"

She forced her eyes to widen. "Who? And with what?"

He grinned and pulled her down onto his lap. She tried to squirm away, but he was too fast and had her pinned under one arm with his other running gently up and down her arm and shoulder. She shivered and he smiled. "Hanlan or Graham, Sylvie?"

She squirmed on his lap trying to touch the floor with her feet. He groaned and buried his face in her hair. "If you don't stop squirming around, you might get more than you bargained for, sweetheart."

She turned her face up to smile at him and it was so real and so bright that he held his breath. "I'm counting on just that, Duncan."

His heartbeat sped up and his loins began tightening. Softly, he touched her side, ran a hand upward, grazed the side of her naked breast. "I think I can get the truth out of you one way or another." He met her brown eyes, held them in his. "What do you think?"

"I think I'll enjoy it when you try," she said boldly, and watched his eyes darken as his pupils dilated. "For the record, Duncan, I'm not going away unless you're with me. I'm going to haunt you and get up in your face and nag at you until you finally get a grip on the fact that you aren't, no, that you could never be like him."

He stared into her eyes wanting to believe her words more than anything, but still too afraid to hope. "How could you even be here with me after all he did to you and your family?" he asked quietly, needing the truth now in this moment more than air to breathe.

"Because I know you, Duncan. I'd put my life in your hands every moment for the rest of it if you only agree to that." She sensed the pain he was feeling and stood taking his face in her hands as she whispered. "You are good, and kind, and thoughtful, and dedicated, and most definitely out of this world sexy," she whispered and with each word she kissed each of his eyes, his nose, his cheeks, and finally his lips.

She felt warm tears against her fingers, and she held his head to her chest wrapping her arms around his neck as he wept. Then, she wept with him. They sat that way for several long minutes before she leaned back just far enough to pull his face up to look at her. "You're beautiful and strong, Duncan Jamison, and together we will get through this."

His blue eyes were shining when he said, "Why would you take the risk?"

She laughed softly. "It's not a risk, honey. It's a promise and I intend to make it to you one way or another."

"But *why* Sylvie? Why after having found out that my da—" he choked off the word. "That Arthur Jamison killed your sister and your dad and all of those other women. Why would you want me, when you didn't even want me before?"

Sylvie got down on her knees in front of him. "I always wanted you, Duncan. *Always.* To the point of obsession. I've wanted you ever since that day you hauled me down the mountain. I chased you for a long time when

you and Elaine broke up for good, but you didn't seem interested and after a while I thought you must be hung up on her." She paused. "Then she died, and I thought that she would forever be the one you loved but couldn't have and I couldn't compete with that."

He was watching her as though debating whether or not she was telling the truth. Finally, he asked, "Why didn't you want a relationship when you first came back then?"

She sighed. "Because I am a fool sometimes. You may as well know that now, since it's bound to come up again in the future."

He raised one eyebrow at her. "I can't be with you, or anyone else for that matter, Sylvie."

She slid her hand down his neck and shoulder. "Is it because you don't love me any more?"

She saw the pained look that crossed his features, watched the inner struggle. "You know that isn't it."

"Do I?" she asked softly.

He caressed her shoulder and arm, then ran a hand down to rest against her thigh. He wondered at the softness of her skin, the sweetness there in her face, and the love she had to give. "I would do *anything* if I thought it could work, Sylvie. But I can't take the risk that everyone is wrong and I'm like him. Not with anyone, but especially not with you."

"It sounds like you have doomed yourself to a lifetime alone."

He shrugged. "It's a price I'm willing to pay to know that you are safe."

"Well, you and I aren't going to get along well then, because I promise that I won't leave you Duncan. If you go, I will find you. I know who you are, and I refuse to leave you while you're wondering about all of this. If you realize you are a good person and then don't want me in your life, I will let you go, but not a second sooner."

"I can leave Chicago."

"Okay, where do you want to go? I'm game."

He groaned. "No, no, no. This is not what I want."

"You aren't going to get your way with this, Jamison. Teach me to fight and shoot, so that I can protect myself from you. Tell me that you don't love me. Tell me that you hate me for all the pain I've caused you. But don't tell me you love me, and then ask me to leave, because I won't," she said with feeling.

He slid his fingers into her hair, rubbed the nape of her neck gently. "I should never have told you how I felt. I have since realized just how selfish I was."

"You don't have a selfish bone in your body."

She settled into his lap and smiled as she felt the familiar hardening of his desire for her. "Give us a little time to figure this out but don't send us away."

He pulled her tight against his chest. "I think you mean don't send you away, sweetheart."

She eyed him. "That's what I said."

He studied her for a long moment, "How did you find me, Sylvie?"

She hesitated, then quietly admitted, "I went back to Idaho looking for you, but you weren't there, so I begged Jackie and Ren until they finally gave in and told me. Don't blame them, Duncan, they only want you to be happy. I think I could help with that, don't you?"

He smiled and she couldn't help noticing it almost looked real.

"You really have no shame when you make up your mind do you?"

She laughed and turned in his lap rubbing against the hard tip of him.

"I'm shameless, but only when it comes to you."

"Why don't you go date one of those other guys you're always bragging about?"

She gave him a narrow stare. "Two reasons. One, you ended things with all of them without me even noticing, and two, I tried that." She watched for his reaction.

She felt his grip tighten on her neck the slightest bit before he forced a relaxed stance. "Which one of them was it?" he asked, forcing a casual tone. "No one you know, and I got through exactly ten minutes before I wanted to throw up so I left the date."

He eyed her, feeling pleased but making sure he didn't show that.

"Keep trying, you'll find someone to love, Sylvie."

"I have found someone I love."

He groaned. "We aren't doing this again, sweetheart." She smiled and wriggled around his lap. "Wanna bet?"

He growled and turned her onto her back as he used his hands and mouth to slowly, torturously, bring her the pleasure they both craved. He lifted his head from her breast. "This doesn't mean anything, Sylvie." He needed her to know he hadn't changed his mind.

She laughed breathlessly. "Now, where have I heard that before, and why do I feel like karma is biting me in the ass?"

Because he couldn't resist, he said, "That's not karma, sweetheart."

She woke alone again the following day and then in exasperation realized that he'd packed up his things and taken them with him. She didn't call Graham this time. She picked up her phone and called Ben. She spent the day alone wondering what else she could possibly do to convince Duncan their relationship was worth a shot.

That night when he slipped into his new hotel room across town, she was already waiting in the bed with a glass of scotch in her hand. He turned to leave but then she lifted the sheet and he realized she was naked.

The rest of the week went the same way with him leaving while she slept and him getting to his new hotel each night to find her waiting there for him. He didn't even try to resist any more when he saw her and that, she thought, was progress.

He also began seeing healthy, happy images of her more often than that of her restrained beaten body. He didn't have a new case yet but was still tying up loose ends with the white-collar crime unit.

The fifth day he didn't bother calling ahead to check into a hotel. He simply drove to one after a long day of work, followed by a two-hour workout. He checked in at the front desk and then made his way up to his room.

Sylvie wasn't inside and he felt disappointed though he'd known she wouldn't be, since she had no way of knowing where he would be. He tried to feel happy about it but when she knocked on his door ten minutes later, he opened it to her. He eyed her, "How did you find me this time? I doubt it's even in the system yet."

She smiled but it looked forced. "When I couldn't figure out where you had booked, I drove to your work and parked a few rows down and followed you here. I'm actually beginning to feel like a stalker." She sounded sad. "Do you want me to go?"

He knew he should tell her yes but the emotion she was trying to cover had him feeling guilty and he couldn't quite get the lie past his lips. Instead, he opened the door wide. "Please don't."

She came inside with only a small overnight bag, and he realized just how much of a toll it was taking on her to follow him around. "Don't you have work?" he asked suddenly, realizing that he hadn't asked her about it for days.

She shook her head. "I quit."

His eyes widened and he took a step forward. "You love that job."

"I did. I love *you* more," she said, and the words felt empty even to her own ears.

He stared at her, torn between his need to offer her comfort and his need to keep her safe. But he hadn't killed her yet... so maybe… He reached for her and pulled her into his arms. It was the first time their lovemaking had been initiated by him since he'd left Wilmington, and she cried in his arms afterward. "I'm sorry about the toll this is all taking on you, Sylvie. This is why I'd hoped you would pick the smart path and give Hanlan another shot."

She slid out of his arms. "I won't lie here naked with you while you talk about sending me to someone else's bed, Duncan." She didn't miss the karmic bite in that either.

Desperate and emotional, she said softly, "I have been chasing you, because I thought we loved each other, but if you don't want me…" She broke off as tears filled her eyes. She wasn't sure she could handle the truth again. She remembered the cold numbness back in high school when she had finally realized Duncan Jamison didn't want her, and she didn't know if she could face that again.

He didn't speak for several moments and when he did, she instantly felt bad for pressuring him. "God, I don't know what to do, sweetheart," he murmured brokenly. "I love you so much it terrifies me, and I want you. God, I want you. But…" He sucked air into his lungs raggedly. "I would never be able to live with myself if you got hurt again because of me. Tell me you understand that?" He waited but she didn't respond because she sensed he needed to talk.

"When Jackie called me and told me it was Dad…" His voice was hoarse as though it took all his effort to force the words through his lips. "I thought that I wouldn't get there in time and then that lady he shot, she was lying there, and I thought she was you. I won't lie, I considered finding him and letting him kill me if you were dead. But it wasn't you and then you were missing, and everyone kept mentioning this old lady.

"I had seen this old lady earlier that day who caught my attention for some reason. Something about her was familiar somehow and suddenly I knew. I knew it was him and that he'd taken you there to that place I'd seen her come from. But that was two miles away and he had fifteen minutes on me, and I thought that if you were dead, I would let him shoot me before I killed him." She looked horrified at his admission. He kept talking. Now, that he'd started saying it all, he couldn't seem to stop.

"I ran until my lungs felt like they were melting but I didn't care and then I broke through the door, and I saw you." His eyes met hers, then he looked away. "You were alive, but his pants were barely up and obviously undone and you, you were all laid out, but bloody and beaten and I knew I was going to kill him. I knew it was only a matter of when and the sickest part is that I wanted it in that moment." He slid his gaze to hers, guilt sheltered there in his blue eyes as he waited for the condemnation in hers.

She shrugged. "So, what, Duncan? If anyone had done that to you, I would feel the same way. I'm honored. Humbled even to know that you love me that much. I was afraid for a long time that you would blame me for having to kill him. You may think that a choice was involved and you're right. The choice was to let him kill me or let him kill you. He was going to, you know. I saw it in his eyes when he ripped down my clothes. I looked into his vacant eyes, and I knew that he was going to rape and kill me. Then you came in and I knew he was going to kill you. All I wanted was to get to you when he fell to the floor. You did have a choice but not the one that you think you did. You chose to live and let me live."

He looked away. Shame burned like acid in his stomach.

"Why, Duncan? Why are you so sure your intentions weren't justified?" She was watching the guilt eat him alive, wanted to cry for the burden of that guilt.

His jaw hardened and he lifted his head, met her eyes and the self-hatred there in his gaze took her breath away. He gulped in air. This was the reason he had left, the reason he had tried to exile himself. She could see it in the way his eyes wanted to look away, even as he forced his gaze to stay steady on hers. She could see it in the rapid ticking of his heartbeat in his neck. "Why, Duncan?" she asked again.

The words tore from his lips like a cry for peace from soldiers, tired and cold, and sick of bloodshed after endless days and nights of just that. "Because, damn it, in that moment, when I saw you, bound and naked, even when I realized that he had probably raped you, and had obviously beaten you, I got hot and turned on, and then I wanted to pull that trigger." He turned away from her stunned and raw reaction.

Jerkily he began to gather his things together. He reached for the dop kit that he had removed before she'd gotten there, and threw it into his bag before he zipped it closed. His hands shook as he reached for his clothes and pulled them on. Sylvie hadn't made a sound and he had used up all his courage to tell her the truth.

Now she would finally move on. Now that she had come here and tortured him into realizing he was never going to be okay without her she would leave. He didn't even realize he was crying until he saw drops falling on his shirt and leaving splotches there. He didn't care. He was broken and lost without a home. He reached for his jacket and his bag and walked to the door, then opened it.

"Are you even going to give me a chance to tell you what I think?" she asked quietly, reverently.

He shrugged and turned back for one last look. "What's the point?"

She rose up, stark naked, and walked to him in spite of the open door.

He closed it. She smiled. "I am truly, madly, deeply, in love with you,

Duncan. So much so, that I fear I will no longer have a heart if you walk out that door one more time."

He stared at her incredulously. "Are you fucking kidding me with this shit?"

Sylvie's jaw went up and out a notch stubbornly. "I'm *not* kidding and if you walk out that door, that's it for us, Duncan. There are no do overs left, no future make-ups." Tears filled her eyes. "If you walk out that door you will break my heart into so many pieces, I won't be capable of putting it back together. I heard every word you said, and I felt how much courage it took for you to say it, and it broke my heart for the pain that you're in, but that won't matter if you leave me now. I *am* beautiful, Duncan. Everyone has told me that for all of my life. And you are handsome and so sexy it takes my breath away every time you strip down."

"I feel out of control when you touch me and tease me, but I let you do it anyway because I trust you to keep me safe even as I'm spiraling into the unknown. You have to trust me too, though. I will keep you safe. If I'm honest with you, I'm wet for you even now because I know how much I turn you on." She set her legs wide. "If you don't believe me, you're welcome to check for yourself."

"Jesus Christ, Sylvie, don't do this," he pleaded as he watched her lower herself and her own pride for him.

She lifted her chin. "I'm not ashamed to admit that I want you, Duncan. Knowing that you still wanted me at what was the most vulnerable moment of my life makes me hot as hell, and I don't care if that seems dark and dirty, because just as I'm beautiful and smart, I have dark parts too. I love you, Duncan, but you have to love you too. You have to love all of you. The part that made you so angry that you wanted to kill a man you knew had inflicted unimaginable pain on so many, as well as the tender part of you that orders room service for me even though you've sent me away."

"And if I can't accept all of it?" he asked quietly.

Her gaze narrowed. "Then you may as well walk out now."

He sucked in a breath and eyed the door. Then he looked at a very naked, allegedly wet, Sylvie, who wanted him and didn't think he was demented. He dropped his bag and jacket on the floor. He wanted to go to her, but his feet wouldn't move. He looked at her brown eyes beckoning him inside, daring him to love her. Her small, upturned nose was still slightly in the air. "I don't deserve you," he whispered softly.

"Why don't you come over here and let me decide that for myself?" she countered.

His feet wouldn't move but then he was striding to her, reaching for her and wrapping her inside his embrace. Touching every inch of her hair, her face, her body, then softly kissing everywhere he'd touched. And if he noticed that she was indeed very wet and hot, well he wouldn't testify in a court of law. He didn't make love to her for a long while, only held and caressed her. Finally, she opened her eyes to look up at him. "Are you ever going to get around to actually fucking me?"

He laughed softly. "Maybe, but first…" He ran a hand slowly up her side to her breast.

She groaned, and in one swift powerful motion, rolled up and over to straddle him. His eyes darkened as she rubbed her core against his jean clad erection. "If you are going to play the slow game after all that cuddling and rubbing, I am going to take charge."

She lay in his arms panting a few minutes later. She ran a hand up and down his chest running her fingers through the sprinkle of dark hair that stretched between his nipples and then sloped downwards. "I have a secret too," she whispered.

He rose up on his elbows to stare at her curiously. "What?"

"I don't want to tell you if you're going to be gone when I wake up again." She looked up at him and waited but he didn't say anything.

"Are you going to leave me again, Jamison?"

He didn't flinch, only held her eyes in his as he laced his fingers through hers and whispered, "Never again."

She smiled radiantly. "In that case…" She hesitated.

"What is it, sweetheart?" "I'm pregnant."

He jerked into a sitting position and raked long fingers through his hair.

"That's impossible. You're on birth control, right?"

She smiled. "I was, yes. I had a couple of days when I took it at odd times but ultimately, I've decided that it was just meant to be." She moved so that she could see his face. "Do you want to be involved?"

He stared at her as fear and excitement warred inside. "Involved in what?"

"With raising our child?"

He looked at her still flat stomach. "And if I don't?"

"Then I take back all the things I said about us being together?" "Why?"

"Because that means I'll be raising him or her on my own."

He hadn't dared hope. "You're keeping it?"

She slapped him. "Of course, I am, you idiot, haven't you been listening to all the sweet things I've been saying to you?"

He grinned impishly. "It's just that you have a career and your dreams, and I thought you'd want to wait."

She smiled. "I've been waiting for eight long years. I'd say that's long enough."

He couldn't stop the nod of agreement. Patience was highly overrated in his opinion.

Chapter 56

Duncan turned to smile at Sylvie as they drove. It had been two weeks since he'd found out that she was pregnant, and they were driving back to North Carolina together in his truck. He still wasn't fully convinced that he should be around Sylvie or the baby she was carrying, and even as he wondered at the wisdom in it, he hadn't been able to walk away from her since that night.

He'd gone to work each morning after their nights of tender lovemaking as usual, finishing up the case he'd been given, but each night he'd gone back to that hotel where she waited with tender hugs and kisses and had usually ordered in dinner for them. Each night, he fell asleep in her arms but with self-hatred for his weakness. His sleep was haunted with dreams of Sylvie dying there in his arms. Still, he came back to her each night.

They were only about an hour out now and he reached for her hand, threading his fingers through her own and holding it tenderly. She knew he wasn't fully convinced in the wisdom of them being together, but she was going to love him until he finally realized what she knew. That he was pure and good and kind.

"I know all of this is still a little hard on you," she said gently.

He merely squeezed her hand as he stared out at the thick trees lining the highway as they drove past. It was beautiful here, he thought, and not for the first time. He could see why she had wanted to stay here after college. He still hadn't allowed his mind to consider having a future here with Sylvie or his baby. He knew that if he let himself imagine that, then he might not ever have the courage to leave, even if he decided his family wasn't safe with him around.

He watched the trees passing by like a balm to his damaged psyche. An eagle soared overhead and then landed to perch on a tree, staring at them as they drove past. He pointed and Sylvie looked out with a smile. They were just coming into the outskirts of town, and he moved into the left lane, intending to go across the bridge and then take the main highway toward

Sylvie's beach house. She frowned suddenly and pulled her fingers from his to touch his arm realizing his intention. "Uh, Duncan, if you don't mind, I'd like to go to your house first," she said quietly, looking for the words to explain what she had done.

Nothing came to mind, and she finally sighed and sat back as he moved back over and took the next exit and then turned right heading out on the tree-lined country road toward his place. He really hadn't spent much time here, since he'd spent most of his time at Sylvie's house, and then had taken off as soon as he'd been allowed to leave by the police department. He turned to glance at Sylvie, "Is there any particular reason you want to come out here?"

She smiled. "Some of my things are there," she hedged.

He didn't dig deeper. Only settled into the seat and turned up onto the narrow road and drove up over the hill. He saw his horses there grazing at the grass, a bright green tint from the fresh rains, and glanced toward the house. The lawn was trimmed, and the horses looked healthy, and he made a mental note to give Jamal a bonus. The kid had kept up on things surprisingly well in his absence.

He parked next to the house and left the luggage in the back, assuming Sylvie was just planning to grab a few things before they headed to her place. She looked uneasily at the bags and the truck but decided to let it go. Hand in hand they climbed the wide stairs to the brightly painted white porch and he reached into his pocket and pulled out the keys. He let them inside and walked with her through the door with a little smile.

He stopped suddenly. Where there had been an empty front room with only the rooster clock on the wall was a beautiful brown leather sofa set and two glass and wood side tables. There was even art on the wall, and he stood, transfixed, as he stared at an enlarged canvas photo of him and Sylvie, arm in arm, with a wide-open mountain behind them as a backdrop.

He remembered her snapping the photo on her phone and turned to stare down at her. "Did you do all of this?"

She looked embarrassed and he smiled gently. She looked nervously at the array of photos she'd arranged over the mantel above the flat stone fireplace. Photos of him and Jackie, one of Jackie and Ren, holding their girls and baby Reagan as they all cuddled on the sofa. There was another of him and Sylvie, this one of them smiling with the cape in the background from when they'd gone downtown to lunch.

His heart began to pound, and pain seeped into his pores as he tried to turn away from this evidence of what could be the promise of a glorious life. He swallowed hard. She still hadn't answered him, and he felt her eyes on him as he struggled for air. He stared at her bright, smiling face and a tear ran down one cheek.

They looked happy together, and he remembered that it was before he'd realized his father was a deranged cold-blooded killer.

"I'm sorry Duncan. I was trying to figure out how to tell you about this..." she offered gently. "I know I shouldn't have, but you were gone, and I couldn't stand the thought of not being near you. I came out here looking for you at first, but eventually I found myself coming out more and more just to feel close to you again." She shrugged. "After several days in the empty house I figured it was time to furnish it."

His jaw was tense, and he forced a smile; he had told Jamal to tell her to do whatever she liked after all. He just hadn't imagined she would do all of this. With his reaction to the simple front room, she was nervous about how he might react to everything else she'd done. Suddenly, she wanted to head to her beach house. "Let's just get out of here. Come on. We can drive over to my place," she said quietly.

He turned to look at her then. He could see the nervousness in her eyes.

"I'm not going to like the rest of it, am I?" he asked softly.

She wouldn't lie to him. She met his searching gaze with a nervous smile, "It depends…"

"On what exactly?"

She looked around the room. "Well, how do you like this room?"

He looked around and smiled. "It's nice."

She squeezed her hands together nervously. "It's too much, I know. I may have been a little obsessed with trying to make sense of how I was feeling and gone overboard, because I had realized I was madly in love with you, but you weren't returning my calls." She eyed his shuttered expression. "Let's just go and I will have it all removed tomorrow."

He didn't know if he could handle the sweetness and evidence of their love when his feelings about it all were still so raw with his fear of being like his father. Still, he turned and looked toward the dining room. This room at least looked much the same except for the wide panoramic black and white canvas of the beach, with the pier cutting out through the center lined with bright lights and a bright moon above, making the waves shine as they moved towards the shore.

He noticed one of the bedroom doors open at the same time she did, and she looked away guiltily as he walked over to peer inside. There were a simple bed and side table sets in there with more impersonal photos of the beach lining the walls. He raised an eyebrow at her. Curiously he turned and opened the second bedroom door. It looked much the same except there were collages of beautiful fall foliage instead of the beach. He laughed suddenly. "And what exactly were you planning to use these rooms for?"

She blushed and looked down at her hands. "Why, for when Ren and Jackie come to visit, of course, after we're married."

His heart ached at the simplicity of her words. If he wanted this, wanted her, he could just reach out and take it. Still, he held back. He walked back out and into the kitchen without saying anything. "Are there any more surprises?" he asked, sounding both pained and amused. She avoided his questioning look and said simply, "A couple, I un- boxed all the things you had shipped."

He nodded and turned toward the stairs but not before he noticed the shiny name brand stainless-steel pots and pans that hung over the island, on hooks that dangled from the massive steel fixture above. When he got to the top of the stairs, he stared out into the room that she had indeed turned into a gym. There was a nice, sturdy looking treadmill, an elliptical and a bench with a full stand of bars, dumbbells, and a variety of weights. He whistled. "Now, that, is state of the art." She smiled, pleased that he seemed to like it, even as he studied the wall-to-wall mirrors and the positive sayings hanging around the room.

She tried to get ahead of him up the stairs, but he grasped her arm and pushed ahead of her. All of it, she'd thought he'd like, had actually designed it with him in mind, but there was one room she didn't want him to see yet, and she couldn't remember if she'd closed the door. In fear, she stared at the door that was opened only a few inches, but if he looked closely… She panicked and rushed forward to close it quickly. "I don't think you want to see in there," she said quietly, and watched a tortured smile turn his lips up. "I didn't know why you weren't returning my calls when I did all of this," she said lamely.

He grasped her hands and gently pulled her away from the door, reaching for the knob. Unable to stop him now, she only hoped that whatever fragile truce she had been able to spin between them in Chicago wouldn't be completely destroyed when he saw the nursery. She watched his shoulders tense as it hit him what she'd done before he forced them to relax casually.

He stopped just inside the cherry-stained, wooden door staring at what could only be described as a child's most cherished wonderland. Fear of the darkness inside him warred with his love for Sylvie and the deep-seated desire to have this beautiful life with her. He sucked the air into his lungs that had expelled at his first glimpse of the nursery.

The walls were painted in long colorful strips in every color that a child might like, boy or girl. A little amused grin turned up his lips as he realized one side of the room was made up for a baby boy, with dark wooden furniture and stuffed animals, blocks, cars, airplanes, while the other side was made up with bright white furniture with rainbows, dolls, more blocks, a different array of stuffed animals. His eyebrows shot up at the lengths she had gone to, to have every type of toy to spark imagination in a toddler.

It was the large black vinyl names with cute little zoo and safari animals parading around them on the wall above each of the softly bedded cribs that had his breath coming in heaves and his hand tightening unintentionally on the doorknob. "No," he said angrily, desperately as he stepped back and away from the door. "Fuck no, Sylvie."

He ran his hands through his hair and then over his taut features. He looked down at his hands in surprise. He hadn't even noticed the tears that were sliding down his cheeks as the torment of what he couldn't have, tore at his fragile mind.

"I'm so sorry Duncan," she said softly, and the truth was evident in her tone. "If I'd known how you felt…" She trailed off even as she moved to him and wrapped her arms tightly around his waist and laid her head on his chest just below his chin. She held him that way for a long moment, regretting what was coming but knowing she had to do it. "I wouldn't have done it this way, Duncan, but it's done now, and you may as well get used to the fact that I am naming our child after you, whether it's a boy or a girl."

He jerked away from her then, anger evident in his blue eyes. "I don't know why in God's name you thought I would agree with this, but it'll never happen." He tried not to think of those small delicately formed letters sprawled out above the beds.

Her chin jutted out a little and she got a stubborn glint in her brown eyes. "I am the mother, and it is ultimately up to me."

He raised his stricken gaze to hers. "Please. If you truly love me, don't do this," he asked in a shaky voice.

She reached her hands up to cup his face in her hands. "I'm sorry that I have to do this. I truly am. But I'm going to have to insist, darling."

He turned his face away from her then, unable to let her see the pain in his twisted features. She reached for his hand and placed it gently on her still flattened belly. "If it's a girl I'm going to name her Rayne Jamison, baby, you can pick the middle name if you want to. And if it's a boy, I'm naming him Duncan Jamison, you can also pick his middle name if you'd like."

He turned to stare down at her, his expression hard. "Why would you insist on doing this, Sylvie?"

She smiled tenderly. "Because I want all of us united in name, Duncan, and I *will* be taking Jamison as my last name when you finally agree to marry me. Also, and this is really important to me, I want he or she to know how proud I am of you, and the strong, honest man that you are. I hope you can come to accept it over time." Her voice was firm, but tender.

He ran his hands roughly through his hair again. "I don't know if I can do that," he said starkly.

She smiled gently. "I will do it for the both of us then until you love yourself enough to accept it as well."

He sighed and she actually led him toward the master bedroom even though she'd been nervously hoping he'd skip that room. He looked around at the walls that were covered in large photos of them in various entangled positions. He vaguely remembered her snapping some photos of them after their lovemaking. They weren't nudes, only showing their bodies entwined down to just below their shoulders. In one her hair was splayed out over his arm as she lay on his chest smiling. In another her arm was thrown over him, her hand splayed tenderly on his face. The honesty of the intimate love between them was obvious and he looked away as his heart stabbed painfully.

He walked toward the closet where she'd told him she had put away his things and chuckled in surprise when he saw not only his things, lining one side, but the other side was also filled with hers as well. "Did you bring all your stuff here?" he asked in surprise.

She laughed softly and shook her head. "No, though most of them are here now. I didn't intend for it to happen, but I was missing you so much and this place was the only piece I had of you, since you didn't leave anything at my place." She aimed it at him like an accusation. "At first, I kept coming to see if you'd come back but then when I couldn't get a hold of you, I'd end up riding and, well working on all of this. Then I wouldn't want to leave just in case you came home in the night, so I'd stay over. Anyway, by the time I realized I'd practically moved in. I had already realized just how big a fool I'd been in pushing you away and so I just started coming straight here each day."

He smiled as he eyed the sleek business suits and dresses lining her side. "You know, I've never even seen you dressed for work."

"I'd be happy to demonstrate if you'd like," she offered with twinkling eyes, knowing that once her clothes were off, he'd take her to bed. Maybe that would help to ease the tension that was palpable between them with what she'd done to his house.

He grinned and nodded. "But first, I may as well go get our bags."

"Deal," she said softly and with tender promise in those brown Eyes that he loved so much.

Chapter 57

Sylvie put a hand on the large mound of her belly and smiled as her son kicked up a storm. "Hey there, baby Duncan, you doing okay this morning?" she asked even as she turned to lift a tea mug to her lips. She'd cut way back on coffee since she'd found out she was expecting Duncan's baby and though she didn't love tea, it felt good to go through her morning routine with a steaming mug of something.

She took a small bite of toast into her mouth and chewed. The sweet, tangy flavor of Mrs Ginny's wild berry jelly burst onto her tongue, and she tipped her head back and closed her eyes. Duncan had kept jars of the jelly in the cupboard since he'd come back. She felt him behind her, and she turned with a smile just as he slid his strong sexy arms around her wide mound cupping his hands over the top. "How are my two favorite people doing today?" he murmured gently against her earlobe sending shivers down her neck.

"Well, little buddy's doing gymnastics and his momma is surviving said gymnastics, so all in all, not bad," she said with a grumpy little laugh. She watched his fingers spread out tenderly over her belly, but he didn't respond. She turned her head up to meet his gaze. "How are you doing today?"

Duncan kissed her neck and cheek and then finally her lips as she lifted her head up to meet his mouth. He looked good this morning, like he'd slept well last night, which hadn't often been the case lately. She pulled her head back a little. "Did you sleep okay?"

He nodded. "Yes, but I always do when I'm here with you."

His hair was freshly cut, and he was wearing a dark blue sweater over tan slacks. Even now, after having him back in her life for nearly six months, that familiar heat began in her core as she looked into his blue eyes. "It's good to have you home with us," she said softly and leaned back into his warmth.

He wouldn't reciprocate her thought, she knew. Even though he'd spent the last six months trying to adjust. He fought day by day with the demons that he simply couldn't seem to quite eradicate. Sylvie knew that he still thought he shouldn't be around her and their son. She knew because she had been teasing him endlessly, about going down to the courthouse to get married and he kept refusing. She wondered if he thought she wouldn't give his son the Jamison name if they weren't actually married.

It wouldn't matter, however, as she had considered legally changing her name even if he never agreed to marry her. It was a stand she wanted to take for Duncan. A stand of solidarity and ownership of the tarnished name because she'd known way more Jamison's with integrity that were good and kind, then that one horrible man who'd rocked the nation with the horrific news of his victims. Duncan didn't want his son carrying the burden of all that, but she wanted their child to know and truly understand the exact kind of miraculous man that his father was.

"How did your case go?" she asked softly.

Duncan had gotten back late the night before from Chicago where he'd been called in on a missing persons case. He'd been gone two weeks, and though he'd gotten back the night before, they hadn't talked much. Instead, he'd spent the night making sweet desperate love to her before they'd both finally fallen to sleep.

He smiled. "We found the missing girl after two days, but I got all twisted up in the case since it broke open a human trafficking ring, otherwise I would have been back a week ago."

She'd been watching the news and following the case, so she already knew the outcome, but it seemed to calm him to talk to her about it each time he'd left and then returned as his cases were closed. "That is good. You really are my hero, Duncan," she said softly.

He snorted. "Sure, right. Because you aren't out there every day making the world a better place yourself." She watched him with a smile. He hadn't argued, or fought, or really ever even allowed himself to be angry around her since he'd driven her back here months ago. She knew it was his careful measured way of trying to assure her that he wouldn't snap and kill her, which was absolute nonsense, but she wasn't going to waste breath telling him that. It wouldn't do any good anyway. He reached around her and poured a cup of coffee that she had made for him. "Thanks for this." He held the mug up toward her. "So, how did *your* case go?"

Sylvie smiled. "I got a guilty verdict, though it was less my success and more the great evidence that the detectives on the case got for us."

He gave her a wry grin. "I'm beginning to notice a pattern with you, ADA Dunlap. Every case you win is because of the detectives' skills, or the CSI evidence, or even the DA himself."

She arched a brow delicately. "What is that supposed to mean, Mr Jamison?"

He didn't wince at the name any more. Probably, partly because she used it often, deliberately, trying to give it a normalcy again with him. He took a sip of coffee. "You are the hero here, not me."

She laughed. "We'll have to agree to disagree."

He nodded with a smile. "Are you hungry? I could whip something up."

Now was the moment to talk to him about the subject she had been avoiding. She couldn't bring herself to talk about it though, so instead she smiled. "I have a better idea. Why don't we go out somewhere and get some breakfast?"

He nodded. "Suits me. Are you going to your place this weekend?"

She looked up at him. "That depends, what are your plans?"

He chuckled. "I have an open schedule." "Do you want to go to the beach house?" she asked softly.

He looked thoughtful; he hadn't been back there since he'd shot his dad across the street. Finally, he nodded. "I'd like that. I can't believe how much I crave the beach and the ocean when I'm gone."

"It gets in the blood," she agreed. "Let's go if you want to. I won't say no to waking up to the sound of waves."

They each threw a few things into an overnight bag and loaded them into the small SUV that she had upgraded to, so she could fit a car seat into the backseat. They drove to a restaurant downtown, near the water, that specialized in morning cocktails and fresh southern breakfast.

After giving the waiter their order. She settled back into the plush booth across from him and reached for her orange juice. He was eyeing her, and she smiled. He didn't smile back, only studied her. After and long moment he set his Mimosa down and asked smoothly, "What are you avoiding telling me, sweetheart?"

She looked down into her glass. Dressed in a long white sweater over blue leggings and a brown belt cinched above her belly that matched her mid-calf brown boots, she was feeling a little warm. She sighed and lifted her eyes. "The memorial is next week, Duncan."

His gaze turned cold. "No," he bit out.

She took a deep breath. "Duncan, I hate to do this, but the families have requested that you be there. Besides that, my dad, Elaine, and your mom, will also be honored there. You don't want to miss that, do you?"

"I already told Jackie that I won't be going. She is going to be there. I don't want to fight with you, Sylvie, so please, just let it go."

"I can't," she said simply. "The families of all the victims will be there, Duncan, and though none of this is your fault, I think it would mean a lot to them to see you there." She felt guilty for using his own guilt against him, but she had already made up her mind to get him there.

He swore low and stood up as though to leave. Sylvie met his blazing blue eyes with her own pleading gaze. "Please don't go. If you don't want to be near me now, then I will go, but you should at least get the breakfast you ordered."

He looked down at her for a long moment before letting a long string of curses out and dropping heavily back into his seat. "It's not you. I just don't think I want to relive all the damage that man did to so many families." She reached a hand toward him slowly, unsure whether he would welcome her touch. He looked at it and lifted his own hand to lay next to hers and slide his fingers through her own. Tears filled her eyes the way it seemed they had been doing since she had first gone back to Idaho. "I know I shouldn't push it, baby, but I really do think that it would be good for everyone if you went. Please just think about it?" she asked softly, as he gave her a warning look.

He nodded once. "I'll think about it." "Thank you, Duncan."

He grinned wryly. "I said I'd think about it. I could get a case next week or just decide not to go."

"I know. I appreciate you at least considering it though." She didn't bother telling him that Agent Graham had already cleared his schedule for the week at her request.

He squeezed her hand and groaned. "How is it that you keep drawing me in again and again, even though I'm determined to stay away?"

Her eyes sparkled as she said, "You love me Duncan, of course you want to make me happy."

He didn't agree, nor did he disagree. He slipped out of the booth across from her and slid in next to her and laid one arm around her shoulders, leaning down to give her a soft tender kiss. "I also happen to think you are very, very attractive."

She widened her eyes. "Even though I'm as fat as a hog?"

His eyes darkened. "Especially because of that. Pregnancy really does look beautiful on you, sweetheart."

The waiter cleared his throat and began putting their plates onto the table in front of them. Sylvie and Duncan both laughed lightly and thanked him before he hurried back away. "Don't you wish it was Nick's baby, Duncan? Then you wouldn't have to come back here and see me all the time."

He growled and she looked up in surprise. He'd been insistently trying to get her to see other people for months now, hoping that she would let him slip away and into the silent hell he believed he deserved. She lifted a hand to her precious mound. "Just think, Nick would be the one feeling forced to come back to us all the time."

"Don't, baby, just don't," he groaned softly.

She looked up at him with a smile. "I could see if Nick would be willing to stand in for you. What do you think of Duncan Hanlan for his name?"

He gave her a cold smile. "I fucking hate it." It was progress and they both knew it.

Chapter 58

The memorial that Jackie and Sylvie had planned together and had built was finished as promised the day after Thanksgiving. The memorial service was planned for the following Saturday. The day Sylvie was scheduled to fly out to Idaho where the event was to take place, Duncan disappeared again. He told her he had some things he had to do. She told him she'd bought him a plane ticket if he wanted to fly out with her, but he only looked hard at her and said, "You shouldn't have done that Sylvie. I'm not going."

At ten thirty she boarded the flight bound for Boise, after waiting as long as possible, hoping Duncan would change his mind and show up at the airport. As she boarded the plane the pilot gave her stomach a narrow look and asked if she had been cleared to fly by her doctor.

She smiled in understanding and pulled out the form her OBGYN had given her. He only glanced at it and nodded, and they welcomed her aboard. She held her breath until she saw the doors being closed as the flight crew prepared for take-off. Tears of disappointment filled her eyes as they taxied toward the runway and took off. She'd hoped that Duncan would change his mind and show up. She wiped her eyes with a tissue from her purse as hopeless melancholy slid through her. She had exhausted every option she could think of to try to help him realize that he was not his dad, but nothing had worked.

Sure, he showed up and made love to her, and they did things together. He always let her know his plans and where he would be, but there was something deeply wrong with all of it. She remembered the version of Duncan who held her and kissed her like he would never let go. She hadn't imagined having his baby and raising it alone but that was closer to the truth than she was comfortable with. Tears ran unchecked down her cheeks as she stared out the window at the clouds below.

"Are you okay, miss?" the older gentleman who sat just across the aisle asked gently, his brow furrowed together in concern.

She wiped at her face and nodded. "Sorry, don't mind me. It's just the hormones."

He nodded and held out an old-fashioned handkerchief. She smiled and took it gratefully. "Thank you, sir."

She tried to get Duncan out of her mind on the long flight and tried to be positive about the progress she'd seen this morning. But the simple truth was that this memorial had been her last idea of how to bridge the void between herself and her baby, and Duncan. He hadn't been interested in going to check-ups or ultrasounds, or childbirth classes, so she had done them all on her own, not wanting to alienate him by asking him to come with her when he wasn't ready. Doing it all alone had taken its toll though, and for the briefest of moments she'd considered calling Nick and asking him to be her birthing coach. She discarded it just as quickly.

Nick would agree, of that she had no doubt, but it wouldn't be fair to him since she could never love him the way she loved Duncan. Whether or not Duncan felt the same for her. She'd truly believed he did love her at one point not so long ago but now, she was beginning to wonder. Maybe he'd never actually intended to marry her despite what everyone had told her.

She swapped planes in Seattle and found herself watching once again for Duncan, on the off chance that he had opted to take a different flight. When a flight attendant announced that her flight was the last one going to Boise for the night, her shoulders sagged in defeat.

When she walked out of the terminal she smiled and waved at Jackie who had insisted on meeting her to give her a ride. Duncan's sister hurried around the silver minivan. "Oh my god, Sylvie, you're huge and so, so, beautiful." She wrapped her friend in a warm hug and took her bags to heft them into the back. Then Jackie stopped and looked around. "No Duncan, I guess then?"

Sylvie swallowed the lump of emotion in her throat and shook her head.

"Unfortunately, not."

"I'm sorry sweetie, I know how much you hoped this would help him finally put it all to rest," Jackie said softly, as she ushered her friend into the passenger seat of the van.

"Yes, well I suppose I should have known he also wouldn't be up for it. Tell me Jackie, you know Duncan better than anyone, should I leave him be and let him go in peace?" she asked, sounding tired, emotional, and a bit desperate.

Jackie shook her head, but then hesitated. "I suppose that depends. As his sister who wants him to be happy I want to say, never give up. But as a mom who knows where you're at and how much energy it takes to first grow and then birth a tiny little human being, you have to do what's best for you and him."

There were tears in Sylvie's eyes when she replied, "That's what I thought." She took a deep breath as every dream she had of what she and Duncan could build together flashed through her mind. Jackie had been her rock, her sounding board through the past several months and she turned to face her friend. "Thank you for everything, Jackie, I couldn't have gotten through all of this without you, you know."

Jackie smiled and nodded as she put on the blinker and pulled out into traffic. "I probably shouldn't tell you this, Sylvie, but I have to admit that I wondered in the beginning, if you had enough courage and strength to handle all of this and still stick by him."

Instead of getting offended like Jackie had expected, Sylvie simply nodded. "And now?"

She smiled. "Now, I think you are the most wonderful sister anyone could ever have, and Duncan is lucky to have had as much as you've given. I love you either way. I hope that you know that, even if you need to move on, it won't change us. I will pester and bug you until you bring my nephew to visit."

Sylvie smiled through her tears. "Deal. In fact, why don't we just decide right now that every year we'll come out in the summer and spend a couple of weeks with you guys, and you can come out in the winter and spend a couple of weeks with us."

Jackie smiled and nodded. "It's a deal." She held her hand across the console and clasped Sylvie's hand in her own. "So, if you decide to quit trying to work things out with Duncan, who is the most likely guy to have a chance with you?"

Sylvie smiled sadly. "If I decide that, and I'll only decide that if it feels like Duncan's vacant presence is more harmful than good, I won't date again. He's it for me. I have given all that my heart has to him so there isn't anything left for anyone else in that way." With a somewhat rueful smile she asked, "Technically speaking, if I've slept with numerous men and had a child but never married could I still be considered an old spinster?"

Jackie laughed. "I don't think so. Are you worried about how he'll treat little junior?"

Sylvie thought about that for a long while before responding. "Not worried exactly, it's just that even when Duncan is with me, there is also always a huge distance between us, and I feel like I can't ever quite reach him. If he's like that with our son…" She hesitated. "I just don't know if it would be better to be able to tell him all the stories about Duncan and see his dad as a hero, instead of always feeling like he's just out of reach."

"I get it. Wouldn't Duncan fight to be involved either way?" she asked quietly.

Without hesitation, Sylvie shook her head. "No, he wouldn't. He would be glad and think that I finally understood how tainted he really is and that I saw his point of view. I think he'd walk away and never look back."

Jackie gasped. "Oh Sylvie, you can't really believe that!"

Nodding sadly, Sylvie said, "I do though." Then more firmly she added, "I know he would."

Not wanting to believe that Duncan was so far gone, Jackie opened her mouth to argue but the stark truth on her friend's face stopped her. She squeezed her hand as tears ran silently down her cheeks. "Regardless, you always have me."

"I do, don't I? Thanks," Sylvie said and determinedly wiped the tears from her cheeks. If Duncan was too much of a fool to love their beautiful, healthy, baby, then that was on him. She was done asking him for more.

Chapter 59

By the time Sylvie was dressed, Jackie and Ren had the twins and Reagan dressed and ready to go. Together they all climbed into the van to drive to the memorial. Jackie had gone to see it already but today Sylvie would get her first look.

The memorial was built on a five-acre stretch of Jamison ranch land next to the main highway. Though Sylvie had helped plan the whole thing, she still stared in awe at the gorgeous fountain at the entrance. It would be dry for the winter but in the spring it would be beautiful. It was a forty-foot circle of beautifully shaped concrete in the form of rock. Above where the water would eventually run down and over those rocks were birds, butterflies, bees, and animals of every shape, distended as though frolicking joyfully for each of the victims. Each shape had been chosen by their families to represent their lost loved one. Across the face of the fountain were large chrome letters extending up out of the water. It read: *Hope Eternal.*

"It's beautiful Jackie."

"It really is. I'm so glad we decided to do this. If you walk over close, you can see each of the names carved underneath on the wings."

Sylvie smiled. "Elaine would love this and so would my dad." She eyed the soaring eagle that she knew was there for him. Then she turned her head, trying to find the large dragonfly that was there for Elaine.

As they pulled around the fountain and the wide concrete drive, she saw the large parking lot straight ahead and noticed that even though they were an hour early, the lot was already quite full. She turned to stare at the large, state of the art, rest area building, that was designed to look like a dome with a rainbow-colored crosswalk that went up over the building before dipping back down below.

Even from here she could see people wandering up there as they looked out over the expanse of the five-acre garden. Inside the rest area she knew, were marbled stones inscribed with the families' final words for their

loved ones, where all who came and went could see and honor them. Every direction she looked from the parking lot, had small brick pathways that wound out away, and even now in the dead of winter had evergreen shrubs and trees planted throughout that gave it a cheerful feeling.

Concrete benches were strewn throughout. Into each seat an image was carved that was the same creature that flew out over the fountain and the names of those family members left behind who would always love and cherish their memories. She knew all of this, since she had helped design it, but up close, even without the blooming roses and flowers that would come with the spring it was breathtaking. She unbuckled and reached for Olivia's seat belt as she breathed. "It's so much better even than I imagined."

Ren chuckled. "You sound just like Jackie did yesterday."

She smiled at Jackie's heart-throb. "It's well deserved. You guys did an amazing job." Ren and his crew had taken hers and Jackie's idea and flown with it. Ren lifted the chunky little Reagan from his seat, and they all walked together toward the tall glass dome building. Out in front she saw that a sound system had been set up and she smiled at Jackie. "I wish he would have come."

Nodding in agreement, Jackie looked around. "Even if it was only to honor Mom's memory." Ren put a comforting arm around her shoulders.

By the time Sylvie took just a minute to read through some of the memorial stones inside, a large crowd had gathered, all donning thick coats and hats, braving the weather to honor their loved ones' memories. Tears once again pooled in her eyes as she stood looking at the two stones next to each other. One was a tan granite; it was her father's and it read:

Reagan James Dunlap, a loving husband, an outstanding father, a champion for the lost he found, the mothers he protected, and all others who needed a protector. May the afterlife reward him likewise.

The other one, a pink rose colored granite read:

Elaine Rose Dunlap. A *sister gone too soon. A daughter mourned in death. The light of shining stars to those who needed to laugh freely. May the hereafter offer her peace, laughter and joy, forever fulfilled.*

She pulled a tissue from her pocket to wipe her eyes and turned in surprise

as strong arms slid from behind to wrap her in a hug. "I'm sorry, I'm a little late…" he began.

Sylvie turned into him giving all the love in her heart as she shook her head and held his blue gaze in her own. "You are right on time."

Together they walked out to where Jackie now stood with a microphone in hand. "Thank you so much for all coming today. It means the world to me and my family that you all came in spite of the cold." She smiled as a few people laughed or smiled at her. "To start things off tonight, we would like to officially turn on the fountain for the first time, even though it won't be running again until it thaws in the spring. After the fountain is running with hope, we will have each of the families come up and share what their daughter, son, grandchild, father, or sister meant to this world and the hope we wish to share in their absence."

With a look at Ren, she said softly, "If you'll all turn to the fountain now, you will notice that from each side, your own representation of your loved one is forever soaring on the wings of hope." There was a small hissing sound and water began rushing out over the top slowly beginning to bubble over until finally it ran and splashed and danced happily. While the fountain hissed and began flowing the speakers slowly started into the beautiful rhythm of Michael Jackson's, 'Heal the World'.

Tears ran unchecked down her face as Sylvie listened to the lyrics and watched the water dance, swerve, splash and run as bright lights slowly lit beneath the rushing water, and then slowly moved up into each soaring figure above. Then slowly all around them the entire garden lit up. Several people gasped as each path slowly lit, lined with lights to show the way to each bench. The arched walking bridge lit up with every color imaginable and it all cast a warm glow across the entire garden. As the song came to a soothing end, Jackie said softly, "May the light of our loved ones warm every heart who passes this way, touch every lost soul, and shine brightly as a beacon for all."

Sylvie took the handkerchief Duncan offered even as she looked up at him in wonder. "This is all so perfect, isn't it?"

He gave her a small smile, but she noticed his eyes were shining as they turned back toward Jackie as she began to speak, her voice wavering with emotion. "Our mother, Mary Jamison was a beautiful, intelligent, witty woman and was always there for us when we needed her. She was the kind of woman I aspire to be. She was the backbone of our family until she died, and I don't think I even realized how much because my brother Duncan Jamison automatically slid into that role as soon as she was gone."

"He suffered the loss much more than the rest of us who he sheltered and protected as though his life depended upon it. Because of that fact, I have a beautiful family, a beautiful life and I am forever grateful for his strength and courage that I know he got from Mom."

She looked at Sylvie, tears in her eyes. "My best friend, Sylvie Dunlap, lost her father and sister and nearly died herself at the hands of our sick, demented father, and I'm grateful every day that my brother had the courage to step up and do what needed doing once again, because otherwise along with each of those we've lost, she would be lost as well. Thank you, Duncan. Today, mom is here soaring for the honorable man that you are." She looked at Duncan for a long moment and then quietly held the microphone out to Sylvie. On shaky legs, Sylvie stepped forward and faced the daunting crowd. "My sister, Elaine, died nearly nine years ago at the hands of Arthur Jamison. She was wild, brave, sassy, and the best sister anyone could ask for. When she died, I knew who had killed her. I'd seen him murder Mary Jamison shortly before, but I was a kid and I was afraid and I didn't have the courage to face what I'd seen, so I buried it in what is called dissociative amnesia."

"When my father was killed recently, Duncan Jamison saved my life or I would have died as well. My father, Reagan Dunlap was a police officer and he stood always for those not strong enough to stand for themselves, and I will forever miss him. Thank you, Duncan Jamison, without you I would be dead and our son who is due to be born in five weeks would be dead too. Thank you for having the strength it took to choose my life over the man who raised you." She lifted up on her tiptoes to plant a kiss on his lips. "You are forever my hero." She turned to Jackie. "Thank you, Jackie, for having the courage and the heart to call the FBI and police the moment you realized that your father was a killer. Without both of you and your integrity, not only would I be dead but so would others he got to when he went free. Thank you, thank you, thank you."

She lifted the microphone into the air as another man stepped forward and took it, talking of his daughter and the life she'd lost. When he finished, he turned toward where Duncan stood. "Thank you, Duncan and Jackie Jamison, for giving us the peace of mind we so rightly deserved after all these years. I once knew a mother who it turned out knew her son was raping women and didn't turn him in because she was both afraid of being associated, and afraid for what would happen to him if she did. So, the fact that you were so quick and so willing to sacrifice your father, to take a bad man off the streets, means the world to us."

As each in turn got up to share about their loved ones, each turned to Duncan and Jackie at the end, to thank them each for the part they'd played. Sylvie stole a glance at Duncan's tight features as one young girl talked about her sister and then thanked Duncan profusely for saving her. She said that she had recently tracked her sister's last whereabouts to this part of Idaho and had been snooping around. She was convinced that, had Arthur Jamison not died, he would surely have killed her when she came looking.

Duncan's grasp on Sylvie's hand hadn't moved and his jaw was set and hard but with each new person who stood and thanked him she felt the tension building. She wasn't sure exactly which way it was going to blow. When all had shared, he still hadn't moved an inch, only giving the merest nod to each who thanked him. Jackie moved to take the microphone from the stand, just as someone in the crowd said, "We want to hear from Duncan Jamison."

Murmurs began getting louder with Duncan's name being chanted around. Sylvie dared a quick look up and saw that he was staring down at her with such stark pain in his eyes, that it took her breath away. Her heart thundered, as she stared up at his anguish. Afraid that it was finally too much for him to handle, she cleared her throat and moved away to grasp the microphone, saying softly. "Duncan has been through so much, ladies and gentleman, how abo—" She stopped as Duncan's hand closed over her own and he took the mic from her cold fingers.

The crowd went completely still and quiet, as they watched the hard-faced man standing in front of them. He took a ragged breath and said softly, "My father was the kind of man that nightmares are made of. I stand before you all as testament of that."

Everyone looked at their neighboring families in confusion as Sylvie tried to pry the mic from his hand saying adamantly. "Don't do this, Duncan! It isn't your fault."

He gave her a cold dead smile and asked bitterly, "Isn't the truth what you want, Sylvie?" She backed up a step, looking afraid, and he laughed softly even as he lifted the mic to his hardened lips again. "The truth is this. If I had insisted on looking through my father's newspapers when I first realized it was odd, twenty-six women might have lived. If I had sent who I thought was a troubled man mourning his wife to a therapist, twenty-five women might still be alive. If I had only taken the time to think about how strange my father had been acting, twenty-four people might still be alive today."

"I have my goddamned Bachelors in psychology, and yet I, the man who lived in the same house with him for eight long years while he hunted and killed and did god only knows what to countless, helpless, victims..." His voice was so hoarse he had to pause and suck air into his lungs. "You should all hate me right now. Because of me, your loved ones are dead." He dropped the microphone on the ground and turned on his heel, ignoring the cries and gasps from the crowd, as well as Sylvie's and Jackie's mouths, which were hanging open in horror.

Suddenly, Sylvie knew he meant to leave and never come back. Fear clenched her stomach in knots as she lifted her long black skirt and rushed after him. "Duncan, don't go please," she begged brokenly. She caught him just as he started around the outside of the crowd. "Don't go, you are every bit as much a victim as we all are."

He pulled out of her grasp and moved away from her. "Stop, Duncan, please don't do this, I love you," she enunciated every word loudly. "Let me hold you."

He stopped for only a second to look back at her and then turned away again. It was just long enough for Sylvie to grasp onto his hand. She held on and wrapped her arms around his waist even as he tried to pull free. "Please..." she begged brokenly. Suddenly, a tall man was there behind Duncan, and he wrapped his arms around them both, then another man stepped forward and another, and another. As tears streamed down her face the entire crowd moved inward, closing around them holding them tight. Close. Warm. She saw his look of disbelief as people slowly crowded in around them in a huge circle. Suddenly his hands went up to his face to rub across it.

In a loud voice against the quiet crowd he said, "Did any of you fools even hear me?"

He heard a chorus of 'yeses', 'yeahs' and 'of courses'. Unable to do anything else he lowered his head into his hands and wept. As he wept, someone sounding suspiciously like Jackie, lifted her gentle voice and began singing.

Where there is hatred, let me bring love, where there is doubt, let me bring faith, where there is falsehood, let me bring truth, where there is pain, I'll comfort you...

As one and then another and other strangers lifted their voices and joined in on a song that had been one of his mother's favorites, Duncan let Sylvie wrap him in her scent. Her essence. Her strength. In that one moment he let the light in and a tiny spark of something inside himself, more than the cold empty numbness he'd felt ever since he knew what his father had done, lit a fuse. He lifted his head and looked down to meet Sylvie's tear-streaked eyes and smiled, then he lifted his head to join in.

When we forgive love, we'll find reprieve.

He didn't even notice Nick Hanlan, Mason Langden and Jonathan Graham who all stood directly behind him until the last bars of the song faded. The crowd around them slowly dispersed, and he turned with his arm around Sylvie to watch the white dove soaring above the fountain that he knew would be inscribed with Mary Leann Jamison just under her wings. He leaned down and gave his very strong, very stubborn, woman a kiss and whispered hoarsely, "Thank you, sweetheart."

Chapter 60

Sylvie dug through her closet in frustration. There had to be at least one pretty dress in here that still fit her. She was forty weeks along and feeling every one of those weeks. She'd had her last day of work the day before and was now officially on maternity leave for the next three months despite her OBGYN having told her that it could still be a week or two before she went into labor. She pulled out a long sweater dress that she had bought a couple of months before and tried pulling it down over her head. It slid on without too much fuss and she smiled. "Finally! Now, if I can only find some boots that will actually fit on my swollen feet," she mumbled as she glanced in the mirror on her way past and then came to a dead stop, as horror filled helpless laughter, bubbled up and out of her throat.

She stared at the sweater dress that had fit well only two months ago and gave it a tug as it now kept slowly hiking its way upward. Her pregnancy engorged breasts and belly pushing tightly against the gabled pattern. She moaned in frustration as the hem slid up again to settle just below her butt and the neckline bunched around her neck in choking fashion. "No, no, no," she moaned as she tugged it down again. She slid onto the dressing stool in exasperation and dejection and watched as her belly wiggled against the restricting fabric with her son's strong kicks. "You are turning me into a house, baby boy," she murmured lovingly as she laid a hand there against the kicks.

The hair prickled on the back of her neck, and she turned to see Duncan leaning one shoulder idly against the door jamb watching her with what could only be described as a tender smile on his face.

"I like it," he said softly as he moved away from the door and came toward her to set warm hands on her shoulders. "It gives me better access to certain, err, cravings of mine."

She stared at him in transfixed horror. "Do you ever think of anything but sex?" she asked accusingly.

He walked around to face her and said in a soft aching voice, "Yes. Right now, I'm thinking about how beautiful you are carrying my son and all worked up over what you are going to wear to a simple barbecue."

Sylvie tried to stand but her feet didn't reach the floor and she had to wiggle forward a little to slide off the tall stool. "It's the first time we will have all of our friends together at once, Duncan, and I want it to be perfect."

He reached out and took her hands in his. "You are perfect, sweetheart, and everything else is going to be perfect just because you're both safe and here with me. All of our friends can suck it if they have a problem with anything." He leaned his head down for a deep kiss, full of feeling.

When he pulled his head up a moment later, Sylvie had tears in her eyes. "Don't cry, sweetheart, you would look beautiful if all you did was wrap in a sheet and cinched a belt at your waist." That image teased at his brain and his mouth went dry. In a choked voice he said quickly, "No, don't do that. I don't want any of the men thinking about you in a bed."

She laughed. "See, you idiot. Sex again."

He pulled her into his arms. "Not just sex, sweetie. Sex with you." She sighed into his kiss and then reluctantly pulled back. "Duncan,

I have to find something to wear! Your sister will be coming here any minute with the kids from the beach house, and Jon is already downstairs, probably wondering where we are right now."

He grinned and she noticed that for the first time in a long time he looked relaxed. She couldn't help giving him a bright happy smile. Then he slid his arms around her again and said softly against her ear, "I'm sure Jon will understand and let in anyone who comes knocking." With that he lowered his head to suckle gently just under her ear and then began making his way downward, even as his hands slid under the sweater and began sliding up her thigh and then waist. "Why don't we get this thing off of you," he murmured huskily.

Sylvie leaned into him with a little moan and then suddenly stepped back. "No way. I still have to get dressed and we are supposed to be outside hosting this thing in…" She lifted his wrist and glanced at his watch. "Five minutes ago!" she shrieked and backed away slowly.

Duncan gave her a small frown. "Can you blame me? I missed you guys all week." He had flown back to Wilmington the day before and they'd barely had any time together because Jackie and her brood were visiting, and Nick had come over. Then Jon Graham had called to ask if he could come a day early since he didn't want to fly back to Chicago, only to turn around and come here for the weekend barbecue they'd invited him to. By the time they'd made it to bed last night, Sylvie had collapsed onto her side and been out like a light. Duncan had spent hours curled around her, hard and contented at the same time.

"We will get some alone time soon. I promise," she said quickly and sidestepped his next advance. She turned to stare across the closet. "Maybe I could wear one of your shirts?"

His hungry sex muddled mind liked that idea. He grinned. "Now, that is just plain genius." He reached into the back of his closet and pulled out an old western style shirt that Jackie had given him for Christmas a few years back. It was black and grey and across the back shoulders in bright white embroidery, said *Duncan.*

Sylvie stared at it as a mixture of laughter, horror, and happy tears all warred inside. Finally, she lifted smiling eyes to his. "Fine, but if you laugh…" she threatened mutinously.

He held up his hands. "My lips are sealed."

She pulled out one of the two pairs of elastic banded, pouched jeans that still fit over her bulging hips and slid them up over her belly. Then she pulled out a white, soft stretch T-shirt and slid it on. She pulled his shirt over the top and rolled up the sleeves and then closed three snaps right in the middle and tied the long tails up under her belly in a cute little knot. She turned to look in the mirror and actually smiled. "It's no dress, but it'll do," she said softly as she turned in a circle for him to see.

His eyes darkened and he moved toward her. With a little squeal she scooted around the stool and made a run for the door. "Don't you dare, Duncan. We have to go down now."

He laughed, then he reached out and snagged her hand. "Can I at least hold your hand, or would that somehow inconvenience one of your old beaus as well?" he asked in a mocking drawl.

She threw a laughing look over her shoulder. "It's *our* guests I'm worried about not some guys that I once dated a very, very, long time ago." She dragged the words out dramatically.

He grinned and then swooped her into his arms and planted a hard kiss on her lips even as he took the stairs carefully downward. Since he was moving in the right direction, she let him keep kissing her. He set her on her feet but then with a little growl pulled her to him again at the doorway of the kitchen. She leaned up on her booted toes and kissed him back.

It was Jackie who cleared her throat. "Um, guys, did we all get the time right or was the barbecue meant to start later?" she asked in barely masked amusement.

Sylvie jerked and turned with a blush to see Nick, Jackie and Ren all sitting at the bar. The twins were on the floor playing with baby Reagan who was sitting happily between their undivided attention. She rushed forward. "Oh god, I'm so sorry. Welcome everyone!" she said and together her and Duncan moved forward for handshakes, hugs and even a kiss on her cheek from a grinning Nick. "I see you guys met already," she murmured to Nick and Jackie.

They smiled and nodded. Duncan moved away to lift each of the twins into his arms for a loud smacking kiss on their cheeks. Both Olivia and Ariana giggled happily, "Hi Unca Dunca," they chorused in unison. He set them both back down and lifted Reagan.

"Well, hello there, big guy, I haven't seen you for a month and you're already nearly as tall as your dad."

He was so involved with the children he didn't see all the adults, including Jon and Mason who had just walked in from outside, giving each other looks and smiles because of him. He lifted the gurgling baby onto his shoulders and asked in a conspirator's tone, "What do you say buddy, want Uncle Duncan to teach you how to impress the ladies and grill up some steaks?" He turned, and with a quick wink at Sylvie, disappeared through the door. Outside were tables of sides, chairs scattered, coolers of beer and soft drinks and the metal trays with prepped seasoned meat that had been set up before Sylvie went back inside to dress.

Mason gave Sylvie a quick hug and she introduced him to Jackie and Ren. "Thank you for all you have given me," she said, with tears in her eyes, quietly looking around the room at each in turn.

They all nodded in understanding. At one time or another each of them had been truly worried that Duncan Jamison might not get back to them. Jon Graham cleared his throat and looked at Mason with a grin. "Do you think Jamison is smart enough to notice we already cooked all of the meat, or will he go put it all back on again?"

Everyone laughed as they made their way quickly outside Duncan's beautiful home. "Good, because I could eat a cow," Sylvie exclaimed happily.

They all loaded up and she in particular heaped her plate high. Five bites later she scooted the plate back and away. "I don't know if I can eat another bite!" she announced. Nick, Jon and Mason all stared in stupefaction at her barely touched food.

Jackie saw their faces and laughingly stated, "Welcome to pregnancy one-oh-one, gentleman." To which all three looked horrified.

A sleek silver car pulled up the road and Sylvie stood. "Good, Ben and Laura are here." The couple slid from the car and Ben reached in to pull out his toddler son and Laura leaned into her side and removed the baby seat with her two-month-old son inside, walking around and toward them. Everyone stood and congratulated them, and Sylvie gave them both a hug. She looked up at Ben. "Are you ready to go back to work, sir? I handled things for you and now it's your turn," she laughed as she patted her tummy.

Nick was standing next to Duncan. With a knowing grin, he turned and met his friend's blue gaze. "I like her shirt," he said a little too smugly.

"Hmm," was the only response he got. Order had definitely been restored and Nick grinned and tucked his hands into his pockets.

After the steaks, thick hunks of ham and chicken wings were eaten, along with potato salad, biscuits, beans, and of course two sweet potato pies that Nick had somehow flounced his mother out of, they all sat back and watched as the children played nearby. It was a warm day for December, with the sun shining brightly down on their little group.

Duncan stood and went inside for a moment and then returned. Sylvie was so busy she didn't notice as she took turns with first Reagan and then Ben and Lauras, Durant. Rubbing a hand over her belly she went to pick at her plate again. She couldn't eat much these days and it meant she had to eat a bit more often. She put a bite of ham in her mouth and moaned as the savory flavor of the steak burst.

"God, that makes me hot," Duncan murmured from behind her. She turned to smile happily up at him and put in another taste.

He was staring intently at her, watching as the sun shone brightly in her streaked hair, her eyes warm and inviting. He put his hands in his pockets and said gently, "I think we can both admit that I have been a bit of an asshole about all of this…" He took a deep unsteady breath, capturing her now curious gaze in his. "I love you. I know I don't deserve to ask you this since I have been trying to run away for months now, but I want, no need, you with me, by my side, always. What would you think about getting married?" He sounded nervous.

Sylvie fought the joyous smile that threatened, and then just because he *had* put her through hell, she took a long time answering. He sucked in air at her hesitation and then just when she was about to say yes, he took her hand in his and got down on one knee, his jaw tight, his eyes serious. "Please, don't turn me down now. I don't want to do life without you for even a day any more. Please, please, marry me." His voice broke and Sylvie leaned forward to wrap her arms around his neck to thread in his hair.

With a happy little laugh, she said softly, "Are you sure this time, Jamison? I won't go easy on you if you change your mind again."

He buried his head against her tummy and groaned. "I'm a goddamned fool sometimes. I know that, but I want you, and this." He kissed her rounded belly. "More than anything in this world."

She reached down and lifted his tear-filled eyes up to her own wet gaze.

"Only if you promise to kiss me right now."

He laughed and grasped onto her neck pulling her down for a deep kiss. Everyone had gone quiet and now they cheered as Sylvie forced Duncan to his feet. "Get up, baby," she said through her happy tears.

Then she leaned toward him and wiped his away as she said softly,

"Everyone needs to cry sometimes you know."

He laughed and then her eyes widened as he pulled a ring from his pocket and slid it onto her finger. Then he leaned down and whispered softly against her lips, "Sometimes even the truth hurts, sweetheart."

Nick sidled up and looked critically at her ring before giving her a happy hug. He shook Duncan's hand and said half seriously, "And just when I was about to step in and take over for you…" He let that sink in, then he said, "I'm glad you got your shit together, finally." He leveled an arched eyebrow at Duncan over his golden eyes. "I'm also surprised you didn't commission the jeweler to make a ring that said, *Duncan*, in gold."

Their friends came and gave hugs and handshakes. As Jackie wrapped her in a tight hug she whispered, "I'm so glad for you both. I wasn't sure you were going to go for tying the knot today being eight months along and all, but I'm so happy for you both."

Sylvie raised an eyebrow. "Come again?"

Duncan grabbed her shoulders and pulled her back against his hard body. "Oh, and by the way…" He held on tight in case she tried to get away. "I may have planned a little ceremony for tonight, just in case, you know?"

She turned her neck to look up at him with mixed adrenaline and nervousness. "In case of what?"

He grinned and said softly, "In case you change your mind in the morning." When she stared up at him with those wide brown eyes, he so loved, he said softly, "I don't want to spend another day apart from you ever again." He spread his fingers over her baby mound and said softly, "Either of you."

She looked up at him and then glanced at Special Agent, Jon Graham. "Do you want me to move to Chicago?" She would if he asked but she really hoped he didn't.

He shook his head even as Jon smiled. "I told the FBI they could suck it because I'm moving back home."

Sylvie shook her head. "No way, Jamison, I'm not letting you quit something that you love and are so good at, for us."

Jon Graham chuckled behind Duncan. "Funny, but that was exactly what Assistant Director Donahue said."

Sylvie turned to eye Duncan. "You're not quitting then?" She directed the question to Duncan who only shrugged.

Special Agent Graham met Duncan's gaze and said firmly, "The director has decided it's a good idea to open up a special task force here in Wilmington and would like Duncan to run it."

"My god! That is amazing," she said excitedly and turned to look up at him again.

Duncan shrugged. "I'm not sure if I'm going to take the job yet."

Several mouths gaped at his casual dismissal of what would be a dream gig. In a slightly confused tone she said, "Why not?"

He met Jon's eyes and gave a tight smile. "Because, they said I could hand pick my team and I gave them my list, and now they are trying to pick my team for me."

Jon held up his hands at Sylvie's questioning glare. "Jamison is exaggerating, a little. We asked him to hand pick ten agents under his supervision in the Chicago field office, that he could offer the positions to. Instead, he came back with a list of people that won't work."

Duncan held his gaze, steady, unbending. "Well, there you have it." He gave Sylvie a quick peck on the cheek. "It turns out that I'm retiring, sweetheart. It won't be so bad though; it will leave lots of time for me to dote on the two most important people in my life."

Sylvie turned to glare hotly at Jon. "Why don't you feds ever just get your act together and do the right thing?" she challenged, completely forgetting for a moment that Duncan was also technically a fed.

Agent Graham gave Duncan a hard look. "Because," he said with a bit of amusement. "Duncan has decided he wants his task force to consist of him, myself, two particular police detectives and ten of our best analysts."

Sylvie's eyes widened in understanding. "I see."

She looked around at Nick and Mason. Then she turned back to Jon. "He has a point though, right? It would be a particularly powerful task force, so what's the problem?"

Nick choked on his beer. "First of all, I ain't no fed." Mason shrugged. "I could get into it, if I had to."

Duncan grinned and Jon Graham finally nodded. "I told Jamison here that if he could get us all here together and get everyone to agree, then I'd make the move." He gave Duncan a hard look. "He's too fine of an agent to let him go again."

Nick tipped his beer back and drained it as Sylvie turned to him with a pleading look. "Just think about all the tools you'd have at your fingertips, Nick."

He laughed harshly. "What happened to your attitude with the feds from a minute ago?"

She pretended not to know what he was talking about. "Why would I say anything like that? Don't you know I'm getting married to a fed?"

Jackie chortled loudly. "All I can say is that I'll take the mountains and ranching any day over all this drama. At least cows are simple," she said half seriously.

Every man turned to stare at her. Duncan was the only one who dared ask, "Have you ever heard of a stampede?"

She grinned and took Sylvie's hand. "Well, you guys can figure all this out later, because right now we need to get Sylvie into her dress, and everyone needs to go get ready, this thing is supposed to happen in two hours."

Chapter 61

Sylvie allowed Jackie to pull her along upstairs. Jackie spent time fussing over her hair and make-up. With a little laugh Sylvie said gently, "I don't know why you are bothering with all of this. I don't even have a dress that fits."

Jackie turned to stare at her in horror. "You were just going to get married in Duncan's old shirt?"

Sylvie shrugged. "It's not so bad. It's actually quite comfy."

Jackie raised twin brows. "Yeah, but this is your wedding day, doesn't that man tell you anything?" She cussed under her breath as she slipped out the door only to return a minute later with a long black bag.

"What's that?" Sylvie asked, only slightly curious.

"It's your wedding dress for god's sake, try to care a little please." Jackie gave her friend, who was sagging into the wide armed chair like she might go to sleep, a frown. "We are supposed to be downstairs in twenty minutes, Sylvie, get up so we can get you into this thing."

Sylvie shrugged. "Okay, I'm just a little tired." She rubbed at her aching back.

Jackie's gaze narrowed worriedly on her friend's face. "Are you okay?"

She smiled and nodded. "Yes, I'm fine." She forced herself up and toward where Jackie had laid the bag. "Let's do this thing."

Jackie rolled her eyes. "Don't sound so excited."

Sylvie turned at her grumpy tone. "I'm sorry, Jackie. I really am thrilled that Duncan is finally ready for this. I just wonder if he couldn't have maybe done it before I'm so far along that I feel like going to bed at seven."

Jackie laughed. "I get it, I do. Now, come over here and let's get you all finished."

Sylvie obeyed. She gasped in pleasure at the white gown with silver beads hand sewn into the delicate bodice and then more into the back of the skirt on the slightly longer curved train. Then she started laughing hysterically. "This will never fit me."

Jackie eyed her with a smile. "Duncan said he got your measurements only a week ago, so I'm sure it's perfect. You feel bigger than you are, I promise."

Sylvie laughed. "Okay, well here goes." She lifted the dress over her shoulders and began shimmying into it. She felt a slight little pop and turned to Jackie. "Uh, can you please go get Duncan for me, Jackie?" she said suddenly even as she lifted the dress back over her head.

Jackie frowned. "Isn't that like, bad luck at this point?"

Sylvie shrugged. "Maybe but I think I need him for a moment."

"Fine but don't fall asleep while I'm gone," she chided.

Sylvie laughed. "I don't think there is any worry of that." As soon as Jackie left, she rushed out and into the bathroom where she grabbed a towel and held it between her legs where water was beginning to seep out. With no one there to hear her, she moaned as the next cramp came.

Duncan came running. "Are you okay, sweetheart?"

Sylvie held a hand against her throbbing back and tried to smile. Duncan was looking very nice in a black and white tux and shiny dress shoes. "How did you put all this together so quickly?" she asked as another wave of pain slid into her back.

Duncan eyed her and the towel. "What is going on, Sylvie?" he asked, ignoring her question, his gaze narrowed in concern.

She turned a wan smile up at him. "Well, either I just did the unthinkable and wet myself, or else my water broke. Take your pick."

He looked pale and then he held onto the door frame for a mere second before he turned and bellowed, "Hanlan, get my truck and pull it around."

Jackie who'd been waiting for Sylvie to finish with Duncan came rushing in. "What is it, Duncan?"

He looked at Sylvie and then back at Jackie. "Sylvie either wet her pants or her water broke."

Jackie smiled at his pale face, then said sweetly, "I'm guessing she wet herself." Just to see if Duncan would fall for it and get himself in trouble.

He gave her a hard look and sprang into action. "All right, I'm here now, what do we do?"

Sylvie moaned and bent over. "I'm really sorry, baby. Maybe we could still get married if we make it quick."

He lunged for her and lifted her into his arms even as she squawked. He turned and strode out the door as she punched his arm. "Put me down you idiot, there's lots of time. First babies take a long time to come. I need to get dressed and get my go bag, and then we can drive to the hospital."

He let her down and stood there, hands in pocket, wondering what in god's name had been wrong with him all these months. He quite literally had no clue what needed to be done. He watched as Sylvie pushed Jackie out the door and then closed it and then began removing her wet underwear. His mouth went dry, and he stared dumbfounded at the huge belly that had a baby inside. How was that thing going to fit out of her slender hips? Terror sunk in. "What is wrong with me? I'm not ready for this. I should have been at your appointments and classes and…" His words faded as Sylvie only nodded.

"Yes, you should have been, but now you get to calm the fuck down! Go get my go bag. It's just inside the nursery, and dammit, keep holding my hand even if it kills you. You got me into this mess, and you are going to help me get out of it." She said curtly, then she doubled over again, breathing hard.

There was a knock at the door and Jackie called, "Nick brought the truck around, Duncan. Sylvie, are you breathing through, okay?"

Sylvie held up her middle finger toward the closed door and then as the pain eased turned to Duncan. "I may have been a bit hasty in saying this will be a while."

He looked thunderstruck. "What the fuck does that mean?"

She glanced at the clock. "Given that my water broke, and the contractions are fairly close together, I'm beginning to realize I've been in labor for quite a while now."

He ran his hands through his hair in agitation. "Why didn't you say anything, for god's sake?"

She smiled sweetly through her teeth. "I thought it was a back ache or cramps or maybe braxton hicks."

He turned and strode out and then came back moments later with a bag he hoped was her 'go bag'. "We're leaving, now," he said firmly. "I'm not taking any chances with those imbeciles down there and you trying to pop this thing out here."

She gritted her teeth. "This thing is your son, and babies don't 'pop' out."

He grinned. "Did I mention I'm not ready for this?"

She gave him the bird and crouched for the next pain, trying to breathe through it. When it was over, she allowed him to take her hand and lead her out. Halfway down the stairs another contraction came, and he stooped down and lifted her into his arms, walking swiftly out to the truck.

Nick was waiting and held out the keys toward Duncan. Sylvie laughed. "You have to drive us, Nick, I need Duncan in the back seat with me. He's doing penance for his absence in the pregnancy."

She heard Jackie laugh softly behind her, as she was plopped unceremoniously onto the back seat and the door slammed shut as Duncan jogged around. He climbed into the driver's seat before he realized what he was doing. Sylvie reached forward and pinched his arm. "I need you back here with me, Jamison, remember?"

He swore and slid out and past an amused Nick, to climb into the back. He stared uneasily at her as she reached for his hand and took it in a death grip as she moaned and gasped for air, as pain surged through her belly and into her back. He eyed that large mound again, tried to imagine a baby fitting through her slender body and a tremor shook him.

For a man who'd been through what he thought was the most

challenging thing possible, he realized that in this moment he was more scared than he had ever been before. Sylvie opened her eyes to look up at him and he tried to force a reassuring smile. She didn't buy it, instead she held his gaze and said quietly, "If you are thinking of changing your mind and leaving now, forget it. I'm not letting you go." She turned her face up toward Nick for a moment. "Stop the truck, Nick. I'm going to need you to back up."

Both men stared at her as though she may have finally gone over the edge. She groaned in frustration. "Now!"

He slammed on the brakes and looked in the mirror at Duncan who only shook his head. Sylvie was trying to get the door open even as the truck skidded to a stop. Duncan swore and grasped onto her until it was fully stopped. She slid away from his grasp and opened the door, "Ben," she yelled so loudly that Duncan winced. "I need you to come with us," she gasped frantically, as another tremor shook her body.

Ben who had come running looked uncertainly between Nick, Duncan, and Sylvie. "Why?"

Sylvie breathed hard for a moment and then lifted hazy eyes and pointed to Duncan. "He is afraid again and I won't be letting him change his mind. That means you are going to have to marry us on the way to the hospital."

Nick laughed, Ben looked unsure of what to do, and Duncan slid an arm around his precious, fiery woman. "Now, sweetheart…" he began.

She turned her brown eyes to him and held up her hands. "I want it in writing today, Jamison." She turned back to Ben. "Get in. Now."

He shrugged and climbed into the front with Nick. The truck slowly began moving again and Sylvie groaned as another contraction came. When it passed, she looked toward Ben. "Do it now, sir."

Duncan frowned. "Sylvie, this isn't necessary, sweetheart. I'm not changing my mind. We can worry about this later."

She shook her head as she looked up and met his gaze. "Uh, uh. I saw the fear and I'll be damned if I'm going to bring our son into this world while wondering if his father might bolt as soon as it's done."

He tried to smile reassuringly but there was still fear in his gaze. "It's not about that, Sylvie, it's just that I'm fairly certain that rather big bump might not fit through."

Ben laughed in the front seat. "I assure you, Jamison, it will all be okay," he said sounding sure of himself.

That made Sylvie at least feel better, since she too had been wondering the same terrifying thing for the past few months as she watched her belly grow bigger. She sighed. "You really think so?"

For some reason the fact that she sounded as scared as he felt, made Duncan calm down. He thought of the cattle and the long, cold nights he'd spent out there waiting patiently for new calves to be born. He thought of the mares and how he'd helped them out from time to time when the mothers became too weak to finish the job. With his thoughts came grounded determination and he grinned. "We got this, sweetheart. I will make sure everything is just fine."

She breathed through another contraction and then leaned forward to touch Ben's shoulder. "Do it now Ben. Please."

Duncan chuckled softly. "We can wait until after, Sylvie, then we can do this thing right."

She shook her head stubbornly and turned to stare up at him. "Do you still want to get married and be with me and baby Duncan, every day?"

He nodded. "Yes but…"

She cut him off. "Just say I do, Duncan."

He groaned and ran one hand through his hair. "Of course, I do, but baby—"

She groaned loudly as another contraction came. As the worst of it eased, she said quietly, "I do too. There, Ben. You see it really isn't all that hard to do." She waved a hand in the air at him. "Now, pronounce that it's done."

He hesitated until he saw the look of pure discomfort on Duncan's face. He grinned, "With the power invested in me online, I pronounce you husband and wife."

Sylvie grinned and leaned toward him for a kiss, but another contraction got in the way. She settled down into the seat and moaned. Forty-five seconds later she straightened up again. "Kiss me, Duncan, you have to kiss before it's a done deal."

He stared down at her beautiful, stubborn face, and her sweet soft body that was going to bear him a son and knew that he was beaten. He groaned and leaned down to take her soft lips in a deep kiss. She pulled back as another contraction came and he sighed and turned her back into his chest as he wrapped his arms around her and held her through the mind-numbing pain. As the contraction ended, Sylvie looked up and asked in a mildly irritated voice, "Well, aren't you guys going to congratulate us?"

Ben laughed incredulously, and Nick tilted the rear-view mirror toward her face. "Not to put a damper on things here, guys, but I've taken enough paramedical classes to know that we have a problem."

Everyone turned to look at him. He pulled to the side of the road as a turnout came into view. "If I'm not mistaken…" he began. Another contraction had Sylvie moaning even as she leaned back into Duncan. He hesitated for several seconds before finishing. "Based on how close the contractions are and the fact that I'm fairly certain she is trying to push…" He let the words hang in the air.

"Spit it out, Hanlan," Duncan growled. "What exactly is the problem?"

He sighed. "She isn't going to make it to the hospital, man."

Ben looked back nervously. "Maybe I should just get out now and walk back to the house for help…"

Duncan shook his head as the steadiness he'd always known settled over his shoulders. "We'll need all the hands we can get." He looked into Sylvie's now terrified gaze and smiled. "Don't worry, sweetheart. I've got this." At her disbelieving frown he chuckled. "I've delivered lots of babies. You are going to be just fine."

She wanted to ask him for clarification, but another contraction set in. Duncan ordered Ben to open her go bag to see what was inside. Before the DA could do that, however, Sylvie opened pain-stricken eyes and said quietly, "There is an emergency birthing kit in the big front pocket."

Duncan was all business then as he instructed Nick to call an ambulance and then to climb into the back and let Sylvie lean against him. Then he slid around to sit across and lifted her feet to rest on top of his legs. "We have to get these pants off of you, sweetheart, okay? We'll do it after the next contraction."

Sylvie groaned and nodded and then reached for his outstretched hands and proceeded to squeeze his fingers until he was sure they might fall off. He didn't complain, just took the pain as best he could, praying that he would make it through this, and that Sylvie and his son would be okay. He deemed Ben the designated one for supplies and spread Sylvie's legs apart as she moaned loudly again.

Ten minutes later, he saw his son's dark hair for the first time. He wanted to cry, but there was still more to be done. Five minutes later she delivered the head and within a minute the rest of his small soft body slid through.

As he stared down at the wiggling pink baby in his arms, he wondered how he had ever thought he might possibly have hurt them. He could never. The love he felt for Sylvie and his son overwhelmed him and even as he told Ben to hand him clamps and scissors, tears filled his eyes. He could never hurt this small wriggling child or his beautiful, beautiful bride. He lifted Duncan Sylvester Jamison onto her chest and said softly, "You did it, sweetheart, he's here safe and sound and all because of you."

As Sylvie held their son, he worked to clamp the cord on both ends before carefully cutting it. He quickly fixed the bulky white plastic clamp at his son's navel and then reached for a small white cotton blanket and wrapped his son up even as his face scrunched up and great powerful cries filled the cab of the truck.

The ambulance came moments later, and he handed his son to Ben and lifted Sylvie into his arms, not caring that his tux was bloodied and smudged. Ben followed and the paramedics got them settled onto the stretcher and then handed the baby back to Duncan.

As the ambulance drove away, sirens blazing, Nick and Ben stood staring, still a little stunned. Nick turned to look at his friend. "So…" he asked with a quirky grin. "How long do you think it will take for her to realize that the many babies Jamison had delivered were cows?"

Ben laughed and gave him a long look. "I don't know. How long do you think it will take for them to realize that they don't actually have a marriage license yet?"

Both men laughed again even as they turned back to the truck eyeing the mess just inside. "Not it," Nick said and they both grinned as they closed the rear doors.

Ben slid into the front seat. "Me neither. Do you think we could guilt Mason or Jon into doing it?"

Nick chuckled as he backed up and turned the truck around and back toward the house. "I don't know, but I bet we could come up with something."

An hour later, Sylvie and Duncan sat together in a recovery suite in the maternity ward. They couldn't stop watching their son as he slept with two fingers crammed into his tiny mouth. Sylvie ran a soft finger over his hand and said in serene wonder, "Did you ever imagine it could be like this?"

He shook his head. "To be honest, I'm still trying to figure out how I ever thought I could or would ever hurt either of you. Look at him. You did the most amazing job, sweetheart. In case I forgot to tell you. Thank you for giving me a son."

She laughed and leaned back against his shoulder where he was propped up on the bed next to her. "I'm so, so, grateful I didn't have to do it alone."

He nodded just as the door opened and all of their friends began filing in. Flowers in vases, balloons, a teddy bear, and last but not least, a large sign that said, *Duncan Jamison's baby*, that Nick delivered with a grin.

They all took turns holding baby Duncan. Even the twins insisted on having turns. When things settled down a bit, Jackie stood next to Duncan and Sylvie. "Sooo…" she said with a smile. "Now that you got that out of the way…" She trailed off.

Duncan grinned but Sylvie raised a brow. "What?"

"When did you want to get married?"

Sylvie met Duncan's eyes and reached to take his hand. She turned back to look at Nick and Ben. "You guys didn't tell them?"

Neither of them said anything so she turned to the room. "Duncan and I got married in the truck, on the way here."

There was a long silence that followed the announcement. Jackie and Laura gasped in horror, and Mason laughed. Ben and Nick stared at each other waiting for the other to speak up. Finally, Ben shrugged. "Uh, about that, guys…"

Sylvie groaned and Duncan slid an arm around her shoulder in an effort to comfort her. “Don’t worry, sweetheart. I will marry you every day for the rest of our lives if that’s what it takes.”

She beamed up at him and whispered, “Me too.” In a silent and a bit awkward moment for everyone else in the room, she leaned up and offered her mouth in sweet surrender. “Just don’t take forever for this one thing, okay?”

He chuckled and sealed the promise with a kiss. A tender kiss that was filled with the promise of family, friendship, loyalty, and above all, hope eternal.